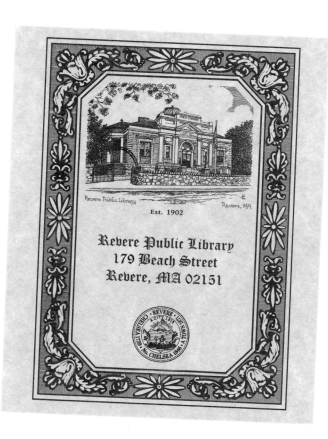

A BAD PLACE
TO DIE

Center Point
Large Print

**This Large Print Book carries the
Seal of Approval of N.A.V.H.**

A Bad Place to Die

A TENNESSEE SMITH WESTERN

EASY JACKSON

CENTER POINT LARGE PRINT
THORNDIKE, MAINE

Library of Congress Cataloging-in-Publication Data

Names: Jackson, Easy, author.
Title: A bad place to die : a Tennessee Smith western / Easy Jackson.
Description: Center Point Large Print edition. | Thorndike, Maine :
    Center Point Large Print, 2019.
Identifiers: LCCN 2018048018 | ISBN 9781643580647
    (hardcover : alk. paper)
Subjects: LCSH: Large type books. | GSAFD: Western stories.
Classification: LCC PS3610.A3496 B33 2019 | DDC 813/.6—dc23
LC record available at https://lccn.loc.gov/2018048018

CHAPTER 1

Tennessee "Tennie" Smith counted nine bullet holes in the RING BIT, TEXAS, sign swaying from one chain on the jail across the street. She glanced at the other buildings in town, most of them new, raw looking, and covered in paint that hadn't yet begun to peel. A third of them had windowpanes with the glass already broken out. She remained seated in the Conestoga wagon, letting the other excited women alight first, while she hoped the man she was supposed to meet had changed his mind.

"Tennie," Winn Payton said, holding his hand up to her.

She looked at the lined face with its wide white sideburns and thought Mr. Payton had aged twenty years since they had begun their journey from a state disseminated by war through a territory of renegade Indians and disgruntled ex-Confederate bandits. She had no choice but to take his hand and get down.

Three dead men lay bound in tarps on the sidewalk, and Mr. Payton began berating several slack-mouthed loafers for allowing the bodies

5

to remain where the women could see them. An older woman took Tennie by the elbow and propelled her to the nearest storefront window to look at merchandise. Instead of looking at lanterns, shovels, and pickaxes, Tennie saw the image of herself reflected in the glass, an eighteen-year-old with soft curling brown hair, dark eyes wide with apprehension, and plummy lips that trembled despite her determination not to cry.

Moving her eyes away, she caught the reflection of a tall, lean man in his thirties walking on the street behind her. His wide-brimmed hat threw a shadow across half his face, but even so, an old scar running downward across both lips, as if made by the slashing of a knife or a saber, was visible. His eyes squinted as he stared at her in passing, causing her to lower her lashes when she realized he knew she had been observing him. She fought the urge to run to him and beg him to please help her out of the plight she was in. Pausing, she turned and watched him stride into a saloon. A man came out of another saloon, followed by a disheveled, dirty, and half-naked woman who screamed obscenities at him.

Winn Payton appeared at Tennie's side. "Tennie," he said in a low voice. "If you don't fulfill your bargain, that's what will happen to you."

She nodded, watching the beleaguered man

push the drunken woman aside when he caught sight of them.

"The women are here!" he hollered at the top of his voice. Men began pouring out of buildings, most of them dressed in pants tucked inside boots with jingling spurs, wearing long-sleeved shirts and bright bandannas around their necks. A few others were dressed in suits; all wore hats. The better dressed ones swarmed the women, and soon, Mr. Payton was introducing a gray-haired man to Tennie as Ashton Granger, her betrothed.

At one time, he must have been considered a handsome man. Clean, dressed in a somber suit and a new Leghorn hat, his blue eyes were kind, but Tennie could not hide the dismay from her face. He was much older than she thought he would be. He, in turn, stared at her in surprise and appreciation before a look of apprehension made a slow march across his face.

Before Tennie could even say hello, they were hustled into the church, and after one mass wedding ceremony, she found herself sitting on a wagon seat by a man she'd just met heading for a home she'd never seen.

"It's not far from town," Ashton Granger said in a deep, likable voice, and Tennie assumed he was talking about his ranch. A series of popping noises came from a distance, and she turned to him.

"The boys in town are just blowing off steam,"

he said. "It's just a little gunfire. No cause for alarm."

Tennie knew it was probably more than that. She had already been warned about Ring Bit by a man who had stayed overnight on their wagon train. He had begged Tennie to run away with him rather than have her go to Ring Bit, but Mr. Payton had chosen that day to have the older women tell the younger ones what would be expected of them on their wedding night. After that, Tennie lost all desire to escape with a buffalo hunter who carried with him the overwhelming odor of something dead. Better to take her chances in Ring Bit, even though he had described it as a wild town unsafe and unfit for women.

Tennie stole short glances at her new husband. His skin was gray, and his breath came hard after every exertion. But he did not force himself upon her, and for that, she was thankful. Tennie knew before the night was over, she was probably going to be crying. To get her mind off it, she asked how the town got its name.

"It's named after a cruel bit used at one time here on wild horses," he said.

Tennie sighed, feeling fate had put a ring bit in her mouth. After that, she remained quiet.

The first sight of his ranch gave the impression of something that had once been worked on with care, but of late, had been neglected. Fences were

8

falling down, the barns leaned, and one of them had a hole in the roof big enough to put a cow through. The porch of the ranch house had poles stuck under it hither and yonder, trying to hold up a sagging roof. Beside a broken gate, three boys with sullen eyes and turned-down lips watched them approach.

Granger helped her down. Taking her by the hand, he led her to the boys. "Tennie, these are my sons. Rusty is thirteen, Lucas here is ten, and little Badger is six. Boys, say hello to your, er—" He paused. "Say hello to Miss Tennie. We were married in town this afternoon."

They mumbled something while Tennie said hello. Rusty had reddish hair and freckles. Lucas and Badger resembled their father, blue-eyed and dark haired. Rusty and Lucas looked as slender as spring grass, but Badger still carried baby fat with him.

"We don't want her here," Badger said. "Why did you marry her?"

The look on his brothers' faces said they agreed.

Tennie felt her heart sink. Mr. Payton had only said the boys were "a little rambunctious," but she recognized malevolence when she saw it.

Granger reprimanded the boys then said, "Come, Tennie. I'll show you the inside."

She followed him through the house. It told the same story the outside did, of something once

9

cared for and let go. The woman in the tintype on the mantle looked like Rusty.

"She's been dead three years," Granger said.

Tennie wished the woman had never died.

Granger indicated a chair for her to sit in. Before sitting down, she gave the cushion a surreptitious shake. Not to her surprise, a small grass snake slithered away. The boys looked at one another from under brows lowered in anger.

Granger looked old and tired. Tennie didn't even try to talk. When the boys announced two riders were approaching the ranch, everyone looked relieved.

Tennie walked outside onto the porch with the others, careful to miss the rotten boards. One man on horseback and another driving a wagon stopped next to the gate. She scanned their faces. With a start, she realized she recognized the one on horseback as the man she had seen in town.

Instead of carrying his guns under a jacket, he had them in the open. Two belts loaded with extra cartridges criss-crossed his leather vest. The collarless shirt he wore belonged to a working-man. Two guns were by his side, one facing butt backward. The one on his left faced butt forward. Both holsters were tied around his striped wool pant legs.

In the dime novel she and the other women had devoured on the wagon train out west, it proclaimed that was the way of a gunfighter, to allow swift removal of a pistol without having it hang in leather. Examining his face closer, Tennie thought him to be in his late twenties or maybe early thirties. By any standard, he looked like a man who knew far more about the bad side of life than he should have.

He sat with ease in the saddle, yet Tennie sensed he took in every corner of the house, every tree, and every shadow by the barn someone could be hiding in. As his eyes fell on her a little longer than the others, she also knew he recognized her. She turned away and studied the man in the wagon.

With thick brown hair poking from his hat, he looked equally tall, but bigger built. He, too, carried a rifle, along with enough ammunition to blow up half an army. The man with the scar began to speak, and Tennie turned back to him.

"Howdy," he said in a deep, clear voice. "My name is George Washington Jones; my friends call me Wash. This is Ben McNally." He motioned his head toward his friend. "We've got a sick man with an arrow in his abdomen. It's too tricky for me to get out. We can't get the doctor in Ring Bit sobered up enough to operate. Somebody in town told us you were a good hand at doctoring."

Granger had been looking at them in consternation, but he responded without hesitation. "Take him around to the sleeping porch in the

11

back. He'll be more comfortable in the small bed there."

"He's a Mexican," the scar-faced man said.

Granger repeated they were to take him to the back. Tennie followed, helping to prepare the bed while the men carried a small, dark, unconscious man onto the porch.

"Tennie," Granger said, "Bring some hot water, soap, and clean towels from the kitchen. There should be some hot ashes left, but you may have to stoke the fire."

She nodded, finding everything as he said.

Carrying basins of hot water, she placed them on a small table next to the iron bedstead. With a start of surprise, she saw Granger had scalpel and forceps laid out among other tools. He rolled up his sleeves, and as he washed his hands and arms, he saw her glance at the scalpel.

"I was a surgeon during the war," he explained. "When I came home, I didn't have the stomach for it anymore."

She nodded. "I've never seen anyone wash their hands before working on a patient."

"It's something I experimented with during the war and had good results . . . although I was never able to convince my colleagues of it. Stand nearby and hand me whatever I ask you for."

"What do you need us to do?" the man with the scarred lips asked.

"You hold his arms down, putting your knee

12

on his chest." Granger turned to the larger man. "You do the same thing with his legs. Put your knee across his legs. I don't want him moving." Tennie watched while he worked the shaft of the arrow in a gentle back-and-forth motion.

"It just might be far enough away from the intestines not to have punctured anything, and at the same time, not be stuck in a bone. There doesn't appear to be internal bleeding," he muttered.

His narrow fingers went down the shaft and probed the wound, while the patient gave a faint groan. Granger removed his fingers, instructing Tennie to wipe the blood from them. She complied, and he selected a wicked-looking knife, making the wound larger in one swift motion. Placing the knife on the table, he picked up another with a wire loop and worked it downward, wrapping it around the arrowhead. With great care, he brought it out, placing it on the table. He straightened and breathed heavily. "Tennie, hand me a clean towel, please."

Tennie gave him one, and taking another, she helped him wipe the blood and clean around the wound.

"He's a lucky man," Granger told the two men. "The arrow appears to have missed the organs. Who is the woman he is calling for? Rosita something?"

"Poco's been calling the name of every señorita

between here and Mexico since he got shot," Wash Jones said.

"Where was that?" Granger asked.

"Near the Brazos. We went to Fort Griffin, but they, along with the camp doctor, were on patrol. Somebody told us there was a doctor in Ring Bit."

Granger concentrated on his patient, but gave Tennie a brief glance. "You are a good nurse."

"I helped my mother during the war," Tennie said. "My father was in the Alabama Brigade. He made it through the war, but he and my mother died of yellow fever soon afterward. I was sent to an orphanage." She stopped, not knowing why she had said so much.

Granger again glanced at her. "An orphanage? Was it bad?"

"Yes."

Granger looked back to his patient, but Tennie thought for some reason her answer had come as a relief to him.

"I'm leaving the wound open to drain," he said when he finished. "There weren't any major arteries cut, and I think he is in more danger of developing an infection than he is of bleeding to death. We'll keep it covered and change the dressings several times a day, though, to see how it's doing."

"Much obliged," Wash Jones said.

Dusk settled, and he and Ben McNally walked

off the porch into the growing darkness. Granger sank down in a chair next to the ill man's side. He appeared exhausted.

"Would you like me to prepare supper?" Tennie asked.

He nodded. "Just bring us all plates of something," he said, his breath coming out shallow and uneven. "I can't face sitting at the table just now."

Tennie nodded. Taking the bloody towels with her, she went into the kitchen and lit the lanterns. Someone had taken the trouble to stock the pantry, and she wondered if it had been done in preparation of her arrival. Disposing of the towels in a bucket of water to soak, she fried the ever-present salt pork and made biscuits and gravy. There was water and coffee, but the milk was canned.

She did as Granger had instructed and made three trips into the darkening evening carrying plates of food along with cups of water and coffee. The men gave polite thanks. The boys said nothing, but the food disappeared. Badger held his plate up and licked it. In a little while, she gathered the dishes and washed them.

Returning to the porch, she saw Granger had placed a chair beside his and indicated he wanted her to sit next to him. "You are not only a good nurse, Tennie, but a good cook. Did you do that at the orphanage?"

"Yes," she answered. "The food was terrible there, full of weevils and maggots, but sometimes they would hire me out to work in the big houses. The former slaves who worked there showed me what to do with better food."

He nodded. "Sometimes the neighbors get together, and we butcher a beef. All of us take some home, taking turns with the best cuts. I haven't felt like participating much lately."

She nodded and listened as he talked about coming to Ring Bit and the changes the war wrought. He wound down, and at the end, asked what brought her to Ring Bit as a mail-order bride. "You are too beautiful to have escaped a hundred proposals, Tennie, regardless of the shortage of men in the South."

"I thought I was signing up to be a missionary," Tennie said, feeling her face turn red.

"What?" Granger asked in surprise.

"It's such a long and embarrassing story."

When Granger did not reply, but sat waiting, Tennie found herself confessing everything.

"One day the matron at the orphanage called me into her office. A man was there who said he was my uncle, and he had come to take me home with him. I tried to tell the matron he wasn't my uncle, but she wouldn't listen to me. She said I had to leave." Tennie's voice rose, almost in hysteria, and she had to calm herself before continuing.

"The man forced me to go with him to a saloon,

where he threw me in a room upstairs. Chains were on the bedstead. He said I was worth a lot of money to him, and if I didn't cooperate, he would chain me to the bed. As soon as he left, I jimmied the window and jumped out, running until I saw a church. I saw some men with the minister, loading up their things. They said, 'Have you come to apply? We are leaving tomorrow at first light.' I told them yes. I thought they were missionaries. They showed me your picture and asked if you were all right, and I said yes again because I thought you were to be my boss at the mission. The minister even put in a good word for me. We had traveled two weeks before I found out I was to be a mail-order bride, not a missionary. Everyone laughed at me. They couldn't believe I had made such a stupid mistake."

Tennie leaned closer to him. "I didn't want to marry someone I'd never met. I waited until there was a full moon. I took some food I'd hoarded, and I was going to leave, but then I looked up in the hills, and I saw a line of Indian warriors in the moonlight. I gave the alarm, and we were attacked. The men managed to repulse them, but they kidnapped one of the women. The next day, we found her. She'd . . . she'd . . ." Tennie couldn't repeat the horror she had seen. "Mr. Payton told me I'd never survive by myself, that I should just come here and do what I had signed up to do." Tennie stopped. She didn't want to tell him Mr. Payton almost had to twist her arm in Ring Bit, too.

"Tennie, Tennie," Granger said, smiling at her in sympathy. "Poor little Tennie." He rubbed her back and squeezed her shoulder. "I have a confession to make, too. I only wanted a wife to look after my sons. My health has been so bad, I haven't corrected them as I should, and they've grown up half-wild. If I died, no one here would want them. When I saw you, I thought my plan had been for nothing. But then you said you grew up in an orphanage, and you know what it's like. Would you promise me, Tennie, if I die, you would take care of my sons? That you would see they didn't get split up and sent to an orphanage? Please?"

He caressed her cheek with one hand, and Tennie found herself nodding her head. "I have to tell you something else, Tennie. I've had another spell with my heart since I sent for you, and I doubt I will ever be able to be a true husband to you. Do you understand?"

Tennie nodded again, and he smiled. "Your eyes are so enchanting. You look like a beautiful little doe. Would you sit on my lap and let me hold you close for a little while?"

Tennie realized she wanted nothing more than to be comforted by him. She moved into his lap and lay her head on his shoulder, allowing him to

18

caress her and kiss her hair. The thought crossed her mind they could be seen and heard by the others, but she was so grateful for Granger's kindness, she did not care.

She looked up into his face, seeing him smile and close his eyes. Many seconds passed before she realized his heart had stopped beating. Not knowing what to do, she stood up. The only name she could think of was *Wash,* so she said, "Mr. Wash. Mr. Wash, would you come here, please?"

CHAPTER 2

Wash had not been far away. He strode across the porch and examined Granger, then turned to his friend. "Ben," he said, keeping his voice down.

The big man lumbered onto the porch. One look, and he, too, knew Granger was gone.

"We'll lay him out on the bed tonight and bury him in the morning," Wash said.

Tennie sat in the chair, put her head down, and closed her eyes. Tears rolled from her eyes down her cheeks, dripping onto her dress, and she didn't even try to understand why.

Wash and Ben placed Granger on the bed, covering him with a sheet. The boys stood silent with them, not asking for an explanation because they already understood. Traditionally, someone was expected to stay up with the body, but in unspoken agreement, they gathered blankets and quilts to sleep on the porch. Tennie stayed close to the patient, Poco, in case he called out during the night, but he slept easier than she'd expected.

The next morning the boys announced they wanted to eat breakfast on the porch. Wash and

Ben nodded in agreement. Tennie handed the boys their plates. They took the food without speaking, refusing to look at her, smoldering with resentment. Ben thanked her when she gave him his. Wash searched her face with his dark blue eyes when she handed him his plate, but she could read nothing in his countenance.

"Thank you, ma'am," he said, his deep voice resonating nothing but politeness.

The men took turns with a pickax and shovel under an elm tree in the backyard. The ground proved so rocky and hard, they couldn't get the hole deep enough. While Tennie cooked dinner, everyone except Poco went in search of stones like the ones covering Ashton Granger's first wife. After dinner, Wash spoke a few words and a prayer over the grave, and Tennie thought it was not the first time he had been called upon to repeat, "ashes to ashes."

Later on, while they stood outside, Tennie made an effort to distract the brooding boys by asking them if they had any school lessons she might help them with.

"We don't have lessons," Rusty said. "The teacher told Pa not to send us back to school."

That knocked the wind out of Tennie, but before she could say anything, Badger burst out in hatred. "We don't want you here."

Lucas and Rusty picked up the cry.

"That's right. We don't need you," Lucas said.

And Rusty said, "You're just a witch who killed our pa, coming here."

The second the word *witch* left Rusty's mouth, Wash made for him. The words, "We can take care of ourselves," crossed his lips seconds before Wash picked him up and threw him in the water trough. He grabbed Rusty by the hair and shoulders and pushed him up and down into the water until Tennie thought he was going to drown him.

"Please . . ." she murmured.

Badger kicked at Wash while Lucas pulled on him, but Ben grabbed each boy in one big hand and threw them in the trough with Rusty, repeating the performance.

When Wash thought Rusty had had enough, he lifted the sputtering boy up to his face and said in a voice so low and mean it sent chills down Tennie's spine, "If I ever hear you refer to Miss Tennie like that again, I won't give you a drowning, I'll give you a licking you'll remember the rest of your life."

Wash threw Rusty down on the dirt while Ben did the same with the other boys.

"You have just as much responsibility to look after her as she has to you, and don't you forget it," Wash said.

From his great height, Ben looked down on them in pity. "Your pa was sick and dying before she got here, and you know it," he said in a gentler voice. "She made your pa a mighty happy man before he died, and don't forget that, either."

With tears in their eyes, the boys stared at the men. They got up together and began running down the road. Tennie started, but Wash stopped her.

"Leave them alone to stew on it," he said. "They'll come back when they get hungry."

Tennie nodded, remembering she had a patient. She washed her hands and began the process of changing Poco's bandage, rolling the sheet down just enough to get to his wound. Wash walked up on the porch, and after a second's hesitation, began assisting her. Poco roused and said a few words in Spanish. Wash answered in Spanish, and Poco closed his eyes and went back into a peaceful sleep.

"You can speak Spanish, too?" Tennie asked.

"Just enough to get by," Wash said, covering Poco when they had finished. "I can speak a little Kiowa, Comanche, and Apache, too, but it didn't stop us from getting attacked. They were after our horses."

"They didn't get them," Tennie said, looking at the horses Ben was brushing down in the corral.

"Not this trip. You probably saved the life of everyone on the wagon train by giving the alarm the night you decided to run away."

So he had been listening. Tennie shrugged.

24

"I never thought of it that way." She rose. "I'd better burn these bandages."

"There are peach trees near the creek making fruit," Wash said. "If I brought you some, could you make a peach cobbler?"

"Bring me as many as you can, and I can make preserves, too," Tennie said. "At least I think I can remember how my mother used to do it."

Ben joined them. "Don't feed him too well, Miss Tennie," he said with a laugh. "You'll never get shut of him."

Tennie smiled. After the emotional scenes of earlier, she would be glad to have something to do to take her mind off the new fix she found herself in. She wondered about the men surrounding her. They went from lightning-fast temper to gathering peaches for her.

Along with the peaches, they brought dressed squirrels, instructing her to fry them like chicken. She took a few of the squirrels, though, and browned them, adding water to make a broth for Poco to sip when he became able.

The boys, as Wash predicted, came home in time for supper. They were quiet and didn't apologize for anything, but no one appeared to expect them to. They sat at the table eating squirrel after squirrel.

Rusty said, "Tomorrow we can have rabbit. Lucas and I know how to find rabbits hiding in bushes and drop a knife to kill them."

"We can shoot good, though," Lucas said. "But rabbits ain't too bright, so we don't have to waste no ammunition on them."

"Do I fry them like squirrel?" Tennie asked.

"Pa liked them stewed," Rusty said.

"With lots of gravy," Badger said. "Pa liked gravy." Tears began to fill his eyes.

Tennie rose. "I have a surprise for you. Mr. Wash and Mr. Ben gathered peaches, and we are having peach cobbler for dessert."

The boys lowered their eyes.

Lucas said, "Thank you, Miss Tennie," in a voice so low it could barely be heard.

Tennie looked at Wash and Ben and gave a slight shrug before fetching the cobbler.

Poco roused just long enough for Tennie to get some broth down him. Even though the bedroom now sat empty, Tennie stayed all night on the porch with the others.

In the morning, Poco regained consciousness. A small wiry man in his twenties, his dark eyes flashed in humor. He teased Tennie while she and Wash changed his bandages, telling her in a weak voice how beautiful she was.

"Am I as pretty as Rosita? As Maria? As Consuela?" she teased back.

"Even more beautiful," Poco said.

"Don't pay any attention to him, Miss Tennie. He's the Mexican version of Don Juan," Wash said as he pulled the covers back over Poco.

26

"Who's Don Juan?" Tennie asked, picking up the soiled bandages.

"Nobody you want to know," Wash said. "Lucas or Rusty can help me change the bandages from now on."

Poco gave a weak smile. "You are a demon."

"No, I just don't want you to get to admiring Miss Tennie so much you bust a gut open."

Ben came around the side of the house. "Buggy coming, Wash."

Poco shut his eyes while Wash and Ben disappeared without seeming to leave so much as a footprint behind.

Wondering what was going on, Tennie disposed of the bandages and waited on the front porch. The boys stood by the gate and watched a buggy with three men bounce down the rutted road to the house. The men pulled up and alighted, knocking the dust from their pants. They raised their hats to her and gave slight bows, their appearance marking them as middle-aged and prosperous.

The chubby one with gray hair wore a gold watch chain hanging across his wide middle. In his hand was a short top hat. The other men held bowlers. One of the men wore a suit even more expensive, but not as elaborate. His face looked as cold and white as the inside of a day-old baked potato. The excitable looking man standing near him, who was bald on top with little gray fringe,

27

at least looked like he had warm blood flowing through his veins.

They began to walk toward the porch. The chubby one turned to the boys and said in a growl, "Beat it. We want to talk to this woman alone." He turned and gave Tennie an ingratiating smile.

She took an instant dislike to him.

The boys frowned but slunk away, and Tennie knew they would stay out of sight but within hearing. She had no idea what had happened to Wash and Ben. She waited on the porch.

"Mrs. Granger?" Chubby asked. "We heard about your unfortunate loss."

Tennie nodded, thinking it odd to hear herself addressed as "Mrs. Granger."

"I am the mayor of Ring Bit. These gentlemen here with me are on our town council," he said, saying their names and introducing the one with the soulless eyes as the banker, and the excitable one as an influential businessman.

"Yes," Tennie said, not understanding what they wanted with her. "Won't you come in?"

They followed her into the house and refused an offer of refreshments. Tennie sat on one end of the sofa while they occupied chairs to her left. She could hear the scurry of feet, and to hide the sound, she spoke. "What can I do for you, gentlemen?"

The mayor looked at the banker, nodding for him to begin.

"I hate to inform you, Mrs. Granger," the banker said. "But the note on this property comes due at the end of the month. Unless you have the money to pay the remaining twenty-five hundred, you will have to vacate the ranch."

Tennie stared at him. He might as well have said twenty-five thousand or twenty-five million.

"And there is no money in Mr. Granger's account to cover that?" Tennie found herself asking, wondering if some other composed woman was talking. Surely it wasn't her.

"No, ma'am," the banker said. "He has a balance of ten dollars."

"Ten dollars," Tennie repeated. They would have to tear the house apart to see if he had stashed any money aside. But even if they found some, Tennie doubted it would be twenty-five hundred. She was finding it hard to breathe.

"Now, Mrs. Granger," the mayor said. "Don't fret. We have a proposition for you that will give you a place to live and an income."

The last proposition she had was to work in a cathouse, and she wondered what theirs would be. It couldn't be worse.

"The thing of it is," the mayor began, "our little town is being overrun by a wild and reckless element. People are leaving and the ones who might settle here are passing us by for safer places to dwell. If this keeps up, Ring Bit could become a ghost town."

The other men were staring at her.

Tennie stared back and said, "Yes?"

"Well, we have a solution," the mayor said, his three chins wobbling. "We want to appoint you as our town marshal. Think of it! The reputation it would give us as a peaceful place."

Tennie thought she had not heard him right. "What?" She shut her mouth, feeling guilty—she hadn't meant to sound rude.

"Mrs. Granger, you won't have a thing to worry about. There is an unwritten law in the West, and one that is perfectly legal in Ring Bit, that if a man kills someone and leaves their children orphans, he is obligated to take care of those children. And let's face it, Mrs. Granger, no one wants to be saddled with those hellion stepsons of yours."

Tennie stared at them, thinking they were crazy.

The nervous one spoke. "You're not putting it right, Horace." He turned to Tennie. "No one is going to hurt a beautiful young woman such as yourself. We don't expect you to wear a gun and go around arresting people. We only want you to use your presence to calm some of the rougher element. You will have to write a few warrants to hand over to the U.S. deputy marshal when he comes, and you'll have to feed any prisoners in the jail. That's all."

The banker crossed his legs and pinched the smooth fabric of his pants. "Really, Mrs. Granger, you have few options. You can farm the boys out to orphanages, because I assure you no one in Ring Bit will take them on, and you will have to support yourself in whatever way you can, or you can accept our offer."

Tennie sat still. She couldn't seem to think straight. Where were Wash and Ben?

The three men stared at her, waiting for an answer.

"I am taking care of an ill man my husband operated on before he passed," Tennie said. "It will be two weeks at least before I can leave here."

"Two weeks will bring us to the end of the month," the banker said, rising.

The other men stood up.

"We'll send someone out for you and your things at the end of two weeks, Mrs. Granger," the mayor said.

Tennie could not understand his suppressed elation or the relief of the other men. It seemed out of proportion to what appeared to be just a stunt. They said their good-byes and left her standing on the porch, watching them go.

The boys crept from the shadows they had been hiding in.

"Do we really have to leave the ranch and move to town, Miss Tennie?" Rusty asked.

"It looks that way," Tennie said, not able to keep the despondency out of her voice. What else was going to happen to her? She looked at the three boys. She hadn't wanted to be a mail-order bride. She hadn't wanted to be a widow. She didn't want to be responsible for three wayward boys nobody else would have. And most of all, she did not want to move into Ring Bit and become the freak of the West, a woman town marshal.

"Let's go see if Mr. Poco is awake. He has two weeks to get better." As they walked to the back porch, Tennie said, "You went to town and told people your father had died, and I had promised to take care of you, didn't you?"

"That's right," Lucas said. "You sure are getting clever, Miss Tennie. Going through an Indian attack and coming to Ring Bit must have made you a lot smarter than when you left."

"No, it didn't," Tennie said. "If it had, I'd be able to think of a way out of this mess."

After checking on Poco, they went through the house looking for money, but all they found was a five-dollar gold piece and a few dollars in Ashton Granger's wallet. There were a lot of papers on the desk, but Tennie couldn't understand any of them. Ben walked in while Tennie sat at the desk, looking at receipts in puzzlement.

"Miss Tennie," he said, drawing near.

"Yes, Mr. Ben?" Tennie answered, grateful to look at him instead of Ashton Granger's crabbed handwriting.

"Wash said not to throw any of your husband's papers away. He said as soon as you can, hire an attorney you trust to look into his affairs."

Tennie frowned. "Why doesn't he tell me this himself?"

Ben paused before continuing. "He's upset about you taking the marshal job. He don't want you to do it."

"Well, what does he want me to do?" Tennie asked, her voice getting shrill.

"He knows you don't have no choice," Ben said, trying to calm her. "He's in a turmoil over it and can't trust himself to talk about it right now. That's all."

"All right," Tennie said, resigned. "I'll keep the papers."

"Miss Tennie," Ben repeated, considering every word before he spoke it. "Me and Wash, we can't help you right now, but soon things will be different. Then we'll be able to do something for you and the boys. We promise."

"What are you talking about?"

"I can't tell you just now. Just don't try to prove nothing with this here marshal job. Just take it, lay low, and wait."

Tennie looked down at her hands in her lap, despondent.

"I promise, Miss Tennie," Ben continued. "I got me a pretty little gal down on the lower Colorado, and Poco's got señoritas from San

Antonio to Chihuahua, but Wash, he ain't got nobody. He ain't gonna leave you high and dry. We'll pull you out of this in time, we promise."

Tennie nodded, but she knew what promises were worth. All the times someone visited the orphanage, vowing to bring them presents of food and toys at Christmastime and never showing back up. Even worse were the ones who brought one turkey and one pie to feed fifty children and expected an enormous show of gratitude for it. As soon as they were gone, the staff devoured the food, leaving the children with cold grits once again. Promises like that meant nothing to Tennie.

She rubbed her forehead and did what she had learned to do. Not get mad, not get excited, and keep her disbelief to herself. "Thank you, Mr. Ben."

At the supper table, the boys talked about the jail. Wash and Ben ate in silence, eyes fastened to their plates. If anything, Wash's eyes narrowed more over his food, and it seemed to Tennie the scar running down across his lips reddened in a fiery glow.

"The living quarters are behind the office," Rusty said. "The jail where they lock up the prisoners is on the second floor."

Wash got up and left the table. Rusty looked after him, his face puzzled.

"He's not too taken with the idea of us moving into a jailhouse," Tennie explained, but it worried her. Why would her taking a nominal job as marshal make him almost blaze in suppressed fury? He knew she had no choice.

Ben, almost always the silent one, told stories on the porch that night, describing the Indian attack that wounded Poco while the three Granger boys listened with wide eyes.

It did not surprise Tennie that the boys appeared to hold no resentment against Wash and Ben for the rough treatment they had received. The fights at the orphanage between boys had upset her when she first arrived, but she'd soon learned to ignore them. The boys wrestled with one another every day and were the best of friends three minutes after knockdown slugfests. The girls had cliques and running feuds that lasted for months and even years, but the boys fought their way through disagreements.

Ben asked Tennie if she was able to talk about the Indian attack on their wagon train.

"It didn't last long," she said. "Some of the women could shoot, but I don't know how. All I could do was cower and hand out ammunition."

"If you were handing out ammunition," Ben said, "you weren't cowering."

"The only help I could really give them was my fervent prayer God would get us out alive."

She couldn't see Wash's face in the dark, but she felt his eyes, silent and brooding, upon her the entire evening.

CHAPTER 3

The next day, Winn Payton and his wife arrived at the ranch. He introduced his tiny gray-haired wife to Tennie, and together they accepted her invitation to come inside. This time, the boys were not told to clear out, and they stood behind the adults, listening.

Mr. Payton started by stating he was against Tennie becoming marshal and suggested she find a man to marry as soon as possible. "The quicker the better," he said. "I don't want men killing one another over you in Ring Bit, Tennie."

Tennie didn't take offense at Mr. Payton's brusque advice. When he'd realized on the wagon train to Ring Bit that her shoes had holes in them, he'd bought her a new pair with his own money at the first opportunity, along with fabric for a new dress because hers was so worn and faded.

He was also fretting over the banker's treatment of her and the boys. "Ashton handed over the money to me to fetch a wife without any hesitation. He never mentioned he had taken out a loan at the bank, but I have no reason to believe the banker is anything but an honest and fair man. Still, Tennie, this bothers me. A lot of things about Ring Bit are bothering me."

"Is there a good attorney in Ring Bit?" Tennie said, feeling shy about asking.

"No, the closest one is in Cat Ridge," Mr. Payton said. "You'd think in a state full of disbarred and bankrupt lawyers swarming in from other places, Ring Bit would have managed to attract one of them. And this scheme to make you a marshal—"

"Now, Father," Mrs. Payton interrupted. "You leave Tennie be about that. She's just trying to keep body and soul together."

Mr. Payton waved his hand in front of his face, but said in agreement, "That's why I'm here. The bank may have a note on the cattle and property, but as far as I know, it doesn't own one on the contents and the other livestock. I'm willing to pay you for the farm equipment and anything else you won't need or be taking with you."

"That's very kind of you," Tennie said. "But I would have to talk that over with his sons first." She turned to Lucas and Badger, but Rusty had disappeared. "Where did Rusty go?" she asked.

They shrugged, and she turned back to the Paytons. "I'm sure he'll be back in a minute. In the meantime, would you come into the kitchen for some bread and peach preserves? There is coffee in the pot."

They agreed, but Mr. Payton wanted to see Tennie's patient first.

"He's a Mexican," he said when he looked down at Poco's sleeping form. Tennie wondered if Poco was pretending to be asleep or unconscious. He lay so still, it looked unnatural.

"He's been very ill," Tennie said. "I hope he's well enough at the end of two weeks to be up and around on his own."

Mr. Payton must have shared Tennie's skepticism of Poco's slumber. He leaned forward and spoke in Poco's face. "Mexican, you hurt this girl or these children, I'll hunt you down clear to Oaxaca to slit your throat." He raised and turned to Tennie. "If he's still not well when you have to leave, send word, and I'll fetch him and take care of him at our place until he can be on his own."

Tennie nodded. Wash and Ben had disappeared again, and she did not know why she said nothing about them to the Paytons. The words didn't seem to want to form in her mouth. Instead, she said, "Boys, go look for Rusty, please. I'll save some bread and preserves for you, too."

On their way to rejoin Mrs. Payton in the kitchen, Tennie wondered if the boys had told anyone in town about the other men at the ranch. Mr. Payton hadn't acted like he knew anything about them, and she thought he would have said if he did. As she sliced fresh bread for her company and put out the preserves, Tennie reasoned perhaps the boys had kept quiet because they did not want to admit the severe discipline they had received at the hands of almost total strangers. Tennie did not know what her reason was.

They had finished their coffee before Rusty returned with the other two boys.

"We want to keep our wagon, our mule, and the two horses. And our Pa's saddle and tack. And his guns," Rusty said without preamble. "You can take whatever furniture we won't need at the jail, along with the rest of the tools and equipment in the barn for a hundred dollars."

The adults stared at the boy. "For somebody who only went to school for a total of two weeks last year, you drive a hard bargain, son," Mr. Payton said.

"I'm going to talk to the teacher about getting them back in school," Tennie said.

Mr. Payton stood facing Rusty. He turned his head an inch to tell Tennie it wouldn't work. "If it was a male teacher, you could turn those big eyes on him and probably get them back in, but it's not, and she's not going to let them return. Not after they hogtied her and did an Indian war dance around her." He spoke to Rusty. "I have to look at what you have first."

"All right," Rusty said, gulping in nervousness, "but nothing less than seventy-five. It's worth more than that."

Mr. Payton stood staring at Rusty for a long time. "Let's see what you got." He walked out the door with Rusty trailing, straightening his shoulders and trying to stand taller.

"Would you like me to go through the house with you, dear," Mrs. Payton said to Tennie, "and help you decide what to take to the jailhouse and what to leave behind?"

"Oh, yes, please," Tennie said, rising. She looked at the door, wondering what was going on with Rusty.

The Paytons stayed on. Just as Tennie was speculating what she should cook for dinner to feed them, the boys appeared with a large mess of fish and more peaches.

"We're smoking some fish down by the creek, Miss Tennie, so we aren't hungry," Rusty said.

Lucas added, "You don't have to worry about us none."

"You boys caught all those fish just now?" Mr. Payton asked in suspicion.

"Uh, we have a trap, sir," Rusty said before Lucas or Badger could open their mouths. "We're heading back now."

Tennie quickly realized where Wash and Ben had disappeared to. She tried not to look troubled and took the fish into the kitchen to fry. She made another peach cobbler for her company.

"I'll say this for them, Tennie," Mr. Payton said. "I've never seen them so well-behaved."

It was on the tip of Tennie's tongue to say she hadn't, either. Whatever Wash and Ben were, no matter why they wanted to hide, they had worked minor miracles on her new stepsons.

The Paytons stayed all day. The boys returned; Poco still pretended to be unconscious, and Wash and Ben remained invisible. Tennie was about to ask the Paytons what they would like for supper when Mr. Payton announced they best be getting on if they wanted to reach home before dark.

"I'll come with some men tomorrow to fetch what we agreed upon," he said, addressing Rusty.

Rusty, looking like a nervous colt, said in a speech sounding rehearsed, "If it is all right with you, sir, I will take my brothers on a hunting trip. It might upset them to see our Pa's things hauled away. We trust you to take what's yours and nothing else."

Mr. Payton again stared at Rusty in puzzlement. "That will be fine, boy." He turned to his wife. "Come along, Mother."

Tennie thanked them for their kindness and saw them to their wagon.

When she came back into the house, Rusty said, "Mr. Wash and Mr. Ben are taking us scouting around and hunting tomorrow. He said to tell you not to worry about being alone with Mr. Poco. He wouldn't hurt you even if he wasn't sick as a dog."

"Scouting what?" Tennie asked, not sidetracked by talk about her safety with Poco.

"Oh, just looking around," Rusty said. "Is there anymore cobbler left?"

Tennie sighed. "Yes, and you'd better fetch Mr. Wash and Mr. Ben. They may want some of that cobbler before you boys gobble it all up, seeing's how they are the ones who picked the peaches in the first place."

Wash wouldn't look at Tennie, and Poco wouldn't shut up. After spending all day dozing or pretending to doze, he wanted to talk. He talked about his mother; he talked about the purity of his sisters, seeing no irony in doing his best to take the virtue away from somebody else's sister multiple times up and down the Rio Grande. He talked about the food his mother cooked. He wanted Tennie to prepare beans the next day.

"I'm not sure you should be eating anything solid yet," Tennie said.

"They will pass through me like grease," he promised. "Mash them and fry them in onion and garlic in bacon fat, and you will make *cerdos* of all of us, señorita."

Ben laughed. "Let him have what he wants, Miss Tennie. If I can find him some *chile pequenos* growing wild, he'll get better even faster."

Late that night, Poco finally wound down.

43

"Tomorrow, I will instruct you how to make tortillas, Señorita Tennie," he said. "The tortilla, the bacon, the beans, *muy bueno.* . . ."

But the next day when Mr. Payton returned with his cowhands to load the things he bought, Poco shut his eyes and refused to open them until they departed. The others had disappeared before dawn, stuffing leftovers from the night before into poke bags and promising to bring back venison.

Mr. Payton brought two young cowhands and a third who appeared older. Tennie smiled and said hello, grateful Mr. Payton was paying enough money for them to survive a while if things went wrong in Ring Bit. The two young cowhands smiled at her, their faces turning red every time she neared them as they hauled furniture from the house. She stood away from them most of the time, but had a hard time controlling her impulsive desire to clean underneath what they were moving before they even had a chance to step away with it. The older cowhand grinned at her and tried to hold her gaze, making Tennie uncomfortable. He seemed content to let the younger men do the work, and Tennie saw Winn Payton eyeing him numerous times.

The men finished with the house and moved on to the barns, where Tennie left them alone. She cooked dinner for them, but Mr. Payton told her to bring it to the barn; they would eat there. She

44

did as he asked and went back into the house to finish cleaning. A while later, she heard them on the porch and Mr. Payton's rusty voice calling to her.

Wiping her hands on her apron, she walked onto the porch. The men had rinsed their plates and stacked them on the porch for her. The young cowboys were in the wagons, while Mr. Payton and the older cowboy were on horseback. Mr. Payton told her they had finished and needn't come back, and she again gave her thanks, throwing a smile at him and the other cowboys that did not rest on any one of them in particular.

The older cowboy, however, drew his horse closer, stopping to stare at her with an intenseness that caused her to feel ill at ease. "I'd like to come back," he said with a smile.

Tennie didn't know what to do. She didn't want to be rude, but she did not want the man to return. She looked at Mr. Payton.

"You!" he barked. "Leave that woman alone and don't show back up here again. In fact, go back to the ranch, draw your pay, take your saddle, and vamoose."

The cowboy glowered at Winn Payton with eyes burning in hatred. He didn't argue, but spurred his horse and galloped away.

Tennie looked at Mr. Payton in concern. She hadn't meant to get the man fired.

"I don't have any further use for that no-good

weasel," Mr. Payton said. "I'm glad to get shut of him." He looked down at Tennie. "That's the kind of shiftless trash you'll have to deal with in Ring Bit, so you better get ready." He turned to leave, saying, "Take care, gal."

"Yes, sir, Mr. Payton," Tennie replied. "Good-bye."

She went inside to try to get Poco to eat a little more, but he refused food. "I have beans cooking for supper," Tennie promised him. "I'll leave you to rest. I believe you stayed up too late last night jabbering."

He nodded. "Tomorrow, I will sit up. But today, I lay down."

Tennie left him to tend to her other chores. As she worked in the front room, she thought of the money Mr. Payton had paid her, which raised her spirits. Maybe they could use the money to move somewhere else, and she wouldn't have to be a marshal. But she didn't know where else they would move. She had made friends with the women on the wagon train. Maybe they would take them in after seeing how much better behaved the boys were. The instant after she thought it, she could almost hear Mr. Payton saying, "Don't move in with some married couple and stir up trouble with the husband, Tennie." He would be right; she didn't need that kind of trouble.

Wash and Ben arrived toting a deer, the boys

bubbling with pleasure. While Tennie fried back-strap, Wash and Ben cut the rest in strips, showing the boys how to smoke the meat for jerky.

After supper, Wash took Tennie aside. "We'll be leaving here next week, and what is facing you in town is going to take all the strength you have. Don't work yourself to death on this house in the meantime."

She nodded, a lump coming into her throat at the thought of moving into Ring Bit.

Wash's nostrils flared, the scar across his lips becoming even more pronounced. "Don't look at me like that. This is hard enough for me as it is."

"Then look somewhere else," Tennie cried, fighting to keep tears down.

An expression of torment crossed his face as if he wanted to say more, but couldn't. He turned and walked out of the house, disappearing into the barn.

They didn't speak the rest of the evening. It grew dark, and Tennie knew she should be sleeping in her own room; she no longer had the excuse of a patient who needed her. She told herself she was too frightened to be alone and placed her pallet in one corner of the porch, far away from the others, and turned her face to the wall. She had to stuff a corner of the quilt into her mouth to keep from sobbing, thinking about Ring Bit.

During the night, she woke up. Propping herself on one elbow, she pushed her tumbling hair from her face and looked around. The others were asleep, except for Wash. He sat in a chair, and even in the dark, Tennie knew he was watching her. She fought an unexpected and overwhelming desire to go to him, put her head on his lap, and beg for a reassuring hand. Instead, she lay down and fell back into a troubled sleep.

Wash sent Rusty to town on an errand the next day. As Rusty readied one of his father's horses and was about to leave, Badger, not allowed to go, fell to the dirt, kicking and screaming. Rusty paused, looking to Wash for guidance. Wash motioned for Rusty to go on, speaking to Badger in a tone filled with as much iron as the guns he habitually wore. "Stop acting like a baby and get up off the ground."

Badger paused in midcry. After a few seconds' hesitation, he jumped up and ran to Ben.

"Don't be coming to me," Ben said. "You know better than to behave like that."

Badger slunk to another part of the yard.

Wash joined Tennie. Watching Badger, he said, "You're going to have a problem with that boy, Miss Tennie."

"His brothers have given in to him and spoiled him, I fear," Tennie said. "I guess that's how he earned his nickname. He badgers them until they give him what he wants."

48

"Don't give in to him too much, and don't let them, either."

Wash looked down at her, and she thought of how weather-beaten his skin looked. She wondered why he did not grow a thick mustache and beard like so many other men would have to camouflage the scar on his lips. Perhaps he wanted the world to see it.

"A Kiowa brave gave it to me," he said, reading her thoughts so clearly, she blushed. "I didn't back up fast enough. But then neither did he a split second later."

She looked down, but looked up again when he spoke her name.

"Those men on the town council will be hiding behind your skirts for a reason; you know that, don't you?"

She nodded, and he asked if it would be all right if he looked through Ashton's papers.

"Yes, please do," she said.

He stayed inside over an hour. She was hanging towels on a clothesline when he came out, looking weary and troubled.

"Don't put your faith in anyone in Ring Bit," he said. "Don't sign anything. If they try to get you to sign something, put them off any way you can until you can get somebody you trust to look at it first."

Lucas, with Badger tagging behind him, approached them. Wash asked what they wanted.

Emboldened, Lucas said, "You promised you'd show us how to clean Pa's old Navy revolver, Mr. Wash."

"So, I did," Wash said. "I know you're a pretty good hand with your pa's rifle, too, for a boy your age. We might as well clean them both." He gave Tennie another look before joining Lucas and Badger.

Tennie went back into the kitchen, grateful to be mistress of her own domain, even if it was one with shelves about to fall down and boards coming loose from the floors. She tried to convince herself the feelings she had for Wash Jones were nothing more than gratitude and a desire to hold on to someone when a frightening unknown loomed ahead of her.

Poco moved from the bed to a chair and spent most of the morning smiling and talking. Tennie waited dinner on Rusty, and when he returned he carried packages with him, handing them to Wash. Wash gave one to Tennie.

"What is this?" Tennie asked, taking a large brown paper parcel.

"It's a small down payment on what we owe you for our room and board," Wash replied.

"I ain't ate so good since my ma died," Ben said.

"You don't owe me anything," Tennie said, but they brushed aside her protests and told her to open her package.

She found it contained yards of fabric, enough

for two dresses. One print had a dark pink background, covered in lighter pink little flowers, flecked heavily in a goldish yellow. The other was dark blue with gold flowers. There was enough ribbon, buttons, and lace to cover four dresses. Tennie had never received such an expensive present. She didn't know what to say. Rusty had brought back the most feminine dress material available, and she wondered if Wash had instructed him to do so for a reason. "I shall be the best dressed marshal in the state of Texas," she said, thanking them and blinking back unexpected tears.

At dinner, Rusty repeated the gossip he heard in town. The cowhand Mr. Payton fired had been found dead in an alley after boasting he intended to go back to the Granger ranch to give Tennie what she had come west for.

"Who would kill him because of me?" Tennie asked. "I don't know anyone in Ring Bit besides Mr. Payton."

"They said if Mr. Payton had done it, he would have said straight up he did," Rusty said.

"He's a good old man," Wash said, helping himself to another piece of bread. "But he doesn't know when to shut his mouth or how to keep a secret."

Rusty bent his head down. They continued eating, but Tennie wondered if Wash had been warning him to be silent.

Wash spoke again without looking up. "I think Miss Tennie made more of an impression on the Ring Bit menfolk than she realizes."

There didn't seem to be any way to answer that, so she didn't.

That evening after supper, Wash and Ben left the ranch, telling Tennie not to wait up for them. Poco brooded and refused to say more than a word or two the rest of the night. Even so, Tennie made pallets for Wash and Ben, finding herself peering into the clear moonlit night for their return.

When she did fall asleep, a creaking board awakened her just before dawn. Opening her eyes, she lay still, watching the two men move to their bedding. Finding the pallets, they lay down like two noiseless cats. Tennie gave a delicate sniff, but if they had been in a saloon drinking all night, she could not smell it. She lay quiet, waiting for the sun to come up.

While she cooked a late breakfast, they rose and went to the water pump in the yard. Peeking at them from the kitchen window, she watched as they stripped their shirts to wash. Whatever they had done during the night had covered them with dirt and grime; even so, she could see old scars telling of previous violent encounters. She leaned back from the window, looking at the kitchen and the food cooking on the stove, almost wishing they had come back reeking of liquor. Men didn't get dirty holding a deck of cards all night.

CHAPTER 4

Wash and Ben sent the boys hunting, asking Tennie to prepare poke bags filled with food so they could stay out all day. Later, while she worked at the kitchen table cutting a dress pattern, the men talked in low tones to Poco. She caught disturbing snatches of conversation.

"He hasn't recognized you?" Ben asked.

"No," came the bitter answer. "I've changed too much. If I'd gotten closer, he probably would have."

"Has he changed?"

"No," Wash said. "He's still the same. . . ." He moved away as he spoke, and Tennie could hear no more.

After dinner, they dozed while Tennie sewed; her fingers busy one way, her mind busy another. The thought of moving to Ring Bit and being thrown into a job in which she had no training and knew little of what would be expected of her made her almost ill. But even that was crowded out of her mind with another worry. Who were these men and what were they doing in Ring Bit? They had been so kind to her, she couldn't bring herself to be rude and ask them, "Just who are you?" Or maybe, she thought, that was just her excuse because she did not want to know.

Tennie half expected, half feared, they would leave again that night. After supper, while sitting on the back porch, Wash opened the other package Rusty had brought from town. Tennie joined the boys in leaning closer to get a look at the book he held in his hand.

"I'll read aloud if you want me to," he said, and the four Grangers wasted no time in telling them they wanted him to very much. "The Three Musketeers," Wash began.

He had the voice of an orator, and before becoming caught up in the hotheaded d'Artagnan and his companions, Tennie wondered if he had been trained in elocution.

Wash stopped reading when it grew dark, but the boys lit a lantern and begged him to continue. Laughing, he agreed to read a little longer, while they sat enthralled.

"*Alguien viene*," Poco interrupted in a quiet voice.

Wash broke off and handed the book to Rusty. "Keep reading. Don't stop. All of you, stay on the porch and don't leave it."

Rusty took the book and hesitated, while Wash and Ben picked up their rifles, stepping off the porch and vanishing into the night.

"Keep reading, Señor Rusty," Poco said. "I cannot understand so many of the words, you see, because that is not my language. But I like to hear the voices."

Rusty bent down and took up where Wash left off. Tennie was afraid to move her eyes from Rusty's face. When she did turn her head, she could see nothing except Poco sitting up in bed clutching a revolver. She looked away, hoping the younger boys would not follow her gaze, but they, too, were afraid to take their eyes from Rusty, who had trouble with many of the words.

"If you don't know the word," Tennie said in a soft voice, "just skip it and move on." She did not want him to stop.

Even though she had been expecting it, Tennie still jumped when she heard gunfire. One shot, another, and four more before it became still and quiet.

Rusty had halted and half-risen, looking in the direction of the barn from whence most of the shots came.

"Keep reading, Señor Rusty," Poco said. "Don't upset the little ones." But he sat poised with his hand tense around the gun.

When they heard the hoot of an owl, Poco relaxed and leaned back into the pillows.

Rusty saw him relax, and bending his head down, he read again, this time with an expression of relief.

It was much later when Wash and Ben returned. They looked loose and almost happy.

"Coyotes," Wash said. "That's enough reading for tonight. Tomorrow Rusty is going hunting with us while you boys stay here with Miss Tennie, who is going to be busy sewing on her new marshal dress."

The younger boys decried the injustice, but Wash told them to hush. "You're going to stay here and let Poco begin teaching you Spanish. You little heathens might as well be learning something."

"Not the dirty words," Tennie said, staring at Wash in the pale flickering light of the lantern. It had not been coyotes firing back at them from another direction. And now he was involving Rusty.

It continued like that for days. Wash and Ben would leave at night, or they would take Rusty with them during the day. In the meantime, they chopped kindling, brought in wood, and did whatever Tennie needed them to during the day, reading to them after supper.

Wash took four limber tree branches, and handing one to each boy, showed them the art of fencing. Ben did not participate; he and Poco watched in appreciation as Wash taught the young ones to thrust and parry while Tennie observed.

During the next few days, Rusty picked up the

sport faster than the others. Wash encouraged him to the next level, and they crossed branches all over the backyard, moving back and forth, Wash instructing while his feet danced across the rocky soil, gamboling over fallen limbs and stones without so much as a slip.

Even Lucas and Badger stopped pounding each other with branches long enough to stop and stare, while Tennie stood nearby, watching.

"He looks just like a jackrabbit, jumping around everywhere." Ben laughed.

Tennie looked down at Ben, who sat chewing on a long blade of grass, the art of fencing as foreign to him as English trifle and plum pudding. Nobody had to tell Tennie only Southern gentlemen from wealthy families with plenty of time and money learned to fence the way Wash Jones knew how.

The day before they were to leave for Ring Bit, Wash informed Tennie he intended on teaching her to shoot.

"They said I don't have to carry a gun in Ring Bit," Tennie said.

"I don't want you to carry a gun in Ring Bit, either," Wash said, no longer playing the dashing swordsman. With his sturdy, plain clothes and solemn face, he resembled an impoverished cowpoke. "But you need to know how to handle a gun. Somebody who knows how might not always be around."

"Oh, all right," Tennie said, not too pleased about it.

"Let's make it a picnic," he suggested, and the others agreed.

Poco would ride in the wagon. Tennie feared he was going to do too much too soon, but he assured her he almost felt like his old self.

Wash and the boys gathered old cans while Tennie prepared a picnic basket for them. After days of being almost ill thinking about Ring Bit, she had resigned herself to her fate and was determined to put on a happy face.

They picnicked near the creek in a grove of oak trees. The trees around Ring Bit were the same live oaks Tennie was used to, but although their circumferences rivaled those in the South, they were only about half as tall. Nevertheless, they made a cool dense shade to place a blanket under. Tennie smiled and laughed.

Wash commented how happy it made him to see her enjoying herself. "You've been like a quiet, worried little ghost the past few days."

"I don't want to leave here," Tennie said. She wanted to add that she didn't want to leave as long as he and Ben and Poco were there, but she did not. The thought of living alone without them on the ranch scared and depressed her. She tried to lighten her mood. "But, since we have no choice, we might as well be excited and hope for the best."

"That's the spirit," Ben said, munching on a handful of cookies.

Wash rose. "Miss Tennie, if you are finished, we'll start our lesson. You boys stay back; I have to try to cram thirty years of artillery knowledge into Miss Tennie's pretty little head in one afternoon."

"My heart's bleeding for you." Tennie laughed.

Wash looked at her for several seconds, his face unreadable. "Come along, then," he said, carrying a burlap sack full of cans in one hand and a rifle in another.

Tennie lifted her skirts, stumbling in the tall grass behind him. When Wash realized she was struggling, he moved the sack and offered her his hand. His fingers felt like tough sinew stretched over rock, the skin covering them as rough as sandpaper. They walked a little away from the others, stopping under a large oak.

"Might as well be in the shade," Wash said. "As much as your laughter charms my soul, I want you to be serious and pay attention. Your life or the life of one of those boys might depend on what I'm teaching you today."

She nodded and tried to be a good student. He took the time to make sure she understood what he was telling her and why it was important. Before he allowed her to shoot, he made her practice loading and unloading. He stood so near her, and the virile odor he carried with him so overwhelmed her, her fingers began to fumble with the cartridges. She had to take a deep breath and force her mind to concentrate on telling her fingers what to do, not how intoxicating Wash Jones smelled standing next to her. She had helped nurse many sick men during the war, and they all had their own scent, some of it awful strong, but none of them had reeked with so much masculinity as the man standing next to her.

"All right, Tennie," he said, his words as soft as a caress. "Let's put the rifle butt up against your shoulder and aim." He stood behind her, helping her to hold the shaking rifle steady. He pressed against her backside, standing back a little at first, but as he instructed her, he came closer until he was against her buttocks. The effect he had on her overpowered all her other senses. She didn't think she could breathe; all her air seemed to be coming in and going out in little spurts.

"Tennie, Tennie," he whispered in her ear, and she felt his lips brushing against her skin. He put his finger around hers. "Pull the trigger slowly," he said.

She couldn't have pulled the trigger if her life depended on it. Her fingers were jelly. He squeezed his finger over hers, until, pushing it back all the way, the rifle fired and plunged Tennie even closer into his shoulders.

Standing behind her, he repeated the lesson multiple times, first with the rifle, later with the revolver. Tennie couldn't concentrate on anything. She might have been firing at the man in the moon. She let him do whatever he wanted; stand as close as he wanted, moving her fingers wherever he wanted them to be. It was the happy screaming of Badger and Lucas playing in the background that made her come up for air.

"Who are you?" she turned her face to whisper into Wash's. "What are you doing in Ring Bit?"

He paused before answering. "It is better for you not to know my business." He took a step back, and the spell Tennie had been under began to dissolve. She handed him the revolver and walked away.

They left during the night without saying good-bye.

The next morning when Lucas and Badger saw the rolled-up pallets and Poco's made bed, the two boys fled to the barn, but Tennie knew without being told their horses and wagon would be gone. Rusty acted as if he had known all along they would leave that way.

Most of the Granger belongings had already been loaded onto their wagon, while the rest sat in a pile by the fence awaiting the wagon and driver who had been promised to take them to the jailhouse in Ring Bit.

The day was so sultry and the absence of the three men so definite, none of the Grangers felt like doing anything. They waited in quiet

61

limbo on the front porch. When a wagon did appear on the horizon, they stared at it with watchful eyes.

"Mercy," Tennie said after getting a closer look at the large, dark-haired man holding the reins guiding two mules. "It's Samson come back from the dead."

"Who's Samson?" Badger asked.

Tennie looked down at him. "I guess they kicked you out of Sunday school, too, didn't they? Did you tie up that teacher, too?"

"No," Rusty said. "They tied her little boy to a tabletop and pretended they were Abraham and he was Isaac. Nearly scared her half to death."

"We weren't going to do anything," Lucas said, tossing his dark head with scorn. "He was awful, Miss Tennie, always bossing us around. Even his own mother was afraid of him."

"Don't let what other people do or think control your own behavior," Tennie said, repeating words from a father who had dimmed into a fading memory.

"What does that mean?" Badger asked.

"It means if I say it long enough, maybe it will sink into your head," Tennie answered, anxiety making her voice sharp.

"Gosh, Miss Tennie," Lucas said. "You sure are snappish since Mr. Wash and Mr. Ben left."

Tennie stared at the wagon making its slow way toward them. "Now that they've deserted us, somebody has to try to turn you into fine little men instead of rotten little boys."

"They haven't deserted us, Miss Tennie," Rusty said, looking at her with concern. "They said they'd be back."

"Don't hold your breath," Tennie said. "You boys better get it into your heads right now, we are on our own, and we are going to have to make it by ourselves." She stood up to greet the man pulling up to the gate.

When he alighted from the wagon, he was even taller than Tennie first imagined. He stood at least six-foot-six and weighed over three hundred pounds, most of it muscle. His face and round cheeks were almost hidden under a long mass of curly black hair. But he smiled at them through his massive beard, and his dark eyes twinkled.

"Hello there!" he called. "I've come to take you little rabbits to town."

Tennie could not place his accent. He sounded Russian, Hungarian, and Czech all mixed together. She introduced herself and the boys to the gentle-looking giant.

"And you are even more beautiful than said to me. But forgive me for slobbering. My name is Michael Rusinko. Everyone calls me Big Mike."

"How do you do, Mr. Rusinko," Tennie said, laughing. "Boys, say hello to Mr. Rusinko."

"No, no," he interrupted. "I do not answer to

Mr. Rusinko. That name reserved for my father. You call me Big Mike. Boys, too."

Tennie glanced at the younger boys, their eyes wide as sunflowers in a meadow. Rusty tried to act calm and knowledgeable, but he looked slightly unnerved, too.

Tennie gulped and said, "Okay, Big Mike." He pitched the rest of their things in the back of his wagon as if he was flicking burnt matches away. He helped Tennie into his wagon, while the three boys clambered into the Granger wagon.

"Giddy-up," he said, popping the reins at the mules, and Tennie dared them to do otherwise.

Taking a deep breath and turning her head to make sure Rusty and the other boys were following, she settled into the seat. "Are you the blacksmith, Mr., er, Big Mike?" she asked.

"That's right. How did you know?"

"Just a wild guess," Tennie said. "Actually, Mr. Payton told me a little about you. He said your livery is next door to the jail?"

"That's right." Mike nodded. "Across the street is butcher and small stockyard. Mr. Milton, the butcher, will give you meat. General store down the street for everything else. You charge, town pays. Last time town had marshal, they give him, what do you call it? Allowance?"

Tennie nodded in understanding. They were going to be on the smelly side of town. "But me?"

"No. Mr. Payton, he go to the mayor and town council, and he say, you give that woman all the food she needs. She feeding three hungry boys and will have men go to jail just so she will cook for them."

Tennie laughed. "They just expect me to be more or less the jailkeeper, don't they? They don't really expect me to round up any bad men, do they?"

"Oh, no," Mike said, reassuring her. "They think just having beautiful young widow in town will make men behave better, that's all."

"Thank the Lord," Tennie said. "I'm going to have a rough enough time trying to keep up with my stepsons. I promised their father I would take care of them, but I don't see how I'm going to be able to keep them out of trouble."

"Yeah, I hear about them boys." Mike laughed. "You have problems with them, you send them to me. I act like big bear and scare them to death."

"Thank you," Tennie said with a laugh, hoping Ring Bit wouldn't be so bad after all.

CHAPTER 5

The jailhouse was one of the few buildings in town made of brick and having a real second story, not a false front like so many of the others. There were bars over the windows surrounded by red brick, but the end bricks were a lighter tannish color, outlining the building. Someone had repaired the broken Ring Bit sign. Next to the door a smaller sign, painted in elaborate letters, proclaimed RING BIT JAIL AND MARSHAL'S OFFICE.

"That's a big jail for a town that's not the county seat," Tennie said.

"They thought Ring Bit would get county seat, but they gave it to another town instead," Mike explained. "The sheriff, he won't come here. U.S. deputy marshal come once every three months. Maybe."

Mike's livery and blacksmith shop stood next to the jail. It had a pump and water trough in front, near the jailhouse. On the other side of the jail was a stagecoach stop and freight office. Beside it was a barbershop and laundry. Across the street stood Milton's imposing painted white butcher shop, but most of its bulk came from sitting high up off the ground and a false front. He had pens of cattle, goats, and pigs behind his store.

Tennie scanned the other signs as Mike slowed the mules to a stop. A feedstore and gunsmith shop, a tack and saddle shop, and a little farther down, the saloons. As Tennie looked down the long stretch of street, she could see after the saloons the shops became progressively more genteel, mercantile stores, dry goods stores, a land office, and funeral parlor, ending with the church and homes on the furthest reaches. Even to her inexperienced eyes, she realized she and the boys would be living on the "wrong" side of town.

Mike put up a big paw to help her alight from the wagon. He opened the door to an office, consisting of a desk and chair on one side of the room, a table with chairs on the other. Tucked in a far corner was a small cot. A potbellied stove sat near the desk, and someone had left an old coffeepot on it. Framed maps hung on the wall along with an empty gun rack. Whoever had been marshal before hadn't taken the time to carry anything but his guns with him.

Mike led her farther into the building and entered a narrow hallway. "Upstairs are jail cells," he said, pointing a big round finger upward.

Ignoring the wide stairs going up, they passed

into the living quarters, a bare room with a few broken pieces of furniture and a cookstove.

She could place her bed in the alcove with enough room to put up a curtain to allow her some privacy. The boys' beds would have to be jammed against the walls. Tennie looked at the room in dismay. "There is no back door. And there are bars on the windows."

Mike nodded. "For reasons to keep safe. No one can escape or get in from back."

"I'll say," Tennie said, feeling morose.

Mike and the boys began unloading their things, asking Tennie where to direct them. She would have liked to clean the place from top to bottom before moving furniture in, but it was already late afternoon, and the others were eager to get things put up and finished.

They did the heavy work, but it would be up to Tennie to see that all the smaller things were put in the right places. Badger and Lucas did not do much, but ran in and out, exploring everything and coming back to report what they had found.

"There are three jail cells upstairs," Lucas said.

"He tried to lock me in one!" Badger tattled.

"Will you fetch me a bucket of clean water from the pump outside?" Tennie asked, knowing the fastest way to get rid of them was to put them to work.

Mike had left with Rusty to show him where to put the wagon. He had said they could keep their mule and horses in his corral until they could repair the one behind the jail. Tennie did as much as she could inside, worrying about what they would do in case of fire. Exhausted, she stood back and looked at the room. A strange sound drifted in from the outside, and Tennie stood listening, wondering what it was.

A louder sound came through the walls, a piecing scream. She turned and raced outside.

In the middle of the street, Badger was being held up by an older, large-framed man with a square jaw and narrow eyes. He was shaking Badger and cursing him.

"What is it?" Tennie cried, rushing to Badger.

The man looked at her with fire and hatred from eyes underneath bushy gray eyebrows. He threw Badger down with so much force, he made a loud thud when he hit the ground. Tennie reached down to help the crying boy up.

"Keep him out of my shop!" the man yelled at her in a rough voice.

"I wasn't in your old store," Badger squalled. "I was just looking in the windows."

"I don't even want you on my porch, you little swine," he said, hollering a stream of curse words as he loomed over Tennie and Badger with hands on his hips.

"Please . . ." Tennie said.

"Send that older boy in the shop for your meat," he said, pointing at Rusty. "I don't want your other monsters even close to my place," and he proceeded to call Lucas and Badger names that would have made a muleskinner cringe.

Tennie found her voice. "Stop cursing these boys."

"I'll do whatever the hell I want." He sneered. "And I don't deal with no meddlesome females, either. So don't you come around."

"Staying away from you will be the easiest thing I'll ever do," she said, beginning to shake in anger, the events she had lived through bubbling inside her until she thought she would explode. "And I'll tell you something else," she found herself yelling. "That meat you give us better not have maggots in it, do you hear me? Because if I find one maggot in it, I'm bringing it back and throwing it in your face. No maggots!"

She burst into tears and ran back into the jailhouse, slamming the door behind her. She circled the inside of the office, sobbing. The boys followed her, silent, with faces solemn.

She forced herself to stop crying. "All right," she said, trying to calm the riot of emotion inside her. "What did you do to make him so mad at you?"

Lucas and Badger looked at the floor.

Rusty sighed. "We climbed on top of his store and poured trash over his head when he walked out. He hates kids, and he's always cussing us, waving his gun at us."

Tennie took a deep breath. "Don't do that again, please. He may deserve it and worse, but please don't do that again. We have to deal with him. He's the one who's supposed to provide us with meat, and if he wants, he can find ways to make us miserable."

The boys looked so sad, it made Tennie feel worse. "We don't have to get meat from him today. We can eat the food I brought from the ranch for supper tonight. Maybe after supper, Rusty will read another chapter of *The Three Musketeers* to us."

Before eating, Tennie opened the windows and gave the bars over them a shake, but they were embedded in concrete mortar. Depressed, she put the food on the table. "I'm going to ask the blessing," she told the boys. "We need all the divine intervention we can get."

Afterward, as they began to eat, she fretted about fire, voicing her concerns about the bars over the windows.

"Maybe we could bust them out with a sledge-hammer," Rusty said.

Tennie shook her head. "No, we'd get in trouble for destroying the town's property." She thought more about it as she sat eating. "Maybe we could borrow a hacksaw or a file or something, and we cut the bars and glue them back in. No one would ever know, but if there was a fire, we could kick the bars out."

The boys looked at one another in excitement. "We could do it at night, so no one would see us," Lucas said.

"That's right, at night," Badger echoed.

"You couldn't tell anyone, Badger," Rusty warned, and Badger nodded, his chubby cheeks grave.

"Do you think Big Mike would loan us a small handsaw?" Tennie said. "And what reason could we have for asking to borrow it?"

They spent the better part of supper making plans to be able to break their way out of the Ring Bit jailhouse if necessary.

"We'll tell him we want to open Pa's strong-box," Rusty said.

"Mr. Wash already shot the lock off it when we couldn't find the key," Lucas said.

"He doesn't know that," Rusty said.

There hadn't been anything in the strongbox except more papers Tennie didn't understand that Wash had told her to hang on to.

The next morning, the boys left to borrow a file or saw from Big Mike. Tennie wondered if Rusty hoped Mike might accompany him across the street to the butcher shop. She was so ashamed of her behavior the previous day, she did not want to show her face outside. Instead, while they were gone, she continued to clean. The desk contained a smattering of papers dating from previous years that meant nothing to her. She placed them in a stack, intending on putting them in the bottom drawer. The bottom drawer yielded, instead of more papers, a pair of shackles and handcuffs. Tennie held them up and made a face, hoping she would never have to use them. She put all the papers in the bottom drawer and placed the manacles on top, vowing not to look at them again if at all possible.

The office, along with everything else, had a dust coating thick enough to write in. Cobwebs surrounded the framed map on the wall; Tennie took it down to clean it. To her surprise, behind where the map had been hanging, she found a small safe buried in the brick wall. It refused to open when she tugged on it. Absentmindedly cleaning the map while alternately staring at the safe, she came upon a small series of tiny numbers written on the back of the frame. Thinking they might be the combination, she tried them on the tumbler.

After a few minutes of turning the knob and wondering if the town council knew anything about the safe, she managed to get it open. Inside, it looked empty except for two twenty-dollar gold pieces, making her almost sure no one but an earlier occupant had known about it. It couldn't have belonged to the previous marshal; he had left in a hurry, but he had taken some things. She didn't know if she should tell anyone what she found or turn the money in. After a few minutes' hesitation, she collected all of Ashton Granger's papers and stuffed them into the safe, along with the gold pieces. She could decide later what to do about them. For the time being, his papers would be securer there than anywhere else. She locked the safe and replaced the framed map over it.

She had finished cleaning the table and chairs when Rusty entered carrying a large chunk of meat and another of salt pork. Lucas had a saw, while Badger toted a file. They were laughing, and it made her happy to see them in a good mood.

"Big Mike said everyone in town is making fun of Mr. Milton, calling him 'Maggot Milton,' " Rusty said. "He's furious, but he gave us a lot of food. Mike said he is afraid not to. You might call him something worse that sticks to him."

"I doubt if he's afraid of that," Tennie said. "He's probably more afraid we'll tell everyone he's starving us."

While she browned the meat, putting it on the back burner to simmer, the boys talked about Mike.

"We told him it was for the strongbox," Rusty said. "He said if we want to sell it, he might like to buy it."

"Yeah, he doesn't trust banks," Lucas said. "Right now, he's got his money hidden in a poke bag."

"But he wouldn't tell us where," Badger said.

Tennie put the lid on the pot. "And I don't blame him."

A high-pitched male voice called to her from the front of the jailhouse. "Mrs. Granger! Mrs. Granger!"

She hurried to the office. The three men who hired her stood waiting, examining the walls and furnishings while the mayor talked.

"We must officially swear you in," the mayor said, trying to sound jovial. He looked nervous. Nevertheless, Tennie smiled and nodded.

With her right hand on the Bible, she swore to uphold the law in Ring Bit. She felt like crossing the fingers of her left hand behind her back, since she had every intention of cutting the bars over the back window, but she supposed there wasn't a law she had to have bars on the windows.

They gave her a badge, but Tennie was too embarrassed to put it on. Instead, she held it in her hand while she asked questions, trying to make clear every detail of what was expected of her, how she was to be paid, in addition to where and what she could charge to the city. They treated her as if they were indulging a child, but it didn't stop her. The last time she didn't ask enough questions, she found herself in front of an altar, marrying a man she didn't know.

Before they left, timidity did overtake her, but she forced herself to ask about the school superintendent. If the teacher wouldn't allow the boys back in school, maybe she could convince the superintendent to use his influence to get them back in.

"It's the undertaker," the mayor said. "If he doesn't have a body, he isn't always at the funeral parlor. If you can't find him there, try his home. It's the third house on the left past the church."

They departed, giving the interior of the jail-house another quick once-over as they walked to the door, the banker's nose giving a slight sniff at the smell of food cooking in the back. If he appreciated it, he gave no sign.

Tennie shut the door behind them and leaned against it with a sigh.

The boys entered the room.

"When can we eat?" Lucas asked.

And Badger asked, "When can we cut the bars off the window?"

Tennie straightened. "You just ate breakfast and dinner's not ready yet. And we have to wait until dark to cut the bars so no one will see us, and we won't get into trouble."

"Then why are we doing it?" Badger demanded, having already forgotten their earlier conversation.

"So if a fire starts out here, we aren't trapped and get burned alive, knucklehead," Tennie said. "I have to change my clothes and run an errand. I won't be gone long."

She changed into the pink dress, with its bows

77

and ruffles. Making sure her hair looked neat, she put on her hat and walked out the door, pausing because the streets looked empty. She began walking down the wooden sidewalk, giving darting glances to the right and left, overcome with the notion she was being stared at from behind closed doors. She did not gape into the dozen saloons she walked by with their opened doors, but was aware the men inside were being still and silent as she passed. She had to step over three drunks propped up on the sidewalks, but they were insensible and made no louder sound or movement other than snoring. Most of the saloons were small; some of them justified the phrase *hole in the wall.* However, when she passed the swinging doors of the Silver Moon Saloon, the sight of an enormous crystal chandelier hanging from the ceiling caused her to gasp and slow her steps. Flocked wallpaper, velvet curtains with gold tassels, and polished wood with brass trimmings were the likes of something she'd never seen or visualized. She had no idea such an elaborate and expensive establishment could and did exist in Ring Bit. She tore her eyes away and hurried down the sidewalk before someone decided to yell out to her. Crossing the street, she looked into the windows of the funeral parlor, but it appeared empty. The sign on the door proclaimed in convoluted script, WILL RETURN SHORTLY.

Tennie didn't wait, but followed the mayor's instructions. It was as she first thought as she walked northward; there were no more drunks lying about, less animal dung in the street, and a general air of increasing refinement permeated the area.

She counted three houses down from the church, stopping in front of a white framed home with touches of fancy scrollwork around its porch. Nice, but not imposing, it nevertheless scared her. She wanted to turn and run back to the shelter of the jailhouse, but her promise to Ashton Granger, who had so willingly placcd a bet on an unknown woman to care for his children, made her walk to the front door and give a sharp rap on the door frame.

She could hear movement within the house, and she took a step back, waiting for the door to open.

A woman with dark, gray-streaked hair opened the door and looked Tennie up and down. She stood taller than Tennie and much stouter, her body encased in a rigid corset struggling to do its job. "Yes?" she said, eying Tennie in suspicion.

"Yes, ma'am," Tennic began, trying to remember how she should introduce herself. "My name is Mrs. Tennessee Granger. I was told your husband is the school's superintendent, and I would like to talk to him about the possibility of my stepsons getting back into school."

The woman's eyes narrowed, and her jaw jutted

farther out. "My husband has nothing to discuss with you. The teacher has made her decision, and he will abide by it."

Deflated, Tennie paused. But the set of the woman's face told her pleading would not get her anywhere. "Thank you," she mumbled and turning to leave, started down the steps. Before she reached the bottom, she was interrupted.

"Mrs. Granger," the undertaker's wife said.

Tennie paused and turned. "Yes, ma'am?"

"We don't want you on this side of town."

Tennie didn't know how she managed it, but she turned, straightened her spine and walked away without looking back. Hearing the door shut behind her, she had only gone a few yards when a slender little man crept from behind the house and approached her. Pausing, still feeling sick at heart and in shock, she looked at him and waited for him to speak.

"Mrs. Granger," the man said. "I am sorry about that. But perhaps if you could come by my funeral parlor later tonight, we could discuss your stepsons' situation together."

Tennie stared at him, wondering what he was talking about. It took a minute for the realization of what he was asking to sink in.

"No, thank you," she said, shaking her head. The memory of the battleax he had to live with made any righteous indignation on her part refuse to even be born. She turned to leave.

"Wait!"

She paused and looked at the small, insignificant little man.

"Wait, please. I'll be right back." He went to the back of his house the same way he had come out. She remained for a minute, wondering if she should leave, but he returned from behind the shrubbery in the backyard carrying a book.

He handed it to her—a *McGuffey Reader*. "Maybe this will help."

She nodded and made to leave.

"No hard feelings?" he said, eyes anxious.

"None," she replied. "Thank you for the book."

CHAPTER 6

Tennie returned to the jailhouse, placing the reader on the table before changing into her oldest dress. The boys were gone, and she could only hope they weren't off raising hell somewhere. Taking hot water from the stove, she poured it into a bucket, carrying it along with soap and rags to the stairs to tackle a job she dreaded.

The upstairs consisted of three disturbing jail cells, the bars surrounding them seeming to scream of the pain suffered within. Four windows ran across the front of the room, facing the street. It had surprised her there were no bars over them, but Rusty had told her, according to Big Mike, the idea had been if someone needed hanging, they could just tie a rope around the prisoner's neck and have him jump or be pushed out the window instead of building expensive gallows.

The large room reeked of urine and stale liquor. Dried feces freckled the floor and walls. Tennie wondered how someone could get feces four feet up a wall, thinking whoever did it surely must have picked it up and thrown it.

The bedding inside the cells was filthy, torn,

full of moth holes, and so infested with lice, she was afraid to go near it. She started to gag and ran to a window, throwing it open and leaning out to gasp for fresh air. She looked down at the tin awning covering the wooden sidewalk. It looked sturdy enough to her, so taking a deep breath, she went back into the cells, picked the bedding up by the corners, dragged them to the window, and threw them out.

They could lay on the awning in the sun until all the lice fried, she thought, and then be taken down and burned. She would have to add dangerous and smelly coal oil to her cleaning bucket to kill the lice, but it had to be done.

Instead of attacking the Ring Bit schoolteacher, the superintendent, the superintendent's wife, her stepsons, and the fate that had put her there, Tennie tackled the filth and lice with enough venom to cleanse the jailhouse of dirt, grime, vermin, along with any lingering evil spirits that dared to stay behind.

Exhausted, bedraggled, she was on her sixth bucket of soapy water and working her way on her hands and knees to the stairwell when a voice startled her, causing her to look up into the face of one of the handsomest men she'd ever seen.

"There is something about seeing a woman on her hands and knees that is so pleasing to a man," he said with a grin.

Tennie got up off her hands but stayed down,

resting on her haunches, her face looking up into his. Dark full hair with wide gray streaks on either side framed his somewhat narrow face. But his blue eyes were large and twinkling underneath arched brows. His clothes were impeccable—a charcoal gray suit with lapels edged in black satin. A narrow silk ribbon bowtie hung from his collar and gold links sparkled against white cuffs. His attire and the whiteness of his skin made her wonder if he was a gambler.

He allowed his full lips and wide mouth to twist into a sardonic grin, and she found herself smiling back at the slender man who leaned, arms crossed, so unconcernedly against the wall behind him.

"My God, they said you were a beauty," he exclaimed, "but I thought they were exaggerating. I can see now they weren't."

Tennie blushed and looked down.

"I'm Lafayette Dumont," he said, with a Southern accent. "I own the Silver Moon Saloon."

Tennie looked up, but could only nod, unsure of how to act around someone so wealthy and sophisticated who had a name like *Lafayette Dumont*. Behind the exterior that read "gambling man" was another layer that said perhaps Lafayette Dumont's family had once been acquainted with presidents and kings.

"How would you like to come to work for me?"

he asked. "No more jail, no more floor scrubbing. You could sing."

Truth loosened Tennie's tongue. "I can't sing."

"With a low-cut dress over that glorious high bosom, no would notice or care," he said, laughing.

Tennie felt her cheeks growing warmer. "No, thank you. My poor parents are probably rolling over in their graves as it is," she blurted and blushed further.

"I'm sure my people would have preferred I stayed home farming a burnt-out plantation and starving to death, but I did what I do best, play cards. Really, Miss Tennie, if you will allow me to call you that, you must get up off your knees. The sight of you at my feet is much too arousing." He grinned and held out his hand.

She took his hand, dry from the constant handling of cards and money. Feeling the slightest pressure of her fingers in his palm would cause him to wrap her in his arms and kiss her, she rose and let go of his hand. She also avoided looking too deeply into his eyes. "How did you happen to settle on Ring Bit?" she asked.

He paused, as a curtain closed behind his eyes, and his face became expressionless, showing Tennie just how good of a gambler he could be. The curtain came up again, however, and he said with another ironic grin, "I had the misfortune of falling in love with another man's wife. My brother's, in fact. My father always said never marry a beautiful woman. He must have known what he was talking about. He did it twice. Ring Bit seemed as good a place as any to spend purgatory."

"I believe in the forgiveness of sins," Tennie said.

He stared at her for several seconds. "Miss Tennie, be careful or I shall absolutely devour your sweet little self."

She did not answer—he was too far ahead of her. He smiled. "Well, if I can't talk you into working for me, I suppose we must get down to other business."

She nodded and he continued. "The saloon owners in Ring Bit usually pitch any trouble-makers out into the street, but occasionally on Friday and Saturday nights, there are pests who won't leave well enough alone, so we have men bring them to the jail cells to spend the night. Don't try to do anything with them or for them. Leave them in their cells until they sleep it off, and then let them go the next day."

She nodded again, dreading the prospect of having drunken brawlers sleeping in the cells above them. "Yes, Mr. Dumont."

"Don't call me that. Call me Lafayette."

"How about I call you Mr. Lafayette?" Tennie said, still a little in awe of the old Southern gentry charm he exuded.

He laughed. "All right. Unfortunately, you'll have to clean up after them. Where's the bedding?" He was looking at the bare beds.

"It was so filthy and lice-ridden, I threw it out the window. After the sun beats on it a few days, I'll have my stepsons bring it down and burn it."

"Good plan." He nodded. "Since most of your inmates will be patrons of the Silver Moon, I'll pay for the new bedding. Go to the mercantile across the street from my saloon. Get what you need and tell them to charge it to me. I'll let them know you are coming."

"Thank you," Tennie said, her voice expressing the relief she felt at not having to tell the town's council what she had done. "May I offer you something to eat or drink? Our dinner should be ready soon."

"No, thank you, my dear girl. I do want to warn you of one more thing before I leave."

"What is that?"

"Don't let your stepsons roam around at night if you can help it. The man across the street is slightly unbalanced, and he may take it into his head to fire a potshot at them. This is off the record, of course."

"Yes." Tennie knew that meant he was willing to warn her, but not testify to it if one of them turned up dead. "I'll try, but I don't know what I can do to keep them inside."

"I hear they are quite good at playacting. Work

on a play for them to put on. Perhaps the *Three Musketeers* book they are reading. Who knows? If they are good enough, I may allow them to use the stage in my saloon. Anything to liven up a boring weekday night."

She followed him downstairs, wondering how he knew what they were reading.

He put on his hat, gray with a wide brim and flat crown, and turned to her at the front door. "And after I leave here, and the men of this town have seen for themselves which way you are jumping. . . ."

"What do you mean?"

"I mean once it becomes known you have turned down the amorous intentions of the married undertaker, and you have refused to come to work for me, they will be knocking on your doorstep, hoping to carry you over theirs." He tipped his hat, opened the door, and left Tennie trying to catch her breath.

Rusty, Lucas, and Badger came creeping out of the back and stood in the doorway.

"Did he mean that about Maggot Milton taking a shot at us in the dark?" Lucas asked.

Tennie took a deep breath, wondering if she should fuss at them for eavesdropping. "Yes, and don't refer to him as *Maggot*. Call him *Mr.* Milton, please."

"Why?" Badger demanded. "Why do we have to be nice to him if he might kill us?"

It made Tennie stop and think. "Hmm, let's see. Mr. Lafayette speaks politely, he runs one of the roughest businesses in town, and I bet he doesn't put up with trouble from anybody. On the other hand, Mr. Milton screams curses at little kids, and I bet you underneath, he's probably yellow. So, you decide what you want to be."

They looked at one another, thinking about what she said. But her mind was already on a different track. Rusty's pants were too short. His hat was decrepit, and he wore the rough worn-out boots of a farm boy. The younger boys were barefoot like every other child in town in the summer, but their clothes were Rusty's hand-me-downs and looked tattered, too.

"I think after dinner we should go to the mercantile and use some of the money Mr. Payton paid us to buy you all new clothes," Tennie said. "But first we need to sit down and make out some kind of schedule for schoolwork and chores. It's not fair to make me do everything around here."

"Can I pick out my own clothes?" Rusty asked, his face anxious.

"What about us?" Lucas cried.

"Rusty, yes. You and Badger, no. Not yet," Tennie said. "Come on. Let's eat. I'll finish the stairwell later."

They started for the living quarters, but Rusty held back. "Mr. Wash was polite, too, wasn't he?" he asked Tennie.

90

"Yes. Yes, he was," Tennie agreed—an extraordinarily polite man with a fierce dragon lurking below the surface. She called into the other room. "Don't go around telling people I said Mr. Milton was yellow!

"I only said he probably was," she muttered.

All conversation ceased in the busy store when Tennie and the three boys entered.

Trying to pretend she did not notice, she handed the bald shopkeeper a list of the bedding she would need for the jail. "Mr. Dumont said I was to put it on his bill, please," she said, wishing her words did not sound so timid. "My stepsons will be needing new clothes, but we have the cash to pay for them."

She tried to get the boys to behave, but Lucas and Badger ran wild in the store, racing up and down the aisles whooping. She finally got them into new overalls and sent them outside to wait. Rusty took his time, examining every shirt and pair of pants. Tennie looked at all the items in the store twice. When she returned to the back of the store where the clothes were, his face still wore the same expression of careful consideration.

"May I buy a hat and boots, too, Miss Tennie?" he asked.

It would be a lot of money, but it had come from his father. It would also mean they would be stuck in Ring Bit until Tennie could save enough money to leave. She nodded, digging into her handbag and handing him enough bills she thought would cover the cost. "I'll wait outside with Lucas and Badger. Take your time and get exactly what you want and think you will get the most wear out of. Just remember you are still growing. If the pants are too long, I can take them up and let them down later as need be."

He took the money and gave her a grateful nod. She left him in the store, walking outside to sit beside Lucas and Badger on a bench. Three young women came out of the Silver Moon, overdressed in the latest fashions. Tennie's hat, a gift from a woman she had done some work for, had been expensive ten years ago. She thought back to then.

The few Southern women who still had money and position preferred to have former slaves serving them. They could either pretend the ex-slaves were deaf, or if they faced the reality that every word they spoke was being listened to, they could tell themselves whatever gossip they shared would only be spread among the Negro quarters and would not make its way into white society. But sometimes they, and especially the wives of carpetbaggers, distrusted the newfound freedom of the ex-slaves, and they would pay the orphanage to have Tennie work in the kitchen amongst the silver and china. Quite a few of them had taken pity on her, remembering her father, while not exactly one of them, had nevertheless been a fine cabinetmaker.

While Tennie's hat, being wide of brim, served her well in the hot Texas sun, it was not the stylish, little floral covered hats worn by the women exiting the saloon. They didn't need wide brims. They had fancy parasols to shield their skin. They made their way across the street in their silk dresses with yards of fabric and huge bustles trailing behind them, causing Tennie to feel a pang of jealousy. She realized they were making their way to the mercantile, and she wished she was somewhere else instead of sitting by the front door with two squirmy boys.

"Well, look who's here," one of the women said. She had dark hair and a face covered in two weeks' worth of powder and rouge. "If it isn't our little marshal."

"Where's your badge, sweetie?" another cackled, while the petite blonde beside her gave Tennie a frosty look before sticking up her nose.

Tennie didn't respond; they hadn't said anything requiring one, but neither did she put up her nose or look away.

They passed her and entered the store, so close Tennie could see the rings of dirt around their collars, and the equally grimy cuffs of their dresses. They seemed to be covered in cheap perfume, but even so, there was an odd underlying scent about them, almost like that of burning syrup.

Mr. Payton, coming out as they were going in, tipped his hat and held the door open for them. After they had entered, he shut the door behind him, greeting Tennie. She returned his hello, saying she hadn't realized he was inside.

He looked down at the new overalls the boys wore. They were as baggy as Tennie felt they could get by with, and the legs were rolled into cuffs. By the end of the summer, they would be too small.

Mr. Payton reached into his pocket, bringing out a penny for each boy. "Go down to the livery and see if Mike has my horse shod yet."

Tennie opened her mouth, but they beat her to it. "Yes, sir. Thank you," and they raced from the bench down the sidewalk to the livery.

Mr. Payton raised his eyebrows at Tennie.

"We had a small discussion about the kind of man who is polite and the kind of man who isn't," she explained. "Don't worry. The world isn't coming to an end. They acted like idiots in the store earlier."

Mr. Payton grunted and looked after them. "Did you buy those overalls with the money I paid you?"

"Yes, sir."

He nodded in approval, taking the seat beside her. "No one has probably told you, but the soiled doves usually do their shopping from two to four in the afternoon, and the other women avoid the stores during that time."

"The undertaker's wife told me I wasn't wanted on their side of town," Tennie said. "So evidently I'm not going to fit in anywhere."

"Well, what did you expect, taking this job?" he demanded.

"And what was I supposed to do?" she asked.

"Be respectable. Marry any of these men in town. All you have to do is point your finger at onc and say 'you're it.'"

"And I would frighten him so badly, he would get on his horse and ride and not stop until he reached California," Tennie countered. She changed the subject. "Why is town so quiet? Where is everyone?"

Pulling out a pipe, Mr. Payton filled it with tobacco from a leather pouch. "There is a little Mexican segment of town to the east of us," he said, pointing to it with his pipe. "And a Negro settlement a mile west of us. Don't go there and don't bother them. They handle their own affairs.

"The men are across the street in the saloons watching us right now. Waiting to see how you handle yourself. Don't go in there, either. For one thing, the saloon girls will try to lure you into taking sides in their constant fights, and it will become a never-ending source of irritation for you. They are sows dressed in silk, but sows nevertheless. The men of the West are so starved for women, they will take anyone, and many a prostitute has found a good man and started a happy life with one out here." He gave a nod of his head to the inside of the store. "But those girls are the hardened ones. They don't want to give up the excitement of the sporting life and won't stop until they contract syphilis or get too old, in which case, Lafayette will put them on the first stage out of town."

"He paid for new bedding for the jail," Tennie said.

"He's trying to get you to feel beholden to him. Don't. That blonde who just walked into the store? That's his mistress."

Tennie had to resist the urge to turn and crane her neck to get a better look.

"I sometimes wonder if Lafayette isn't trying to get shut of her," he mused. "He hired a slick piano player last year and talked up how exciting life could be on a Mississippi riverboat, but Arabella wouldn't take the bait. She dallied with the piano player for a while, but in the end decided what she had here was too good of a nest to fly away from, so she let one of the other girls run off with him."

"I won't pretend I understand any of that,"

Tennie said. "All I know is he said he fell in love with the wrong woman and that's how he ended up in Ring Bit."

"The brother's wife?" Mr. Payton said. "Did he tell you he killed one of his brothers in a duel over that woman?"

Tennie shook her head. "No."

"He did. I talked to my relatives in Alabama about him when I went there to fetch you girls; they told me about it. The brother's wife became so distraught over the havoc she caused, she went into mourning and hasn't come out of it to this day."

"Well, that's a little foolish," Tennie said.

"To you and me, yes," he said with a dry laugh. "But to those wealthy, inbred old Southern families, no." He took a long drag on his pipe. "The thing to remember about Lafayette is everything boils down to business with him. He's here to make money—I guess to prove something to his family. I don't know. His parents disowned him."

"He hasn't tried to go back?" Tennie asked. "Surely his family has forgiven him by now."

"Maybe, but her family hasn't," Mr. Payton said. "She had an uncle who used to go to town wearing a woman's camisole and corset under his shirt. He'd preen like a peacock when people would notice. He wouldn't hurt a fly, but there was a stern younger brother who would kill

Lafayette in a heartbeat if he ever showed his face back there. It's surprising to me he hasn't come looking for him."

Rusty walked out of the store, looking self-conscious in his new clothes. Tennie had feared he might decide on something inappropriate, but he had made good choices. It came to her with a start they were replicas of the ones Wash Jones had worn, right down to the high-topped boots with the pants legs tucked in.

"Oh, here," Rusty said, thrusting into her hand the money he had left over.

Mr. Payton nodded in approval. "You know anything about horses and cattle, boy?"

Rusty nodded. "Yes, sir. I helped my pa with our cattle before he got so down."

"You're old enough to go on the roundup and trail drive next spring," Mr. Payton said. "I'll take you on. I won't be going next year, but my men will. I'll see you have a place with them."

"Thank you, sir," Rusty said, surprised and pleased.

That night, amidst a flurry of whispers, Rusty worked on the outside cutting the bars with a saw, while Lucas and Badger took turns with the file from the inside.

It grew so late, Tennie told them they would have to stop for the night. "We still have so far to go."

CHAPTER 7

By Friday afternoon, Tennie decided the men must have tired of sitting inside of buildings watching her, because the sidewalks were filling with people, almost all of them male. The streets became noisy with the sounds of men shouting and animals barking and braying. Maggot Milton ran out of his store twice waving a gun and cursing children to stay off his sidewalk and away from the animals in the pens behind his building. By evening, the streets were full of horses tethered to hitching posts in front of the saloons, and gunshots were heard being fired all over town. The sounds of laughter and cursing filled the night, all of it raucous. It seemed to Tennie it happened in front of the jail more than anywhere else, as if she was being dared to come outside.

She stayed huddled with the three boys in the living quarters. Rusty tried to read, but the noises outside were so loud, they had trouble hearing him. He stopped when a particularly vile stream seemed to be coming their way. They had the door between the living quarters and office open, and from where they sat, they could see the outside door. When the cursing became its strongest, it sounded just outside the door, and all four of them jumped when it was kicked open.

"We got one for you, Miss Tennie," a man shouted. He and another man were half carrying and struggling with a man so drunk, he could hardly hold his head up. He nevertheless managed to squirm and spew obscenities at his captors.

Tennie jumped up, grabbing the key ring from the wall.

"Stay back, Miss Tennie," the bigger of the two men wrestling their prisoner said. "He's liable to kick you. He's a mean jackass when he's drunk. Oops, pardon my French, ma'am."

Tennie nodded and followed from a safe distance as they took the prisoner upstairs. They threw him unceremoniously into the farthest cell and slammed the door behind him. Tennie locked it with shaking hands. He jumped unexpectedly, and she barely made it out of his reach before he grabbed her, calling her foul-sounding names she didn't know existed. One of the men took a pistol and, using the butt, reached through the bars and struck him in the head with a blow that should have knocked him out, but only sent him reeling back.

"Don't pay him no mind, Miss Tennie," the other man said. "Believe it or not, he's a real nice fellow when he's sober."

They didn't waste time, but tromped back down the stairs, spurs jingling, with Tennie behind them. Reaching for the door, they stopped. "Lafayette said to remind you not to be outside if you can help it."

Tennie nodded, and they left, shutting the door behind them.

The prisoner, however, continued his tirade. Tennie returned to their living quarters and the table the boys sat around, but the man's continual cursing above them amplified throughout the room. Rusty tried to read and couldn't. As the prisoner cursed everyone who locked him up, he began banging the slop bucket against the bars as loud as he could.

Badger began to cry. "I want my pa. I want to go home."

Lucas began to weep silent tears, while Rusty looked like he was about to. Tennie stared at them, feeling helpless.

"Wait a minute," she said. "We have some buttermilk pie left over from supper. I think it would be a nice thing if you took it over to Big Mike and perhaps visited him for a while."

The younger boys wiped their tears. "Really?"

Tennie nodded, but Rusty looked hesitant, as if he didn't want to leave her alone.

"I'll be fine," Tennie said. "You boys go. But don't wear out your welcome."

She got the pie for them and thrust it into

Rusty's hands as the sounds above them increased in ferocity. They walked into the office.

Opening the door, Tennie peered into the night. "Okay, go there and straight back. Don't dare go anywhere else."

She stayed at the door, watching through the dark night. Mike had his doors open and lanterns lit. She could make out the dying embers in his forge and the shadow of the boys as they walked past.

She shut the door and went back to the table. She placed her hands over her ears and put her head down, but she couldn't block out the screaming filth above her head. She kept her hands over her ears, her eyes shut tight, hoping he would tire of yelling and beating on the bars soon.

She felt someone's presence in the room rather than heard it. She jerked her head up and removed her hands from her ears. Rusty had come back, carrying the pie.

"Mike said Mr. Lafayette and Mr. Payton both warned him about eating us out of house and home, so he can't take the pie," Rusty said. "But he sent me back to fetch you. He said you can sit with us; we can watch for anybody coming who needs locking up tonight."

Tennie nodded in thankfulness. She took the keys from the hook on the wall and followed Rusty to the livery as the man in the cell above cursed Tennie, Lafayette, and Lafayette's mother.

Mike sat in a chair just outside the door, facing the jail, and he had placed another chair for Tennie a little farther back in the shadows, so she could see but not be seen. The boys sat around them on the ground.

"Thank you, Big Mike," she said, sitting in the chair he pulled it out for her. "It is nice of you to let us come over."

"Nice?" his big voice boomed. "No, not nice of me. Nice for me."

She couldn't place his accent. "Are you Polish, Mike?"

"No! I am Ruthenian," he said, beaming in pride.

"What's that?" Badger asked.

"Here, I show you. Come closer to fire." Mike took a stick and drew circles on the ground. "See, here is Russia; here is Poland; here is Hungary. Here is where I come from," he said, pointing the stick. "And here," he said, moving the stick far from the circles, "is where I am now. The people where I am from, they are all small people. I don't fit in so good there. But here, I fit in better with tall Texans."

Tennie laughed and agreed, moving back to her chair. Mike took his place as sentry and began telling them about his home in the foothills of the mountains, his big voice booming over and drowning out the sounds of rinky-dink pianos, shouting, fights, and the occasional gunfire floating in from the street. Tennie listened, but waited, nerves tense, for her job to begin. Mike hadn't been talking long when he stood up. Tennie rose and went to the door, seeing two men dragging a writhing third toward the jail.

"I have to go," she said. "I'll be back. You boys stay here with Mike."

They followed her to the front doors of the livery as she hurried to do her job. She made a motion for them to stay back and called out to the men in front of her. "I'm right here."

The men looked up. One was the same man who had come the previous time, a heavyset, stoutly built cowboy. The other man grappling with the drunken cowboy who seemed intent on escaping their grasp was a different helper.

Tennie opened the jail door and stood back. They headed for the stairs with the battling man muttering they were to let him go so he could kill them or some other peckerwood, Tennie wasn't sure. When the other prisoner heard them coming up the stairs, he began his ruckus again.

The men threw the thrashing man into one of the empty cells and slammed the door behind him. Tennie locked it as quickly as she could and drew back. One of the men yelled at the first prisoner.

"I told you to shut up! Now shut your mouth. You ain't going nowhere." His words had no effect on the jailed man's tirade, and he shook his head in disgust, heading for the stairs. Tennie followed the two men out.

"Go ahead on," the first man said to his helper. "I'll be there directly."

He nodded and left. The heavyset cowboy turned to Tennie. He looked older and wiser than an ordinary cowboy in the dim light of the lanterns, a man with dark sad eyes and a square chin. "Name's Jeff Hamilton, Miss Tennie. You and them young'uns staying over at the livery?"

"Nice to meet you, Mr. Hamilton," Tennie said, grateful to hear another Southern accent. "All that hollering was upsetting the boys, so I sent them over to Big Mike's. He sent them back to fetch me, saying it would be all right if we just watched the jail from the livery for a while."

"We'll be working together, Miss Tennie," Jeff said. "You might as well call me Mr. Jeff."

"Of course, Mr. Jeff," she said as they walked together.

"Don't worry about Honey Boy; he'll calm down and fall asleep in a little while. You won't have to be up too late. Most of the vinegar is out of them a little after midnight; after that, they quit wanting to fight. Then we'll just roll them onto the sidewalks when they pass out."

"Honey Boy?" Tennie said with a questioning raise of her eyebrows.

"It's the nickname his mama gave him and it

stuck," Jeff said. They had reached the door of the livery. He tipped his hat. "I'll be getting back. I'll tell Lafayette where you're at."

"Is Mr. Lafayette . . ." Tennie began. "Is he the boss of the town?"

"No. It'd be a da . . . er, dag-gum sight better place if he was, though," he answered and moved through the night.

Big Mike and the boys were in the middle of telling ghost stories. Tennie sat down once again, but got interrupted just as Mike began a narration about something he called a *vepyr*, a bloodsucking man who haunted castles.

"Thank goodness there are no castles around here," Tennie said before she hurried away. That was all she needed, hollering men and children screaming from nightmares about a *vepyr*.

The three men were from another saloon. When their prisoner saw Tennie, he mistook her for another woman and began cursing her violently.

One of the two men holding him gave him a vicious strike across the face. "That's not Marguerite! That's Miss Tennie!"

They pushed him inside the jailhouse, up the stairs, and into the third cell. Honey Boy began banging his bucket and hollering again, some-thing about Lafayette being some kind of mother Tennie didn't understand. She only knew it drew a violent response from the men who had brought the third prisoner in.

One of them drew his pistol and fired it into the cell. "Shut that up or the next bullet goes in your gut," he hollered.

"Please, I'm going," Tennie said, heading back down the stairs. The two men followed her, escorting her to the livery.

"Don't pay him no mind, ma'am," one of them said. "He's got the manners of a donkey."

"I won't," Tennie promised, thanking them before escaping back into the livery where Mike had gotten off the subject of the bloodsucking count and was telling them about a headless man who rode through the countryside looking for his wife.

Tennie had never met anyone so full of lore and superstition as Big Mike. She was listening to a story about his grandmother, who knew his ill father was going to die because a bird tried to get into the house, when Jeff called to her from the doorway.

She started and jumped up.

"One more, Miss Tennie," Jeff said, but his voice lacked the rougher edge he had used before.

He had yet another helper with him, but they didn't bother to have the cowboy between them in a hold. Their prisoner barely made a shadow, he was so small. In the dim light, he looked as mild as a bowl of oatmeal. Tennie hurried to the jailhouse, wondering what he had done. She opened the door for them, but they didn't warn her to stay back. Instead, they allowed the prisoner to climb the stairs ahead of them.

"You may be keeping him for a while, Miss Tennie," Jeff said. "He knifed a friend of his, but the man ain't dead yet. Doc passed out earlier tonight, and when we managed to wake him up, he had sobered enough to work on him, so he may live."

Tennie didn't know how to respond. When they reached the top floor, she said, "The cells are full. I don't know where to put him."

Jeff looked at the three men. "Honey Boy's finally out. We'll put him in there with him. They're pals."

"Uh, do you think we should search him for more weapons?" she asked, feeling timorous, but not wanting Honey Boy to be knifed, too.

"Two-Bit, you got any more weapons on you?" Jeff asked the prisoner.

He shook his head. "Nope."

"He's all right, Miss Tennie," Jeff said.

Tennie unlocked the cell, hoping the sound of the key being turned didn't awaken Honey Boy and turn him into a crazed maniac again. Jeff opened the door, and Two-Bit walked in.

"Roll Honey Boy off the bed," Jeff instructed the prisoner. "He ain't gonna feel nothing for a long time."

Two-Bit nodded, pushing Honey Boy aside. Tennie scrunched her eyes shut and heard a thud, but when she opened them, Honey Boy was lying on the jailhouse floor, mouth gaping, still snoring and looking none the worse.

She locked the door and followed Jeff and his helper down the stairs.

"Lafayette will send word what to do with him, tomorrow or the next day," Jeff said. "It depends on if the man he knifed lives and wants to press charges. They usually don't."

"Oh dear," Tennie muttered.

Jeff held the door as she walked out. "Don't fret, Miss Tennie. When Doc is sober, he's a dang good doctor."

She walked back into the livery, feeling exhausted. Badger and Lucas had fallen asleep on the ground. Mike and Rusty were discussing the best way to shoe a horse. Tennie wanted to cry, but was too tired to shed tears.

It wasn't much later Jeff returned. He was by himself. "Lafayette sent me to tell you to go on to bed now, Miss Tennie, if things have quieted down in the jail."

Rising, Tennie started to pick up Badger, but Jeff leaned down and tossed the sleeping boy on his shoulders. Rusty shook Lucas awake, and the three of them followed Jeff. He walked into the jailhouse and headed straight for the back, pausing until Tennie told him where to put Badger. He gave their living quarters a brief once-over before heading to the stairs.

Tennie followed him, thankful all the prisoners were asleep. "May I blow out the lanterns now?" she whispered to Jeff.

"Sure," he said and helped her extinguish the flames.

She followed him down the darkened stairs to the front door. "Thank you, Mr. Jeff. Give my regards to Mr. Lafayette, and my thanks, too."

"Yes, ma'am," he said, tipping his hat before walking back into a dark night that had become noticeably quieter.

Tennie checked on her prisoners throughout the next morning, but it was noon before any of them awakened. She still hadn't heard word about the knife attack. Two of the prisoners were sullen, and Tennie was glad to be rid of them. Honey Boy, however, while groaning and carrying on about how bad he felt, repeatedly asked Tennie if he had been obnoxious, all the while apologizing because he knew he had.

"We are about to eat dinner," Tennie said, trying to divert his flow as they walked down the stairs. He was a strapping young cowboy, and Tennie hoped he wouldn't stumble and fall on her. "Would you care for something to eat?"

"Ugh," he moaned, holding his attractive blond head between two large hands. "I couldn't eat a thing."

They had reached the front door, and he seemed reluctant to leave. "Is there anything I can do for you to make up for my bad manners, Miss Tennie?"

"I'll need to feed the man upstairs," Tennie said, looking at the ceiling. "But I haven't had a chance to clean up there, and it smells so bad." One of the sullen ones had vomited.

"I'll fetch Two-Bit down here, Miss Tennie," Honey Boy said. "He can eat at this here table, and then I'll take him back up for you."

She wasn't sure what the protocol was for feeding prisoners, but Honey Boy's plan sounded all right to her. While he went for Two-Bit, Tennie made plates for the boys in the back and brought the rest of the food out to the front. When Honey Boy saw it, he decided he was hungry after all. Tennie had made extra food, but even so, she had to put small portions on her plate to make sure her two guests had enough. For someone who complained of a sick stomach, Honey Boy managed to eat three platefuls without slowing down.

They ate without talking, and when they finished, Honey Boy, becoming loquacious again, took the mild-mannered Two-Bit back to his cell, all the while fussing at him for getting into a knife fight that might keep him from being back at work on Monday.

Tennie, noticing Two-Bit did not seem the least perturbed about missing work, followed to lock the cell door, telling him she would return in a little while to clean the other cells. She managed to get Honey Boy to leave, and by the time she cleaned the kitchen and the upstairs cells, there was a riotous dogfight outside. The boys ran to watch, and Tennie looked, but couldn't stand watching the bloody, snarling teeth and had to go back inside. Just in the short time she had been outside, the amount of money bet on the two dogs staggered her.

If she had harbored any ideas of Saturday night being milder than Friday, it proved wrong. It was a louder, more violent, repeat of Friday. Big Mike again encouraged them to seek sanctuary in his shop, although once or twice cowboys drifted in, looking for a place to spend the night, but left again when they saw Tennie and the boys.

Honey Boy was back, rowdier and blaring even more curse words at the world. As she followed Jeff down the stairs after locking him up once again, she asked if Honey Boy was a married man.

Jeff gave her a sharp look. "No, ma'am."

"That's good. It would be horrible to think he had reproduced. I don't know how children could stand living with someone whose personality changes from warmhearted to brutal so quickly."

Jeff laughed. "Oh, he's been drinking all afternoon. You're just catching the brunt of it."

"I guess better me than some poor woman with a lot of little children," Tennie said with a sigh.

It wasn't just Honey Boy spewing filth at the top of his lungs; two other prisoners screamed and rattled the bars so hard, Tennie worried they wouldn't hold. The jail cells filled with brawlers who wouldn't stop fighting, plus Two-Bit, who lay on his cot and stared at the ceiling. Tennie and Jeff tried to keep the others away from him, but they were soon overcrowded. The last two prisoners of the night started arguing, and within five heartbeats were trying to choke one another.

Tennie screamed, "Stop!" but they didn't even appear to hear her.

Jeff took her by the elbow and led her down the stairs. "Leave them be, Miss Tennie."

She nodded, feeling her nerves were shot to a frazzle. Jeff took her back to Mike's, and it was with the greatest relief when he returned to tell her Lafayette said to go to bed.

CHAPTER 8

Late Saturday night, three men in town were robbed and left for dead in different alleys. At ten o'clock on Sunday morning, there was another knifing at the regular weekend cockfights in the Mexican section. A fight broke out between the Anglos and Mexicans leaving ten wounded and one man dead. Tennie wouldn't have known anything about the crimes, but Rusty heard about them and told her.

The church bells rang, and Tennie paused in her cooking to listen. The undertaker's wife had said they weren't wanted on that side of town, and Mr. Payton had said nothing to contradict it. When it came to worshipping God, they were on their own there, too. She bent down and concentrated on preparing food once again.

Jeff called to her from the office and walked into the living quarters, his spurs clinking. He took a quick sideways gander at what was cooking in the pots and told her to release Two-Bit. His friend lived and wasn't one to hold a grudge.

"What about the four dead men?" she asked.

"Miss Tennie," he said. "Nobody claims to know anything; nobody claims to have seen anything. Even if we had a male marshal, he wouldn't be able to do anything. The last one we had left so fast, we didn't see nothing but the dust he kicked up fleeing. The two before that were shot."

"Did they have family?" Tennie asked, thinking of the gold coins.

"Nope," Jeff said. "None of them, fortunately." He looked at her, his face kind. "I know you are in a tough spot. But don't trouble yourself unduly over it."

"I really don't understand why the town council wants me here," Tennie cried.

"Come on, now, quit that," Jeff said. "Let's go get Two-Bit."

Two-Bit wasn't anxious to leave. "Do you mind if I try to wake Honey Boy? We cowboy together at the Bar S."

Tennie didn't mind as long as Two-Bit was doing the shaking and not her. She and Jeff stood by while Two-Bit roused Honey Boy. The other men, mindful of a cockfight they wanted to attend, had managed to roll out of bed earlier and asked to be released, so Honey Boy and Two-Bit were her last prisoners.

A contrite and groggy Honey Boy followed them down the stairs. All the men seemed reluctant to leave, even Jeff.

Tennie, however, was prepared. "I have cooked a big Sunday dinner. Would you care to join us?"

Jeff laughed. "I believe I better leave you to it. Joe Lee, Lafayette's cook, gets his dander up when he puts out food, and nobody is there to eat it."

Honey Boy and Two-Bit, however, stayed.

"Do you mind if we all eat together since it is Sunday?" Tennie asked.

"No, ma'am! That would be fine, wouldn't it, Two-Bit?" Honey Boy said.

"Yes, ma'am, we'd be plum grateful, we would."

Tennie nodded, calling the boys and bringing the food to the office. The boys lugged in chairs, and they crowded around the table. Two-Bit reached his fork for the braised roast swimming in gravy and potatoes, but Honey Boy knocked his hand away.

"Where's your manners, you East Texas hillbilly?" Honey Boy said. "Miss Tennie has to ask the blessing first."

Tennie bowed her head and said a quick one; she didn't want praying to get in the way of Two-Bit's appetite. Honey Boy gave Two-Bit a withering look and turned back to Tennie. "That's why he's called that, because he ain't worth two bits."

"At least my name is not Honeee-Boyyyy," Two-Bit said, making his voice sound girlish.

Before Honey Boy could respond, Rusty spoke. "Three men were found dead in alleys last night, and another one got killed at the cockfight this morning."

But they had started eating and refused to talk until they were finished. Tennie had never seen men so intent on eating. Her father and mother always had lively discussions over the dining table, and in the big homes she sometimes served in, bright conversations flowed. In Texas, it seemed men believed in eating without speaking.

Honey Boy chewed his last bite and nodded his head. "Lots of nefarious goings-ons, even for Ring Bit, but I've heard tell of worse Saturday nights. Good thing I got drunk and was locked up."

"I shouldn't have knifed that man," Two-Bit said. "But he shouldn't have insulted me like that."

"How did he insult you?" Honey Boy asked.

"I don't remember. I just remember I felt highly insulted," Two-Bit said, looking mournful. "He ought not to have said whatever it was he said."

"I heard talk there has been a lot of rustling going on around here," Rusty said. Although he had tried to sound casual, Tennie caught a note of intentness in his voice and turned to stare at him.

When Honey Boy nodded, Rusty asked if he knew who was behind it.

"No, we can't figure out what's going on. It's

like those cattle just disappear," Honey Boy said. "The Bar S has really caught it, and the boss is fit to be tied over it, but we haven't been able to put a stop to it."

Two-Bit agreed. "Before I got locked up, I heard vigilantes or somebody is really cracking down on them over at Mills Creek. They've been finding men dead with running irons in one hand and pistols in the other. There's been stories about men disappearing, only to find out later they've been thrown into a pokey somewhere far away."

"What's a running iron?" Lucas asked.

"It's a short piece of iron that rustlers use to change the shape of a brand," Honey Boy said.

After having lain on a cot silent for two days, Two-Bit, now garrulous, explained. "A regular branding iron is over three feet long; a running iron is barely two feet. Sometimes it will just have a point on it so a rustler can draw a new brand. Or it might be in the shape of something that can change a brand into something else right quick."

"Either way, if anybody is caught with one, it means a fight between Gabriel and Old Scratch over who gets to take what's left," Honey Boy said.

"Who's Old Scratch?" Badger asked.

"The devil," Lucas said, his voice full of scorn. "Didn't you learn nothing in Sunday school?"

"I didn't get to go that long before they threw me out," Badger said, defending himself.

"Where is Mills Creek?" Tennie asked.

"It's way on the other side of Cat Ridge, the county seat," Honey Boy said.

Tennie stole another look at Rusty, wondering why he was so interested in cattle rustling. Badger began to chatter, demanding to know if Tennie had made dessert, fussing he didn't like what she had cooked, and in general, making a pest of himself.

"Hush up, boy," Honey Boy said.

Badger crossed his chubby little arms over his chest. "I don't have to do what you say," he pouted. "You're not my pa."

"Listen, kid," Honey Boy said, turning from genial guest into a man to be reckoned with quicker than a woman could change her mind. "I don't put up with trash from nobody, from six to sixty. Now you either hush your mouth or I'm taking you out behind this here jail and wearing your tail out."

Badger's lips puckered and trembled, and he looked at Tennie and his brothers. "Are you going to let him do that to me?" he demanded.

"I don't think we could stop him, Badger," Tennie said quickly. "He's just trying to keep you from spouting off and getting your head blown off when you get older. Or knifed like Two-Bit's friend." She turned to Honey Boy. "Please don't get up. Badger isn't going to say another word." And she gave Badger a look that said he was going to get taken outside by somebody if he did. It was not lost on her that Honey Boy had chastised Badger for the same thing he was guilty of, but she needed all the help she could get.

Between two sips of coffee, Honey Boy went back to being convivial. He and Two-Bit began one yarn after another about cowboying, enthralling the boys and entrancing Tennie. Nevertheless, as used as she was to the hair-trigger temper of Southern men, she could not get over the impression Texans were much worse. So full of incredible friendliness one minute and so ready for violence the next.

After they departed, she found on five separate occasions bouquets of wildflowers left on the doorstep of the jail office. Once she caught the retreating figure of one of the sullen men from the night before. She sighed and put the prettiest ones in between the pages of the Granger Bible.

On Monday morning, Rusty came back from his errand across the street and threw the meat provided from Maggot Milton onto the table. "I hate that old cuss!"

"What happened now?" Tennie asked.

"Oh, he was just fussing and carrying on about us feeding prisoners when we don't have to," Rusty said.

"Don't pay any attention to him. If the mayor

and the councilmen don't like it, they can tell us." But she worried over it, nevertheless. "Come on. Let's do some lessons before I have to do laundry." She fretted over the school lessons, too. It was almost impossible to get the boys to sit still, and she felt bad she was such an inadequate teacher.

Lafayette came Monday afternoon after all the washing was done. He was dressed in a suit of exquisite cut, his eyes weary and puffy from the weekend. Sitting down at the office table, he asked, "Is there any coffee in the pot, sweet Miss Tennie?"

"No, it's filled with hot water because I was drinking tea, but I can make you some coffee." She rose.

"No, make us both some tea, please, ma'am," Lafayette said, rubbing his brow. He watched her as she prepared the tea. "Jeff said you had a rough couple of nights."

"Yes," Tennie said, placing a mug in front of him. It wouldn't surprise her if he had a set of Haviland china for his personal use in the Silver Moon. "Mr. Jeff was very kind to me. And he appears devoted to you."

"He was a major under my command in the army," Lafayette said thoughtfully, stirring sugar into his tea. "He has a younger sister who some-how got lured by the lights of San Francisco and ended up in its sewers. I used my influence to extract her from her difficulties and had her put into a convent until she could overcome her problems. She's now happily married to a devout Methodist in Mobile. So, you can see why Jeff is loyal to me." He drew in a deep breath. "And now, my dear Miss Tennie, I must speak to you like a Dutch uncle."

"Oh, no," Tennie said. "What have I done wrong?"

"You haven't done anything wrong yet," Lafayette assured her. "But you are about to."

"What do you mean?"

"Mike Rusinko is a lonely bachelor. He's an immigrant who never fit in well with his people, and he's still on the outside of the circle here. And suddenly he has this beautiful young woman visiting him at night. He's already madly in love with you, you know."

Tennie didn't know, and she blushed, looking away.

"He's over at the livery threatening to never change another shoe off any horse belonging to Honey Boy or Two-Bit," Lafayette said.

"I have no interest in anyone!" Tennie exclaimed. "And if I did, it would not be Honey Boy or Two-Bit. Mike has been a friend, that's all."

"Then don't lead him into believing there will be more."

Tennie looked away, saying nothing. She

realized Lafayette was telling her not to go to Mike's at night, but what did he expect her to do?

"In addition," Lafayette continued, "I make my money off cowboys coming into town on the weekends—so does Mike. He takes care of their horses and provides them with a place to stay in the stables should they not be able to afford a room. When you are there, they are too embarrassed to go into the livery to sleep. That interferes with Mike's business, and ultimately, it might interfere with mine."

"And that's all that matters, isn't it?" Tennie said, looking back at him.

He stared at her for several seconds before answering. "Perhaps."

She knew she was being unfair. "I don't want to lead Mike on, and I don't want to interfere with his business or yours," she said, feeling defeated and depressed. "But I don't think I can handle staying in the jailhouse and listening to the rantings of drunken men half the night."

As soon as she said it, she felt like biting her tongue off. Lafayette endured that every night. She looked down at her hands folded in her lap.

A poker player accustomed to reading faces, Lafayette placed his hand over hers and squeezed it. "You don't have to bear it if you are willing to go next door to the stagecoach station instead. I've talked to Shorty, the stationmaster, and he's agreeable for you and the boys to come over there whenever you wish. He's a grouchy old curmudgeon, but if you can put up with Winn Payton, you can put up with any other grumpy old man."

"Won't I just be trading one lusty man for another?" Tennie demanded.

Lafayette laughed, throwing head back. "No," he said, still chuckling. "Shorty has made no secret in town that the cucumber on his vine dried up a long time ago."

Tennie turned red. "I guessed I asked for that."

He rose. "Come along. I'll take you over there and introduce you."

Once outside, he took her hand and placed it on his outstretched arm. They walked together, and Tennie couldn't help but be thrilled being so close to such a handsome man.

"Have you ever drunk champagne, Miss Tennie?" Lafayette asked.

"No," Tennie said, trying to keep her head. "Have you ever listened to your pa playing 'Oh, Susanna' on the banjo?"

"My father thought fun was a four-letter word, so no, I have not," Lafayette said.

They arrived at the station, a narrow building with two large plate-glass windows on either side of the door. The station stood next to the jail, but on either side were alleys wide enough for a wagon to get through.

The door of the station was open, and as they crossed the threshold, Tennie looked around in dismay. There was a counter, a safe behind the counter, and a door leading to the back. On one wall was a bench, on the other side of the room were chairs placed around a small table. It was as stark and uninviting as one could possibly make it. The only thing of interest were the wanted posters on the wall. Tennie shrank at the prospect of having to spend time there.

"It's just a swing station," Lafayette said. "A place to change horses and allow passengers to get out for a few minutes. The home station where they feed and house the passengers is at Cat Ridge.

"Shorty!" he called.

"Uncock your pistol, I'm coming," a crabby voice came from the back.

Tennie swallowed again.

A small man entered the room from the door behind the counter. He wore his thinning white hair combed back, rimless glasses, a light shirt, and a dark waistcoat containing a pocket watch. He reminded Tennie of a fussy old maid, and she saw why Lafayette was so confident of the little man's ability to be a chaperone and nothing else, especially in the eyes of everyone in town.

"Shorty, this is Miss Tennie, the marshal," Lafayette said.

"How do you do, Mr. Shorty?" Tennie said,

126

giving a nod of her head and an almost imperceptible curtsy.

"We're getting one thing straight right now," the old man said in a precise tone. "The name is Shorty, and I don't put up with high-tone women. If you're going to get high-toned in here, you might as well turn your little bustle around and head right out that door and don't come back."

Tennie stared at him, realized her mouth was hanging open and shut it. "Yes, Shorty. I mean, no, I'm not a high-tone woman." Of all the things she ever expected to be accused of, it wasn't being high-toned.

"Did Lafayette explain the conditions for your coming here?"

Tennie shook her head, almost afraid to remove her eyes from him.

Lafayette told her in an aside. "He expects you to play dominoes with him and be nice to his dog."

"I don't know how to play dominoes, but I would very much like to learn," she said, still scared to take her eyes away. "And I like dogs." She imagined a mean little feist nipping at her heels.

"I'm not putting up with anything from Ashton's boys, either," Shorty said.

Tennie nodded her head. "I'll warn them." She could just imagine the uproar this news was going to cause.

"All right," he said with as much ungracious-ness as could be put into an answer. "Come over whenever you feel like you have to. I don't owe Lafayette a flying fig, but Winn Payton speaks highly of you, even if you are something of a nitwit."

"And that, my dear Miss Tennie," Lafayette said, steering her to the door, "is why Shorty has never married."

"I see that," Tennie said, taking a deep breath of fresh air. They took two steps and were stopped by Shorty's voice behind them.

"Herd up the biscuit eaters and bring them here to meet Bear," Shorty told her. "I want him to get used to their scent and know they're all right before they come busting over here."

"Bear?" Tennie asked. "Who's Bear?"

"My dog, featherhead." Shaking his head in disgust, he went back into the station.

Tennie looked at Lafayette. "Oh, this is going to be so much fun."

Lafayette laughed at her. "You'll have that old man eating out of your hand in two weeks' time."

Tennie laughed back at him. "Mr. Lafayette, you are bad!"

"One of these days, Miss Tennie," he replied, "I'm going to insist you stop being so high-toned and call me Fayette."

"One of these days I might," Tennie said with a smile.

They stopped at the jailhouse door. Lafayette stopped smiling and said in kind and measured words, "It's fine if you and your stepsons want to visit Mike during the day, especially the boys. But don't let them go there at night."

Tennie searched his face. "What are you hiding from me?"

"Nothing I can talk about. Just take my word for it. Things go on in Ring Bit at night that are best for them not to get involved in."

Tennie nodded, looking southward to the livery. "Should I say something to Mike?"

"You don't have to," Lafayette replied. "Jeff will talk to him and explain it is bad for your reputation to be there at night, and the boys need to stick with you."

Tennie nodded again. "Thank you."

He left, and as she stood watching, it seemed to her his posture and stride appeared jauntier than when he'd first entered the jailhouse that afternoon. As she started to go inside, she caught sight of the blonde prostitute, the one Mr. Payton had said was Lafayette's mistress, standing farther up the street, staring at her.

Tennie turned and went back inside. She sat at the desk and rubbed her forehead, telling herself not to depend too much on Lafayette's kindness. It might not last.

Rusty opened the door, and all three boys came in.

She looked up at them. "We have to go meet a dog."

Just as she thought, they were irate about not going to Mike's in the evenings.

"I don't want to go over to that old station-master's place," Rusty said. "He's as mean as old Maggot Milton."

"Don't call him Maggot," Tennie said.

"I don't understand why we can't go to Mike's," Lucas complained.

"I told you. Go during the day all you want," Tennie said. "But Mr. Lafayette said he preferred you didn't at night. He thinks you need to stick with me."

Lucas frowned.

"Look," Tennie said. "The stationmaster is going to teach us how to play dominoes. And we have to be nice to his dog. We can take books over there and read them, too, I imagine."

"Dominoes," Rusty said, his eyes widening. "Miss Tennie, our mother wouldn't let us play dominoes. She said they were the instrument of the devil."

"Well, we're just going to have to pray to Jesus to keep the demons away because we are going to learn how to play and that's that. Now come on, let's go meet this pesky little dog."

CHAPTER 9

The giant that greeted them with a wagging tail and a tongue hanging out, each looking almost a yard long, weighed at least a hundred pounds even without counting the six-inch-long black and gray fur covering him.

"I thought he was a little dog," Tennie said, wide-eyed.

"Miss Tennie, he said his name was Bear," Lucas said. "What did you think?"

"I guess I wasn't thinking," Tennie replied.

"Don't you dare devil this dog or tease him," Shorty said. "And don't try to give him any food. I've got him trained not to take food from strangers."

"Isn't this the dog that was in the dogfight last Friday?" Tennie asked. "The one that almost killed the other dog?"

"That's right," Shorty said. "Bear doesn't go looking for fights, but he doesn't back down from any, either. Let that be a lesson to you boys."

"May we pet him?" Lucas asked.

"Yes, let him smell the back of your hand first," Shorty said.

Tennie gulped, but soon she was down on her knees, rubbing her hands all over the luxurious fur of the dog. She realized Shorty must take extraordinary care of him. She stood up. "What do you want the boys to call you?"

"I told you my name is Shorty, woman! Don't tell me you've already forgotten it?"

"No, I haven't," she rushed to say. "We'll be back then, Shorty. Thank you."

She herded the boys back to the jailhouse, grateful they were enthralled with the massive dog and hoping he wouldn't eat them alive. She stayed behind to start supper while they left again. They had only been gone a short time when they burst back in.

"Miss Tennie, Miss Tennie!" they hollered.

She ran into the office. "What is it?"

"It's Mike," Rusty said, out of breath.

"He's over there threatening to kill Mr. Lafayette," Lucas said.

"He said he's going to the Silver Moon and kill Mr. Lafayette," Rusty repeated.

"What?! What did you tell him?" Tennie demanded.

"We didn't tell him anything, honest!" Lucas said.

"That's right, Miss Tennie," Rusty agreed. "He was ranting and throwing things when we got there."

Tennie wiped her hands on her apron. "Oh

dear." She didn't bother to remove her apron but headed for the door.

Mike stood in the middle of the livery, lifting a massive wagon wheel and roaring. He lifted the wheel over his head and threw it across the building.

"What are you doing?" Tennie cried.

He turned a furious face to her. "I go kill Lafayette Dumont for telling you not to come here."

"He's just trying to protect my reputation!" Tennie cried. "He says it looks bad, an unmarried woman visiting a man at night, and he's right."

"No!" Mike roared. "You marry me and everything will be right!"

"I don't want to marry you!" Tennie hollered. She took a deep breath and looked around, suddenly realizing the place was full of onlookers. "I don't want to marry anybody right now!" she added, trying to soften her words.

"But perhaps one day?" Mike asked.

Tennie felt like crying. "I'm not going to commit myself to anyone right now. Not you or anyone else."

"Okay," Mike said, anger spent.

"You aren't going to try to kill Mr. Lafayette?" Tennie asked.

"No, I let him live."

"Thank you." Tennie looked at the astonished faces of the men around them then turned and fled the livery. "I can just hear Mr. Payton say, 'I told you so, Tennie,'" she muttered as she reentered the jail. "Oh, my supper!" and she raced to the kitchen.

That night, they blew out the lanterns and continued sawing on the window bars, although it was slow going. Lucas and Badger, exhausted from the weekend and all the excitement of the day, fell asleep, leaving Rusty and Tennie to finish.

"Miss Tennie," Rusty said, after looking to make sure his brothers were asleep.

"Yes?"

"I think someone came in here and went through our things when we were at Mike's Saturday night."

Tennie stopped sawing. "What?"

"Yes," he whispered. "Things were changed around, put back different."

"But we don't have anything," Tennie said. "Oh no, our money!"

"It's okay," Rusty said. "I know where you hid it. I looked, and it's still there."

Tennie stayed silent, trying to think. "There is a safe in the office hidden behind one of the maps on the wall. I put your father's papers in there. Tomorrow, when the sun is reflecting off the windows and people can't see in, I'll put most of our cash in there."

"I can stand in front of you, too," Rusty said, "to block people from seeing in."

Tennie agreed and began sawing again, wondering who would rifle through their things and why.

"I think we got it, Miss Tennie," Rusty said in an excited whisper. He pulled on the bars. With a scraping noise, they came out. "Gosh, they're heavy." He put them back in position. "I think they are going to stay just like that. We don't have to glue them."

Tennie breathed a sigh of relief. "Okay, we'll check how they look in the morning. Let's go to bed."

The bars were still in place in the morning, and they all agreed it would fool the casual observer.

"This is just for emergencies," Tennie warned them. "Don't be using this as a shortcut to the privy."

They had finished the breakfast dishes and were working on lessons when a loud commotion sent them running out of the jailhouse. Three cowboys on horses in the middle of the street had a steer between them with horns ranging eight feet, and they were firing pistols in the air. Two were young, but the third was a much older man with a face looking as hard as a weathered rock on a tall mountain.

"Milton, come out of that store!" the older man hollered, firing his pistol in the air while the other horses danced in nervousness. He glanced at Tennie and nodded.

Maggot Milton came out of his shop wearing a bloody apron. "What do you want, Davis?" he barked.

"I'm here to tell you, and I'm here to tell that fat mayor and those lowdown worms on the town council I better not hear one peep out of their sorry mouths if that little gal marshal wants to feed any cowboy from the Bar S. I'm donating this here steer and more to come when need be."

He turned to Tennie. "You hear that, gal? You feed Honey Boy, or Two-Bit, or any other cowhand from the Bar S what gets thrown in jail, and you feed 'em good."

Tennie, speechless, could only nod her head.

"And I don't want to hear nothing from nobody, understand?" the old cowman hollered, looking around at the onlookers he had attracted. "And that includes Dandy Dumont over there at the Silver Moon. If any of you don't like it, you can take it up with me, but you leave this here little gal alone."

He motioned to his men holding the steer. "Take him around back and put him in Milton's pens."

Maggot Milton growled, went back into his shop, and slammed the door behind him.

Tennie stood in awe as she watched the old cowman urge his horse closer to her using the minimum of pressure on the reins. His feet and legs didn't appear to even so much as twitch.

136

It was as if the horse could read his mind.

He looked down at Tennie. "Two-Bit lives up to his name, but Honey Boy is my top hand. Every few months or so, he has to go on a bender and raise hell, but there ain't no harm in him."

Tennie nodded.

The old man turned his gaze to Rusty. "I heared Winn Payton tapped you to go on the trail drive next spring. You come out to the Bar S come September, boy, for the fall roundup. You'll do well to learn everything you can from Honey Boy."

"Yes, sir," Rusty said, stealing a glance at Tennie. "Thank you, Mr. Davis."

The old cowman looked at Tennie, sweeping his hat off to show a thatch of white hair. "I forgot to introduce myself, ma'am. Shep Davis, owner of the Bar S."

Tennie nodded. "Tennessee Granger. Most everyone calls me Miss Tennie."

"Well, Miss Tennie, pleased to meet you. I just might land in your jail one Saturday night, too. There may be snow on my roof, but a fire still burns in my hearth."

"Uh, yes, sir," Tennie said. "Pleased to meet you, too, Mr. Davis." She watched as he rode down the street, horse and rider as one.

"I don't want Rusty to leave," Badger began to wail.

"Hush," Tennie said. "We can't expect Rusty to

137

babysit us forever. There's Bear. Go give him a big hug."

She turned to go back inside, but came to a dead stop when she caught sight of a familiar Stetson and lean legs with pants tucked inside tall boots. Wash Jones walked along the sidewalk. He looked at her as he strode by. Tennie's heart gave a thump, and she began to put her hand up to wave, but Wash, looking her in the eye, turned away and kept walking.

She stared, unbelieving. He had seen her, knew it was her, and yet had just kept walking without acknowledging her in any way. She watched as he crossed the street and entered one of the smaller saloons, a place he knew she would not follow.

Fighting unexpected tears, she turned and entered the jail office, shutting the door and leaning against it. It took her several minutes to collect herself, to slow down her beating heart and fight down the stormy emotions making her want to weep in pain.

Someone knocked on the door and turned the handle. She stood back, wiped a tear from her eye and hoped for one wild second it would be Wash.

Instead, Big Mike came in, looking forlorn and abashed. "Miss Tennie. Still friends?"

"Of course," she said, trying to smile.

"Boys are at stables now."

"That's fine; they adore you," Tennie said. "It's just at night they need to stay with me."

He nodded. "Okay, as long as you not mad."

"I'm not mad. You're not mad at me, are you?"

" 'Course not!" he bellowed.

She tried to smile again. She fought the urge to place her head against his big chest and burst into tears, letting his massive arms envelop and comfort her.

"It's okay, then?" Mike asked.

"Of course, it's okay," Tennie said.

"Okay, I go now," he said, leaving her to her miscry.

She spent the rest of the morning wondering why Wash Jones had snubbed her. Was he still mad at her for taking the marshal job? With a sudden feeling of shame, she remembered how close she allowed him to stand behind her when he taught her to shoot. Should she have pushed him back? Did he think she was some kind of a whore who sat on strange men's laps and allowed cowboys to hug her from behind?

By dinnertime, besides being hurt, she was angry, shoving pots across the cook stove with more force than necessary. Rusty didn't come back for dinner, and Lucas said he was squirrel hunting and would be gone all afternoon.

"Why didn't he take you and Badger?" Tennie asked, feeling cross and showing it.

Lucas shrugged. "I don't know. He just said

he wanted to go by himself. Maybe he's jealous because Mr. Lafayette is paying me to find empty bottles and take them to the saloon."

"Empty bottles?" Tennie asked.

Lucas nodded. "They wash them and put beer and stuff in them. I made ten cents."

"Good for you," Tennie said. "But please be polite and don't cause Mr. Lafayette any trouble. And I'm not sure the saloon is the best place for you to be hanging around."

"I don't," Lucas said. "They make me take the bottles to the back door. I'm going to save my money and buy some clothes like Rusty's."

That's all she needed, Tennie thought. Two boys who wanted to look like Wash Jones.

"Shorty said Bear is a papa," Badger said. "He said if I behave, when the puppies get bigger, he'll give me one if it's okay with you."

"The only way I would let you take a puppy is if you promise to be good to it. No pulling on its ears and tying cans to its tail or anything like that," Tennie said.

"I promise. Shorty says everybody in town wants one of Bear's puppies just so they can turn them into fighting dogs, but he wants to give me one because he said he knew you wouldn't let me use it as just another fighting dog."

"Well I'm glad somebody in this town has a high opinion of me," Tennie grumbled.

Tennie had two visitors that afternoon. The

banker arrived holding a sheaf of papers for her to sign concerning the overdue mortgage on the ranch. She tried to read over them, but the light, impatient tapping of his fingers on the table made her so tense, she couldn't make out any of the complex language used in the documents. Placing them on the table, she asked him to leave the papers so she could examine them better later on. He insisted it was simply a formality that had to be done.

Tennie stared at the papers, upset at the banker's increasing annoyance with her. Wash Jones had told her not to sign anything, but she was so furious at Wash for slighting her she felt like grabbing the pen, dipping it in ink and signing *Tennessee Granger* in as big letters as she could make.

She took a deep breath, trying to calm her heart. "I can't sign these right now," Tennie said, trying to sound firm and nonchalant at the same time. Let the old bloodless buzzard fume, she thought. She didn't care.

He controlled his anger, but Tennie had the feeling that underneath, he was furious at her. He gathered the papers and rose, telling her he would return. "The mortgage goes through whether you sign them or not, Mrs. Granger. This is just a formality," he repeated.

She did not argue with him, and he left, taking the papers with him.

Later that afternoon, while sweeping the office, she heard women's voices and saw the three saloon girls peeking through the window at her. The beautiful blonde swept in through the doorway while the other two stood near the windows.

"Yes," Tennie said. "Can I help you?"

"I'm here to talk about Lafayette," she said, trying to look royal and impervious.

"Won't you sit down?" Tennie said, indicating the same chair at the table the banker had used.

Her visitor sat in the chair as if afraid it might have dirt on the back and soil her dress. She looked around the jail office with unabashed curiosity.

Tennie took the other chair and waited.

The other woman turned to her. "Do you know who I am?" she demanded.

"I think," Tennie said, "that you work in the Silver Moon."

She laughed, a cheap imitation of a laugh given by someone Shorty would accuse of being high-toned. She gave Tennie a look of fake indulgence while the girls outside on the sidewalk made little pretense of not staring. "Hardly that," she said with a tinkling little laugh. "My name is Arabella, by the way."

"And mine is Tennie."

"No one has probably told you, but I am Lafayette's fiancée."

Tennie shook her head, and Arabella continued.

"That's right. As soon as Lafayette can get away from business, we're going to be married."

Tennie nodded. As far as she knew, it might be the truth.

Taking Tennie's nod as a sign of belief, Arabella began to weave a story. Lafayette was madly in love with her; he had named the saloon the Silver Moon after the color of her hair. He was going to take her to Paris on their honeymoon. Lafayette had told her he would die without her.

Tennie could believe everything except that. She could not imagine Lafayette telling any woman he would die without her, much less the over-made-up little doll with petulant lips, reeking of cheap perfume and waving a lace handkerchief that hadn't been washed since Abraham Lincoln was president. Tennie's opinion of Lafayette's taste plummeted as she listened to the stream of lies pouring from his lover's lips, and she became distressed he was involved with someone who claimed to be the daughter of an English count. Tennie was sure counts had daughters, but she didn't think they spoke with Midwest accents and declared their castles were on the Potomac River in Scotland.

Arabella, sensing Tennie's skepticism and aware of the audience outside, stopped almost in midsentence. Opening her purse, she pulled out a small silver dagger, holding it across the table while staring at Tennie with menace. "Now you listen to me, you prissy little two-faced meddler," she said, dropping any pretense of gentility. "You try to cut me out with Lafayette, and this goes straight into your heart, understand?"

The situation upset Tennie and embarrassed her.

Arabella took her response for fear. "As long as we understand one another," she said, sneering in spite. She flounced from the office and rejoined her friends. She talked to them while looking through the window in triumph, laughing with her friends while they joined her in ridiculing Tennie from outside the jailhouse.

Tennie watched in dismay as they gave her one last glance of derision through the window before parading away. She folded her arms across the table and put her head down, not thinking of anything, listening to the sound of her heart beating.

After a while she rose and walked next door to Shorty's. She found him outside behind the station where he kept the spare horses. Bear came to her and nudged her hand. The first time she had seen the dog, he'd had blood dripping from his teeth. She bent down to pet him anyway. It felt good to hug him and cover his head with kisses.

She talked a little while with Shorty, asking him about the puppy, explaining she had not had a dog since childhood and couldn't remember how to take care of one. Shorty didn't seem to mind her ignorance and promised to guide her and Badger in caring for the pup when the time came.

When she got back to the office, she found a newspaper lying on the desk. She looked around, but the jailhouse was empty. Sitting down, she began to read the *Brushwood Gazette*. She rose and looked at the map, finding Brushwood to be a larger town between Mills Creek and Cat Ridge. Returning to the desk, she saw by the date it was several days old. Scanning the headlines and wondering why someone had placed it on her desk, one headline caused her to stop and suck in her breath.

**First Woman Marshal
Appointed in Ring Bit**
In an unprecedented move, this week the town council of Ring Bit swore in Mrs. Tennessee Granger as town marshal. The former Tennessee Smith arrived in Ring Bit as a mail-order bride. Her betrothed, longtime Ring Bit rancher Ashton Granger, did not survive the wedding night, but left three sons in her care. The new Mrs. Granger agreed to keep the law in Ring Bit, apparently unaware the last town marshal escaped an angry lynch mob by the skin of his teeth, the previous two

marshals were killed in the line of duty, and there were at least thirty unsolved murders last year in Ring Bit.

It is not known if she realizes the infamous outlaw Harden Kane was released from prison in Huntsville last week. At the time of his sentencing, Kane swore to return to Ring Bit and kill those he felt had framed him on bogus charges of saddle stealing. An itinerant cowhand testified against Kane only to end up in an alley several months later shot through the head. Kane declared at his trial several important businessmen were behind what he called "a put-up job." The men, all presently on the Ring Bit town council, denied Kane's allegations, stating the U.S. deputy marshal had found the saddle in Kane's possession after a tipoff from the cowhand; he had been duly tried and convicted, and they had nothing to do with either the accusation or arrest.

However, they have placed a comely young widow in the position of town marshal just as Kane is leaving prison, reminding citizens the law states anyone harming a parent and leaving their children orphans shall become legally responsible for said children. To refresh the memory of our readers, last year it was reported the Granger boys knocked over fourteen outhouses and threw trash on leading citizens from atop their storefronts. In addition, after being kicked out of school for roping the teacher and doing a war dance around her, and being banned from Sunday school for also tying up another student and threatening him with his life, the boys are said to have placed a small trunk holding a stray cat where the town's minister would find it, take it home, and open it. The resulting scars required sixteen stitches. And in a lesser degree of devilment, they turned around the saddles of every horse tied to all the hitching posts in town and also placed numerous burrs under saddles.

Town councilmembers and the mayor have refused to comment whether or not they hope this will be a deterrent, one to prevent Kane from returning to Ring Bit.

Tennie put the paper down, pausing to take several deep breaths. She picked the newspaper back up and searched the rest of it. Other headlines spoke of the rash of cattle rustling in the area and holdups along the roads, but nothing else mentioned Ring Bit.

Someone had taken pains to let her know why she had been hired, and an outlaw could possibly be on his way to Ring Bit to wreak havoc. *"They are hiding behind your skirts for a reason,"* Wash Jones had warned her. Ben had told to lay low and wait for them. Wash had just proved the futility of that. She sat, leaning back in the chair and staring out the window for a long time, obviously waiting for something, but for what she did not know.

CHAPTER 10

Rusty came into the kitchen holding several dressed squirrels as she was about to prepare supper.

"Did you offer Mike and Shorty any?" Tennie asked.

"I took Mikc somc," Rusty said.

"Maybe it would be neighborly if you asked Shorty if he wanted a couple," Tennie said. "We have plenty." Anyone who made an offering of skinned squirrels could never be accused of being high-toned.

"I'll go, I'll go," Badger said.

Tennie nodded and Rusty handed a couple of the squirrels to Badger. He returned later saying Shorty was proud to get them.

Tennie finished frying the squirrels, put supper on the table, and watched the boys eat. "Please don't put any more live cats in suitcases. A person who is cruel to animals is the lowest kind of person there is. We have to kill animals for food, but we don't have to torture them."

"Who told you about that?" Rusty asked, embarrassed.

"The newspaper," Tennie said. "Besides, that poor man could have gotten his eyes scratched out."

They set up a wail of protests, defending their actions, but Tennie cut them off. "I don't want to hear about it. That's in the past and doesn't matter anymore. Just don't do it again. If your father was alive, I think he would agree with me. In the little time I knew him, that's what impressed me the most. How kind he was."

Lucas began to sniffle, and Badger began to wail. "I'm sorry, Miss Tennie. I'm sorry we're so bad."

"That's enough of that," Tennie said. "You are just boys, that's all. If you were perfect, nobody would like you. Just don't be cruel to animals anymore, please."

They promised they wouldn't. They practiced sword fighting until they tired. Rusty began to read from *The Three Musketeers* while Tennie wondered what kind of mess she had gotten them into.

The next morning, she had trouble holding them to their lessons.

"Tennie, Tennie," two female voices called to her from the office. Recognizing them, she excused the boys from lessons and went to greet her visitors.

On the wagon train from Alabama to Texas, some of the women had behaved little better than Arabella, Lafayette's mistress. Others had, at first, looked down their noses at Tennie, just as a matter of principle, she guessed. Still others had been kind and fun to be around. All of them had laughed, some gently and some harder, at her mistaken belief she had signed up to be a missionary out West, not a mail-order bride. Nevertheless, no collection of women could have gone through the hardships they'd endured and not come out closer to one another.

The two women waiting for her in the office had shared recipes and sewing tips, along with teaching her how to dance. They were older than the others and had given up hope of marriage in the war-torn South until Winn Payton decided to visit relatives in Alabama and bring back brides for any man in the Ring Bit area who wanted one and could afford to pay her way out.

Tennie hugged them. Small women with sweet round faces, twins so much alike, she could never remember who was which. She begged them to sit down while she brought them tea. After the usual inquiries about how things were going, they put their mugs down.

"Tennie," the first twin said. "Our husbands are waiting for us in the wagons so we can't stay long. We came here for a reason."

The second nodded her head. "Yes, dear. It's like this, Tennie." But she paused, giving her sister a look of helplessness.

151

The first twin took a deep breath and plunged on. "Tennie, we can't even come to town on Saturdays, things are so bad in Ring Bit. All the cursing and shooting off firearms."

"And the men, Tennie!" the second one said. "They . . . they . . . urinate right in the street in front of everyone!"

"It's not just what we see and hear," the first one continued. "Our husbands are afraid we'll accidentally get shot or worse!"

"And it's not just on Saturdays. We had to beg our husbands to allow us to come today so we could talk to you."

Tennie listened in dismay as they continued their tale of woe. On Sundays, they could attend a small country church with a handful of members, but otherwise, they were cut off from the rest of the world. They had gone from living in a large city to being stuck alone on a ranch, and the only town within reach was such a pit of vipers, it was not safe to visit.

Sounds of a tirade coming from across the street and shots being fired halted their discourse. Tennie leapt to the window, afraid it was one of her boys. Maggot Milton was waving a gun and cursing a man in a wagon in front of his shop, yelling at him to move out of the way. The two husbands sat in another wagon in front of the jail, their faces stony hard, and Tennie knew how angry they must be.

"See what we mean?" the women cried.

Tennie sat back down. "I don't know what I can do," she said, feeling miserable.

"Tennie," the first one said. "You were the sweetest little flibbertigibbet, but somehow or another you always managed to get done whatever needed to be done."

"Half the time I was told how dumb I was, and the other half how bossy," Tennie said. "And I hear it now from my stepsons."

"That was just jealousy talking, Tennie," the second twin said. "Please, Tennie. Try to figure out something."

She nodded her head. They rose to leave, and she hugged them again.

After they left, she put her forehead against the doorframe, closing her eyes. In frustration, she beat her fist against the wall. She didn't want to have to do something about an outlaw coming to shoot up the town! She didn't want to do anything about the situation in Ring Bit! People were asking too much of her, and she burst into tears. "I can't do it!" she cried. "I can't do it!"

By the time the boys came back, her tears had dried. They wanted to know who her callers were and what they wanted.

"They were women I was on the wagon train with," Tennie said. "They wanted to visit and tell me how awful Ring Bit is." She looked at the three boys. She had gotten them and herself in a fine mess, but she didn't know what would have happened to her or them if things hadn't worked out the way they did. "Rusty, do you know anything about carpentry? And how long it takes to get to Cat Ridge on horseback?"

Later that afternoon, at different times, five cowboys came by the jail to tell Tennie when she decided to get married, they would like to be considered as a matrimonial partner. Four said Big Mike was tall on muscle and short on brains. The same amount commented Lafayette was no longer a young man in addition to belonging to a disreputable and unstable profession. Two added Jeff Hamilton was already approaching old age, and another that Shep Davis, owner of the Bar S, had almost as much hair growing out of his ears as he did on his head. Three wanted to remind her Honey Boy owned nothing and was only a hired hand. All five said Two-Bit was so lazy, if he caught on fire, his sparks wouldn't even bother to fly upward.

All she had to do was accept one of their sweet proposals, and she could forget about outlaws and men pissing in the street. She could have her own home without drunks screaming obscenities at her from above her head. She could hand over Ashton Granger's papers and say, "Here, you handle this." And she would be welcome on the other side of town.

But not one of the men who came by that afternoon had aroused enough emotion within her to make her want to spend the rest of her life with him.

On the other hand, she could go to work for Lafayette and become as happy and carefree as the hardened prostitutes who worked for him appeared to be, as long as she didn't get stabbed by Arabella.

Rusty returned home, telling her it would take all day to ride to Cat Ridge and back.

Tennie felt like screaming that she did not want to go to Cat Ridge. Trying to put a rein on her feelings, she weighed whether she really needed to go and how afraid they would be riding back in the dark if it took longer than she thought. She tried to remember what the night before had looked like. Had there been a moon? Was it cloudy or clear?

When the younger boys heard there was a possibility they would ride to Cat Ridge the next day, they clamored to go.

Rusty assured her the Granger horses and mule could stand the trip easily. "They need to be ridden, anyway, Miss Tennie. They need the exercise."

"We'll talk about it tonight." She didn't want them blaring it all over town that they were going to Cat Ridge the next day. She'd made her decision. That was where she was going, not to the altar again and not to work in the Silver Moon.

When dusk was about to settle over the town, Jeff stopped by to tell her he thought the coming weekend would be quieter for her—Honey Boy, for one, had decided to check on a line shack on the far reaches of the Bar S and would probably not return for the weekend. "You had a lot of company today," he added.

Tennie nodded. "They just came by to say howdy."

"Is that what they call it nowadays?" He looked around the room. "Where's the table?"

"Rusty has it in the back working on it," Tennie replied, trying to sound casual. "Mr. Jeff, do you think it would be okay if I took the boys to Cat Ridge with me tomorrow? I want to introduce myself to the sheriff there. But I would have to be gone most of the day."

Jeff gave her a steady gaze. "You'll be gone all day and part of the night, but I imagine it would be all right if you asked Big Mike and Shorty to keep an eye on things. Were you planning on making this trip by yourself?"

"Well, just me and the boys," Tennie said.

"Bandits travel that road," Jeff said. "Lafayette goes to Cat Ridge once a month or so. Why not wait and go with him?"

"No!" Tennie said, giving a start. She forced herself to relax. "I mean, no, I want to go tomorrow."

156

Jeff stared at her for several seconds before speaking. "Well now, I have a little business I have to take care of in Cat Ridge myself. So why don't I ride with you and the boys?"

Tennie breathed a sigh of relief. "That would be fine. Should we be ready at dawn?"

"Ten years ago, I would have said get those boys up and going by four-thirty; it's better to leave early than come home late. But tonight, I'll be rolling drunks out the door, and you'll be playing dominoes far into the next few nights, so I reckon dawn it will be."

Tennie nodded. "Okay. I'll go ask Mike and Shorty to keep an eye on things."

"You talk to Shorty," Jeff said. "I'll tell Mike to have the horses ready. It's going to take a lot of explaining and listening to him roar, so you better let me do it."

The first thing Shorty said when Tennie told him she was going to Cat Ridge was, "Jeff taking you?"

"Yes," Tennie said, wondering how he had figured that out so fast. "Do you mind keeping an eye on things?"

"Nope," he replied. "But I've got some papers I want you to drop by the home station."

"What days do the stages run?" Tennie asked, although she thought she knew the answer.

He answered while rummaging through pigeon-holes. "Leaves Cat Ridge heading this way on

Tuesday, Thursday, and Saturday. Comes in from the other way on Monday, Wednesday, and Friday. I forgot to turn those papers over today, that's the reason I'm asking you to take them tomorrow. No sense waiting till Friday."

"I understand," Tennie said. "That's fine."

He stood up. "Wait a minute. They are probably in the back. I was looking at them last night."

As soon as he disappeared into the back room, Tennie ran to the wanted posters and scanned them as quick as she could, but she couldn't find the one she was hoping to see. He came back in, and she twirled around. "Thank you, Shorty."

He handed them to her, rolled up and tied with a string. She made sure she petted Bear before leaving.

Jeff stopped by on his way back to work. "Mike said you better stick with the gray dun and let the boys ride the mule and the buckskin. Let them have it out tonight over who rides what. I don't want to have to listen to kids fighting first thing in the morning."

"I'll tell them." She didn't know why she said it; they probably had their ears up against the wall as it was.

Jeff was right; there was a terrific argument over who had to ride the mule. In the end, they decided to take turns, but let Rusty be on the buckskin when they rode into Cat Ridge. He was getting offers to cowboy, and he had his reputation to uphold.

Tennie had them ready on time, poke bags full of food she had prepared the night before. Mike was getting their horses ready when they entered the livery, but Jeff had not yet arrived.

"What you want to go to Cat Ridge for?" Mike demanded as he put a halter on the mule. "You want to move there?"

"No," Tennie said. "I want to meet the sheriff. I think that's what town marshals are supposed to do. Meet the county sheriff."

"Humph!" Mike grunted. "He no good."

"Probably not," Tennie agreed.

"Men in Cat Ridge—all cowards," Mike said. "All no good. All what you say, Nancy boys."

"What's a Nancy boy?" Tennie asked.

"Wears apron and prances around like woman." Tennie laughed. "Probably so."

When Jeff walked in, she felt a wave of relief. She didn't want to take much more of Mike's disapproval and grumbling.

"We'll see you tonight, Mike," they called as they left.

Once on the road, Jeff apologized for being late. "If you think you had to listen to Mike grumble, I had to listen to Lafayette carrying on."

"Is he mad at me because I'm not at the jailhouse?" Tennie asked, upset she might get into trouble.

"He thinks it's too dangerous out here for you, and you have no business in Cat Ridge, anyway."

Tennie didn't know how to answer. The sun was making a slow appearance amidst a backdrop of red and purple sky. The land they were traveling lay flat in spots, hilly in others. Passing a grouping of large boulders, Tennie looked up, half expecting to see someone watching them from behind. "Is there a shortcut back to Ring Bit from here?" she asked, instead of answering Jeff's unspoken question.

Jeff nodded, but it was Rusty who answered.

"I've been on it," he said, shutting his mouth after he said it and looking as if he wished he hadn't.

"It's too rough a trail for a wagon, but a man on horseback or mule can use it," Jeff said. "It's harder on horses, so most folks generally use this road."

Tennie wondered why Rusty had blurted the answer out and straightaway acted like he regretted it.

"Mr. Payton said Indians don't attack this far south," Tennie said to change the subject.

"Not anymore," Jeff answered. "The soldiers at Fort Griffin hold them back. There are still uprisings around the Red River. And I heard there was a skirmish or two around the Brazos here while back."

"That's where we were attacked. Near the Red River," Tennie said.

"Winn said his guard had fallen asleep, and you were the one to sound the alarm. 'Cause you had some fool notion you could make it on your own."

Tennie turned red with embarrassment. She would never live that down.

"He also said when he started out he was full of vim and vigor and when he got back, most of his hair had fallen out and all of it had turned gray, mostly due to worrying about you," Jeff said with a laugh.

"Oh, that's just an exaggeration," Tennie said.

Jeff laughed again and started telling stories about the time he and Lafayette were attacked by Indians on their way to Texas. The boys listened, captivated, while munching on biscuits tucked with slices of bacon. Tennie rummaged in her poke bag, grateful Mike had put her on the gentlest horse, and handed Jeff some. She couldn't imagine anyone with guts enough to attack Lafayette. All he would have to do would be to give that uppity look of Southern steel, and anybody with any sense would back off.

But she did not want to discuss Lafayette, and she let Jeff entertain the boys without comment.

CHAPTER 11

Later in the day, the boys, anxious to get to Cat Ridge, rode ahead of them.

Jeff talked to Tennie about Ashton. "He settled here before Lafayette and I came. He had a reputation of being a brilliant surgeon, but he wouldn't do it after the war unless Doc was so drunk and the situation was so dire he felt obligated to help. They had a big Indian conflict north of here with dead and wounded soldiers all over the battlefield. The army came and got Ashton, and they gave him one of those arrowhead removing tools. I hope you still have it."

"Oh, yes, we kept all that," she said. A buzzard flew overhead, and she watched, wondering how such an ugly bird could look so beautiful in flight.

"Winn said Ashton removed an arrow from a Mexican before he died."

"Yes, he did," Tennie answered, looking back to Jeff. "I saw immediately how skilled he was."

"And the Mexican lived?" Jeff asked.

"Yes. He stayed with us for a while and then moved on. He wasn't any trouble at all." She looked down at her horse, wishing Jeff would talk about something else.

"Winn said you were a pretty good hand at nursing yourself," Jeff said.

"Oh, not really," Tennie said, relieved to change the subject. "My father wasn't making any money in Tennessee, so my parents moved to Alabama into a small house next to a big estate. After my father went to war, they turned the estate house into a hospital. My mother would nurse the soldiers, but she didn't want me there at first. Later on, when the war kept getting closer and things got so bad, she let me work in the kitchen. I realize now she was trying to make sure I didn't go hungry. A cook can always nibble on food here and there. After a battle when the wounded were pouring in, I would help her nurse, though. They didn't like little girls doing that, but things were so dreadful, and my father was out there somewhere, possibly in the same circumstances, so my mother allowed it."

"You must have seen a lot," Jeff said.

"She wouldn't let me help when the doctors were doing amputations. But sometimes at night, when I'm sad and depressed, I can still hear those poor men screaming."

"I think that's what's wrong with Honey Boy," Jeff said, shifting in his saddle. "He went to war when he wasn't much older than Rusty, and he saw too much to forget. It builds up in him, and the only way he can get shut of it is to go on a three-day drunk."

"I had no idea," Tennie said.

"And after the war?" Jeff asked.

"My father came home; we had a joyous reunion; my parents came down with yellow fever and died."

"And you went to an orphanage," Jeff said.

"Yes. There are nice orphanages overseen by kind, dedicated people, but I wasn't in one of those. Because I had kitchen experience, they put me to work cooking. They started hiring me out to the big houses to help cook for parties and things." Tennie shook her head in disgust at the memory. "They would tell me no one wanted to adopt me. Later, I found out they wouldn't let anyone adopt me because I was making them too much money on the side. I was so stupid."

"Now, Miss Tennie, how were you supposed to know?"

"You're right," Tennie said. "But it still galls me I didn't have any better sense than that. And then the other girls started leaving. I would sometimes hear whispers about what they were doing. I really didn't understand; I just knew it wasn't something good. So, I stayed at the orphanage cooking, and I guess Mr. Payton has filled you in on the rest."

"Winn never was one to shy away from talking," Jeff said.

"Mr. Jeff, you've had me doing all this chattering, and you haven't told me one thing about yourself."

He laughed. "There ain't nothing to tell. I haven't lived nearly as exciting a life as you have, gal."

"I don't believe that," Tennie said with a smile.

Jeff encouraged her prattle, and she was happy to be away from Ring Bit and have someone to talk to. It was almost like being on the wagon train again, except Jeff's eyes never stopped roaming, and nothing escaped his notice. He broke Tennie off in midsentence to call the boys to halt. He rode forward and shot a coiled diamondback rattlesnake in the road they had neither seen nor heard. The younger boys begged for the rattles. Jeff dismounted, stepped on the still-writhing body and cut off its head, kicking it far away with his boot. He handed his knife to Lucas and let him remove the rattles.

"I think it's fifteen of them, Miss Tennie," Lucas called.

Tennie grimaced. Badger wanted to eat it.

"I have plenty of food in these poke bags," Tennie said. "I don't need to be eating no rattlesnake." The snake, still twisting, terrified her, and she wanted to move on.

Jeff smiled and got back on his horse. "Well, boys, Miss Tennie said no." They grumbled, but passed the rattles to one another as they rode on

166

their way. They tired after a while, and Jeff had to tell them if they asked one more time how much farther it was, he was going to jerk them off their horses and wear their butts out.

Before reaching Cat Ridge, they stopped to eat near a grove thick with oak trees and yaupons. Tennie got down from her horse, but stood next to it while they checked for copperheads. After eating, she found a long stick to poke the ground and make noises with to scare away any snakes while she went behind the thick trees and yaupons to change out of her dust-covered old dress into her fresh blue flowered one. She wiped her face with a wet handkerchief and tried to make herself as presentable as she could.

"Can we leave now?" Badger said when she returned.

"I'm ready," Tennie said, but knew she was lying. She wasn't ready to face any of the things she had to do, but there was no turning back.

Cat Ridge proved to be the opposite of Ring Bit. Instead of new buildings and bare streets, Cat Ridge had stately brick edifices and trees lining an avenue. Rusty remembered going to Cat Ridge with his father, but the two younger boys had never been. It was not even close to what Tennie had left behind, but she found herself in awe anyway. They found a corral, and while Jeff, Rusty, and Lucas watered and fed the mule and horses, she and Badger climbed the corral boards and stared at Cat Ridge like it was an oasis in the desert. She remembered Shorty's errand and removed his papers from her saddlebags, asking Rusty to hold on to them.

They left the corral together, following Jeff, who took them to the sheriff's office. "When you get finished with your business, Miss Tennie, meet me on the south side of the courthouse square. It's one street to your right."

She nodded and hoped Jeff could not see how scared she was. When he had walked away, she turned to the boys. "Do not say a word in there. No matter what the sheriff says, no matter what I say, just keep your mouths shut. The first one who says a word is not getting any pie the next time I make one."

She looked at the brick building and wished she had a large elm tree shading her jailhouse door. She glanced back at the boys, thinking they might be mutinous, but they looked frightened, too. She remembered the Indian attack and how afraid she had been. Why should a sheriff scare her? She straightened her shoulders and opened the door.

A brawny older man with puffy eyelids hanging partway down over his eyeballs sat in a chair behind the desk. He rose when he saw her. Tennie nodded, moving her head enough to get a brief glimpse of the polished furnishings surrounding her.

"Hello, my name is Tennessee Granger. I'm the new marshal from Ring Bit."

He scowled and sat down. There was a chair beside her, and rather than stand and be embarrassed by not being asked to sit, Tennie sat down in the chair and began her business. "I read in the *Brushwood Gazette* that Harden Kane has been released from prison. It also said it had been his intention to come back to Ring Bit and exact revenge on the people he felt had framed him."

The sheriff stared at her in dislike. She stared back.

He shifted in his chair. "Let's get this straight, Mrs. Granger. I don't go to Ring Bit; I don't have anything to do with Ring Bit; and I try to keep that trash from Ring Bit out of my town."

"Do you know if Harden Kane is on his way to Ring Bit?" Tennie asked, ignoring everything he said.

He swelled like a mad horned toad about to spit blood, every gesture making it obvious he did not want to have a conversation with her and was doing so against his will. "He left Huntsville. The last sighting of him was in Waco. He's not in a hurry, but he's making a beeline in this direction. If he continues to travel like he's been doing, he should be in Ring Bit sometime next week.

"Let me tell you something, woman," the sheriff continued. "I don't give a two-day-old fart what he does in Ring Bit. If he comes here, I'm going to ask him to move on, that's all."

Tennie nodded. "The paper said he felt he had been framed, but it didn't explain why someone should frame him."

"How the hell do I know? He's killed a dozen men the law has been unable to pin on him to hang him from a tree which is what he deserves. So what if someone framed him for stealing a saddle to get rid of him?"

"Do you have any wanted posters of him? Wasn't he wanted at one time? Was he tried and got off?"

"Yes, he scared the hell out of some jury so bad, they brought back a verdict of not guilty."

"I'd like to have any wanted posters you have of him," Tennie repeated.

He glared at her, wanting to refuse. Instead, he jerked open a drawer, brought out a stack of papers, and went through them in jerky motions. He took out two and threw them across the desk to her. "You can't miss him. He's the ugliest SOB I've ever seen."

Tennie took the posters. They showed a good likeness of Kane, a man with a thin V-shaped face, narrow eyes below sharply arched brows, and an equally long and thin nose ending in wide chiseled nostrils. She silently agreed it was not a pleasant face. "Thank you." She rose. "Is there an attorney in town?"

"Yes, he's on the left just down the street. But he's a Jew."

"I don't care," Tennie said, heading for the door. "So was Jesus Christ."

"Hell, I know that," the sheriff said, getting up. "I just meant he's going to demand money up front. Or maybe you figure you got another way you can pay him."

Behind her, Rusty gave a start, but stopped himself. Tennie gave the sheriff a long look before turning to open the door.

"And another thing," the sheriff said. "Keep those boys out of the stores. They're not welcome in any of the shops here, and I'd appreciate it if you took them and yourself back to Ring Bit as fast as you can."

"It will be a pleasure to shake the dust of Cat Ridge from my feet," Tennie said and left.

Rusty was the last one out and shut the door. He joined Tennie and the others, shaking in fury. "My pa would have killed him for talking to you like that," he said through gritted teeth.

Tennie was almost as angry as he was. She took several deep breaths, trying to keep from crying. "Perhaps he's just upset because he knows as county sheriff he should be doing something about Ring Bit, and he feels guilty because he's not."

"Or maybe he's just a Nancy boy," Lucas said with venom.

Tennie burst out laughing, and the others joined her. "I'm no better than he is. I can't do anything about Ring Bit, either."

"But the difference is at least you try, Miss Tennie," Lucas said.

Tennie smiled again. They began walking down the street, looking for the attorney's office. When they found it sandwiched between two large mercantile shops, she stopped and told the boys to wait for her nearby, but stay out of the stores.

"Do you want me to take these papers to the stationmaster at the stagecoach stop?" Rusty asked.

"You can find out where it is, if you want," Tennie said. "But I have to go there myself when I'm finished here."

They skittered away, and Tennie turned, knocking on the door. She turned the handle and entered, going into a hallway. There was an opened door to the right at the end, and she walked to it, pausing in the doorway.

A slight young man sat behind a wide, solid desk in a room surrounded by bookshelves teeming with books. In between the books were various knickknacks—a globe, a wooden box, and on one end, an odd-looking skull.

She looked back at the lawyer who was giving her a piercing stare through round wireframed glasses. He had a head of longish, curling dusky hair that matched his dark brown eyes.

"May I help you?" he asked, his voice as dry and crisp as a fall day in the mountains.

"Yes, if you are Levi Myerson, the lawyer whose name is on the plaque outside."

"Yes," he said, closing his book and leaning back, interlacing his fingers and placing them across his stomach. "Sit down and tell me your name."

Tennie sat down. "My name is Mrs. Tennessee Granger. I am the new town marshal in Ring Bit."

"Is this a professional call or private business?" he asked.

"Private," she answered.

"Then I must tell you I charge a fee upfront. I don't give away advice for free, Mrs. Granger."

Tennie colored. "I have money to pay you, and I don't expect anything for free."

"Good, as long as we understand one another. Now tell me what your problem is."

Tennie began at the beginning, of coming to Ring Bit, marrying Ashton Granger, his death, the visit from the town council and the banker. The banker's assertion Ashton had mortgaged the cattle and land. The suspicion someone was hunting through their things searching for some-thing, and the banker's insistence she sign papers he refused to leave behind for her to look over.

"And what do you want me to do?"

Tennie drew in a deep breath. "I want you to tell me if I should sign those papers. I want to know

173

if the bank's claim on the property is valid."

"First of all, did your husband leave a will?"

Tennie bit her bottom lip. "I didn't find anything that looked like a will in his things."

"Then he died intestate. And since he owned the property before he married you, that also changes things. I have to tell you the laws in Texas are quite different from other places because they still adopt some regulations left over from the Spanish. In Texas, when a man dies, his estate is divided between his widow and his children."

"I'm not trying to take anything away from his children," Tennie said. "I would feel guilty taking anything, seeing as how we were only married a few hours. But I promised him I would look after his children, and that includes protecting their inheritance."

He gave her another intense gaze. "This is what you are entitled to," he began, reeling off words about probate and affidavits of heirship that made little sense to her. She could only nod and try to keep up.

He rose from the desk. "I want to show you something." He went to one of the shelves and took down a newspaper, bringing it back and placing it in front of her. He pointed to a caption above a long paragraph.

Tennie read it aloud. "Railroad to be built across Texas." She looked up. "What does that mean to me?"

"It means, there is a possibility your late husband's property is worth a great deal to someone if the railroad buys part of it to run their lines. Is the ranch near the town of Ring Bit?"

"Yes," Tennie nodded. "It's very close."

"So far, if what you are telling me is true, the banker has skirted every law concerning the repossession of property. You were right not to sign anything. I want you to go home, look through your deceased husband's papers, and collect three samples of his signature if possible. Go through every paper and set aside anything that concerns the property, the bank, and finances. I will also need your marriage certificate.

"On this end, I will go to the courthouse to get your late husband's affairs settled legally and see if the banker has filed the correct papers. He has a certain amount of time to do so, so don't come back with your records for three or four weeks. You may send them by the stagecoach if you wish. After I look them over, I will have to confront him personally in Ring Bit. We may end up going to court if he cannot produce the proper documentation. It will cost if we have to go to court."

"I have two twenty-dollar gold pieces," Tennie said.

He sighed. "You can leave five dollars with me today. Do not let him talk you into signing anything." The lawyer reached over and pulled

175

two business cards from a small box at the corner of his desk.

"Don't discuss it with him if he comes back. Just hand him one of these cards and tell him I have advised you not to sign anything, and he must take this up with me. If he does not have a legal right to the property, he will be wise to drop the matter. If he does have the correct papers with a valid signature, you will pay the remainder of my fee, and the matter will be closed."

Tennie nodded, "I understand."

He took a deep breath. "I do not mean to insult you, but most people, particularly a woman alone, would not have the courage to question such a leading citizen. May I ask why you did?"

Tennie flushed. "I had a friend who advised me not to sign anything and to find an attorney I could trust. I hoped since you were in Cat Ridge and not Ring Bit, I could trust you."

"You had a very good friend, madam."

"There is one more thing," Tennie said. "And this is on a professional level. Were you the defending attorney for Harden Kane?"

For just a second, Tennie thought she could read surprise in his eyes.

"Yes, I was."

Tennie tried to choose her words carefully. "He claimed he was innocent. Did you believe him?"

"I will tell you what I told him and what I tell all my clients. It is not what I believe that is important. It is what I can prove. I was unable to prove him innocent."

"But personally?" she asked.

"Did I think he was innocent of being a cold-blooded killer out to make a reputation for himself? No. Did I think he was innocent of stealing a saddle? Yes."

"He also claimed he was framed," Tennie continued. "Did he tell you why he thought he was being framed?"

The lawyer drummed his fingers lightly on the arm of the chair before answering. "What a client tells me is privileged information. But since he clearly made it a matter of record in every bar in town, I will tell you. He said he accidentally opened the door of a roomful of men who appeared to be having a meeting. They did not notice him at first, and when they did, they seemed greatly disturbed. He heard none of their business, but they weren't sure how long he had been standing there. He thinks he was railroaded out of town and put into prison to keep him from investigating further into their affairs."

"He swore he would get revenge," Tennie said. "He's been released from prison and appears to be heading for Ring Bit right now."

"My dear woman, if I had a dollar for every time I heard the accused say he was coming back for revenge and never followed through, I would be a very rich man indeed. However, I will give you my opinion for free. If he comes back to Ring Bit, he will come when night falls. He will not take the chance of a sniper shooting him in the back in daytime. He is not the brightest specimen of mankind, but he is not entirely stupid, either."

Tennie nodded. She dug into her handbag and placed a five-dollar bill on the desk. While the attorney wrote out a receipt, her mind was busy thinking about Harden Kane riding into Ring Bit at night, rather than daytime. She thought perhaps he would.

She folded the receipt and placed it in her bag. "Thank you so much, Mr. Myerson," she said, rising.

He followed her to the door. Before opening it, he asked, "You are a Christian, I presume?"

"Yes," she nodded.

He gave a sigh. "Too bad. I would propose marriage to you myself, but my family would never approve."

She smiled at him, and he opened the door for her. "On the other hand, I am in Texas, and they are in Boston, and there is always the option of changing your name to Esther."

Tennie smiled again. "Thank you, Mr. Myerson. I will see you in a few weeks."

"I hope so, my dear Mrs. Granger. You are living in a very corrupt place."

CHAPTER 12

The boys met Tennie as she walked down the sidewalk after consulting the attorney.

"What are you grinning about, Miss Tennie?" Lucas asked.

"Because I went from being insulted to being called *my dear* and almost proposed to. Of course, one had to talk to me, and the other one was getting paid to talk to me, so that might make a difference."

"Well, come on," Lucas said, taking her by one hand while Badger took the other. "We found the stagecoach station. It don't look nothing like Shorty's place."

"It doesn't look *anything* like Shorty's place," Tennie corrected.

"That's what I said!" Lucas retorted.

They were right, however. Tennie stood in front of a large two-story building with wide verandas on both stories. "Oh, my. I guess you boys better go to the back and look at the horses. I don't think they would mind. I'll meet you there."

"Okay," Rusty said, handing her Shorty's papers. "Come on. Let's go," he told the younger boys.

Tennie walked up the wide stairs, opening double doors into a large dining room filled at the moment with travelers. Some of the stations they had stopped at while on the wagon train had been little more than four stone walls and a leaky roof. This was clearly one of the better ones.

A baldheaded man wearing a visor and sleeve garters stood working behind a counter on the left side of the room. She made her way to him.

"Excuse me. Are you the stationmaster here?" she asked.

"That's right, ma'am," he said. "What can I do for you?"

"I'm Tennessee Granger, the new marshal in Ring Bit. Shorty sent some papers with me to give to you."

"Oh, yes, Miss Tennie. I've heard about you. Thank you very much."

Tennie took a deep breath. "I have some other business to talk to you about and a favor to ask. Is there someplace private we can talk?"

"Of course," he said in surprise. "Come this way, Miss Tennie." He opened the swinging door for her to enter behind the counter.

She followed him into a small office.

"Please sit down," he said, taking a chair behind a desk.

Tennie sat in one on the other side. "You have a very nice establishment here," she said, looking around.

He smiled in gratitude and pride.

After exchanging a few more pleasantries about Shorty, Tennie got down to business. She pulled out one of the rolled-up wanted posters and handed it to him. "This man is no longer wanted, but he is on his way to Ring Bit to cause trouble, I fear. If it is at all possible, I'd like to know when he will arrive in town. Is there any way your drivers can keep their eyes and ears open, sending word to me when he has reached Brushwood? He doesn't appear to be in a hurry, and I think the stage might come in from Brushwood through Cat Ridge and into Ring Bit before he makes it there on horseback."

"Of course," the stationmaster said, to Tennie's relief. "Let's go outside and talk to one of the drivers. He's here right now."

She followed him outside, where she found Rusty, Lucas, and Badger petting the massive horses, all of them fourteen hands high or more. An older man almost as large as Big Mike saw them coming. He had on a disreputable-looking hat with holes in it, a long salt-and-pepper beard with tobacco juice caught in the whiskers, a gun belt holding an ivory-handled pistol, and boots covered in dust and mud.

"Packer Jack, this is Miss Tennie, the new marshal Shorty told you about."

"How do you do there, ma'am?" he said in a gruff voice.

"Nice to meet you, Mr. Packer Jack," Tennie said.

"Oh, Packer Jack or just plain ole Packer will do."

"Packer Jack is one of the company's most skillful drivers, Miss Tennie," the stationmaster said. "He's gotten our stagecoaches through some rough rides. Besides carrying the mail, the army uses us to transport their payroll, and we're always careful to change the dates and times of our shipments, but Packer has had to outrun bandits several times now.

"But enough of that. Miss Tennie has a favor to ask you, Packer."

Tennie repeated her request while Packer listened, keeping his eyes fastened on her. She handed him one of the wanted posters. "Just keep it. I hope you can help me."

"I'd be pleased to help you, but just what are you aiming to do, young lady?" he asked.

"I'm not sure."

Ben McNally had advised her to lay low and not try to prove anything. On the other hand, her friends had begged her to do something about Ring Bit. And somewhere in the middle lay the fact that she was the town marshal whether she liked it or not. "Maybe there is nothing I can do," she admitted. "But I would like to be forewarned of his coming."

"I can understand that, and I'll put the word

out quietlike that I want to know if and when this here fellow shows up in Brushwood."

"Please don't put yourself at danger," Tennie said.

"Don't you worry about that none," Packer said. "Old Shorty shore speaks highly of you."

"No one in Ring Bit would ever know it," Tennie said with a laugh.

The men laughed, too, and Tennie turned to the boys. "We best get going. I imagine Mr. Jeff is waiting for us."

As they were leaving, she called, "Thanks again."

On the way to the courthouse, she paused long enough to fold her remaining wanted poster and place it in her bag. She only had the vaguest shadowy idea of what to do about Harden Kane, and she wasn't ready to discuss it with anyone.

Jeff was sitting on a bench, talking to other cowboys. "Did you get your business taken care of?"

"Yes, but we aren't in a hurry; we can wait over yonder while you visit some more," Tennie said.

He rose. "I've jawed enough." He said good-bye to his friends. "Let's stop at the store and get some candy to suck on, on the way home."

"We can't go in the store," Badger said.

"That's right," Lucas said. "That mean old sheriff told Miss Tennie we couldn't go in any of the stores and for her to take us and get out of town."

"Oh, fiddle," Jeff grunted, herding them into the nearest store anyway.

Tennie was a little wary, but with Jeff present, the boys didn't act like Genghis Khan set loose on the prairie. When Jeff asked them what they wanted, they told him, taking what he gave them and giving polite thanks. She wasn't sure if they were frightened of Jeff or if they had something to prove.

On the way home, Jeff asked about the sheriff, but Tennie glossed over it. Feeling guilty because she didn't want to talk about Harden Kane, she told him about going to the attorney instead.

"Please don't tell anyone, Mr. Jeff," she said. "I don't want the banker to get so mad at me for questioning his honesty he kicks us out on our fannies."

"Miss Tennie, by the time we get back to Ring Bit, it will probably already be all over town you went to see a lawyer."

"Really?"

"Yes. But it may just get out in the saloon tonight that you were unsure of Texas law and wanted to ask someone how soon a widow could get married again."

Tennie paused to think about it. "You mean, if I had a friend like you who told that story in the saloon tonight?"

"That's right," Jeff said nodding his head.

"Thank you, Mr. Jeff," Tennie said, feeling humble. "There's one more thing. I found a safe behind one of those maps hanging on the wall of the jailhouse. Inside were two twenty-dollar gold pieces. Is it finders, keepers, or do I need to report it? I was going to use them to pay the lawyer."

"It's finders, keepers, and don't tell anyone about the safe," Jeff said. "You might want to hide something in it one of these days."

"I already have," Tennie said. "That's where Ashton's papers are." She explained about someone going through their things, and the lawyer's suspicion it might have something to do with a railroad being built through Ring Bit.

Jeff ruminated on this for a while. "A railroad coming through, eh? They'll probably use the stage route, and that road goes right through Ashton's ranch. You know that, don't you, Miss Tennie? That he let people cut through his property?"

Tennie shook her head.

"I'm not going to be blabbing this all over town, but I am going to tell Lafayette and Shorty a railroad might be coming through Ring Bit, because it will affect their business in one way or another."

"Of course," Tennie agreed. She shifted in the saddle, trying to ease her discomfort. Her rear end was going to be sore for at least a week, and balancing while riding sidesaddle with one leg wrapped around a saddle horn was no easy feat. Weariness beginning to set in, she encouraged Jeff to talk so she could expend less energy by listening rather than speaking.

Just when she was breathing a sigh of thankfulness her stepsons had managed to behave on the trip, they got into a fistfight at a midway stop over who had to ride the mule next. While blood spurted from Lucas's nose, Badger began kicking Rusty. Heretofore, Rusty had always humored Badger and let him get by with such behavior, but this time, he threw a punch that sent the smaller boy flying.

Jeff grabbed Tennie's arm before she could do anything and propelled her to her horse. "Come on. Let them fight it out. They'll work it out and catch up with us."

"I survived the War; I survived the orphanage; I survived an Indian attack; I survived being a bride and a widow all in the same day, but I don't think I'm going to survive them," Tennie said when they were on their way.

Night came before they made it back to Ring Bit. A three-quarter moon kept sliding in and out of the clouds, throwing everything into shadows and light. The boys had quietened down. Jeff had grown silent. On top of a swaying horse, Tennie's eyes fell shut.

"Stick your hands up!" a muffled voice said.

Tennie's eyes flew open to see a man dressed in dark clothes with half his face covered standing with a gun in his hand. In the next instant, she saw a flame of fire shooting from Jeff's revolver, along with the roar it caused. The man crumpled to the ground.

She and the boys sat openmouthed and paralyzed, but Jeff dismounted, kicking the pistol out of the man's outstretched hand. He wasn't moving.

Tennie asked, "Is he dead?"

Jeff bent down, pulling the kerchief from his face. He lit a match to get a better look. "Yes."

Tennie and boys dismounted.

"Who is he?" Rusty asked as they stood over him.

"Just some young drifter who was in the saloon last night," Jeff said.

Tennie bent down beside him, looking at the smooth face of the boy in the moonlight. "He's so young." She ran her fingers down his cheek. "God rest your soul," she murmured.

Jeff rose. "Rusty, he's got a horse around here somewhere. Will you boys look? It's probably tied over yonder," he said, indicating a dark clump of trees.

They took off and Jeff called to them, "Don't go stomping around and step on a snake. Slide your feet a little."

He took Tennie by the elbow and helped her up. "You can see why I wanted you to ride with me or Lafayette to Cat Ridge."

"I can't go with Lafayette," Tennie said, tired and depressed. "Arabella threatened to kill me unless I left Lafayette alone."

Jeff uttered something that sounded like a strangled curse word. "Don't pay her no mind. She doesn't mean a thing to Lafayette, and the only thing he means to her is a free meal ticket."

"Well, she doesn't want me interfering with her free meal," Tennie said. "And she must mean something to him; he keeps her around."

"He can't get shut of her," Jeff said. "Look, don't be too hard on Lafayette. He's a fairly young man still, and he doesn't fit into society any better than you do."

"All right," Tennie said. "I won't be hard on Mr. Lafayette. But what about you? Were you ever married?"

Jeff paused, looking at the boys who had found the horse and were bringing it back. "Yep. And she's the reason I swore off women for the rest of my life."

He put the dead boy on the back of his horse, tying him to it. He tied the horse to the saddle horn on the mule Rusty was riding. "Stay behind us," he murmured to Rusty.

Just as Tennie fell into the bed exhausted, she heard the sound of thunder, thankful they had made it home before the rain. Already half asleep, she thought of the lawyer's final words. Levi Myerson hadn't told her she lived in a dangerous place. He had labeled Ring Bit "corrupt." She fell asleep wondering what he meant.

They slept late the next day, and Tennie spent most of the morning cooking food for the coming weekend.

That afternoon, she swept the sidewalk in a desultory way, unable to summon much energy. Mike came by before she finished, and they sat on chairs in front of the jailhouse and talked for a while. He wanted to know about her visit to Cat Ridge, but she wasn't inclined to talk much about it. He wasn't interested in the details anyway, only that she had not liked it. They watched as Maggot Milton came out of his shop waving a fist at someone and cursing.

Tennie winched. "The way he behaves, how does that man manage to have any customers?"

"Him?" Mike said. "He's not too bad once you get to know him."

Tennie eyed Mike in surprise and suspicion. "If you say so."

"Important businessman with lots of money," Mike said.

"Well, so are you," Tennie said.

"Me? No. I no own the building. Just work there."

"I never believe men when they tell me they

are broke, and I never believe men when they tell me they have a lot of money, either," Tennie said.

Mike blushed. "Aw, Miss Tennie."

After Mike left, Tennie took up her broom again, looking down the street. Someone had pointed the doctor out to her soon after she'd arrived, and she watched now as he entered a tiny saloon, thinking him nondescript and devoid of personality. He was a slender man, never standing hunched over, but never standing quite upright, either, with thinning, graying light brown hair and colorless features. He had a habit of entering every saloon in town and staying a little while in each one before going into the Silver Moon, his last stop, as if putting off the inevitable, or what he felt was unescapable.

In front of the same saloon, Apache John lay sprawled on the sidewalk, already unconscious. Men stepped over him without a thought. Jeff said he wasn't really Apache, but a member of one of the lesser tribes the Apache had annihilated. Nor was he full-blooded, either, but a mixture of Anglo, Mexican, and Negro. He looked older than he probably was, with chiseled features alcohol was slowly obliterating.

Tennie, who had seen enough lice-covered soldiers to recognize it, avoided him drunk or sober, crossing the street when he was passed out so she didn't have to step over him.

She was starting to recognize the habits of the

citizens of Ring Bit. Shorty, who kept Bear in at night and let him out every morning at dawn; Big Mike banging away on an anvil late into the night, keeping the longest hours of anyone in town; there always seemed to be someone coming and going to his establishment and to the slaughterhouse across the street. The men who flocked to the café in the mornings for coffee and breakfast. The mayor, the banker, and the other town councilmen kept to the north side of town except late at night when she would sometimes catch sight of their shadows creeping to the south side.

She finished her sweeping and was about to go inside when Lucas came running down the street. "The undertaker says they are about to bury him, Miss Tennie," he said when he reached her.

"Thank you, Lucas." Tennie went inside and put the broom away. She removed her apron and put on her hat, tucking a stray brown curl underneath the band.

She had not requested the boys go with her to the funeral of the young man killed the night before, but they followed her anyway. Along the walk up the hill to the cemetery, she stopped to pick a few wildflowers, fresh after the rain, and Lucas and Badger joined her.

The preacher walked ahead of them, giving no indication he knew they were behind him. The gravedigger, the only person at the burial site, stood leaning with one arm on his shovel, watching them through narrowed lids and pragmatic eyes. The preacher was already repeating a few Bible verses when they reached the grave. The scar from the cat scratch was still visible on his cheek, and after a quick prayer, he departed without speaking to her.

Tennie cast her flowers on top of the casket and picked up a handful of damp dirt and threw it in also. The younger boys copied her. She nodded to the gravedigger, turned, and left. They had been the only mourners to appear in the cemetery.

On the way down the hill, Badger wanted to know why she had thrown dirt in the grave, and Lucas wanted to know why they had gone in the first place.

"Y'all ask the hardest questions." Tennie sighed. "It just doesn't seem right for a person not to have somebody at his funeral."

"What about the dirt?" Lucas asked.

"I don't rightly know, except it is sort of symbolic. Maybe it shows you know they are in God's hands, and there is nothing else you can do for them in this life but help bury them." After that, she had to explain what *symbolic* meant.

They met Jeff coming out of the Silver Moon. "Did you go to that boy's funeral?"

"Yes," Tennie said, looking down to find Badger hiding behind her skirts. She wondered what was the matter with the child. "It wasn't much of one," she told Jeff. "But we showed up anyway."

"We threw dirt on his grave, Mr. Jeff," Lucas said. "Miss Tennie said it was a symbolic act."

"You did, did you?" Jeff said. "Well, that was probably the kindest thing anybody had done for him in a long time. You boys ready to learn how to play dominoes?"

"You bet," Lucas said. He looked at Tennie and added, "sir."

"We'll see you later, Mr. Jeff," Tennie said.

Before she could leave, Arabella came to the swinging doors of the saloon, giving Tennie a confrontational stare, her eyes moving to Badger hiding behind her skirts. Her lips curved in a sneer, and she turned, going back inside.

"I'll see you later, Miss Tennie. Don't forget what I told you," Jeff said, motioning his head toward the inside of the saloon.

Tennie nodded.

Jeff left them, going in the opposite direction, and she tried to walk with Badger hanging onto her leg.

"Badger! What is wrong with you?"

"I'm scared," he mumbled, hiding his face in the fabric of her dress.

"Of what?" Tennie asked.

"Lucas said Mr. Jeff is going to shoot me," Badger cried.

"Oh, for gosh sake. What did you tell him that

for?" Tennie said, glaring at Lucas. "He's not going to shoot you, Badger, unless you hold a loaded gun on him and try to rob him. Mr. Jeff was trying to protect us, that's why he shot that man. Now don't be such a fraidy cat and don't be believing everything Lucas pours into your ear."

Lucas tried to defend himself, but Tennie only nodded, not willing to be drawn into any more arguments. She had seen so much of death at an early age; she chastised herself for not remembering her stepsons had not. They had lived on a ranch and acted bad after their mother died; now they were finding out what bad really was.

CHAPTER 13

Tennie had just finished striking matches to the jailhouse lanterns when the first prisoners began to arrive. Two men from one of the smaller saloons pushed in three drunken soldiers on leave. The soldiers were rowdy, complaining they were being picked on by ex-Confederates, referring to them as grayback parlor boys, making themselves as obnoxious as they could.

Tennie followed them up the stairs, standing aside while the men threw the soldiers in one cell. She locked the door, in the back of her mind thinking it odd they appeared to avoid looking at her. She followed the other men downstairs, taking a minute or two to speak to them before shutting the door.

The boys were waiting in the living quarters whcn she walked in. "Are you about ready to go to Shorty's?" she asked.

Before they could answer, a thumping sound came from the ceiling above.

"Hey, we got a sick man up here," a muffled voice called out. "We need to get him to a doctor quick!"

"Wait a minute," Tennie told the boys. She went to the stairwell, grabbing the keys along the way. The soldiers continued to shout, and she lifted her skirt, hurrying as fast as she could.

One of the soldiers lay on the bed groaning.

Tennie started to unlock the door, but thought better of it. Something felt wrong. "Bring him here," she said, standing at the door. "Lay him on the floor."

They protested, but she refused to open the cell door. When they saw she wasn't going to give in, they picked up their friend and brought him to the door, placing him on the floor next to the bars. Tennie glanced at their insignia—two privates and a corporal.

She knelt by the bars with the corporal on the other side on the floor. He didn't look ill, but his eyes were shut, and he was groaning. She placed the keys on the floor, pushing them out of reach of the prisoners' arm. Reaching into the cell, intending on placing her hand on his heart, he caught her off guard by snatching her wrist and pulling her up next to the bars. His hands were around her throat in a flash, and he pulled her face hard against the bars.

"Throw them keys in here," he growled, his whiskey face inches from hers. He throttled her, and she put her hand on his fingers, trying to pull them away. His face came forward, and he put his lips on hers. The hold he had on her neck wouldn't allow her to turn her head, and all she could do was press her lips together as firm as she could while his lips crushed against hers.

He backed off, talking into her face, his breath so foul she had to shut her eyes. "Listen to me. We got a wagon in the back ready, and you, me, and the privates are going for a little Friday-night ride together. Now throw the keys!" he screamed, his hold on her neck tightening even more.

Tennie tried to nod, but he wouldn't let go. She felt around behind her until her hand touched the keys. Grasping them, she flung them toward the wall behind her as hard as she could.

"Why you!" he said, strangling her so hard, she almost lost consciousness.

"You've killed her!" one of the privates shouted. The corporal let go, and Tennie fell back, rolling away from the bars as quick as she could.

They called her every filthy name they could think of while she sat out of reach, gasping for breath, her gullet feeling crushed, her neck a ring of fire. They told her she was sleeping with all the other prisoners, shouting they knew she was letting every man in town poke her, why not them?

The boys came up the stairs, terror showing on their faces as they stared at her reddened neck.

Tennie got up. "Downstairs," she rasped, picking up the keys. She was so weak-kneed, Rusty and Lucas had to help her.

They took her down the stairs and to the back, helping her into a chair.

"Thank you. Let me think. Let me think." She shut her eyes. She couldn't handle those prisoners. She couldn't let them out in the morning, nor could she feed them or empty their slop jar.

"Lucas," she said, opening her eyes. "Take the bars in the back window down. Go to the Silver Moon through the alley to their back door. Ask if there is a high-ranking army officer in the saloon. Preferably a major if you can find one. Tell him I need to speak to him. Do you have that?"

"Yes, Miss Tennie."

"If you are by yourself, go the back way and come in through the window. Don't use the front."

"Yes, ma'am," he said, his face anxious.

"Okay, vamoose," she croaked.

Rusty helped him with the bars. Lucas scampered out; she could hear him hit the ground with a thud and the sound of his little footsteps fading away. She crossed her arms, placing them on the table, and lay her head down.

"Are you all right?" Rusty asked. "Would you like a glass of water?"

She raised her head, forcing herself to appear normal. "Yes, I'm fine. But I would like some water, please."

She drank some of the water and waited,

thinking herself the worst marshal in Texas, unable to handle three drunken soldiers.

It was some time before they heard Lucas opening the front door, pulling a major by the hand, followed by Jeff and two other men from the Silver Moon.

She tried to give a brief and calm explanation of what had happened even though her voice betrayed her by shaking. "I think this falls into the army's jurisdiction," she told the handsome young major who was staring at her in dismay and concern. "They can stay the night, but you'll have to come get them at first light and escort them back to the fort."

He apologized profusely for the behavior of his men. "Should I post a couple of guards here tonight?" he asked Tennie.

"For their own protection, you better," Jeff interrupted. "We'll stay here while you find some of your men." His fingers brushed against the blackjack hanging from his belt.

The major left, and Tennie hoped whoever he found was at least somewhat sober. She didn't need two more drunken soldiers to contend with.

"You best take the boys over to Shorty's now," Jeff said.

Tennie nodded and herded the boys out the door. She paused by Jeff and whispered without looking at him, "Please don't kill them."

"We won't," he said, patting her shoulder.

Shorty awaited them with lanterns lit, leaving the front door open to catch the breeze. He had a table with dominoes ready and with painstaking exactness led them through the rules of play. Tennie tried to concentrate and forget about what had happened, but she couldn't seem to block out the soldier's face in hers, the feeling of his hands around her neck, and she shuddered every time she thought about it. Since only four could play at a time, she teamed with Badger, but he caught on faster than she did. She hadn't realized there would be so much counting in dominoes, and it pleased her to see how fast the boys could add scores.

"We've been trying to keep up with school lessons," she said, putting her hand down to stroke Bear's thick fur.

The dog licked her hand, and she rubbed his ear.

"That's good," Shorty said, keeping his sharp eyes on what he called the "bones."

"Aw, schoolwork ain't no fun," Badger said.

"Humph, maybe not," Shorty said. "But when I was with the Rangers, it sure hurt some of the men."

"You rode with the Rangers?" Rusty asked.

"Yep," Shorty replied. "The men who couldn't read or write couldn't rise up in the ranks. Many a good man felt cheated by not making captain because he couldn't read or write."

Tennie felt like leaning over the table and

planting a kiss on Shorty's whiskered cheek. Play slowed down as Rusty and Lucas questioned Shorty about his ranger service—who he rode with, where they went, who they fought. Somehow, he didn't seem like a fussy old maid anymore.

To Tennie's surprise, nothing else happened that night, and Jeff came by early to tell them to go to bed.

They thanked Shorty for his hospitality and headed with Jeff back to the jail. "The soldiers are still drinking and spending money," Jeff explained, "but they've had their horns polled and aren't causing any more trouble tonight. The major asked permission to sleep on the cot in your office."

"Of course," Tennie said, relieved there would be an officer in command on the premises.

Jeff stopped at the door. "How did Lucas manage to get to the saloon without Shorty seeing him?"

Tennie paused. "Come along." She took one of the lanterns hanging from the office wall and led the way to the living quarters and the window in the back. She held the lantern over the window while Rusty demonstrated removing and replacing the bars. They waited for Jeff to chastise them.

"I had a fear of being trapped in here during a fire," Tennie said.

The only comment Jeff made was to tell the boys to keep their mouths shut about it. "Are you going to be okay?" he asked before leaving.

She nodded. "I think so."

The next morning, Tennie fried salt pork, putting the slices between biscuits she wrapped in paper, placing them in a poke bag for the prisoners and guards to take with them. The major, angry at the soldiers and upset they were cutting into his leave, sent them, or what was left of them—there was not a spot on their bodies that wasn't bruised—back to the fort under the guard of a second lieutenant and two privates, none of whom looked too happy at having their leave cut short, either. He said nothing about the blood covering the prisoners, only apologizing to Tennie again. Tennie tried to be gracious, but she wanted them out of Ring Bit.

With their embarrassing comrades out of sight and therefore out of mind, the other soldiers went back to living it up in Ring Bit on Saturday night. Jeff brought in one; the smaller saloons sent another. But other than wanting to fight every man who wasn't in uniform, they were as polite to Tennie as falling-down-drunk men could be.

She and the boys played dominoes again with Shorty, with Rusty spending part of the night reading the rest of *The Three Musketeers* to them. Jeff showed up with another prisoner, but this one didn't have to be manhandled. Tennie rose and went to the door.

"Miss Tennie," Jeff said. "You'll have to keep Apache John in a cell tonight for his own protection. Some of the boys have really been deviling him."

Tennie frowned. The last person she wanted in one of her cells was Apache John. Everything would have to be stripped, boiled, and washed down the next day to kill the lice he carried. Still, she couldn't refuse him or Jeff.

"Okay," she said, not feeling the least cordial. "I've got two soldiers in one cell; he can have the one farthest away from them." Jeff had already warned her to keep the soldiers together and out of cells with civilians.

Apache John went along with them quietly. When the soldiers saw him, they raised a ruckus about being in the same jail with an Indian, but Jeff ordered them to shut up. Apache John acted like he heard nothing, walked into the cell, pulled the blanket off the cot, and placed it on the floor, where he proceeded to lie down without a word to anyone.

Jeff shrugged. Tennie locked the door and followed Jeff downstairs.

"John doesn't live here in town?" Tennie asked as they walked back to the station.

"No, Winn Payton lets him live in a tiny shack on his place," Jeff said. "Say, I think I saw that little Mexican tonight, the one you patched up here awhile back."

"Poco?" Tennie asked in surprise. "He didn't come by to say hello."

"That's gratitude for you," Jeff said, leaving her at the station door.

The major wanted to sleep on the cot again. Tennie wasn't sure how it would look having a strange man, and a handsome young one at that, sleeping on the cot in her office two nights in a row, but she wasn't thrilled about having more unruly soldiers upstairs, so she agreed. Besides, she thought, she had three chaperones and anyone could look in the window at any time during the night and see the major sleeping alone. With other soldiers running loose in town, Jeff hadn't told her not to, either.

However, she offered the major breakfast before releasing his men. He was a lonely young man, far away from home, and she felt sorry for him. He had been a West Point cadet, and the life he had to live on the frontier of Texas was so wildly different from the one he had back East, he was eager to talk about his home to anyone with a sympathetic ear.

Tennie listened, learning all about his father, his mother, and his sweetheart.

When at last he left the table to get his prisoners, they found Apache John awake and sitting on the floor, staring at the wall.

Tennie sighed. She unlocked the door to the cell the soldiers were in, telling the major goodbye and good luck.

They left, and she returned to Apache John's cell, unlocking the door. "Mr. John, you are covered in lice, and I don't want someone with lice sitting at my table. If you want my boys to help you bathe and delouse your hair, we'll do that. I'll boil your clothes for you, too, if you want me to. Otherwise, you'll have to take your breakfast outside in the back."

Apache John looked straight ahead. "Breakfast in back."

"Okay," Tennie said. "Suit yourself. I'll have it out to you directly."

She followed Apache John down the stairs. The major had not left, however.

"Miss Tennie," he said with concern. "You don't intend on feeding that Indian, do you? You don't have to do that."

Apache John went out the door as if they were speaking about someone else.

"It will probably be the only decent nourishment he gets all week," Tennic said. "The corn he lives on comes liquefied in a bottle. Now, if you'll excuse me. . . ."

The major surprised her by grasping her hand and kissing it. He reddened, and clicking his heels together, bowed and turned, marching out the door.

"Good heavens," Tennie said and went into the kitchen.

The boys were almost as enthralled to be around a real live Indian as they were to be around a former Texas Ranger. Tennie prepared a plate of eggs and fried salt pork for Apache John, hoping he could keep it and the biscuits down. Handing the plate to Lucas, she warned him and the other two boys, "Don't sit too close to Apache John. I don't want lice jumping from him onto you."

He could not only keep what she put on his plate down, he demanded seconds. Using his fingers, he ate hungrily from both plates. Grunting as he handed the plate back to Lucas, he left without giving so much as a nod of thanks.

"Don't worry," Tennie muttered to his retreating back. "I'm getting used to gross ungratefulness." She remembered as an orphan, how much she'd hated being forced to make huge shows of gratitude for what amounted to a little of nothing. It shamed her she had expected the same thing from other people.

That afternoon, Tennie went for a walk by herself, escaping to the only place she knew she could be alone, the cemetery. She sat down on the ground with her back against a tree, looking out over the green grass covering the graves and the crosses placed above them. She put her head down and cried and cried and cried.

That evening, she explained to the boys what they would have to do.

"Don't you think we ought to tell Mr. Jeff and Mr. Lafayette, and just let them handle it?" Rusty asked.

Tennie sighed. "Believe me, I would like nothing better. But it is not their responsibility. It's my responsibility. And I have every intention of deputizing you, so it will be your responsibility, too."

"Deputizing us?" Rusty asked.

"Are we getting paid?" Lucas wanted to know.

"Unpaid deputies," Tennie stressed. "This time, you are going to be working on the right side of the law instead of against it."

They went over her plans, making suggestions, helping her modify them into something that might work. A sheet over the window was deemed too flimsy and might show a shadow, better to hang a quilt instead. What chair would he insist on taking? He could possibly have any three, but Tennie had to be in one in particular, preferably the one directly across from his. Badger and Lucas would have to practice. "But not upfront where anyone can see," Tennie said.

For the early part of the week, they waited. The boys were not inclined to roam all over town and stayed nearby, visiting with Big Mike and Shorty, playing with Bear, and practicing their sword fighting. Jeff came by and wanted to know why Lucas hadn't brought them any bottles, and his brothers hastily helped him gather the loose ones thrown around town and take them to the back door of the Silver Moon. Lafayette stayed away, and Tennie felt alternately grateful and disappointed.

On Tuesday, Tennie met the stage, but Packer Jack had no word for her. On Wednesday evening, Rusty told Mike he wanted to saddle the buckskin to hunt coyotes. Instead, he waited for hours at the boulder on the road between Ring Bit and Cat Ridge. At midnight, following Tennie's directive, he gave up, coming back home.

Every day, Tennie cooked massive amounts of food. Delectable pies and cookies had to be made, consumed, and more made again. She and the boys ate whatever they could to keep the food from spoiling, only so she could cook fresh the next day. Shep Davis from the Bar S came by with Honey Boy and Two-Bit to say howdy, and Tennie fed them so royally they had trouble getting up from the table, they were so stuffed.

"I thought some ladies I knew on the wagon train were coming to visit," Tennie improvised. "But they must have been held up."

"Lordy mercy," Shep exclaimed. "How big a' heifers are these women?"

On Thursday, Tennie waited outside for the stage. As soon as she saw Packer Jack's face, she knew he had news. She ran up to him before he even had time to dismount.

"He was at Brushwood day before yesterday," Packer said, climbing down from the stagecoach. "He should be coming this way this evening or tomorrow."

"Thank you," Tennie said, gulping in nervousness. She thrust a poke bag full of cookies into Packer's hands.

He protested it wasn't necessary, and Tennie said she knew that, but she appreciated his help. He started eating the cookies and left off further protesting.

Tennie did not think Packer Jack told anyone else Harden Kane was on his way to Ring Bit, but by noon, the town had all but shut down. The saloons would stay open during the Apocalypse and the Second Coming, but every other business, including the butcher shop across the street locked its doors and put a CLOSED sign up. Even Mike, who normally kept both of his big doors open day and night, shut them. He and Shorty, at separate times, told the boys to get inside and stay inside, instructing them to have Tennie lock the door.

Rusty had kept his buckskin tethered to the yard in the back, telling Mike they wanted the horse to eat the grass down. At dusk, just as the sky was beginning to darken, he slipped out the window and rode away.

Tennie sat the table, half hoping Harden Kane was coming so they could get it over with and half hoping he wouldn't. Her hands shook as she lit the lanterns. "Are you ready?" she asked Badger and Lucas.

"We're ready," Lucas said, giving a solemn nod.

"We've been practicing," Badger added.

In less than an hour, Rusty was at the window, taking the bars down with excited hands. "It's him!" he whispered. "There's no mistaking. It's him."

"Okay," Tennie said. "Remember, stay in the back until you hear my signal."

"Okay, okay," Rusty said, helping her out the window and onto the horse.

Tennie had her hair down, her full pink skirt and petticoats spread over one side of the saddle. Only a blind man would mistake her for anything but a woman on a night with a Comanche moon.

CHAPTER 14

Tennie rode toward Cat Ridge, her hands shaking so much she could hardly hold the reins. She kept the horse at an easy plod—there was no hurry. In the moonlight, she could see the figure of a rider approaching. When he caught sight of her, he reined his horse in, placing one hand near the butt of his revolver before continuing, but she kept her steady pace, willing herself to be calm and remember death only came once.

"Mr. Kane?" she asked when she reached him.

He pulled in the reins, halting his horse. "Who wants to know?"

Tennie reined her horse so it could be in line with his. "I'm Tennessee Granger, the new town marshal of Ring Bit," she said, making her voice a shade more feminine. "I'd like to ride with you a spell and ask a few questions of you."

She could feel, rather than see, his perplexity. He put his heels to his horse's flank, and she joined him, matching her horse with the slow pace of his.

"I heared they got a woman marshal," he said. "You ain't armed, are you?"

"No, I'm not armed," Tennie said.

"What do you want to ask me about?"

Tennie had thought long and hard how to approach Harden Kane, and she still wasn't sure. But the truth seemed the best place. "There's something going on in Ring Bit, and I don't know what it is. The town is awful, and it's not just all the saloons. There are saloons in most every town in the West, but none of them seem as bad as Ring Bit."

She had his attention, puzzled though it was. "It is like there is a cancer that needs to come out. But I don't know what it is or where to look. Or if I could even do anything about it.

"Your attorney told me you figured you were framed because men thought you heard something you shouldn't have."

He grunted. "My attorney! That shyster got me a year and a half in prison."

"He believed you, you know," Tennie said. "He told me he thought you were entirely innocent of stealing the saddle."

That seemed to surprise Kane. "He told you that? Really?"

Tennie nodded. "Yes. Really. He said you told him you walked in on a group of men in a room. Was it in the Silver Moon?"

"Nah," Kane said. "It was in one of those little saloons down from it. I was looking to go to the back to the privy and took a wrong turn. I was slightly inebriated. That's lawyer talk for *drunk*."

Tennie gave a brief smile. "Who were the men? Did you recognize them?"

He reeled off names, all the men on the town council who had visited her at the ranch and a few others she had a nodding acquaintance with.

"And you can't remember any word you heard them say?" Tennie pressed.

"Nah, lady, I was too soaked."

Tennie sighed. "Well, it was worth a try, anyway. Whereabouts are you from, Mr. Kane?"

"I'm from all over the place, but most of my raising was in Kansas. Bloody ass-backward Kansas. My last known address was cell number three hundred and twenty-five in Huntsville."

Regretfully, Tennie knew nothing about Kansas. She wracked her brain trying to think of something to say to keep the conversation going. Hadn't Two-Bit once mentioned he came from near Huntsville?

"I heard there are a lot of beautiful pine trees in Huntsville, but it's very humid," Tennie said.

"Oh, my God, lady. You have no idea. And ticks! Every time they put us to work in the fields, I came back pulling more ticks off me than a dog has fleas."

He warmed to his subject, and Tennie had no trouble keeping him talking about how horrible prison life had been. Unfortunately, that got him started on how he was going to kill the lowdown skunks who put him there.

They were approaching the edge of town. "Have you had supper?" Tennie asked as innocent as she could. This was the crux, the moment when everything would swing one way or another.

"Not really," he said, suspicious. "Why?"

"I have supper on the table in the office. Just some ham and potatoes. A little fresh okra and black-eyed peas. Some light bread. A couple of chess pies and a few cookies. I have three stepsons, but they decided to leave early to visit friends. Now I'm stuck with all this food." She prayed God would forgive her lies, and Harden Kane would believe every one of them.

He eyed her in suspicion, but the desire for woman-cooked food trumped his doubts. "Who's there? In the jailhouse?"

"Nobody. My prisoners only come in for the weekend."

He grinned, and Tennie almost wished he hadn't. "All right."

They dismounted near the water trough to let the horses drink, and Tennie prayed Big Mike was not watching. After the horses had their fill, they walked to the hitching rail in front of the jail and tied them there.

At the jailhouse door, Kane pulled his revolver, motioning for her to let him go in first. He turned the handle and kicked the door in. When nothing happened, he walked in, gun in hand, looking in every corner. All the lanterns were lit, and he headed for the living quarters in the back.

Tennie followed him, holding her breath he did not try the bars over the back window. Pulling a small rocker on a rug in front of the window as they left had been Rusty's idea. Instead of moving the rocker, Kane walked to a window on the side of the room, checking the bars and peering outside. Satisfied, he left the room with Tennie following.

When he turned to go up the stairs to check the cells, Tennie expelled a breath of thankfulness. Everything was moving along as planned. Now if he would just sit in the right chair.

Placated, he bounded down the stairs and looked at the table spread with food. "I guess you weren't lying, woman." He glanced at the window, covered in a quilt so thick, no one could see a shadow through it. He grabbed the chair she and the boys had thought he would take, the one with its back to the side wall of the room, where he could see the door and the windows.

Tennie sat down opposite of him, her back to the rest of the office.

He removed his hat and began eating as if he hadn't eaten well in a long time, his head with its thinning sandy hair bent low over the plate. She tried to make small talk to drown out any bumps in the night he might hear, even though anxiety made her almost unable to swallow.

Kane began to talk about his plans, or lack of them, openly. He wanted revenge and talked about shooting people who had crossed him, but he didn't appear to have any idea how this was going to be accomplished. After he satisfied that desire, he thought he would head farther west, perhaps to Tombstone. Tennie let him talk, hoping it was steam he was blowing off, not building up.

"What are you looking at?" he demanded when she ran out of things to say.

Tennie looked at him in surprise, but answered truthfully enough. "I was thinking you are not what a woman would normally call handsome, but instead, you are a striking looking man."

He thought about it and decided to be pleased. "Unforgettablelike," he said in good humor.

"Entirely," Tennie agreed.

When he quit, after topping everything off with one whole pie, Tennie took a deep breath and did what she knew she had to do. She reached under the table to the open-faced drawer Rusty had built for her and pulled out Ashton's old Navy revolver.

She aimed it at Kane's belly, cocking the hammer, watching as his face drained of every color and emotion except pure shocked white.

"Now, Mr. Kane," she said, "I want you to

stand up slowly and remove your gun belt just as slowly."

He belched out a word that sounded like "What?"

"Just stand up and undo your gun belt, letting it drop to the floor," Tennie repeated. "Please don't do anything that could make me nervous. I'm afraid this gun is going to go off accidentally as it is."

"You and me both, lady!" he managed to blurt. He stared at the revolver, gulped, and rose slowly.

She had every intention of shooting him if he tried anything, and he must have realized she planned to do so if he did not comply, so he followed her instructions, letting the gun belt go to the floor with a clunk.

"Rusty!" she called.

The boys ran in, Rusty snatching the gun belt while Badger and Lucas snapped leg irons around Kane's ankles so fast, he did not have time to realize what they were doing. Rusty removed the gun belt to the back of the jailhouse, leaving it in their living quarters. Coming back, he searched Kane for more weapons, while Kane looked at Tennie in dismay.

"You didn't play fair, lady!" he complained.

"Mr. Kane," Tennie said, heaving a sigh in relief, "women never play fair."

Rusty found a derringer in Kane's coat pocket and a knife strapped to his calf. When he was sure the man had no more weapons on him, he nodded to Tennie.

"Please sit down, Mr. Kane," Tennie said. "But keep your hands up."

Lucas and Rusty wrapped rope around Kane's middle, leaving his hands free, tying him to his chair.

"What are you aiming to do with me?" he asked her, his face full of bewilderment.

"I aim to keep you here out of harm's way until the stage comes in, then I'm putting you on the stage with a ticket for Tombstone, if the stationmaster agrees your horse is worth that. If not, he'll get you a ticket to El Paso."

"I've never been on a stagecoach before," he whined.

"It will be a new experience for you," Tennie said. "You may take your saddle."

"Can I tie his hands up, too, Miss Tennie?" Lucas asked. "Please!"

"That depends on Mr. Kane. Are you going to sit here, nice like, or are you going to give us trouble? My stepsons are very handy when it comes to a rope."

"I already heared that," Kane said, sweat popping out on his forehead. "Don't let them boys tie me up further," he pleaded with Tennie.

"I don't think it is going to be necessary, Lucas," she said.

"Aw, heck." Lucas moved to the desk, where he

leaned against the corner rubbing his hand on the rope and keeping brooding eyes on Kane.

"Would you like to play dominoes?" Tennie asked. "Our neighbor has a set he'd loan us, I think."

"I don't like dominoes," Kane said, pouting like a child. "I got a deck of cards in my saddlebags."

"We don't know how to play cards, but you can teach us if you want to."

"I'll learn you a new way to play poker. I run across it in Waco. Five-card draw."

"Sounds wonderful," Tennie said. "Rusty, while I guard Mr. Kane, would you tend to the horses and bring Mr. Kane's saddle inside? Lucas, you and Badger will have to clean the table and put the food away like we discussed, remember?"

"Shucks," Lucas grumbled, a sentiment echoed by Badger, but Lucas put the rope where he could get to it, and he and Badger began removing dishes from the table.

"There ain't hardly no food left to put up," Lucas groused as he gathered the empty bowls and plates. "Some folks eat like hogs."

"Don't pay any attention to him," Tennie told Kane. "He's just mad because I won't let him really go to town tying you up."

Tennie followed Rusty to the door, her gun raised while she looked across the street at Milton's butcher shop.

"You a-feared of that man across the street?" Kane asked.

Tennie nodded. "I think he's a little unbalanced. He's hates us, anyway. Although I think he hates Rusty the least."

Rusty, coming back in with Kane's saddle and saddlebags, said, "He scares me to death every time I have to go over there." He threw Kane's things in the corner, and they shut the door. Tennie sat down at the table again while Rusty rooted in the bags and found the deck of cards.

"Miss Tennie . . ." he said, setting the cards on the table.

"I know," Tennie said. "Your ma was agin it, but I think she would allow it this time so we can keep Mr. Kane entertained while he waits for his stagecoach."

"Ain't we gonna play for money?" Kane asked.

"Oh, no," Tennie said. "We don't have gambling money."

"Then we ought to play for matches or toothpicks or something," Kane said.

Badger ran to fetch matches, and they sat down at the table, four eager faces staring expectantly at Harden Kane.

He raised a doubtful eyebrow around the table, but sighing, took a deep breath and said, "Well, first off, we have to shuffle the cards."

"Why?" Badger asked.

Tennie silently blessed Harden Kane's heart as

he gruffly explained the rules and object of the game and why they had to do every step. Once she picked it up, Tennie enjoyed poker. After a streak of beginners' luck, she realized how peeved Kane was getting that she was winning, although he didn't seem to resent it when the boys did. She began losing on purpose, and it put Kane in a much better mood.

A knock came at the door. Lafayette and Jeff entered as if making a casual visit.

"My dear Miss Tennie," Lafayette said. "What do we have here?"

"Mr. Kane is teaching us to play five-card paint," Tennie said.

Six voices rose in unison to correct her. "Draw."

"Oh, that's right," Tennie said. "Five-card draw. It's something he learned in Waco. Do you know it, Mr. Lafayette?"

"I am acquainted with it, yes," Lafayette said, a smile playing at his lips. He came around the table and stood behind Tennie, watching her play. When she discarded two aces, he gave an almost imperceptible start. Tennie turned and gave him a glance telling him she knew what she was doing, and he made an ever-so-slight nod of understanding.

"Perhaps Mr. Kane would care to play cards with myself and other men for real cash?" Lafayette asked.

"You got it, friend," Kane said.

Lafayette sent Jeff to the saloon to fetch his dealer and see if he could pull Shorty into the game. When the three men arrived, Tennie got up from the table, grateful to let them take their places. Jeff did not play, however, but took a chair in the corner, stretching his legs out and lowering his hat over his face. The night's activities were beginning to tell on Tennie and the boys. She sat on the cot with Lucas on one side of her and Badger on the other, while Rusty took the chair behind the desk. Lucas and Badger did not last long before falling asleep, and soon Tennie felt her head begin to nod.

She didn't know how long she slept. She was awakened by a shrill voice. She opened her eyes, realizing she had leaned over and had her head on the cot while her legs hung limp over the side.

"Well, isn't this a cozy little scene," Arabella said, hands on hips. Small plump breasts spilled from the lowcut dress she wore, her elaborate hairdo beginning to show signs of falling apart. The heavy makeup on her face made the creases in the frown around her mouth more pronounced.

Tennie sat up, but said nothing. No one said anything. Disgusted, Arabella gave Tennie a hard stare before letting her lips curve upward in a smirk. She walked behind Lafayette, who sat with eyes intent on the cards, and draped her arms around him, kissing his neck and shoulders while stealing glances at Tennie and smiling.

Arabella began rubbing her hands up and around Lafayette's shoulders. He continued to play as if she wasn't there. Her hands began stroking lower and lower on his chest, until they disappeared under the table. Tennie could not see the dealer's face, but Harden Kane's had suffused a nasty red, and his eyes scorched in fire. Shorty looked aggravated and glared at Arabella. She paid no attention, but let her arms take on a pulsing up-and-down motion under the table. Tennie felt her own face burning; she turned and looked at Jeff.

"Miss Tennie," he said, pushing his hat back. "I shore would like some coffee. Would you be so kind as to make some?"

Tennie nodded in gratefulness. "Yes," she replied, and disentangling herself from the sleeping boys, left for the kitchen.

It took a while to get the coals in the stove stoked, and Tennie did not hurry.

Jeff came into the kitchen and stood beside her at the stove. "I hope the man who marries you"— he kept his voice low—"realizes he is going to go gray overnight."

She turned. "What do you mean?" she whispered.

"I mean every man in town had sense enough to lay low when news came Harden Kane was on his way. And what happens? Here comes Shorty into the saloon, saying, 'Jeff, you and Lafayette better get over there to the jailhouse. You'll never believe it, but I think Tennie has Harden Kane in there playing cards.' "

"Well, I had to do something with him to keep him from trying to escape and getting his fool head blown off or somebody else's, too," Tennie said.

"How did you get him in here?" Jeff asked.

Tennie explained, adding she intended on putting him on the morning stage with a ticket for Tombstone if Shorty would agree his horse was worth it.

Jeff gave a quiet laugh and shook his head. "I think you could charge his ticket to the town, and you wouldn't hear peek nor peck about it from anybody."

Jeff stayed in the kitchen with her until the coffee was ready. He took the pot while she carried the mugs into the office, but Arabella had left, to Tennie's relief. The men continued to play into the early hours.

Tennie prepared ham and cheese sandwiches they could hold in one hand. Lafayette never made eye contact with her, never seemed to acknowledge anything else in the world was going on except the card game. She noticed Kane's pile did not go down much, and as it drew closer to the time for the stage to arrive, his pot increased from when it first began. Tennie wondered if the players had done it on purpose, sensing they would have less trouble out of him.

When she heard the sound of horses coming, she stood. "Mr. Kane, that's your stagecoach."

While Lucas and Rusty untied Kane, Lafayette drew her aside, taking her hands in his and kissing them. "My dear lady, I apologize if my association with certain people has caused you embarrassment."

She didn't know what to do or say, except to squeeze his hands in return.

She turned back to Kane. "Now please walk close to me, Mr. Kane. You are less likely to be shot that way."

He did not disagree, but picked up his saddle and went with her out the door. Jeff, Lafayette, and Shorty followed. Packer Jack sat on top of the stage watching them with his head cocked and his eyes half-closed. Kane threw his saddle on top of the stagecoach, opened the door, and climbed in.

Before shutting the door, Tennie leaned forward. "Mr. Kane, do me one last favor."

"What is it?"

"Lay your head down on the seat until you get out of town," Tennie said with a smile.

He drew closer. "Miss Tennie, go with me to Tombstone. We could get married. I wouldn't let nothing happen around you like what happened in there tonight with that ole gal, I swear. I'd take good care of you and them boys."

"You know, I believe you would." She smiled at him in kindness. "Thank you, but I must say no." She leaned forward and kissed his cheek.

He surprised her by taking his hands and placing them on her cheeks, planting a big kiss on her lips. He leaned back grinning.

She smiled. "Lay down now," she said, and shut the door.

He did, and Packer Jack cracked the whip, hollering, "giddy-up."

Kane's head stayed down as the stage left, but he threw his hat up in the air inside the coach.

Someone fired a bullet through it.

CHAPTER 15

As Tennie sat with Mike on the bench in front of the jail, he fussed at her for being sneaky. "I know nothing about what you were doing," he boomed. "Why don't you come to me for help with your plans? Why go to fancy man Lafayette?"

"I didn't ask for his help," Tennie said. "He just showed up."

"Shorty, he should have come got me," Mike grumbled. "I could have handled Harden Kane criminal just like that," he said, waving a big paw.

"Then why were your doors shut?" Tennie asked.

"Because people tell me to shut them, say bad outlaw is on his way to shoot up town. I don't go looking for trouble like Miss Tennie."

She laughed.

He wanted to know all the details, what they had done, what they had talked about. She left off telling Mike of sharing with Harden Kane her fears about the town, but told him everything else. Except, of course, the part about the bars in the back window being sawed off. She didn't mind Jeff knew, but she didn't want it to get all over town she and her stepsons had desecrated jail property.

She half expected the town councilmen to hand her walking papers—she had, after all, accomplished what they'd hoped, gotten rid of Harden Kane. Although Jeff assured her Maggot Milton probably had a rifle trained on Kane the entire time he had been in Ring Bit. But the councilmen did not come around, and it was only through hearsay she learned they were pleased with the job she was doing.

The problem with Harden Kane had only been a temporary one. The townswomen stayed locked behind closed doors from Friday to Sunday morning, when they felt it prudent enough to walk to church. During the week, they were close enough to be able to judge when things were slow, and it was safe to come out. The country ladies did not have that recourse. Tennie began sitting outside the jail more and walking up and down the sidewalks when she had time. She wondered if it was just her imagination the foul language had diminished, the shooting had lessened, and the daytime drunkenness had decreased.

Much to her disgust, Jeff brought Apache John back in. "Why do they keep picking on him?" Tennie cried once they were back downstairs.

"Maybe to get a rise out of you," Jeff said.

228

"They know you feed Apache John whenever he comes begging."

"Well, I'm not settling their arguments," Tennie said. "Somebody else is welcome to the marshal job if they don't like it."

"Pipe down," Jeff said, laughing at her. "Don't get your drawers in a wad."

"Easy for you to say," Tennie pouted. "Everyone expects me to perform miracles around here."

Jeff opened the door for her. "Scoot," he ordered.

She walked outside taking a deep breath of the night air. Turning to Jeff as he shut the door, she fell into step with him back to Shorty's.

"You need a break, gal," Jeff said. "Winn Payton's been after me to bring you out there for a visit. What say I take you out there Wednesday to visit? Or Lafayette could take you in the buggy."

"I'm not going anywhere with Mr. Lafayette. He and Arabella made it abundantly clear he belongs to someone else," Tennie said.

Jeff stopped, and Tennie paused to look at him. "Miss Tennie, what if I told you most of that is just part of the job?"

"Then I would say he has a sorry job. And so do you."

"And so do you," Jeff countered.

"Can't argue with that," she said as they began walking again. "What about the boys? Are they going with us? Mr. Payton didn't exactly welcome us to come to his ranch when Ashton died. His answer to my problem was to pick a man and get married—any man. Just do it."

Jeff grinned. "Don't hold that against him. He's an old man, and he knew those boys would be too much for him. Besides, you need a break from them, too. Shorty wants to take Rusty fishing, and Mike will keep an eye on Lucas and Badger. For all his faults, he likes kids. And to tell you the truth, I wouldn't mind getting away from all the drama that goes on in that saloon for a while, either."

"Okay," she agreed, giving him a smile before going inside the station.

They were back to playing dominoes, with occasional games of five-card draw. Tennie watched Shorty play, and she later told Jeff she thought Shorty had been holding back when he played with Harden Kane. Jeff laughed and told her Shorty was such a cardsharp, he wasn't allowed in any of the saloons anymore.

"I haven't caught him cheating," Tennie said in disbelief.

"He don't need to cheat," Jeff said. "He's just that dang good."

"He must be holding back with us, too," she said. "Badger beat him last night."

The next evening, before dark, two cowboys Tennie had never seen dragged a couple of unwilling and belligerent cowhands into the jail.

"These boys are causing trouble, Miss Tennie," the taller one said. "They're better locked up for tonight to cool off before they cause real problems."

Both prisoners protested and put up violent struggles. In response, their handlers shook and slapped them.

"Shut up!"

"Keep quiet!"

By now, Tennie had an acquaintance with all the men the saloons used to get rid of troublesome customers, but she had never seen these fellows before. Reluctantly, she fetched the keys and followed them as they pushed the men roughly up the stairs, shoving them with more force than necessary into a cell. She locked the door and followed the handlers down the stairs.

"Don't pay no attention to them, ma'am," the taller cowboy said. "They're better off up there for their own protection."

Tennie nodded. The boys had come inside and watched the men leave.

From upstairs came the sounds of two men calling her. "Ma'am! Ma'am!"

Tennie climbed the stairs, with Rusty, Lucas, and Badger following behind.

Her prisoners were holding onto the bars, two weather-beaten young men who didn't look any

231

scruffier or meaner than any other cowboys who roamed the streets of Ring Bit.

"Ma'am," one of them spoke. "We're drovers from down south around Pleasanton. We got three hundred head of cattle south of here with only a couple of green wranglers watching them. If we don't get out of this here jail, somebody's gonna take off with our cattle."

"Please, ma'am," the other cowboy said. "Let us out of here."

Tennie didn't know what to do. She went to the windows, standing to one side so she wouldn't be so visible. The men who had brought the cowboys in were loitering across the street in front of the butcher shop.

"I think they are waiting to see if I let you go," Tennie said. "If I do, they will just waylay you in an alley and possibly kill you. I don't know why they brought you in here to me and didn't do that in the first place."

"They are just testing you, Miss Tennie," Rusty said. "To see if they can keep using you."

Tennie gave him a stare. "Where'd you learn something like that?"

Rusty turned pink. "Shorty. He tells me stuff like that."

Tennie nodded, looking back to the window. She couldn't smuggle the men out the back. The other cowboys would figure out she had a back entrance, and she didn't want that known.

"Where are your horses?" she asked, turning to the jailed drovers.

"In front of the Silver Moon saloon," one said. "Two appaloosas branded with a lazy J."

Tennie nodded. "Rusty, would you and Lucas slip into the alley and bring their horses around to the back? Then create some kind of disturbance down the street so those cowboys in front of Mr. Milton's will leave to see what's happening. Don't do anything that's going to get you into major trouble."

"Yes, ma'am, Miss Tennie!" Rusty said.

He and Lucas were only too happy to snatch horses and create a ruckus. They left, bounding down the stairs with Badger behind them.

Tennie stood at the window and waited while the cowboys across the street continued their bored loitering. When she judged sufficient time had passed for Rusty and Lucas to have brought the horses around to the back, she unlocked the jail cell door and led her prisoners down the stairs.

"Stand back so you can't be seen and wait," Tennie said, walking to the edge of the window and trying to peer down the street without being noticed. Several minutes passed, and the drovers behind her began to get restless.

"Those men are still across the street," Tennie told them. "Don't worry. My stepsons are experts at causing commotions. They'll clear the way for you."

She had no sooner spoken when the sound of Lucas hollering could be heard. "Catfight! Catfight in the Silver Moon!" he yelled, repeating it as he ran down the street.

The bored cowboys in front of the butcher shop perked up and looked at one another. A crowd was already gathering in front of the Silver Moon, and they decided to join the other men, craning their necks to see what was happening.

"Okay," Tennie said. "Let me go first."

She opened the door and looked at the thickening gaggle of onlookers at the saloon door. Men drew back, almost tripping over one another, while two women catapulted into the street, kicking, screaming, and pulling hair.

"Now," Tennie said, motioning the men. They slipped behind her and hurried around the back of the jailhouse.

Tennie walked closer to the melee, wondering if she should do something to stop the two women. One of them already had claw marks down the side of her cheek. The other was throttling her, and with a shock, Tennie realized the would-be strangler was Arabella, Lafayette's mistress.

Winn Payton had warned her not to get involved in the saloon girls' spats. However, she was afraid if someone did not stop Arabella, she really would murder the other woman.

The victim quit pulling at the fingers around her neck, hauled back, and hit Arabella in the eye as hard as she could. Tennie winced, but Arabella shrieked and loosened her hold enough for the other women to get free. She ripped the front of Arabella's dress, screaming, "You are crazier than ten drunk Mexicans!"

Tennie felt a hand on her elbow and someone drawing her back. She turned and looked at Shorty.

"This is no place for you, Tennie," he said, and she allowed him to lead her back to their part of town.

That evening, while they sat at Shorty's, planning strategies to beat their opponents at dominoes, Jeff walked in and threw a piece of paper on the table in front of Tennie.

"The next time your boys decide to steal horses and start a catfight in the saloon, Lafayette said to tell you he'd appreciate it if you had them draw the women outside first," Jeff said. "Those wildcats ruined three chairs, a table, and a mirror costing in the hundreds before they got pitched outside."

Tennie looked at the paper and the words written in Lucas's childish hand. "That other saloon womin with the red hair said you is gettin old and fat, and she is goin to take your man. He is already makin eyes at her."

She looked up at Lucas. "We are going to have to work on your spelling."

"I did it that way on purpose, Miss Tennie.

Honest!" he protested. "I told Miss Arabella a cowboy had given it to me to give her, and everybody knows cowboys can't spell."

"Some of them can," Tennie said. "Shorty was a cowboy, and he can spell better than anyone at this table."

"Miss Tennie!" Jeff interrupted.

She turned and apologized. "There is a reason for this," she said, and the four of them explained.

The men exchanged long glances. When she finished, Shorty said, "Can you describe the men? The ones who brought the drovers in?"

Tennie shut her eyes, willing herself to remember the men standing in front of her at the jail. "The tall one had a brown mole about as big around as a pencil in the middle of his cheek. The shorter one was slight, with heavy eyebrows. Even though they did not resemble one another too closely, I got the impression they might be brothers, but I can't tell you why I thought that."

"Yes, I think I know who they are," Shorty said. "You did right, girl." He turned to Jeff. "Tell Lafayette I said the wages of sin are death and broken mirrors. Now either sit down and play or leave us alone."

Jeff sighed. "I have to go back to work."

Tennie followed him outside and stood on the sidewalk with him. "I just told the boys to create a disturbance. They dreamed that up on their own."

236

"Knowing them, I have no doubt that is true."

"Mr. Jeff," Tennie began, unsure of what to say. "I know it's not my place, but I don't think Miss Arabella is entirely right in the head. She could hurt Mr. Lafayette."

"You're preaching to the choir, sister," Jeff said. "The doctor came over and gave her a dose of morphine, so she's out of it now."

"I wonder why he drinks all the time," Tennie mused.

"If I was doing to those girls what they are asking him to do, I'd stay drunk all the time, too."

"What things?"

"Things I hope to God you never know anything about. I've got to head on back. I'll tell Lafayette it was something the boys cooked up to help you get those men out of town. Go back to your domino game. Try to stay out of trouble the rest of the night, little sister."

During the noon hour the following day, Tennie fed, along with her stepsons, two of Shep Davis's cowhands who had gotten into a brawl over one of the Silver Moon's saloon girls, ruining even more of Lafayette's furniture. Tennie suspected the girl of being jealous over the attention the previous catfight had created and therefore egging on the argument between the two cowhands over her. For whatever reason, they had carried the fight too far, and Lafayette had them thrown in jail, but not before they had given Jeff a black eye and more bruises.

In the middle of the meal, the U.S. deputy marshal walked in to introduce himself to Tennie, and another chair and plate were hastily placed at the already crowded table.

Tennie, not hungry, picked at what was left on her plate, while throwing occasional glances at the lawman who ate in silence like the cowboys. She had envisioned the marshal as being a middle-aged man with gray hair, a mustache, and a paunch. He had the mustache, but it wasn't gray, and he wasn't anywhere close to forty yet. Under a mane of thick brown hair and straight bushy eyebrows rested a pair of sparkling green eyes, and even though he spoke little, Tennie found herself liking his quiet, self-assured manner.

The cowboys had to return to work and would probably take a cussing from Shep Davis for being late. They apologized to Tennie, thanked her profusely for the food, and sent her regards from Honey Boy and Two-Bit.

Before they could leave, Lafayette stopped by to remind them he expected full remuneration on the next payday. Looking sheepish, they agreed to pay, donning their hats, full of good spirits and stories to tell the other cowboys around the campfires during the coming week.

"Mr. Lafayette, would you care for a piece of pie?" Tennie asked.

Lafayette looked down at the table. "I'm not going to take your last piece of pie, Miss Tennie."

"Don't be ridiculous. It will save a fight over who gets it later on. Let me get you a plate."

She asked the boys to help her clear the table. When she returned with more coffee, the two men were discussing county politics in a desultory manner, neither man appearing to like, nor dislike, the other. Just as Lafayette was finishing his pie, Mike walked in and told the marshal his horse had a loose shoe, and after that brief discussion ended, he appeared reluctant to leave. Shorty came by, sat at the table without being asked, and demanded to know the news. Meanwhile, the boys, having been banished to the back or outdoors, slowly made their way through the group of men, going outside to loiter by the jailhouse windows so they could overhear what the men said.

Tennie sat, listening and waiting. At last, when the other men finally left, the marshal looked across the table at her and said, "Is there someplace private we can go to talk?"

She nodded, rose, and went outside. They could walk up the hill to the cemetery easy enough, but Tennie had learned on her trek out, western men did not like to walk if a horse was anywhere near handy.

"Rusty, would you saddle a horse for me? And bring along the marshal's horse if it's ready?"

"Can we go?" Badger asked.

"No, you heard the marshal," Tennie said.

They didn't try to pretend they hadn't been listening. Rusty came back with the horses, and with the help of a nearby mounting block, Tennie got on hers while the marshal swung a long slender leg over his saddle. She led him the short distance to the cemetery, where they could be seen by anyone nosy enough to look, but not be surprised by eavesdroppers.

They dismounted, leaving the horses and strolling an aimless path around the graves while talking.

"Do you always have a crowd like that around?"

Tennie laughed. "I have three stepsons. I have a crowd with just them around."

The dashing marshal smiled. "When I heard Ring Bit got a female town marshal, I was prepared to dislike you. I expected an old boozing, sometime prostitute, dressed in men's clothes."

"I'm glad I disappointed you," Tennie said.

"And then when I heard how you got rid of Harden Kane, I admit to suffering from admiration mixed with envy. Nobody else could have gotten that sorry piece of backwater sludge out of the countryside so fast."

"Thank you. But I did have help. I only fear by letting him go, I may have been signing a death warrant for someone else."

The marshal grunted. "Don't worry. I don't

imagine he'll make it past El Paso alive anyway."

Tennie paused. "What is it you really want to talk to me about?"

He stopped walking, fingering the brim of the hat he held in his hand. "Two drovers caught up with me and complained of being harassed by a couple of cowboys here in Ring Bit. They told me you got them out of town, and they were able to move their herd farther north."

"That's right. I didn't know the cowboys who wanted them jailed, but Shorty, the stationmaster, thinks he does."

"I'll talk to him then before I leave town," the marshal said. "There's been a rash of rustling going on in this part of the state for a long time. I'm trying to stop it; there are other men trying to stop it. I came here mainly to warn you to stay out of it the best you can. You did right by not confronting the two cowboys and bypassing them another way. These men are ruthless. I don't think they'd kill a woman or children, but they could do other things that could make you wish you were dead."

"I understand. I have no desire to saddle up and go chasing rustlers. I can't even keep law in Ring Bit. I thought they just wanted to use me, to hide behind my skirts hoping I could charm Harden Kane into leaving them alone. But, they still have me here. And I don't know why."

She could see the marshal struggling, wanting

to tell her something, yet fearing he shouldn't. In the end, he chose to remain silent.

"I can't do anything about the shootings, the drunkenness, the waylaying of men in alleys to beat and rob them," Tennie said. "I've been trying not to hide in the jailhouse, hoping just having a woman around will give them something else to think about besides death and destruction."

"That's probably true." The marshal ruminated in thought a moment. "Try not to show too much favoritism or get too involved or you'll just cause fights. Remain as aloof as you can." He grinned. "But don't be surprised if you have men causing trouble just so they can be thrown in your jail. I'd be tempted."

CHAPTER 16

After the deputy marshal left town, seven men at different times just happened to drop by the jail, and just happened to mention to Tennie the marshal had a sweetheart on the other side of Brushwood. They left satisfied that the news did not appear to affect her one way or another.

The following day, Tennie baked three pound cakes. One to take to the Paytons, one for Rusty and Shorty, and the other for Mike, Lucas, and Badger. Lucas had already told her Mike intended on teaching them how to fry steak and bake biscuits in a Dutch oven over the forge coals, and there was no need for her to leave food for them.

"It's almost as easy to make three pound cakes as it is to make two," Tennie had told the boy. "You might as well take one and tell Mike I insist."

As the cakes cooled, she stepped outside to get away from the heat of the kitchen. Across the street, she could hear Maggot Milton going strong from inside his shop. She turned and looked toward Shorty's and gave a start. Rusty stood with his back to her next to the entrance of the alley, talking earnestly with Wash Jones.

Wash wore the same long-sleeved and collarless cotton shirt, the same vest, and the same striped pants. He had on only one gun belt, but it contained the same two crossed pistols. His hat shaded his eyes, but the scar across his lips shone bright in the sun.

If Wash saw her, he made no sign of it, but he and Rusty, walking together, made a smooth movement of disappearing into the alley.

Tennie took a deep breath and tried to calm herself, to think with a clear head. Enough men had been peeved at her to snub her from time to time to show their displeasure, but she didn't believe that had been Wash's intention. He hadn't looked at her to make sure she was watching; he had just silently melted away.

He didn't want people to know they knew one another. He had hidden at the ranch, and now in town, he was pretending they were strangers, even though he did not mind speaking to Rusty. What had their earnest conversation been about? Tennie wiped an unwanted wetness from her eyes and went back inside the jailhouse.

Rusty did not come home for dinner. Lucas said he went swimming with friends.

"Why didn't he take you?" she asked.

"He wouldn't let us go," Badger said. "I wanted to go, but he said no. I hate Rusty sometimes!"

"You better kiss the ground Rusty walks on for sticking around to help take care of us," Tennie said, distracted.

Lucas didn't seem upset Rusty hadn't taken them, and he kept his eyes on his food while he ate. Tennie was sure he was hiding something.

When Rusty came in for supper, his freckles popping out from the sun, he laughed and talked, joking with his younger brothers, and Tennie chided herself for trying to borrow trouble. Nevertheless, she could not bring herself to question him. It was humiliating enough Wash did not want to acknowledge her and refused to tell her why. But if she was a marshal, and he was an outlaw . . . ? She did not want to think about it.

"I've got a new book," Rusty announced when supper was over. He pulled it out of a poke bag, with Tennie and the other boys crowding to have a look.

"*The Headless Horseman: A Strange Tale of Texas*," Lucas read. "Sounds great!"

"Where'd you get it?" Tennie asked.

Rusty kept his eyes on the book and paused before saying, "Shorty. Shorty gave it to me."

Late that night, when everyone else was asleep, Tennie sat in the office. One lone lantern cast a feeble light across the office desk while she searched through the wanted posters the marshal had left behind, hoping she did not find one of a man with a scar running across both lips.

The next morning, Rusty left early for Shorty's but came back. "Shorty said to say thank you for the cake and to take the musketeers book out to the Payton ranch with you. Somebody out there will want to read it."

Shorty was either in on the conspiracy or he really did give the headless horseman book to Rusty, Tennie reasoned while berating herself for being such a suspicious, distrustful person.

She gave Lucas and Badger a lecture about not bothering Mike and making pests of themselves, which they ignored.

"I might as well have been talking to the wall," Tennie lamented to Jeff when he fetched her.

"You've got a buggy," she said when she walked outside.

"Yeah," Jeff said. "Lafayette said to take it. He has a favor he wants from you, and he's trying to butter you up."

"Okay, it's working," Tennie said. "Help me up, please. I haven't been in a covered buggy since only God knows when."

The buggy looked almost new, a covered two-seater with thick tufted padding on the seat and a wide space in the back to hold belongings. After giving her a hand, Jeff went around the other side and got in.

"What kind of buggy is this?" Tennie asked as Jeff told the horses to giddy-up.

"An expensive one," he replied. "Some kind of phaeton is all I can tell you."

Tennie leaned back in the seat, unused to such luxury. "What does Mr. Lafayette want of me?"

"Let it keep for a while, Miss Nosy. We got all day to talk about it, and we might as well wait until we at least get out of town and away from prying ears."

"Okay," Tennie agreed, and she remained silent until they had gotten well away from Ring Bit.

They passed through small bare hills, gullies thick with oak trees on either side, the road becoming more rutted as they traveled. Jeff had to watch what he was doing with the reins and try to keep the horses from landing the wagon in holes so deep they would have difficulty pulling it out.

Tennie did not mind any of it. "It feels so good to be away from the jailhouse for a while. This reminds me of when we were on the wagon train. It was so much fun. Well, getting attacked by renegade Indians and bandits wasn't so much fun, but traveling together, stopping to cook together, not really having any responsibilities, that was better than a European vacation."

Jeff gave a grunt of a laugh. "What do you know about European vacations?"

"Nothing," Tennie agreed. "Mr. Payton bought a diary for me and told me to write down every-thing that happened day by day. The first thing I wrote was Mr. Payton bought me a new pair of shoes today."

"He's a good old man," Jeff agreed.

"That's what—" She broke off, about to say, "That's what Mr. Wash said," but amended it to "That's what everybody says." To hide her fluster, she added, "The country ladies want me to do something about Ring Bit so they can come into town. I have no idea what to do."

"Maybe you don't realize it, gal," Jeff said, keeping his eyes on the road that was little more than a wide cow trail, "but you've already calmed it down considerably. It hasn't hurt the Silver Moon's business any. Men flock in there, hoping me and Lafayette will tell them all about you."

"I thought my ears were burning," Tennie said. "I hope you aren't telling them the whole truth. No need for the whole world to know what a knucklehead I really am."

Jeff laughed and she continued. "It upsets the ladies to see drunks peeing on the sidewalks in front of them. Mr. Milton's blasphemy and the cursing of other men like him makes them and their husbands uncomfortable. I don't have a husband who cares what I have to listen to, but these women do."

"I'm going to ignore your 'poor me' account since you could have a husband any time you wanted one."

"Yeah, yeah, yeah. You and Mr. Payton. I told

the deputy marshal all I could do was try not to hide in the jailhouse."

"Is that what you were talking about with him up on the cemetery ridge?" Jeff asked.

"Yes." Tennie turned her head to look at cows grazing in a nearby field. "That and the rustling that's going on. He told me to stay out of it, and I told him I had no intention of getting involved in it. Somebody else can hunt them down. I wouldn't even know where to begin."

"There is such a thing as lady rustlers, you know," Jeff said.

"I can't imagine any in Texas. Women can own land in Texas. Why go thieving when you can have a place of your own?"

"You have Queen Isabella of Spain to thank for that," Jeff said. "A lot of the laws here were passed down from when Texas was under Spanish rule."

"I am much obliged. But I don't need to be chasing after any rustlers, male or female." She grew serious. "I get so tired of cooking and cleaning all the time, Mr. Jeff, but keeping food on the table for those boys and having work for them to do is the only way I can think of to keep them home and out of trouble. And they are so smart! I feel bad they can't go to school. I try, but I'm not much of a teacher."

Jeff's face grew pensive. "I get tired, too. Sometimes, I want to escape somewhere where there's no drunks to collar, no war memories to push down, no leftover pain caused by unfaithful women. To just be at peace."

He seemed so sad, Tennie didn't know what to say.

He roused out of his reverie. "That's kind of what I wanted to talk to you about."

Tennie stared at him. "What?"

"Lafayette. He realizes you don't want to work in a saloon. But he's been nosing around, and he believes that railroad line will be put through Ring Bit. He's quietly started buying up property, and he wants to build a hotel. A big fine one for wealthy cattlemen to come to. You know Lafayette, everything has to be covered in gilt. He wants you to help him run it."

"Me? I don't know anything about the hotel business."

"Neither does Lafayette. But he doesn't mind going out on a limb if he thinks there is fruit at the other end."

Tennie took a deep breath and pondered the request. "No offense, but why did he send you and the buggy to butter me up about it?"

"In the first place, he still feels guilty over that fiasco with Arabella at the jail. He spends every day all day long trying to hide his feelings from other people—it's part of his work. He distances himself from any true emotional scenes; I'm not talking about the fake hysterics the saloon girls throw every five minutes, but the real thing. He knows you have a right to lay into him about what happened that night."

Tennie made a face. "I'd just like to forget it. What's the second place?"

"Lafayette is under the mistaken belief I have some kind of influence over you, and I can get you to agree to help him with this hotel venture. Sis, he'd pay you enough to hire a tutor for those boys. And you'd be over people doing the cooking and cleaning."

"Just because I get tired of cooking and cleaning doesn't mean I don't like doing it," Tennie said. "And nobody takes my bossing seriously."

"Think about it. Right now, Lafayette needs you, and you need him."

Tennie didn't want to delve too deeply into that. "I don't have to think about it. If he'll let those ring-tailed stepsons of mine help me, I'll do it.

"Plus," she added. "I'm counting on your help, too."

Jeff laughed and looked relieved. "You got it. It will be a while, yet."

A picket fence surrounded the Payton ranch house. Trees had been planted on either side of the one-story structure, with wide porches flanking every side. It had a homely prettiness about it, an attractiveness sometimes a plain, but friendly, girl could generate. Mrs. Payton came out onto the porch to welcome them, and Tennie's heart leapt to see a friendly woman's face.

Jeff helped her down from the buggy. Mr. Payton came around the side of the house and greeted them, after which the men disappeared while Tennie and Mrs. Payton went inside the comfortably furnished home.

To Tennie's surprise and delight, Mrs. Payton had invited two of her nearest neighbors to visit, too, and the four women spent the day in the kitchen laughing, gossiping, and sharing news while they cooked and later cleaned. Tennie enjoyed their company, but she had so little in common with them, most of the time she remained silent. They would be horrified if she shared that one of her prisoners pulled down his pants in a drunken stupor, exposing himself to her, and Tennie was afraid they would disapprove of her for having a job where such things could happen.

Mrs. Payton hinted of a surprise, yet refused to tell Tennie what it was. "I'll let Mr. Payton tell you."

When Jeff said it was time to leave, Mr. Payton followed them outside. After Tennie climbed into the buggy, Jeff got in beside her.

Unable to stand it any longer, Tennie looked at Mr. Payton and blurted, "Mrs. Payton said you had a surprise for me."

He smiled in amusement. "This weekend, we

are having a dance," he explained. "People will be coming here from miles around."

Tennie's mouth dropped. "A dance? Can the boys come, too?"

"Yes, but lay down the law to them. I don't want my barns burned down."

"I will. But"—her heart failed—"but I can't come!" she cried. "I have a job. I have to be at the jail." She turned to Jeff in misery.

"I reckon I can manage the jail for you," he said. "Won't nobody be in town anyhow. They'll all be out here. I'll come out later. Just save me a dance."

"I will," Tennie promised.

"Honey Boy and Two-Bit are going to fetch you and the boys," Mr. Payton said.

"Honey Boy?" Tennie said, her heart falling into her shoes once more. "But Mr. Payton, the last time Honey Boy was drunk, he threatened to kill me."

"He won't be drinking," Mr. Payton said. "He promised, and for another thing, when Two-Bit wants to, he can handle Honey Boy better than anybody and keep him straight. That's the only reason Shep keeps him around."

"All right. If you say so," Tennie agreed. She took a deep breath in happiness, talking nonstop to Jeff about it on the way home, pumping him for any information he could give her about the kind of get-togethers people in Texas put on.

When she entered the jailhouse, she could hear voices coming from the back.

"He had one," Lucas was saying. "I saw it! It looked just like what Two-Bit said."

Tennie burst into the room. "Guess what? The Paytons are having a dance this weekend, and we are invited."

"A dance?" Rusty said.

"If you all don't behave at that dance," Tennie threatened, "I'm going to skin you alive! And everybody might as well put their old clothes on, because tomorrow, I'm washing everything. And baths for everybody Friday."

"Aw," Lucas moaned.

Badger wanted to know what a dance was. Rusty wondered how many girls would be there.

"Plenty," Tennie said. "And I don't care if your mother thought dancing was right up there with the other seven deadly sins, we're going."

Tennie went to get her pink dress to examine it for stains, while Rusty said he and Lucas were going to talk to Shorty.

"Okay," Tennie said. Something in the back of her mind sent up a signal, but she ignored it. She had other, more important things to think about.

Friday night, they played dominoes with Shorty as usual even though it was an abnormally quiet evening in Ring Bit.

"Is Mr. Lafayette going to the dance?" Tennie questioned Jeff.

"Oh no," Jeff said. "Winn Payton would welcome Lafayette, naturally. But his neighbors would pitch a fit if Lafayette showed up there with Arabella."

"I'm surprised they'll let me come," Tennie said.

"You have Winn and his old lady's blessings," Jeff said with a laugh. "Arabella doesn't. Anyway, she is making life unbearable for Lafayette over that dance. She's so afraid he's going to go without her, his life wouldn't even be worth living if he went."

CHAPTER 17

Jeff had told Tennie all the house parties were potluck. The Paytons would provide much of the food, but it was considered polite for the women to bring more, along with extra utensils. Tennie almost went into a tizzy worrying over what to prepare. Because of her precarious social standing, she felt an overwhelming desire to please without making it look like she was showing off. She ended up cooking for two days, and at the last minute, baked more.

She forced herself and the boys to take naps, hoping they wouldn't be tired and cranky before the night ended.

Honey Boy and Two-Bit arrived early, and they had to wait for Tennie to finish getting ready, but they didn't seem to mind. They carried the food to one of Shep Davis's wagons while Mike stood nearby talking, and Maggot Milton watched from his front porch.

"Are you going to the dance, Big Mike?" Tennie asked, a little out breath when she did make it outside.

"No," he bellowed. "I have to work. Someone

has to stay here and work while others go out to play."

"Oh, Mike," Tennie fussed. "I think you could come for a little while."

"Well, maybe later," he admitted, gratified she had asked.

She looked across the street at Milton, thinking she should be neighborly and say something, even though he habitually rebuffed any overtures of friendship, no matter how slight. He had such an odd grimace on his face, as if happy to be rid of them for one night, any wave or word of friendship died, and she climbed onto the seat of the wagon. Honey Boy tossed Badger into the back of the wagon, who squealed with happiness, with Rusty and Lucas climbing in.

Tennie was quickly wedged in between the solid muscles of Honey Boy and Two-Bit's slight frame. Honey Boy gave the horses a good-natured holler and popped the reins. It relieved her to see him at his jolliest self, while even Two-Bit, habitually looking like he'd lost all his money in a poker game, almost smiled.

The three talked on the way to the Payton ranch. Tennie confided her fears of not being able to dance well enough to keep up. Or she would be a wallflower—no one would ask her to dance. Or no one would touch the food she brought, and out of everyone's on the table, hers would be uneaten.

They gallantly dismissed all her notions,

declaring they would eat everything she brought and dance with her no matter how bad she was, which made her laugh.

As they neared the Payton ranch, Honey Boy teased Tennie. "Sometimes you are so quiet, Miss Tennie, a feller thinks you've had your tongue cut out. Other times, you chirp and sing like a happy little songbird."

From the back, Lucas interrupted. "Shorty said Miss Tennie's petticoats start fluttering every time a handsome man comes around."

Tennie turned around and gave him a hard look. "Don't be telling everything you know about me," she warned. "And you all better behave, no matter what devilment the other boys try to pull you into. We'll never get invited anywhere if we're not careful."

She knew they were more afraid of Honey Boy's and Two-Bit's disapproval than they were of her threats and hoped that would help keep them straight. She left that worry in the hands of God and concentrated on being pleasant company the rest of the way to the Payton ranch, laughing and talking with the two men on either side of the wagon seat.

They were early, but others had arrived even earlier. Empty wagons littered the perimeter of the yard, while corrals were beginning to bulge with a variety of horses and mules. The boys jumped out and joined another group of boys loitering around the corral, while Honey Boy helped Tennie from the wagon. Grateful Jeff had taken her to the Payton ranch beforehand, it was still daunting to walk into the almost unknown. Once Honey Boy and Two-Bit deposited the food in the kitchen on tables already overloaded with food, they disappeared to converse with the men, and Tennie had to get accustomed to the women all on her own. Fortunately, many of them were the same ones she had come west with, and the kitchen overflowed with sounds of laughter and happy chattering.

The Payton cowhands had removed most of the furniture in the front parlor onto the porches, rolling up the carpet and setting it aside. All that remained in the room were a few chairs lining the walls, and a long sideboard containing a waiting punch bowl and cups. In the dining room between the parlor and kitchen, tablecloths covered old doors laid across sawhorses to hold food, in addition to the long wide mahogany table in the center of the room.

Under Mrs. Payton's patient guidance, Tennie began to transfer food from the kitchen to the dining room while the house filled with people. Men bringing fiddles and guitars congregated at one end of the room. They rosined their bows, and when they drew the bows across the strings, a thrill from the crowd seemed to bounce all the way to the ceiling.

The Paytons led off the dancing with a Grand March, a promenade signifying the trials of life, of coming together, quarreling and separating, only to be rejoined again. Honey Boy grabbed Tennie's hand, and they joined the other party-goers, holding hands in a ring while they walked around the room's perimeter. The dancers separated, with men going one way and women going another. After circling again, the partners rejoined, and Tennie squeezed Honey Boy's hand in happiness. They joined hands with another couple, a grinning little wizened man and his plump jolly wife. After circling the room, the men and women split from one another again, only to rejoin to form an arch with their hands as each couple took turns going under. Honey Boy was so tall, it was a tight squeeze, and women squealed as they stood on their tiptoes with arms outstretched so he could pass under.

The band went into a two-step, and Mr. Payton clasped his wife and led the others. This time, Two-Bit claimed Tennie from Honey Boy, and the night of merrymaking began.

Tennie danced the two-step, the waltz, and did Western square dances with every man there, including Shep Davis, who swung her so robustly around the floor he left her gasping. A group of girls grabbed Rusty, pulling him and other adolescent boys into one corner of the room and soon had them doing steps. Even Lucas got swept up by a girl in pigtails. Badger was at the food table, sampling everything his little fingers could reach before being shooed away by the older women who told him the children would have to wait until the grownups had eaten.

Tennie danced many times with Honey Boy, who, despite his size, was nimble on his feet. Other times her feet were crushed, and a few times, her own landed where they weren't supposed to, but instead of causing anger, it added to the frolic.

Mr. Payton stopped the players around ten o'clock to ask the blessing, and afterward the hungry partygoers descended upon the tables. It gratified Tennie to see the food she had brought consumed, and she wouldn't have to depend on the kindness of Honey Boy and Two-Bit, although between the two of them, they could have emptied half the platters on the table with ease.

When it came time for the children to eat, she found Lucas and Badger running and squealing through the yard. She caught them and said, "You haven't tied anybody up or done anything to the horses, have you?"

Lucas assured her they had just been playing hide-and-seek in the dark.

"Well, come eat so I can go back to dancing," Tennie said.

The musicians, having had their fill, plus,

Tennie suspected, a few trips outside to tipple out of a brown jug, began playing again. Later she noticed several men slipping outside, but there seemed to be more going on than just an occasional nip.

Rusty came inside, and Tennie made her way through the dancers to talk to him. "What's happening out there?"

"Some of the other cowboys are fighting with Honey Boy and Two-Bit over you, Miss Tennie."

Tennie looked at the door and gave a start, but Rusty stopped her. "Don't go out there, Miss Tennie. You'll just make it worse."

"I don't know what to do."

"Just smile and laugh and keep dancing like you don't know anything, I guess." He held out his arm. "Here, you can dance with me. I think I'm getting the hang of it."

"All right," Tennie said, thankful Winn Payton had insisted all guns be deposited by the door for the night.

Later, men drifted back inside, along with Two-Bit and Honey Boy, who looked a little rougher, but not too bruised up. Tennie didn't ask them anything, and they didn't volunteer information. She was glad to see whatever happened outside had not put a damper on their mood.

Their boss, however, decided it was time to leave. "Fightin's over. Time to go home," Shep said, giving everyone a cheerful good-bye.

"He acts about that ranch like a mama cow acts with her baby calf," Honey Boy told Tennie. "He don't like to be away from it too long."

Jeff walked in at two a.m. and went straight to the food table. When he finished eating, Tennie took a break and joined him.

"I thought you were going to claim a dance," she said.

"So I did, but I don't want to interrupt your fun."

"You're not," she said, taking his hand. "Come on."

Like Honey Boy, Jeff proved light on his feet for a big man.

"How are things in town?" Tennie asked. "How come the mayor and the rest of those townies aren't here?"

"Things in town are slow, and they think this is too hick for them."

"Then they are silly. But to tell you the truth, I'm glad they aren't here."

The two-step ended, but Jeff kept her for the following waltz.

"I hope my stepsons are behaving and aren't setting fire to anything. It's been a while since I checked on them."

He laughed. "They're all right. Badger is asleep on one end of the sofa on the porch, and Lucas is fighting sleep on the other end."

Tennie felt herself wearing down, too, but other

than resting a few times on one of the chairs lining the room or helping out in the kitchen, she continued to dance, several more of those times with Jeff.

Jeff nodded to the door. "You haven't slipped outside with any of the men tonight, Miss Tennie?"

The thought had never occurred to her. "No. None of them have asked me to. Even if I did, I'd have three boys suddenly awake and following me, wanting to know what I'm doing."

"Well, now," Jeff said with a grin. "If they haven't asked you, it's only because they are afraid some other lovesick fool would shoot them. And as to the boys, what happens to you, happens to them, so I reckon they'd have a right to be interested."

"I hadn't thought about that." Then she added, "I am having such a good time."

"You can thank the Paytons for that. They haven't put on a to-do like this in years. They think mighty highly of you, Miss Tennie."

"And I them. But I can't believe this was all just for me."

"Maybe, maybe not," Jeff said and swung her around.

It was only later, while dancing with Honey Boy and noticing by the variable lantern light the bruises beginning to darken on his cheeks, that Tennie wondered why Jeff didn't come in for the same thing. At times, she thought men were jealous of her attachment to Jeff, but other than a few offhand comments about how old he was, no one had threatened to beat him up or kill him.

Big Mike came in and stood at the door just as she was thinking about him. She smiled, and he immediately claimed her for the next dance.

"I'm glad you could come," Tennie said.

"Yeah, me, too," he said, talking loud as always.

About four in the morning, the dancing began to get a little wild. The men began a somewhat frenzied stomping, especially Mike, who rattled pictures on the wall, while the women began to exhibit a feverish giddiness. Honey Boy claimed he was hungry again, and Tennie walked to the table with him. It appeared almost wiped out, but Honey Boy spotted a roll. Taking the roll and declaring he was thirsty, too, they walked back into the parlor to the sideboard, where Tennie managed to dredge the last remaining drops of punch into a cup for him. Before she could hand it to him, a sleep-deprived dancer bumped Honey Boy's elbow, sending the roll flying under the sideboard.

Laughing, Tennie said, "I'll get it. We can wipe the dust off."

She put the cup down and bent down. Without looking, she reached under the sideboard. She had no sooner placed her hand under it than she felt a searing pain as if a bear had clamped down on her hand, and she heard the nightmarish sound of rattling. Screaming in pain, she jumped back, staring at two small pinholes in her hand.

"Snake!"

Women began screaming, and suddenly a rush of people moved frantically around the room. The pain in Tennie's hand was so intense she was only vaguely aware Honey Boy was stomping on the head of a rattlesnake. A man ran to the fireplace, pulling down Winn Payton's shotgun, and he blasted the snake at close range, even though Honey Boy had stomped it to death.

She could hear herself sobbing. Jeff grabbed her hand, cutting into the flesh with his knife and putting his lips to the bite mark to suck out the poison. In between spits, he yelled, "Get a bucket of coal oil."

There was another mad scramble for coal oil. Tennie stared in agony at her hand, watching the swelling traveling up her arm. Jeff guided her to a chair, where he plunged her hand into a bucket of coal oil, sending her into another spasm of pain and causing her to cry out.

Faces surrounded her, faces drained of blood and white with fear. Jeff hugged her shoulders, and she stared at him through her tears. His eyes were filled with anxiety, and she cried out to him. "Don't leave me, Mr. Jeff. Don't leave me."

"I'm not going to leave you. Old Jeff is right here."

"Please don't leave me," Tennie cried. "Don't leave me!"

"I'm not, I'm not," he assured her.

"Shouldn't we go for the doctor?" Honey Boy asked, his face drawn with fear.

"He'll be so drunk you won't be able to rouse him," someone else cried.

"Doctor!" Tennie screamed in horror. "Mr. Jeff, don't let the doctor near me!" She began to cry hysterically. "He'll cut off my hand. He'll cut off my arm. Don't let him touch me! Don't let him touch me; he'll cut my arm off."

She knew she was hysterical, but all she could think of was the surgeons during the war. "My mother would cry," she screamed. "She would come home in tears because doctors would be cutting off arms and legs that could be saved! But there wasn't time! There wasn't time!" She began sobbing and begging Jeff again not to let the doctor near her.

"Apache John has a mad stone," Honey Boy blurted.

"He's drunk in town, too," a woman cried.

Jeff stared hard at Honey Boy. "Get it. Tear his shack up if you have to, but find it and get it."

Honey Boy nodded and pushed his way through people before they could even register the errand he was on.

"Shouldn't we go for the doctor, too?" a quiet voice asked Jeff.

Jeff nodded without speaking, and Tennie began to weep again.

"I get him," Big Mike said, for once keeping his voice down. "If I have to tie him up, I bring him." He turned and left.

Through a fog of pain and tears, Tennie became aware of the terrified faces of her stepsons. She tried to stop crying. "Mr. Jeff," she said between tears, "I'm ruining the party. Can you take me somewhere else? But I want to hear the music again. Please, Mr. Jeff."

"Sure, Miss Tennie," Jeff said. "Just keep calm. You're going to be okay. Everything will be okay."

He motioned for someone to get the bucket, and with one swift movement, he picked Tennie up and carried her outside to the sofa on the porch. He set her on the end, with her hand dangling into the coal oil, while he sat beside her, his arm around her shoulders.

She placed her head on his shoulder and tried to stand the waves of pain coming up her arm from her swollen hand. "I don't want to stop the party. I want to hear the music again. Please."

Jeff nodded to the people standing around them, and they backed away. In a few minutes, the band began playing again, but softer, tender, music.

After a while, she was able to stop crying and endure the pain. She waited for what seemed like a long time, her head resting on Jeff's shoulder, wondering if she was going to die and what would happen to her stepsons if she did.

She became aware of a commotion, of people rushing out of the house again, and Honey Boy calling for a bucket of warm milk.

Someone brought a lantern and held it over her while people crowded around her. In the faint light, she saw them making way for Apache John. When he reached her side, he put his hands up around his neck and pulled a round stone from a pouch, dropping it into the bucket of milk hastily placed in front of him. He lifted her hand out of the coal oil.

"Must wash off," he said with grunt, and a flurry of skirts headed back into the house for soap and water.

Tennie stared at John's head, thinking of all the times she was aggravated to have him in her jail, mad at him because he had lice and stayed drunk all the time. But in the flickering light of the lantern, she caught a glimpse of something else. For a few brief seconds, she didn't see a dissolute face, didn't smell or see filth, didn't even see an Indian with dark skin. She saw the strong face of the inner man, the true man before it had become mired down with cares and worries of the world, and she wondered if that was the way God saw him all the time.

As quickly as the image came, it left, but the

feeling lingered. She knew if she lived, in two weeks' time, she would be fussing at John about his lice again, but she didn't think she would ever forget what she'd witnessed.

He cleaned the oil off her skin and patted it dry, not unaffected by her involuntary cries of pain. He fished into the pail of milk and brought out the stone, placing it over the snakebite.

Tennie stared, thinking it odd the stone stuck to her hand. After a while, it turned a putrid shade of green and fell off, but Tennie's hand felt better. John again soaked it in milk and reapplied it.

"Look!" someone cried. "The swelling is going down!"

"Praise God!" a woman whispered fervently.

Three times he applied it, and each time it stuck. And each time, Tennie's hand felt better. On the fourth time, the swelling had almost disappeared, the pain so faint to be almost nonexistent, and the stone refused to stick again. After that, Tennie knew she was going to be all right.

Watching John, Tennie asked how she could ever repay him. He remained so silent, she thought he wasn't going to say anything. But then she saw the slightest upward curve of his lips.

"Bake John pound cake, too."

Tennie gave a weak laugh. "You've got it."

Jeff wanted Tennie to stay quiet for a while, although she assured him she felt fine, just tired.

271

The sun was coming up, and Big Mike arrived with the doctor. He shook off Mike's assistance getting down from the wagon. He looked at the house, stalked toward Tennie, and examined her hand, giving a snort.

"You people got hysterical over nothing," he said in a bad humor. "She was obviously bitten by a nonpoisonous snake. You get out here and get wound up like a bunch of heathens, and then drag me from town for nothing."

Nobody said anything.

The Paytons came forward. "We'll make it worth your while, doctor," Winn Payton said.

His wife placed her hand gently on the doctor's arm. "Come into the kitchen, doctor, and we'll make you breakfast," she said in a soothing voice, leading him away from the mute crowd.

"Are you ready to go home, Miss Tennie?" Jeff asked.

She looked at Jeff and turned to stare at Two-Bit and Honey Boy. She turned back to Jeff. "I thank you kindly, Mr. Jeff, but I think a girl is supposed to go home with the ones who brought her."

Jeff smiled and stood up. He looked down on her, shaking his head and still smiling then turned and walked away.

The women prepared a pallet in the back of the wagon and insisted Tennie lie down on it. Even though she protested she could walk, Honey Boy lifted her and placed her on it. Three somber boys climbed in beside her.

Jeff, leading his horse, walked to the wagon and ordered Tennie to spend a couple of days in bed. "You boys see to that," he told Rusty and his brothers.

Three heads nodded.

CHAPTER 18

Tennie slept almost the entire Sunday. She could hear the boys rattling pans on the stove and vaguely smelled bacon frying, but she didn't rouse enough to want any. She heard voices of people coming to check on her—Shorty, Shep Davis, Honey Boy, and Two-Bit.

On Monday, she dressed, but lay back on the bed, although she thought she would be fine if she moved around. The boys left to go squirrel hunting, but came back and fought over how to prepare them.

The mayor dropped in that afternoon to see how she was. She sat up in bed, but he insisted she not get up.

"I heard you gave everyone at the dance quite a scare," the mayor said, trying to sound merry. He turned to the boys. "You boys run along. I'd like to talk to your stepmother alone."

Tennie's heart lurched. She hoped she wasn't in trouble. The mayor continued to talk about the snakebite, the coal oil treatment, and the mad stone. Tennie thought he was just killing time until he felt like mentioning what he really came for.

She searched around, trying to think of some complaint he might have against her. "I know we've been going through a lot of groceries at the jail. It seems the prisoners don't want to wake up and get out of here until they smell dinner cooking."

His only reaction was to smile, and Tennie added, "Although I know Shep Davis is bringing in extra beef espccially for his cowhands."

"Oh," the mayor said, dismissing beef, "we've got plenty of cattle in Texas. Don't you worry your pretty little head about that."

Tennie gave a small sigh of relief.

"I heard the U.S. deputy marshal came by to see you." He said it so unstudied, for a split second, Tennie almost let her guard down.

She threw it back up, but tried to keep her answer lighthearted. "Oh, he just brought some wanted posters by. I didn't recognize anybody."

"But you had a long talk with him at the cemetery," the mayor pressed.

Tennie didn't know what to think. She lowered her eyes so he couldn't see the suspicion in them. "The marshal is a mighty handsome man," she said, turning to look at the wall as if embarrassed.

The mayor laughed. "That he is. He's got a sweetheart in every burg, but I think the one on the other side of Brushwood is about to lasso him."

"So I've heard," Tennie said, forcing herself to give a lopsided smile.

The mayor leaned forward, and just as Apache John's face had momentarily been transformed for her, the mayor's countenance seemed to do so, too. Instead of a chubby, jovial old soul, she saw one corrupted by greed and hardened by a desire for power.

He leaned a little farther. "We wouldn't want that deputy marshal to involve our little town marshal in things that really aren't her concern, would we?"

"Like what?" Tennie pretended to demand like an insatiable old gossip.

He leaned back and laughed, evidently lulled by her performance. "Nothing, little gal. I'm just talking." He stood up. "You rest now, and don't worry your pretty little head about a thing."

Jeff entered without knocking as usual. "Mayor," he said, removing his hat and nodding his head in greeting.

"Jeff"—the mayor smiled—"she's feeling much better." He turned to Tennie. "Take it easy now. We don't want anything bad to happen to our little marshal."

Tennie tried to smile and nod. "Thank you for coming by, Mayor."

When he left, she threw her head back on her pillow and shut her eyes.

"Did he upset you?" Jeff asked.

"I almost got snakebit again," Tennie said, opening her eyes. "He was warning me to keep my nose out of any business the deputy marshal has. The mayor's doing something; he's up to something, but I just don't know what."

Jeff sighed, dragging a chair nearer the bed and sitting down. "For now, leave it alone," he advised.

"I have to," Tennie said. "The deputy marshal doesn't want me involved in anything, either. All I am is cook and housekeeper for a bunch of drunks. And I can hear that dad-blasted Mr. Milton yelling cusswords at children from across the street all the way in here. And I had to sit here and listen to that fat old rooster mayor try to intimidate me like I was a five-year-old!"

"So what do you want me to do about it?" Jeff said, raising his voice.

"Nothing! Just listen to me complain!" She looked at him and calmed. "Mr. Jeff, thank you for saving my life." When she saw him about to protest, she interjected, "Yes, you did. At the very least, you, and Honey Boy, and Apache John saved me from getting my arm amputated. Thank you."

Jeff rose, leaned over, and patted her shoulder, making Tennie feel better. "Rest up," he said. "You're still tired and overwrought. Don't let the old fat rooster get in your craw. He's not worth worrying about." He put his hat back on.

As he was leaving, Tennie leaned over her shoulder and called to him, "Mr. Jeff! I had a great time at that dance. Except for the snakebite part."

He stopped and pushed his hat toward the back of his head with his forefinger. "So did I," he grinned. "Especially the snakebite part."

He left the room, and she heard the sound of someone's else's footsteps.

Jeff said loud enough for her to hear, "Watch out, Winn. She's on a tear."

"I am not!" Tennie called.

"What's the matter with you?" Winn Payton said, entering the room. He removed his hat and fanned his face with it. "You must be feeling better."

"I am. I mean to pay you back for whatever you had to give the doctor for coming out to the ranch."

"No, no, no," Mr. Payton said, taking a seat. "Our dogs and cats got old and died, and we just didn't have the heart to replace Buster, the last dog we had. We've had mice here lately, but thought we'd gotten rid of them with traps. After everyone left, we pulled the sideboard away from the wall and saw where they had gnawed a hole in the floor. That snake has been living there no telling how long, eating those mice. I said, 'Mother, we have got to get us another dog and some cats, even if we are getting so old they'll outlive us.' We felt terrible about that happening to you, Tennie."

"Don't. I had the most wonderful time of my life at the dance, Mr. Payton. Thank you so much for having us."

"It was our pleasure. I imagine it won't be easily forgotten by anybody." He rose. "I'm off to Shorty's to see if he'll still let us have one of his pups."

"I think he's holding one for Badger right now," Tennie said.

He nodded and went to the window, leaning forward and looking out. "You boys go to the wagon and bring in the food Mrs. Payton sent along. You've eavesdropped enough for one afternoon."

She heard them mumbling, "Yes, sir."

That night, Rusty and Lucas took turns reading from *The Headless Horseman,* and Badger said he was getting a puppy the next day.

The ball of dark fur Shorty brought looked like a miniature of his father.

"I'm going to name him Rascal," Badger said. "Because Shorty says it fits both of us."

Tennie laughed and took her turn holding the puppy and playing with him.

A summer storm came through, and they spent the day cooped up, except for every two hours or so when Tennie had them take the puppy outside. She spent a good part of the day cleaning little puddles and messes, and the other part of the day trying to stay out of the way of their mock sword fights. The switches Wash Jones had provided them had long since broken, but Rusty had cut more. When they tired of thrashing around with the sticks, they played with the puppy.

"He is a rascal." Tennie laughed when Jeff stopped by to see the dog. "He's into everything."

Jeff bent down and rubbed the squiggling puppy's little belly. "How are you getting along today?" he asked her.

"I'm fine. I should be baking Apache John a pound cake, but I'm not sure when he's coming into town, and I want it to be fresh."

Jeff stood up. "That's one reason I'm here. John won't be coming into town anymore. Found him dead in his shack yesterday. They've already buried him out on Winn's place."

Tennie didn't want to believe it. "What happened?"

"Just old and living too hard," Jeff said. "Winn said he must have gone home Sunday morning and died sometime during the night. They couldn't find the mad stone."

Tennie gasped. "Were there signs of a struggle?"

Jeff shook his head. "Nothing like that. Somebody probably went in there, saw he was dead, and decided to take the stone. Winn swears it will be useless now; in order for a mad stone to work it has to be given. It can't be bought or stolen."

Tennie sank down on a chair and shut her eyes. "When I think of all the times I got so aggravated at him . . . it makes me so ashamed of myself." She rubbed over her eyes with her fingers. "Why hasn't Mr. Lafayette been by to see me? I would have thought he would have stopped by."

"He's locked in his room, drunk," Jeff said. "He started drinking the day of that dance, and he hasn't stopped since."

Tennie's head jerked up. "Is that like him?"

"Hell, no," Jeff said. "When they are playing those late-night poker games, and he has the bartender bring out a bottle of his special liquor, it's just watered-down tea. That's one reason he wins so much money. His opponents are all getting drunker and drunker, and he's as sober as a judge. But they don't know it."

Tennie shut her eyes again. She couldn't do anything for John except pray God put him in a beautiful place to roam free from the problems that dragged him down. But Lafayette . . . "Tell him *The Three Musketeers* is a little too complicated for us to put on as a play, but Big Mike has been telling the boys all sorts of stories, and we would like to act one out for him." She looked at Jeff. "Will he come here for that?"

Jeff nodded.

Tennie told the boys Mr. Lafayette wasn't feeling well and asked if they would be willing to put on a short play of one of Mike's tales to cheer him up. They jumped on the idea and began fighting over which one. They wanted the bloodsucking *vepyr*, but realized it wasn't enough of a story. Somehow or other, in a process Tennie could not later recall, they decided to act out the sleeping princess who is saved by the handsome prince, but he was going to have to fight an evil *vepyr* to get her.

Badger began screaming and crying they were leaving him out. Rusty and Lucas got into a fistfight over who would play the *vepyr*. Tennie got so fed up with them, she walked outside and stood under the awning, watching the rain and thinking about Apache John.

When she walked back in later, they were sitting in three corners of the room, sullen and throwing hateful glances at one another.

"Rusty will be the *vepyr* because he is bigger and scarier looking," Tennie said. "He'll also have to be the narrator and the king. Lucas will play the part of the queen and the handsome prince. Badger is going to be the evil witch who casts the spell and the good witch who tries to break it. Now let's get to work."

It became a nice way to spend the days inside during stormy weather, and Tennie doubted she could have kept them practicing otherwise. Mike loaned Rusty a cape from the old country that would work for the *vepyr*. Using walnut hulls, Tennie dyed flour sacks to make a dark witch's

283

outfit for Badger. She bleached other flour sacks for his appearance as the good witch. Lucas refused to wear a dress, but agreed to wrap Tennie's shawl around his middle and wear a wig made of a horse's tail he'd begged off Mike. They fashioned crowns out of paper.

When Jeff heard their plans, he donated a red silk sash for Lucas to wear as the prince. "Don't ask me where it came from. I don't want to talk about it."

Badger wanted to show off his powers by pretending to put a spell on Rascal and having him play dead. He worked with the puppy over and over, and despite Tennie's warnings the dog was too young, refused to give up. In desperation, he turned to Shorty.

Shorty walked into their living quarters with Bear. "Why didn't you tell me you wanted a dog that could play dead?" he said with a querulous scowl. By the end of the afternoon, he had Bear rolling over with his paws up every time Badger waved his "magic wand" over him.

Jeff took over the reins of other parts of their production. He informed Big Mike and Shorty they could attend the boys' play, but it was for Lafayette's benefit, and he didn't want them blabbing about it and having every bowlegged cowboy in the county showing up at the jail Tuesday evening. He watched Tennie and the boys practice; afterwards, he cut boughs they could use to show how the forest had grown up around the sleeping princess. The boys wanted to do an elaborate sword fight between the prince and the *vepyr*, but Tennie was afraid they would knock over the coal oil lanterns and set the place on fire. Jeff said he would take care of the lanterns.

"He is coming, isn't he?" Tennie asked.

"I haven't told him," Jeff said. "People like Arabella have a sixth sense when something is going on. She and I know all the moves to make one another depressed. On Tuesday, I'll start yanking her chain enough she'll get so miserable, she'll send for the doctor. When she's in that faraway land where she thinks she can turn into vapor and wisp through keyholes, I'll tell Lafayette you and the boys have a surprise for him. But not until then."

"Mr. Jeff!" Tennie said, aghast at the life he led in the saloon. "But won't she suspect you?"

"I'll make sure she doesn't."

The subterfuge depressed Tennie, but she felt she must go ahead in hopes it might help Lafayette.

On Friday and Saturday, she and the boys practiced at Shorty's. Tennie had only a couple of lines, so her periodic absences did not interrupt their rehearsals. Shorty, however, grew weary of their pretend swordplay and demanded they break to play dominoes.

285

On Monday, Tennie cleaned house. That evening, they had a dress rehearsal with Jeff helping to move props around. On Tuesday, she baked a cake and cookies.

They were all nervous and bickering. She had to send the boys to the creek, telling them not to return until suppertime.

At dusk, her guests arrived. Big Mike, loud and antagonistic toward Lafayette, but not so much it would cause a fight. Shorty brought Bear, trying to suppress his eagerness at showing off what his dog could do. Jeff brought Lafayette along. Tennie gave a start at his appearance. He looked dapper as usual, but in the short time, he had lost much weight, appearing gaunt and aged.

"My dear Miss Tennie," Lafayette said, having lost none of his suave manners. "I am truly astonished you would go to so much trouble for me."

"You haven't seen us perform yet," Tennie said, feeling a little sick to her stomach.

The guests took their places in chairs placed in front of a makeshift stage. The stage consisted of three chairs facing the audience, next to the bare kitchen table. The office table had been brought in and placed by the cookstove to hold desserts for later.

Rusty, having the most difficult job, stood up with a nervous start, clearing his throat. "Gentlemen, tonight we tell a tale about a kingdom long ago and far away . . ."

He had notes, but tried to use them only to prompt his memory. When he finished the introduction, he went to the side of the room and placed a crown on his head. Tennie sat in one of the far chairs. When Lucas appeared wearing his horsehair wig and paper crown, his bottom wrapped in Tennie's shawl, it brought smiles and gentle laughter. He and Rusty took their places as the king and queen, sitting on their thrones.

The men tried not to laugh at Badger in his witch's costume. Rusty and Lucas fed Badger his lines, apologizing to the witch for forgetting to invite her to their feast.

The witch yelled, "You should have!"

The king and queen pleaded with the witch not to put a spell on them, especially not on their daughter.

Again, the witch yelled, "When her finger gets pricked by a needle, she will die!"

The king and queen went through elaborate motions to show their fear and foreboding.

Forgetting the story, Badger, whose main concern was to show off the trick Bear knew, said without prompting, "To show you what a mean, evil witch I am, I will kill your dog." He waved his pretend wand, and Bear performed his trick of playing dead, causing the men to grin and Shorty to almost burst trying not to be proudful.

Tennie tried not to look at the audience, but she couldn't help but steal occasional glances at Lafayette. To her relief, he smiled much of the time, laughing and sometimes clapping.

Rusty removed his crown and announced the second act. Badger, still as the evil witch, sat in a chair pretending to be sewing.

"I've never seen anyone sewing," Tennie said. "May I try?"

Badger handed her the needle. Tennie pretended to prick herself and slumped down as if dead. While Tennie played dead, Shorty helped Badger out of his bad witch costume and into his good witch one.

Rusty removed his crown and took up his role as narrator again. "The bad witch has caused the death of the princess, but the good witch is going to try to break the spell."

Badger arrived again, this time in his white flour sack with its white hood. "She won't die, but all of you will sleep for . . . for. . . ."

"A hundred years," Rusty hissed.

"A hundred years!" Badger shouted.

Jeff turned down the lanterns. Tennie took her place, lying flat on the table. Lucas sprinkled flowers around her while Jeff placed brushwood around the table to symbolize the encroaching forest. He removed the lanterns to a safer distance, turning up the wicks.

Rusty's narration took a turn from the traditional story. "The mean witch sees the handsome prince arrive at the castle, and she sends an evil, bloodsucking *vepyr* to stop him from finding the princess and kissing her back to life, awakening the whole palace."

Bear, trained by Shorty, pretended to be asleep next to the table. Lucas arrived with his red sash and pretend sword, while Rusty put on Mike's cape. Cracking her eyelids just to peek, Tennie was surprised to see Rusty had taken charcoal and made wide black circles around his eyes. He had let what Tennie hoped was beet juice dribble from the corners of his mouth to look like blood. He made a scary spectacle, and he advanced menacingly on Tennie. Lucas yelled and waved his sword. Rusty pulled his out, and they began thrusting and parrying, going throughout the room, jumping on chairs and down again, dancing around light on their feet as Wash Jones had taught them.

Tennie tried to play asleep, but she couldn't help turning her head a smidgen, opening her eyelids just a slit to see the men's reaction. Big Mike was smiling big and slapping his thigh in laughter. Jeff sat grinning while a smile played at the corners of Shorty's mouth.

But Lafayette sat motionless, watching the boys with such intentness his face appeared frozen. It puzzled her so much, she shut her eyes and refused to open them until Lucas had killed the evil *vepyr* and kissed her cheek to awaken her. During rehearsals, he had pretended to kiss her, or only lightly grazed her cheek. To her surprise, he planted a big wet one on the side of her face.

She and Bear awakened. Tennie exclaimed with hands over her heart she had been saved by her prince, while Lucas grinned.

Rusty removed his cape and gave his face a quick wipe with a damp washcloth before announcing, "Everyone lived happily ever after, except for the evil witch, who was so frustrated she went into a cave and hid for another hundred years."

The men stood up and applauded, Mike's thundering praise reverberating throughout the room. Tennie and the boys smiled and bowed. Only Lafayette did not clap. He rose slowly from his chair, and Tennie hastily said there were refreshments for everybody at the back table.

Lafayette stood, staring hard at Lucas and Rusty, his voice coming out flat and demanding. "Where did you learn to swordfight like that? Country boys don't know these things. Who taught you?"

CHAPTER 19

Everyone in the room grew quiet.

Rusty responded evenly enough. "A cowboy came by the ranch. You know how Pa was; he opened the door to anybody. The cowboy stayed a few days and left."

"What was his name? What did he look like?"

Badger opened his mouth, but before any words could come out, Lucas said in a loud voice, "There's a spider on your head," and he slapped Badger's skull.

Badger rubbed his scalp and looked daggers at Lucas, but said nothing. Tennie held her breath, not understanding why they couldn't talk about Wash Jones, yet unwilling to break some unwritten code of her stepsons.

"He was just some drifting cowboy, Mr. Lafayette," Rusty said. "Stayed a few days and left," he repeated.

Lafayette continued to glare at the boys, but after several uncomfortable seconds, his ingrained sense of *noblesse oblige* took over. He forced a smile and gave his heartiest thanks for a fine performance. "Miss Tennie, you and your magnificent stepsons have overwhelmed me."

His eyes began to glitter, and he smiled. "And, my dear young lady, you have given me a glorious idea." He picked up her hand and turning it over, placed warm lips against her palm.

And twice that night, Tennie was surprised by a kiss.

Although Big Mike had kept his promise not to spread the word about Tennie's small production, he could not stop himself from bragging about it afterward. At first, Tennie had no clue to the extent of his gossip. She cooked, she cleaned, she swept, she walked up and down the street as far as the saloons went, greeting people early in the morning before the doxies got up and the drunks became obnoxious.

One morning, she noticed a small group of women knotted in front of the bank. The full dresses they wore were dark and somber, their hats black and placed squarely and resolutely atop hair pulled back in tight buns. They were making angry gestures at the mayor, who appeared to be trying to calm them down. When one of them caught sight of Tennie, she pointed her finger, mouthing harsh words Tennie could not make out. She stopped and looked behind her, but no one else was on the street. Not understanding what was going on, she turned and went back to the jail.

Lucas came in later to tell her. "The townswomen are all mad at you. They told the mayor you were laid splayed out on a table in front of a bunch of men and with children present."

"What?" Tennie exclaimed. "Didn't they understand we were putting on a play about a fairy tale? And I was not 'splayed' out."

"They didn't care," Lucas answered. "They said it was scandalous the town marshal should be acting that way, especially in front of children."

Tennie took a deep breath, fighting back tears. It devastated her to think something that had seemed so innocent could be taken so harshly. Lucas was staring at her with concerned eyes, and Tennie found herself getting furious at the people who were upsetting this boy.

"Well, so what if they don't like it? What are they going to do? Kick you and your brothers out of school? Oh, they've already done that. Kick you out of church? They've already done that, too. Run us out of town? Big deal," Tennie said, waving her arms in anger. "We'll just pack up, go to Cat Ridge, and see if Packer Jack can help me find a job as a cook at a stagecoach stop somewhere. I hate this job anyway."

"But they might try to take us away from you, Miss Tennie," Lucas cried.

"Don't worry," Tennie said, hugging the boy. "Nobody else wants you. And if worse came to worst, we'd just head out, and they'd never find us."

The door flew open and Arabella stormed in. She screamed at Lucas, "Beat it, you little brat!"

Lucas turned and placed himself in front of Tennie, mouth tight, eyes mutinous, but Tennie patted him on the shoulder. "Run along. Everything is going to be okay."

He looked Arabella up and down, giving her a hard stare before leaving through the door she had left open.

She started in on Tennie. "You and Jeff Hamilton think you are so smart, don't you?" she ranted. "The two of you are plotting to get rid of me so you can have Lafayette all to yourself!" She raged in that vein for several minutes, calling Jeff and Tennie the foulest names she could think of.

When she finally stopped to heave and take a breath, Tennie said, "I am not in cahoots with Jeff to try to capture Lafayette. We are his friends, and we knew he was depressed, so we were just trying to cheer him up. That is all!"

"Yeah, but you—"

"I'm not trying to get rid of you," Tennie said, her voice rising louder and louder. "I'm not making a play for Lafayette. Get that through your head!"

"Oh," Arabella said, drawing herself up in anger. "So, Lafayette's not good enough for you, is that it? You're just too good for our kind." She stopped shrieking and spit into Tennie's face.

Tennie wiped the spit away. "Get out. Get out."

Arabella slapped her so hard, Tennie had to brace herself to keep from falling backward.

"Out!" she said again, pointing at the door. "Out! Out! Out!"

Frustrated, Arabella left in a fury. Tennie sank down in a chair and tried to stop shaking.

Lucas wanted to throw trash all over town, unhitch all the horses, and scare them away, along with putting coal oil in everybody's well to dispel any notion anyone might get of replacing Tennie as their caregiver.

Rusty, however, talked him out of it. "Shorty said just leave it alone; it will all blow over."

The next day, the Paytons came to town. Sitting at the office table, Mr. Payton began chastising Tennie all over again. "What were you thinking of, Tennie? Lying on top of a table in front of a roomful of men."

"It was a fairy tale!" Tennie said. "Mr. Lafayette has been depressed, so we tried to cheer him up by putting on a play for him. That's all."

"Well, he's not depressed now," Mr. Payton said.

"Perhaps if you had invited some women, too, dear," Mrs. Payton said.

"What women?" Tennie replied. "The women in town won't have anything to do with me."

"Well, they certainly aren't going to now," Mr. Payton said. "Tennie, Lafayette is too old for you."

"And Tennie," Mrs. Payton added, "you know yourself you'd never be happy having a husband who ran a saloon crawling with loose women."

"I'm not trying to catch Mr. Lafayette as a husband," Tennie said, wondering what they would think of her if they knew she had slept on the back porch with Wash Jones and his men.

Tennie didn't think Mike knew of the havoc his loose mouth created. Every time he saw her, he boomed, "You liked my stories, eh?"

Friday night came, and Tennie found herself looking forward to a routine of locking up drunken men that would make her forget all about putting on a play and lying on a table. The evening looked like it was going to be the usual miscreants, and she suddenly missed Apache John. He'd always left a mountain of work for her, but he'd never caused her any trouble.

She played dominoes with Shorty and the boys late into the night. Badger had already fallen asleep. Jeff appeared at the door, and Tennie looked up, thinking he was going to tell her Lafayette said things were quiet enough they could all go to bed.

Instead, Jeff motioned her outside. "It's Honey Boy. He's been on a rip-snorting tear. He demolished two of the smaller saloons, but they couldn't hold him to get him to the jail. He came into the Silver Moon, and it took three men to get him down."

"Oh, no," Tennie said with a moan.

"They're bringing him now, but I think you'd better give me the keys and let me lock him up."

"All right." She went back inside for the keys, and handing them to Jeff, she looked up the street to see three men struggling with Honey Boy. For the rest of her life, Tennie would wonder why what happened next seemed to be slowed down by time, as if everyone was moving in a sluggish dream. She saw Honey Boy break free from his captures, saw him running in their direction, heard him shouting at Jeff he was nothing but a sheep-humping scoundrel. He reached Jeff, and putting his hands around Jeff's neck, began to strangle him. In the struggle, Tennie fell when she tried to move out of the way. The last thing she remembered was getting up behind Jeff and seeing Honey Boy, arm reared back, with three men behind him, trying to take him down.

When she came to, she was lying on the sidewalk, with Jeff and Shorty calling her name. They kept asking her if she was all right. She struggled to sit up. She nodded, but put her head down in pain. Jeff lifted her face while Shorty held the lantern over her.

"God almighty, he almost put your eye out," Jeff said. "Do any of your teeth feel wobbly?"

Tennie rubbed her tongue over her teeth and shook her head, tears of pain wetting her cheek.

"I dodged that big fist coming," Jeff said. "I

had no notion you were standing behind me."

"Where is he?" Tennie said.

"He's knocked out in his cell," Jeff said, and Tennie had never seen him so distraught. "I think we may have crushed his skull; I don't know." He stood up. "Stay here with Shorty for now. I'm going to see if I can sober Doc up to look at you and Honey Boy. I'll tell Lafayette I'm spending the night on the cot in the jailhouse tonight."

Tennie didn't protest, even though she knew it would be just more fuel added to the fire already surrounding her. She let Jeff and Shorty assist her back into the station where she curled into a corner and sobbed. Shorty said nothing, but brought her a blanket and a pillow. He helped her up while he spread the blanket on the floor, but she crawled back onto it and into the corner as soon as he finished, where she continued to weep.

It was over an hour before Jeff returned with the doctor.

He got down on his knees and looked into Tennie's eyes, asking her questions she thought were stupid until it dawned on her he wanted to know how cognizant she was. He checked in her ears for signs of blood. "You'll be all right. Do you want something for the pain?"

Tennie's skull pulsated in agony, but she shook her head.

"You boys get over here and talk to her," he

ordered. "Don't let her go to sleep for at least another hour to make sure she's okay." He stood up.

Tennie finally remembered her manners. "Thank you, doctor."

He paused. "I know what you think of me," he said, his face twisting in bitterness.

"I think you are a good doctor," Tennie answered. "Please make sure Honey Boy will be all right."

He shook his head, stuffing his instruments into his bag. "Women!"

After he left, the boys crept over to her, unsure of what to say.

Lucas finally thought of something and asked, "Do you want us to go over our lessons for you?"

"You must really feel sorry for me if you are willing to do that," Tennie replied. "Yes, please do."

Jeff slept on the cot in the office that night.

In the morning, he roused all but one prisoner and told them to get the hell out. Honey Boy, his hair encrusted in dried blood, slept on.

"Are you sure the doctor said he would be okay?" Tennie asked, staring at Honey Boy through the bars.

"Yes," Jeff said. "He's going to want to kill himself when he sees you, but Doc said he would probably sleep most of the day."

Jeff left. Big Mike stopped by, his jaw dropping when he saw her. Jeff and the other men were paid not to talk about what the customers of the Silver Moon did while intoxicated. Tennie gave Mike the same account she had given the boys; Honey Boy had been drunk and had accidentally fallen against her, knocking her into the wall. As stout as Honey Boy was, Mike was stronger, and he could crush what three men with pistols butts and blackjacks could not. If other men—the ones who left flowers for her and stopped by to talk every day—found out, they might put a bullet in Honey Boy.

When he roused in the late afternoon, he gaped at Tennie. "What happened to you?"

"Come on downstairs. I want to wash the blood out of your hair."

Although Tennie realized his head must have felt like leaden cotton wads, he sat at the table with his eyes closed and allowed her to clean his scalp with a wet washcloth.

When she did not speak, he said with his eyes still shut, "Miss Tennie, don't tell me I did that to you."

"You were aiming for Jeff but got me instead," Tennie said, patting his scalp with the cloth, trying to be gentle.

Lucas entered the room and sat down at the table, staring with solemn eyes at the young cowboy.

Honey Boy's Adam's apple bobbed several times, and two tears rolled down his cheeks from behind closed lids. "Two-Bit usually keeps me from going too far, but he was feeling poorly and didn't want to come to town."

"Miss Tennie says we have to depend on ourselves," Lucas said.

"Lucas," Tennie said, "you go outside. Mr. Honey Boy doesn't feel well."

Lucas got up from the table. When he reached the door, he turned to Honey Boy. "Mr. Jeff said you almost put her eye out."

"Lucas!" Tennie warned.

He went out the door, and Tennie put down her washcloth. Honey Boy rose, giving her an agonizing stare.

"Run along," Tennie said, sighing. "It will be okay."

He nodded and shot out the door, stumbling over the sill.

Jeff came by later to see if he had gone. "Lafayette and I discussed not serving him any more liquor at the Silver Moon, but he'd just go somewhere else and drink it. At least there, we can keep an eye on him."

"I didn't invite him to our little play, and that probably set him off. But he's got something deeper than that going on inside of him."

"How did you get so wise?" Jeff said.

"Staying up all night praying for it," she said.

301

"Don't worry. Shorty calls me flea-brain enough times to keep me humble."

"Miss Tennie, Honey Boy ain't the man for you," Jeff said.

"I know that. I've known that from the beginning."

"Then why were you crying over him so?" Jeff asked. "Shorty said you were caterwauling like an old maid whose last hope just married somebody else."

"A girl can shed a few tears over a fellow without wanting to be his bride, can't she?" She started to tell him of Arabella's visit, but thought better of it. No use in stirring up more trouble.

On Monday, Tennie went into the general store to buy flour and canned tomatoes. She walked to the counter just as one of the townswomen finished her business.

"Thank you, kindly," the woman told the grocer in a voice as syrupy and sweet as a clover honey then turned and caught sight of Tennie. "Hussy!" she hissed. "You no doubt got what you deserved."

"No doubt," Tennie said, but the woman was already heading out the door.

"Don't pay her no mind, Miss Tennie." The grocer then added, "Your eye is looking a mite better today."

"Thank you. It feels better."

During the next two weeks, her face healed.

Honey Boy stayed at the ranch. His boss, Shep Davis, burst into the jailhouse and demanded Tennie explain what she had been telling Honey Boy.

"He's suddenly come up with this here notion he can't depend on me to take care of him the rest of his life, and he wants me to begin selling him parts of the ranch bit by bit so that when I die, it'll be his."

"I didn't tell him anything," Tennie said. "Lucas told him he shouldn't be depending on Two-Bit to keep him out of trouble. Sort of."

"Dang. I don't want to lose Honey Boy." Shep's busy mind changed the subject. "Say, what are these signs Lafayette is having posted all over town?"

"I don't know." She followed Shep outside to look.

Jeff stood next to the station wall, hammering nails into a poster.

Shorty came out. "You can just take that down right now," he demanded.

"It ain't hurting nothing, old-timer," Jeff said. "Might even bring you some business."

Winn Payton walked from across the street to join them.

Tennie read aloud, "Come see the world famous singing sensation, Fanny Boulet," except she pronounced it Boo-let.

Jeff corrected her. "Boo-lay."

"Fanny Boo-Lay," Tennie repeated, standing corrected. "Watch as she performs her daring act on a high-flying swing."

The poster showed a scantily clad, buxom young woman on a swing, her red hair and tissue-thin costume flowing enticingly behind her as she stared at her audience with parted lips and half-closed eyes. The artist had emphasized a pair of large nipples pushing naughtily against the thin fabric that barely covered them.

"Oh my," Tennie said.

"What is Lafayette up to now?" Winn Payton grumbled.

"I don't know," Shep Davis said, "but I'll be there. When is it? Tell me, Miss Tennie. I don't have my glasses on."

"Saturday night two weeks from now," Tennie told him.

"Not this Saturday, but the next?" Shep demanded.

"That's right," Tennie said.

"You better brace yourself, gal," Jeff said. "This town will be busting with soldiers from the fort and every cowboy within two hundred miles of here."

Tennie took a deep breath in dismay.

"Don't feel too bad," Winn Payton said. "Lafayette has given the women of this town something to complain about besides you."

CHAPTER 20

When the cowboys arriving for an evening of Friday night revelry learned Fanny Boulet was coming to Ring Bit, the mood of the town shifted. Every store that carried an article of men's clothing sold out, from neckerchiefs to bowties. Many of them left Ring Bit and headed for Cat Ridge and beyond to find something that might make them stand out in Fanny's eyes. The owner of one of the mercantile stores told Tennie the only other time he had sold so much men's toggery was the day she arrived to be the marshal.

Every bit of gossip anyone had ever gleaned was shared and repeated a thousand times. Tennie was kept from learning the more salacious ones, but she still nevertheless heard about the duels fought over Fanny, how she had been married to a count who shot himself over her unfaithfulness, of being banned in Boston and run out of town for indecency. How she was indecent, Tennie never found out.

Lafayette walked the sidewalks of town whistling and smiling. Jeff shook his head and mumbled something about Lafayette playing with fire. When Tuesday's stage from Cat Ridge came in, Tennie went outside and stood on the sidewalk in front of the jail while a group of at least fifty men crowded around the stagecoach. Lafayette had to struggle to get through the mob, but he reached the stage and was the first to hold open the door, extending his hand. A lace-covered glove reached out to his, the ribbons shining golden on a dark green satin sleeve.

There was an intake of breath, and Fanny Boulet, in all her glory, stepped down from the stagecoach.

Tennie strained to look over the heads of the men crowded around Fanny. All she caught was a glimpse of a buxom woman with an hourglass figure wearing a fabulous dress, her red hair flaming underneath a matching green hat covered in feathers, one of them over two feet long.

"Lafayette, darling!" a musical voice rang out.

Tennie saw Lafayette bend down, she guessed to kiss Fanny's hand. Packer Jack unloaded bag after bag, along with a huge trunk. Lafayette spoke to someone, and several men began fighting over who would get to carry a bag. He led Fanny and her admirers back to the Silver Moon, an entourage of men bunched behind them.

"Whew!" Tennie looked over to see Shorty's sour face.

"Lafayette is a fool," Shorty said with so much acidity, Tennie was glad she didn't have an elm tree shading the jail. It would have curled up and died.

At the supper table, her stepsons did not follow the local custom of refusing to speak until after eating. The conversation centered around Fanny Boulet.

"Mr. Lafayette said we could come in through the back, stand hidden in the wings of the stage, and watch Miss Boulet's performance," Rusty said. "You wouldn't mind if Lucas and I did that, would you, Miss Tennie?"

Tennie thought about it, trying to decide what kind of trouble they could cause or be subjected to. She didn't answer right away, and Badger began to beg to go along.

"No." She knew that much.

Badger looked as if he was considering throwing himself on the floor in a fit, but three pairs of defiant eyes dared him to try it. He sank back down in the chair, and the pout he gave was a small one.

"Mr. Lafayette won't want Rascal in his saloon, anyway," Tennie said.

Besides sleeping together, Badger walked around holding the dog almost every waking moment.

"Mr. Lafayette said you could come, too, Miss Tennie," Lucas said. "But Mr. Jeff said no, you had to be at the jail. Then Mr. Lafayette got mad and told Mr. Jeff he was quick enough to offer to do your job so you could go to a dance, and Mr. Jeff said it wasn't the same thing.

"What's a monkey on somebody's back, Miss Tennie?" Lucas said, continuing to chatter. "Mr. Jeff said all the saloon girls had monkeys on their backs, but I've never seen any monkeys there."

"I don't know," Tennie responded. She saw Rusty give Lucas a look and a frown indicating *I'll explain it later.*

"I don't know why everybody thinks Miss Boulet is so special," Lucas said between bites, refusing to let Rusty's warning looks stop him. "She looks kind of long in the tooth to me."

"Lucas, shut up," Rusty said.

"Shorty said it!" Lucas said, defending himself. "He said if Miss Fanny was a horse, it would be about time to start filing her teeth down."

Tennie resisted the urge to smile. "She's still beautiful, though, isn't she?"

"Oh sure," Lucas conceded. "They said Miss Arabella is fit to be tied over Miss Boulet coming. I could hear her screaming and throwing things yesterday when I took bottles to the back door."

"What's a monkey?" Badger asked.

"Don't you remember?" Lucas said. "Pa let some gypsies stay down by the creek, but they had a monkey they had trained to steal, so Pa had to ask them to leave. That's how our barn got that big hole in it; the gypsies put a curse on it when they left."

"Mr. Wash said they tampered with the roof before they left, and the first big wind that came along put a hole in it," Rusty said, disparaging Lucas's theory. "He got up there and looked at it."

Lucas finished eating in silence. The boys asked to be excused and went outside while it was still daylight left, Rascal trotting behind them. Tennie cleaned the table, wondering why just mentioning Wash Jones's name could put a stop to Lucas's gossipy prattle.

After Fanny insisted on getting her beauty rest because of her tiring journey, she allowed Lafayette to escort her all over town, taking her on picnics down by the creek, along with buying her every trinket, hat, or dress her eyes happened to light upon in Ring Bit. The merchants were ecstatic and made sure they placed their most expensive items prominently in their store windows hoping to catch Fanny's gaze. It was said the milliner only got about three hours of sleep a night; as soon as she made one outrageously expensive hat, Lafayette would purchase it, only to replace it the next day with a newer model that caught Fanny's fancy.

Lucas reported Arabella picked the youngest, strongest, and most handsome cowboys to escort her up and down the streets, too. Instead of having them buy her things, she would squeeze their arms, remarking how strong they were. She alternated between seething every time she looked at Fanny to staying hours in her room, not appearing to care about anything.

Saturday night was to be Fanny's big performance, with Lafayette hinting it would be the first of many. By Friday morning, the town pulsated with strange men riding in. Big Mike did a brisk business and had Rusty and Lucas helping him. Even Badger put Rascal down long enough to run errands for them. The stagecoaches were coming in full to capacity, sometimes squeezing more men on top in addition to Packer Jack and the helper who rode shotgun for him.

Tennie had finished the breakfast dishes and was about to start putting things on to cook for dinner when Lafayette entered the jailhouse, calling to her.

She walked into the office, wiping her hands on her apron. Lafayette stood with Fanny by his side. Tennie smiled and greeted them, but Fanny barely gave her a chance to say hello.

"Darling," Fanny addressed Lafayette. "Don't tell me this is your little marshal? But where is her gun belt? Where are the pistols?"

Tennie stood wearing an uncertain smile, while Fanny continued to burble. "I'm so disappointed; she looks like a little girl. Not a marshal who arrests bad men and locks them up."

Her stream of one-sided conversation gave Tennie an opportunity for a closer look. Although turned out in expensive clothes, Lucas had been right; Fanny was not a young woman. A heavy corset could not totally control her thickening waist, nor powder hide the lines around her eyes and mouth.

"I'm sorry to disappoint you, Miss Fanny," Tennie said. "People coming in here wanting to see a female marshal usually are."

"Do you have a badge under that apron?" Fanny asked with obvious curiosity. "Really, darling, you should at least wear a badge."

Tennie looked at Lafayette, who appeared amused by the exchange. She smiled nervously again. With a start, she realized there was a line of gray hair next to Fanny's scalp. She had never seen anyone with dyed hair before.

"What is it, darling?" Fanny asked.

"Your hair," Tennie said, then added, "It's beautiful."

"Darling, you are so sweet," Fanny purred. "I will let you in on a little secret. One word. Henna." She reached out and touched Tennie's brown curls. "It would do wonders for your looks, darling. You should let me try some on your hair."

"Don't touch her hair," Lafayette said, his voice so forceful, it startled both women.

They stared at him.

A slow dawning of realization came over Fanny's face, and she began to eye Lafayette in amusement. "Darling, Lafayette," she chastised, shaking her head. "Shame, shame on you. This is going to cost you so much more money. So much more money." She gave a short laugh. "And to think I believed you really wanted to see me again. Oh, Lafayette."

Tennie had no clue what was going on. Lafayette, always a master at hiding his feelings, nevertheless looked uncomfortable, much to Tennie's surprise. Fanny did not look anything but amused, allowing only a fleeting gloat of avarice to cross her face.

"We must be going," he said. "Miss Tennie, the offer to watch Fanny's performance from the wings of the stage still stands."

"I'm sure it will be wonderful," Tennie said.

"Darling! Of course!" Fanny said.

Tennie had only ever stepped foot in one saloon, and it had been against her will. In Ring Bit, she had followed Winn Payton's advice to stay out of them. She did not even have to consider whether or not to go to Fanny's performance; she knew she wasn't. She said nothing about Lucas and Rusty going. She neither gave them her blessing nor forbade them. She trusted Jeff and Lafayette to either keep them out of harm's way or to send them home if they aggravated anyone.

It did not matter anyway. At six o'clock on

312

Saturday, just hours before her big performance, Fanny had come out of Lafayette's upstairs office and walked down the stairs, exclaiming Lafayette wanted her to give special instructions to Joe Lee, his half black, half Chinese chef. He was to prepare a special supper for just the two of them after the performance.

As she walked by Arabella, she gave her a dismissive wave of her hand. "Really, darling. Don't try to intrude. You are not wanted."

Before anyone could stop her, and in front of at least a dozen witnesses, Arabella withdrew from her bosom the same small dagger she had threatened Tennie with and rushed to Fanny, stabbing her in the back. The dagger went in so deeply, it entered the heart, killing Fanny almost instantly.

Pandemonium broke out in the saloon. The doctor was present and not so drunk he could not pronounce Fanny dead. Jeff and a helper grabbed Arabella and began hauling her kicking and screaming outside.

When she realized they were heading for the jail, she screeched, "What are you doing? Nobody goes to jail for murder in Ring Bit." She began calling for Lafayette and cursing Jeff.

Upstairs in his office, Lafayette heard the commotion and came out in time to see Arabella being dragged away. When he walked down the stairs and saw Fanny lying with Arabella's dagger, what he had always referred to as her "plaything," in Fanny's back, witnesses said he paled so white they thought he would faint.

Tennie knew none of this at the time. She was bidden to the front of the jail by the sounds of Jeff calling her name and Arabella's screaming.

The two men shoved Arabella inside.

"She's killed Fanny," Jeff said. "Quick! The keys!"

Tennie stopped gaping and hastened to fetch the keys, racing ahead of them up the stairs. With fumbling hands, she opened the door to the farthest cell. Jeff and his helper threw the screaming, kicking woman into the cell and slammed the door behind her. Jeff grabbed the keys from Tennie's hand and locked Arabella in. Taking Tennie by the elbow, he pulled her as quick as he could back down the stairs.

"What? What?" was all Tennie could say.

Jeff repeated what had happened in the saloon. He turned to his helper. "Get somebody to ride with you and fetch the sheriff from Cat Ridge as quick as you can. Telegraph the deputy marshal while you're there."

The man nodded and hastened from the jailhouse. Jeff stopped to take a breath. Above their heads came the sounds of Arabella's screeching.

"Fanny's had her knife in Arabella since she got here," Jeff said. "After Lafayette brought her here to meet you, they had a big powwow in Lafayette's office, and he sent me to the bank to withdraw a godawful amount of money. That's when Fanny pulled out all the stops. She did everything she could to humiliate Arabella, deriding her every chance she got."

"Oh, Lord," Tennie said, so upset she could hardly think. "That's no excuse for murder!"

"I'm sure she didn't intend for it to work out that way," Jeff said, shaking his head. "God help us. What a mess."

As Arabella continued to curse and yell, Jeff paused. "Don't let anyone, and I mean anyone, in there to see her. Don't let them go up the stairs. Lock the door and refuse to let anybody in."

Tennie looked up at the ceiling. "The doctor?" she queried. "Should the doctor look at her? She's hysterical."

She had never seen Jeff look so indecisive. He always knew exactly what to do.

"Mr. Jeff?" Tennie said.

Jeff took a handkerchief from his back pocket and wiped the sweat from his face. "I'll send the doctor over to give her something to knock her out for the night. After that, I don't know. I don't know anything, Tennie."

Tennie nodded. Jeff left, and she locked the door behind him. She turned and saw the boys lined up by the door.

"Miss Tennie?" Rusty said. It was more of a statement than a question.

They looked up at the ceiling as Arabella began banging on the bars with something heavy, probably her shoe. "You ugly sow!" she shrieked. "You get Lafayette over here this instant!"

Jeff came back with the doctor. Tennie unlocked the door and let them in. The doctor reeked of liquor and lurched as he headed for the stairs. Jeff and Tennie followed.

Arabella was still cursing Tennie when they reached the second floor. When she saw Jeff, she began to curse him.

"Bella," the doctor slurred. "I'm going to give you something."

To Tennie's amazement, Arabella immediately calmed down. She lay down on the bed expectantly, rolling up one sleeve. Unlocking the door to let the doctor enter the cell, Tennie could see marks up and down Arabella's arm.

Tennie turned her head as the doctor shakily filled a needle. She looked at Jeff and he nodded. She didn't have to be told what the monkey was on Arabella's back.

The doctor left the cell; Tennie locked it behind him, taking one last look at Arabella, who lay waiting expectantly, then followed Jeff and the doctor down the stairs. As the doctor opened the door and left, she placed her hand on Jeff's arm and looked at him.

"It's a way of life for those women, Miss Tennie," he said when the doctor had departed.

"And Lafayette?" Tennie asked.

"It's like trying to corral cats. He lets them do what they want as long as he can make money off them. That's the ugly truth of it."

Tennie sank into a chair, placing her elbows on the table and shading her eyes with her fingers.

"He's been trying to get rid of her for months, even before you came," Jeff said.

Tennie jerked her head up. "Why not just put her on the stagecoach?"

"I can't answer that. Look, with any luck, the sheriff will be here by morning, and we'll be shut of her. She'll have to stand trial in Cat Ridge."

But the sheriff did not come in the morning. He sent word the judge had traveled to the capital and would not be back in Cat Ridge for at least two weeks. Until then, Arabella was to stay in Ring Bit with a woman as her jailer. He also sent instructions Tennie better have Arabella dried out by then; he wasn't putting up with no degenerate opium addict.

The deputy marshal likewise sloughed off any responsibility. It was a county murder and would have to be tried in Cat Ridge. He did, however, advise Tennie to interview all the witnesses and write down their depositions, making sure they were signed.

There was a constant round of meetings at the jailhouse. The town council arrived in force in a turmoil, offering no advice or help. The only clear directive from their meeting was Tennie should under no circumstances allow reporters to speak to Arabella.

Jeff came several times, still adamant Tennie was not to allow Arabella any visitors except for the attorney Lafayette had sent for.

"She'll have them smuggle no telling what in to her," Jeff said of visitors. "She'd kill you too without batting an eyelash."

One by one, he brought the witnesses who had been in the saloon at the time of the murder. He set a table up outside for Tennie to write on, and she painstakingly took their statements. Many of them could not sign their names, and she had to get Mike or Shorty to witness their mark. Their stories were all the same. Fanny Boulet had been taunting Arabella, and Arabella had responded by putting a knife in her back.

When the last man left, Tennie turned to Jeff. "What about the saloon girls?"

"They were all occupied upstairs," Jeff said. "They didn't see anything."

"Oh, all right," Tennie said, not thinking anything about it. She looked up and wondered why her answer caused him to give her a piercing stare.

He lowered his eyes and picked up the sheaf of papers. "Here, let me help you get this stuff back inside."

Winn Payton and Shorty walked into the jailhouse as they finished putting the table back in place.

"It's going to get bad, Jeff," Winn warned. "She may still be knocked out, but when she wakes up, the doors of hell are going to open."

Tennie sat down at the table and let them converse without interruption. They could talk all they wanted to, but in the end, the responsibility of taking care of Arabella for two weeks was going to fall on her shoulders, and she knew that.

CHAPTER 21

Tennie worried how she would handle taking food in to Arabella, not to mention buckets of water and taking out chamber pots.

Jeff had already told her not to even let Arabella have utensils. "She could rush you with a spoon and put your eye out. Let her eat with her fingers. I've seen her do it enough times."

The boys hovered, listening to everything. Tennie debated whether to shield them or let them in on what was happening. In the end, she did not have the heart to shut them out.

By late afternoon, Arabella had awakened and started screaming obscenities that could be heard all over town. When Tennie and Jeff tried to bring her food, she threw the plate at them. They narrowly missed being covered in urine when she let fly with the slop bucket.

The boys fled the jailhouse and did not come back until almost dark. Jeff and Shorty walked in just as they returned.

While they were there, Shep Davis banged on the locked jailhouse door. "Let me in," he roared. "It's Shep!"

Shorty, standing closest to the door, opened it for him.

"These boys can't stay here with that witch spewing filth twenty-four hours a day," he said, brusque as usual. He had to talk loud to be heard over Arabella's screams. "I'll take the two oldest boys home with me. There's always plenty to do on a ranch, and they can earn some money while they are there."

Shorty eyed the frightened boys. "Badger and Rascal can bunk with me and Bear."

Lucas drew closer to Tennie, standing behind her chair. "I thank you kindly, Mr. Davis," he said, surprising everyone, "but I'm staying here with Miss Tennie."

Tennie turned to stare at him in surprise. Before she could say anything, Rusty agreed. "I'm staying, too." He turned to Badger. "But Badger, you and Rascal might be better off at Shorty's."

Badger began to cry. "I don't want to leave Miss Tennie," he sobbed.

"I'll bring some cotton for you to stuff in your ears," Jeff said. "We'll see what we can do in the morning."

When Tennie looked at herself in the mirror the next morning as she washed her face and combed her hair, all she saw was a face pinched with worry and eyes with dark circles under them.

Jeff arrived early, banging on the door and calling, "It's Jeff!"

She opened the door, letting him and two men carrying toolboxes in.

"How was it?" Jeff asked.

"She never slept a wink last night," Tennie said.

When Arabella heard Jeff's voice, she called out to him. "Jeff Hamilton, you turd-eating rat, you get the doctor over here right now, do you hear me? You get him over here right now or everybody in town is going to hear what really happened between you and your old lady. You hear me?!"

Jeff looked at the men. "Come along." He led them to the living quarters while Tennie followed. "They're going to put in a back door, Miss Tennie. Lafayette is sending some other men over to put up a tent for you to sleep in. You'll still hear her, but it won't be right over your head."

Tennie almost wept. "Thank you."

"Shorty said Bear could stay with you at night," Jeff continued. "Nobody will bother you with Bear around."

Big Mike arrived, instructed by Lafayette via Jeff to make a small door in one of the jail cells Tennie could pass buckets and food through so she wouldn't have to risk going into Arabella's cell.

When the mayor saw the workmen putting in a back door, he went into an unexpected fury, his fat chin quivering in anger, raging at Jeff. "You and Lafayette had no right to desecrate town property."

"What are you talking about?" Jeff snorted. "Mike's going to build bars over the door that can be locked from the inside. It will be as safe as it ever was."

"That's not the point," the mayor shouted. "You had no right."

"Maybe not," Jeff said. "But what difference does it make?"

"Because, because . . ." the mayor flustered.

"Why?" Jeff demanded. "Why?"

The mayor had no answer. He turned to Tennie. "As soon as that woman leaves, you go back in that jailhouse, lock this door and don't use it again. Do you understand me, young lady?"

Tennie nodded and watched as he left in a cloud of temper.

Afterward, it occurred to her that she had not heard Arabella screaming in a while. She no longer demanded Lafayette—it was the doctor she wanted to see.

Tennie entered the jailhouse and looked up the stairway. She could hear the clanking of Mike's tools and the sound of Arabella's voice. Climbing softly on the treads, she went far enough up the stairs she could see Mike on his hands and knees working, but Arabella was hidden from her view.

"You dumb ox," Arabella was saying. "Everybody in town is laughing at you because you think that backstabbing little halo-rubbing tramp likes you. She's just using you like she's using every other man in this town. She probably laughs at you behind your back. Dumb foreigner. You'll never fit in here or anywhere else." Arabella continued to taunt Mike every way she could think of.

It relieved Tennie that Mike appeared to ignore everything Arabella was saying. Then he turned his head to reach for a tool, and Tennie saw his face was wet with tears.

She crept back down the stairs, feeling helpless and sorry for Mike.

Giving thought, she wondered if what she'd heard was true? Was she using every man she had contact with? Or were they using her? What did it matter? They were all in the cesspool named Ring Bit together.

When Mike finished, he tromped down the stairs to fetch Tennie so she could see what he'd done and how the door worked. Jeff heard him and followed the two of them up the stairs.

When Arabella saw Tennie, she raced to the front of the cell, grasping the bars like a spider. "You get that doctor up here right now, you whey-faced little toad," she screamed. "Right now!"

Jeff put his hand on Tennie's arm. "We have to look at Mike's handiwork, first, Arabella. Calm down."

He stooped down and examined the door Mike had built on the cell next to Arabella's. Made floor level so things could be slid in and out, it was barely big enough for a bucket, too small for a person to squeeze through.

Nevertheless, Mike had put a lock on it. "Same key open cell, open this."

"You are very talented, Mike," Tennie murmured.

"Shut up and get the doctor!" Arabella yelled.

"Tennie, get this cell ready, and we'll move Arabella into it while we are here," Jeff said.

Tennie hurriedly put a bucket of clean water and another bucket for waste in the cell. She asked Jeff if she might put a small table and chair from downstairs in the cell, but he shook his head. "Not now, she'll break it and use it to club you with if she gets the chance. Maybe later."

All the while, Arabella screamed at Jeff. She would get even with him. When Lafayette got her out, she was going to find a way to fix him for good. Every sentence she spoke was peppered with invectives, but no one even looked at her.

When it came time to transfer Arabella to the other cell, Jeff moved with lightning speed once the door was open. He grasped her wrists while Big Mike got behind her and picked her up. Letting go of her wrists, Jeff stepped aside while Mike moved the kicking and screaming woman from one cell to the other.

When Mike got out, Jeff slammed the cell door shut. When Tennie tried to lock it, Arabella reached out and scratched her face. Jeff walloped her with a brutal punch, sending her backward.

Arabella stood heaving, some of the fire knocked out of her. "I want that doctor," she said without hollering.

Jeff looked at Tennie and nodded to her.

"Miss Arabella," Tennie said, her voice shaking. "The sheriff at Cat Ridge sent instruction we have to dry you out before you go there to stand trial. The judge is out of town, so it will be two weeks before we can take you to Cat Ridge. You'll have to stay here for now and without the doctor."

Arabella seemed to have trouble comprehending what Tennie was saying. "What do you mean, stand trial in Cat Ridge? What are you talking about? I want out of this jail cell now! People get killed almost every day in Ring Bit. Nobody gives a rat's ass! Nobody stands trial."

"Arabella," Jeff said. "People die in fair fights; people get killed in dark alleys. When people murder somebody in broad daylight in front of a dozen witnesses, they are going to go to jail and stand trial no matter who they are, and that includes you."

"You're just trying to get rid of me," she screamed. "This is a plot between you and that revolting little do-gooder."

Jeff took Tennie by the arm and they went down the stairs with Mike following them, Arabella's rants scorching their ears on the way down.

"Get that doctor now!" reverberated in their ears as they walked outside.

Mike grumbled as he worked on the door of iron bars. He did not like going against the mayor's wishes, and he told Tennie several times, "I do this just for you, Miss Tennie."

She thanked him repeatedly. "But Mr. Lafayette is paying for this, isn't it?"

"Mr. Fancy Pants pays, but I no work for him," Mike said. "I do this just for you."

Tennie felt no guilty qualms about the money Lafayette was spending. She was more than a little angry with him for becoming involved with Arabella and the drug-peddling doctor in the first place. In between the anger came great stabs of thankfulness he was doing so much to make her life bearable.

No one knew where the tent Lafayette had put up came from or what it was originally intended for—he had won it in a poker game. The handsome army major who had slept in the jailhouse when his men were incarcerated loaned Tennie four cots to put in it. Rusty and Lucas took a hatchet and went looking for willow trees. After numerous trips, they had enough to build a small brush arbor.

When Mike finished the back door, he warned Tennie not to use it after Arabella left. "Mayor right. Don't use door after bad woman leave. Promise me."

Tennie did not understand how using the door to go to the backyard of the jailhouse was such a big deal. All that was there was a line of privies and horse pens on either side. The corral boards had never been repaired. Beyond them lay a flat field with nothing but hills in the distance. Nevertheless, she promised.

After he left, two saloon girls came to the jailhouse. Tennie opened the front door, but went outside to talk to them.

"We demand to see Arabella," one of them said.

"No one is allowed to see her right now," Tennie said.

A screaming match ensued when Arabella heard their voices. She commanded Tennie to let them up; the women screamed at Arabella that Tennie was denying her the right to visitors, and it ought to be illegal. It went back and forth, with all three shrieking obscenities at Tennie.

She turned, went back inside the jailhouse, and locked the door.

The doctor did not appear.

That night in the tent, they could still hear Arabella's shouts for the doctor, as could everyone on the south side of town. But being outside, it was somewhat tolerable. Bear, once Shorty made it clear to the dog what he was to do, lay by the front flap of the tent all night long, and Tennie slept without fear, despite the strong odor coming from the corrals and privies around her.

The next morning when she checked on Arabella, she saw vomit all over the cell. Feces caused by severe dysentery spread out on the floor. Arabella's eyes were ringed in black hollows, her hair a tangled mess. She stared at Tennie.

Tennie thought Arabella would begin another tirade. Instead, she took another tack that at first puzzled Tennie.

Arabella came to the door, placing her hands around the bars as she stared at Tennie. "Tennie," she said, making her voice soft. "You know, if you brought me a bottle of laudanum, I could make you very happy."

"Miss Arabella, I can't bring you a bottle of laudanum."

"No, Tennie, no. Listen to me," Arabella said. "I know you like men; everybody in town knows you like men. But you're probably afraid to sleep with them because you're afraid of getting pregnant. That's right, isn't it?"

Tennie did not have a clue what Arabella was getting at.

"But Tennie, I know a way to make you happy where you wouldn't need a man. I could do that, Tennie. I could kiss you places that you never dreamed of that would make you feel so wonderful."

Kiss her places? Tennie stared at Arabella uncomprehendingly.

"I just need a bottle of laudanum, Tennie,"

Arabella continued. "You could help me out, and I could help you out."

Tennie recalled the kisses Wash Jones had placed on her hair and his warm breath against her cheek. She remembered the feeling it gave her inside. She looked at Arabella and recoiled. "No!" She turned and headed for the stairs.

"I need that bottle of laudanum!" Arabella screeched, pulling wildly on the bars. "I need it! I have to have it!"

Arabella screamed for laudanum off and on while Tennie cooked breakfast. She handed plates to the boys, and they took them outside to eat. Jeff knocked on their new back door.

"Come in," Tennie said. "Have you had breakfast?"

"Yes. I was going to ask you how she is, but I could hear her as I came up the street."

"I don't think she closed her eyes at all last night, either," Tennie said, and proceeded to describe the state of the cell. "I need to get in there and clean and at least try to get her to eat."

"Get the handcuffs," Jeff said. "I'll handcuff her to the other cell while you clean hers."

As they went up the stairs, Tennie said, "At least she's not as violent as she was yesterday."

"Don't let that lull you," Jeff said. "It could change in a heartbeat."

With Arabella chained to the bars on another cell, still demanding laudanum, Jeff looked out the front windows while Tennie scrubbed the cell and changed the soiled bedding.

"We're in for it now," he murmured, and Tennie turned to see what was the matter. He glanced at her from his spot by the window and shook his head.

Jeff managed to put Arabella back into the cell and get the handcuffs off, narrowly missing a kick in his groin. He helped Tennie carry her cleaning buckets down the stairs.

"What is it?" she asked.

He put the buckets down and went to the windows, staring out. "Reporters. Hanging on to every bar on the stagecoach like a passel of possums."

"Is the mayor going to talk to them?" Tennie asked, peering from around his shoulder.

He turned back. "The mayor is going to hide and let you bear the brunt. I'm sorry, Miss Tennie, but you're the one who is going to have to go out there and talk to them."

"What do I say?" Tennie said, looking at the men unloading small valises. "Wait a minute, I think that's my attorney out there. Levi Myerson."

"Lafayette sent for him," Jeff said.

Tennie turned to Jeff. "What does Lafayette plan on doing?"

Jeff gave a deep sigh. "He'll pay for her attorney. No doubt she'll get off because she's a woman. He'll give her enough money to get to

San Francisco with the promise of more waiting for her to make sure she goes there."

"San Francisco?" Tennie echoed.

"That's where she's always wanted to go, and he doesn't care," Jeff said.

Tennie sighed, too, giving a small shake of her head. If Lafayette was sending Arabella to San Francisco, he truly did not care about her. She looked out the window. "I don't want to go out there and talk to those men," she cried. "I don't know what to say!"

Jeff looked at her with sympathy. "Do it and get it over with."

Tennie took a deep breath.

"Wait a minute," Jeff said. "Put your badge on."

"Oh, for land sakes!" She went to the drawer and pulled out her unused badge, pinning it on her shoulder with trembling fingers, praying she would say the right thing.

"Now, Miss Tennie," Jeff said in mock reprimand. "Don't you start that cussing just because you have to hear it from Arabella night and day."

Tennie laughed, but tears were fighting their way to the surface. "Here goes nothing." Opening the door, she stepped over the threshold and onto the sidewalk.

CHAPTER 22

The reporters fired questions at Tennie from every side. Had she seen the murder? Where did it happen? What were Fanny's last words? Why did the saloon girl stab her and with what?

In the middle of trying to respond, Maggot Milton stomped across the road, black hat stuck belligerently on his head, his fingers resting on the six-gun in his holster. "Get these people out of here," he ordered Tennie. "I have a business to run, and I don't want the road blocked."

"Mr. Milton," Tennie said, trying to stay calm, "they have a perfect right to be here."

The reporters ignored Maggot. "When can we interview the prisoner?" one reporter demanded.

"You won't be able to interview her for a while," Tennie said, fighting to keep her voice from rising hysterically. With an effort, she lowered it. "She's not well."

They wanted to know what was wrong with her. Before Tennie could answer, a shriek was heard from upstairs. "Hot spit and hellfire! Somebody get me a bottle of laudanum! I can hear you jackasses down there. Bring me a bottle of laudanum!"

Their pencils flew across paper even faster. To Tennie's further dismay, she saw a group of the townswomen coming her way, headed by the undertaker's wife.

"Has a doctor seen her?" the reporters demanded. "Is she under a doctor's care?"

Tennie stared at the approaching women. "A doctor has seen her, yes." She didn't tell them being under a doctor's care had a great deal to do with her prisoner's present state.

The group of women reached her as Arabella continued to scream cursing demands for laudanum.

The undertaker's wife took the role as spokeswoman for the group. "Mrs. Granger, we demand you do something about that woman," she barked. "You are the town marshal, and you must do something about that screaming. It's upsetting everyone. It's bad for the children."

"I imagine the children are getting a lesson in the uses of opium they will never forget," Tennie said, biting her tongue as soon as the words left her mouth. From around her, pencils scratched hurriedly.

One reporter in the back hollered, "Are you a married woman, Marshal?"

Tennie answered, wondering what difference it made. "No, a widow."

The women swelled to a greater degree of self-righteousness, especially when Arabella's wailing grew in intensity.

"Do something!" several women demanded.

"Gag her immediately!" the undertaker's wife ordered.

"I will not gag her," Tennie said. "She is retching constantly. A gag would cause her to choke on her own vomit."

"That's just what she deserves," came the reply. "You are no better than she is."

"Don't you talk to my stepmother like that!" Lucas said.

Tennie had to grab him to keep him from kicking the undertaker's wife in the shins. She had not realized the boys were anywhere near.

"This is all Lafayette Dumont's fault!" the undertaker's wife said, looking around at the other women. Heads nodded and she continued. "He's the one who brought that jezebel here in the first place, and he's the one who encouraged no telling what goes on in that saloon."

"I don't think *encouraged* is the right word," Tennie said. "*Allowed,* yes, but not *encouraged.*"

No one paid any attention to her. The reporters were all over the undertaker's wife, wanting to know about Lafayette. She obliged by giving them an earful. Jeff slipped out of the crowd and headed for the saloon to await the onslaught. Tennie turned and herded the boys back into the jailhouse, locking the door behind them. She leaned against the door and took a deep breath.

From above their heads, Arabella shouted, "Bring me a bottle of laudanum before I tear this place apart!"

"Come on," Tennie said, ignoring her. "I'll help you work on your brush arbor. You'll just have to tell me what to do."

While Tennie helped tie a latticework of willow branches on a pole frame, three Mexican men came into the yard carrying shovels and trowels, pushing a cart filled with mud. Without asking, they began to construct something that soon took the shape of a large beehive.

Tennie got down from the ladder borrowed from Shorty and walked to the men. She didn't know Spanish, and she wondered if they knew English. When they saw her approach, one of them stopped working, raised up, took his hat off, and gave her a little bow.

Tennie smiled and pointed, raising her shoulders and opening her palms as if to ask *what is this?*

The Mexican man nodded. "*Cocinar, cocinar.*"

One of his helpers interjected. "Cook."

"Oh," Tennie nodded in understanding. "It's an oven, isn't it?"

The man in front gave her a pleasant nod whether he understood her or not. Tennie wondered what on earth possessed them to enter the jailhouse yard in the white section of town and start building an oven. A thought popped into her head, and she said, "Poco?"

"*Sí, señora*," the man said, and the other two echoed his words. "*Poco amigo*."

Tennie smiled and nodded. She tried to say thank you, and managed to remember the correct Spanish word. "*Gracias, gracias*," she said, smiling and backing away, returning to the brush arbor.

"What is it, Miss Tennie?" Rusty asked. "What are they doing here?"

"Poco sent them to build an outdoor oven. I really don't know why, except maybe he heard we were being bombarded and thought I would rather cook outside than in."

"We can make a fire ring, too!" Lucas said.

"Let's get finished with the brush arbor first," Rusty said.

Levi Myerson came around the jailhouse, wiping sweat from his forehead with a clean white handkerchief. He wore a black suit, and Tennie didn't know how he stood the heat in it. She greeted him and implored him to sit in the shade while she fetched a glass of water.

When she returned, he had taken his jacket off and was watching the boys work on the brush arbor. She handed him the glass and sat next to him.

"Your stepsons are full of energy."

"If they wanted to build a fort out here, I would

let them," she replied. "Anything to keep them occupied and out of trouble."

He finished gulping the water and handed her the glass, refusing more. "The stagecoach driver delivered the papers you sent. I could find nothing that would indicate your husband took out a loan."

"And the papers at the courthouse?" Tennie asked.

"Nothing was ever filed," Levi said. "Since Mr. Dumont sent for me, I took the liberty of killing two birds with one stone. I went to see the banker when I arrived here and confronted him. He claims it was entirely a misunderstanding on your part."

"But, there were witnesses!" Tennie said.

"None that would testify against him, I daresay. I again took a liberty and pretended to go along with him. You must keep your job here until we get your late husband's affairs settled at least, and it is better not to antagonize him too much. I will pass the information I have on him discreetly to other people who will just as discreetly look into his affairs."

Tennie nodded. "What about the ranch?"

"It is yours and your stepsons'." He again explained about her legal responsibilities. "He should have left a will, but he didn't."

"Thank you," Tennie said. "What do I owe you?"

"It's been take care of by Mr. Dumont." When Tennie started to protest, he stopped her. "He realizes his actions have caused you an enormous imposition. He's going to lose a great deal of goodwill in this town before this is over, and he is desperate to keep yours."

"He doesn't have to buy it," Tennie said. "He has been a greater friend to me than I could have dreamed of."

"Well, I'm not going to go into that," Levi said. "I was informed you took the depositions of witnesses. If you please, I'd like to read them now."

"Of course," Tennie said. "I'll fetch them."

She went into the jailhouse and returned carrying the stack of statements. Leaving them with Levi, she went back to the construction of the brush arbor, continuing to tie willow branches while giving occasional glances at the attorney.

He read through each deposition with care, taking his time, his face reposed in absorption. When he finished, he sat looking ahead with an unseeing stare, while she continued her work. Looking down for perhaps the tenth time, she caught him staring up at her as she stood atop the ladder.

"I'm ready to talk to Miss Van Buren now," he said.

"Miss Van Buren?" Tennie asked with a puzzled

frown as she stepped down from the ladder. "Who is Miss Van Buren?"

"Your prisoner," Levi said, rising. "I have no doubt that is not her real last name, but it is what she goes by."

Tennie opened the back door and pointed to the stairwell. "She's in a cell at the top of the stairs. I will wait for you outside."

The Mexican men had finished the oven and were preparing to depart. Tennie tried to ask them how she was to use it, but they just smiled and nodded their heads as they collected their tools. She gave up and smiled her thanks.

Big Mike joined her and watched the men depart.

"They built an oven for me," Tennie said, "but I'm not sure how to use it."

Mike barely gave it a glance. "Is easy. I will explain." He turned and told her how it worked.

"Mike," Tennie said, "I hope you realize you are a lot smarter than you think you are."

He stared at her. "Is more important to me you should think so," he said with a grunt and left.

The attorney stayed with Arabella almost an hour. While he remained upstairs, Tennie prepared a simple supper—but not in her new oven. She would experiment with that later. When Levi opened the back door and stepped into the yard, he patted his face again, this time with relief.

"She is," he told Tennie, "in many ways an

abnormally intelligent and cunning woman. She is also one of the most thoroughly compulsive liars I have ever run across. There were times I think she actually believed what she was saying."

"I wondered," Tennie said.

He looked at Tennie sharply. "I knew as soon as she told me you tried to make love to her."

"What?!" Tennie shook her head in disgust, thinking she should have known Arabella would twist the truth around. "What are you going to do?"

"I obviously can't put her on the witness stand. She would hang herself. We'll plead temporary insanity, and they will let her off. Especially if I can convince the jury she would leave Texas immediately."

Tennie nodded. "Yes, I heard that was Mr. Lafayette's intention, to get her out of town and out of the state."

"Yes," Levi said. "It would be easy for me to cast Lafayette Dumont as the villain in this piece, but since he is paying my salary, I will use other methods to elicit sympathy for her."

He gave Tennie a piercing stare from over his glasses. "Under no circumstances is she to have drugs of any kind. She must be completely sober when she goes on trial, or she will find herself in the Walls Unit of the Huntsville penitentiary."

Tennie nodded.

He continued. "I'm stating this as plainly as

I can. She will do anything, pull any trick, any stunt, tell any lie she can think of to get you to supply her with drugs. Stand firm no matter how sick she gets. I talked to the doctor, and he said her withdrawal symptoms should peak in about five days and hopefully be gone in ten. You can stand it that long, can't you?"

"Yes," Tennie said. "I'll have to."

"It won't mean she's cured; it will just mean the physical symptoms of withdrawal will be gone. Do not trust her. I want her delivered to the Cat Ridge jail clean and sober."

"I understand, but it's all so confusing," Tennie cried. "Will there be justice for Fanny? If Arabella is freed, will she kill again? At the same time, it's not like she ran into a church and murdered somebody."

"Welcome to my world," the attorney said. "I'm sorry you have to deal with this."

Tennie felt the burden of Arabella's future rested on her. She shut her eyes. Opening them, she said, "The sheriff wants Arabella to be sober, too. I will do everything in my power to make sure she is. What happens to her after that is not in my hands.

"And now, we would be honored if you would eat supper with us."

Surprisingly, he agreed. An even bigger one came after supper, when after removing his glasses and placing them in a case, he announced he would like to play baseball. Rusty and Lucas first stared at him with wide eyes, but ran to fetch a bat and ball. Badger and Rascal followed.

As they began playing in the field beyond the jailhouse corral, Tennie cleaned the dishes. She could hear Arabella moaning and crying her name, but she ignored her until she finished her chores.

Trudging up the stairs, she found Arabella lying on the cot, the back of her hand pressed against her forehead dramatically. "Get the doctor," she said in a weak voice. "I'm burning up with fever."

"No doubt you are feverish," Tennie said. "But I'm not getting the doctor."

Arabella jumped from the bed and hit the iron bars of her cell with her fists, beating on them and screaming. Tennie left her and went outside to watch the others play ball.

The school summer term would be over soon, but even on a school night, the town boys were ready to forget homework and play ball in the field. Tennie stayed near the back door watching the attorney playing with boys of all ages. She wondered what brought him to Texas, a Yankee in an ex-Confederate bastion, and if he felt like Mike, a stranger wherever he went.

Tennie caught glimpses of shadows peeking around the corner, but disappearing as soon as she turned to look. She had no doubt they were reporters hoping to sneak in the back way to interview the shrieking, cursing Arabella.

At dusk, the game ended. Levi returned to where Tennie sat, wiping sweat from his face with a handkerchief. "I've never played on a field so full of horse manure and holes left from hoofprints."

"Hoofprints and horse manure?" Tennie asked, puzzled. "No one keeps horses back there."

"Someone has run a lot of horses through there," he said. "And the prints all lead over there," he said, pointing to Mike's livery.

"Well, that's the stable," Tennie said, but she still wondered. She looked back to the attorney. "We can offer you a bed in the jailhouse, if you think you can stand it."

"Thank you, my dear Mrs. Granger," he said with a laugh, rising from his seat. "But Lafayette has offered me sleeping accommodations in his saloon."

That night, with the jailhouse locked tight, Bear stood up in the tent several times, hackles raised, growling. After a while, he would lie uneasily back down, but he did not leave his post until morning.

The next day, the scene in the cell upstairs was repeated. The broth Tennie had made especially for Arabella, hoping she could keep at least some of it down, was strewn all over the floor, the bowl it had been in lying upside down in the corner.

Jeff came once again to restrain her while Tennie changed the bedding and scrubbed the cell.

After breakfast, she built a fire under the wash pot outside, keeping the back door unlocked as she went back and forth into the kitchen. She praised the brush arbor, and the boys took the ladder down to return to Shorty.

Before they left, Rusty spied a billow of smoke coming from the north side of town. "I wonder what that is?" he said, pointing.

"Maybe it's just someone burning a brush pile," Tennie said. Before the words were out of her mouth two seconds, they could hear shouts coming from uptown.

"Something else must be burning!" Rusty said. "Come on," he told Lucas and Badger.

"Be careful," Tennie warned, but they were already around the corner. She went back to her wash pot, but sounds coming from the other side of the jailhouse arrested her attention.

"Help me, help me," a man's voice moaned.

Tennie cautiously made her way to the edge of the jailhouse and peered around the corner. A man was lying between the jailhouse building and the livery. He rolled over and moaned again.

Tennie hurried to his side. "What is it?" she asked, bending down.

He wore a houndstooth suit and a little derby hat, and she recognized him as one of the reporters from the day before. "Are you all right?" she asked as she tried to help him up.

"I think so," he said, rubbing the back of his neck. "Somebody coldcocked me and took my wallet."

"Just now?" Tennie asked. "I didn't hear anything."

He nodded his head.

Tennie continued to stare at him in concern. "Do you think you will be okay? Can I get you anything?" She looked around, but there was no one else in sight. "I don't think we'll be able to catch who did this to you. I'm so sorry. Usually this sort of thing happens at night in dark alleys in Ring Bit."

He shook his head, suddenly looking much better. "I'll be okay. It's nothing. They didn't get that much."

"I still feel terrible about it," Tennie said.

He brushed her concerns aside, saying he would be fine and must be going. "I'll let you get back to your washing," he said and left.

Tennie wondered how he knew she had been washing, but reasoned he must have been peeking around the corner when he got attacked from behind. It worried her the criminals in Ring Bit were getting more brazen than usual.

She went back to her wash pot, taking a long stick and stirring the soiled bedding. After several minutes, she paused, her glance returning to the corner of the jailhouse. She pivoted and looked at the drifting smoke on the other side of town. Moving her eyes from the diminishing smoke, she stared at the back door. Arabella had not screamed in some time.

She threw the stick down and went to the back door, opening it gently. Taking soft steps across the wooden floor, she could hear the sound of voices coming from up the stairs. Staying close to the wall, she again crept up the treads.

"Yes, I was a virgin when Lafayette seduced me," Arabella was saying. "I was living with my parents in a mansion in New York when he convinced me to leave and come out west with him. I could have been on Broadway. Everyone said so."

Tennie came in view of a line of reporters standing in front of Arabella's cell. Not noticing her arrival, she watched as they exchanged glances of disbelief over Arabella's tale.

One of them turned and remarked, "But Miss Van Buren, a saloon girl said Lafayette picked you up in a cathouse in New Orleans."

"She's lying!" Arabella spat out. She continued in a calmer voice. "They're jealous of me. They've always been jealous of me."

Tennie took another step up, enabling her to see Arabella. She sat at the foot of the cot in front of the men, drinking from a tin cup, her blonde hair loose and in a tangle of knotted mats. One shoulder of her dirty saloon dress had been pulled down so her breast hung out. She had raised her ruffled skirt around her waist, spreading her legs open, revealing private parts coated with dried filth.

A wave of shame went over Tennie—shame for her prisoner for exposing herself, shame for the looks of hunger mixed with disgust on the men's faces, shame because she had to witness it.

Tennie took a step forward. "Out," she said, looking at the men and pointing down the stairs.

She'd startled them, and they flinched. She repeated "Out," in a voice neither angry nor weak. They had no choice but to leave.

"Wait a minute!" Arabella said, jumping up when she realized they were going. "You promised. You promised me the bottle!"

Tennie caught sight of the bottle of laudanum one of them was trying to hide in his pocket.

He looked at her shamefaced. "We only gave her a little. We had diluted most of it with whiskey."

"Please leave now," Tennie said, too upset to say anything else.

They tramped down the stairs and out the back door, Tennie behind them, with Arabella's cries trailing at their backs. When they disappeared around the corner, Tennie sank to the earth and beat the ground with her fists.

CHAPTER 23

"Miss Tennie, Miss Tennie!" Lucas called. "Somebody set fire to the church house privy. It wasn't us, honest!"

"I know it wasn't," Tennie said, looking up.

Shorty joined the boys circling Tennie. "Tennie, what is it? What's the matter?"

She told him what happened.

"Lucas," Shorty said. "Go to the back door of the saloon and ask to speak to Jeff or Lafayette. Tell them what Tennie said."

"Yes, sir," Lucas said, glancing at Tennie before taking off for the saloon.

Lafayette responded by sending men all over town to buy every bottle of laudanum, warning merchants they could no longer expect his business if they ordered more in the near future.

"There will be a lot of surprised families when old grandma starts carrying on like Arabella," Jeff said later. "Don't feel bad, Miss Tennie. It could have happened to anyone."

The reporters must have been telling the truth about the amount of laudanum they gave

Arabella. Late that afternoon, she began piercing screams, crying for help.

They sounded real to Tennie, and she raced up the stairs to see what was the matter. Arabella stood in the middle of the cell, crying and clawing at her dress.

"They all over me, Tennie, do something!" she cried.

"What, Miss Arabella? What?" Tennie asked. She couldn't see anything.

"The worms! Can't you see them? They're all over me!"

No matter how much Tennie tried to reassure Arabella, she could not convince her there were no worms. Looking out the window, she could see a crowd of people gathering in front of the jailhouse.

"What's going on up there?" a man hollered.

A woman echoed his question. "What's the matter with her?"

"Rusty!" Tennie called down the stairs. "Go outside and bring the preacher up, please!"

"Yes, ma'am," he hollered, and unlocked the front door. In a minute, he came back in, dragging the preacher inside and locking the door behind them.

"Please, sir," Tennie called down the stairs. "Please come up here."

He mounted the stairs slowly, staring at Tennie when he reached the top.

"I want you to see for yourself what is happening to her, so you can back me up," Tennie said.

He turned and watched Arabella clawing away at her dress, scratching her skin with her nails, trying to remove the imaginary worms, all the while screaming for help.

He bowed his head and said a silent prayer then turned to Tennie. "Yes, Sister Granger, I see." He started back down the stairs with Tennie following him.

She went outside with him to face the crowd of angry faces, explained that Arabella was hallucinating, and there was nothing they could do.

"Is that true, Reverend?" a woman asked.

"Yes, sister, it's true. We must pray for that poor misguided soul."

They weren't ready to pray. They were ready to string somebody up. They looked angrily down the street at the Silver Moon.

The newspapers begin pouring in Thursday. Rusty entered the jailhouse carrying an armful. He, Tennie, and Lucas pored over them, reading parts aloud to one another. "Famed Singer Fanny Boulet Killed by Opium Fiend in Jealous Rage. Saloon Owner's Den of Vice Becomes Scene of Murder."

As the lawyer predicted, reporters found it all too easy to cast Lafayette as the villain. He was described as having "satanic raised eyebrows" and being "a cold, uncaring seducer of young women, luring them into a life of depredation and misery by ensnaring them with drugs."

Lucas looked troubled. "I don't think Mr. Lafayette lured Miss Arabella into anything."

"He didn't," Tennie said. "They are just trying to sell newspapers by making it sound even worse than it already is."

A firm knock at the door caused them to look up. Rusty opened it.

"I see you've got the news," Jeff said as he came in.

"It's not good," Tennie agreed.

Jeff picked up a newspaper and threw it back down. "The saloon is deserted. Doc and the girls lit out on the first stage this morning, one step ahead of an angry mob. You won't have to worry about where to put any other rowdy inmates tomorrow night, Miss Tennie. There won't be any."

He pulled out a chair in the corner and sat down heavily, legs stretched out. "Fanny would have been proud. She comes off as a pure, beautiful young woman who sang like a nightingale, instead of a greedy, middle-aged strumpet whose voice had begun to crack at the high notes."

"What's a strumpet?" Lucas asked.

"Shorty needs help at the station," Jeff said. "He's overrun with people leaving town to gamble in Brushwood. At least somebody is doing a brisk business."

The boys left to help Shorty and Mike. When they shut the door behind them, Tennie locked it then turned to Jeff.

"An epidemic of smallpox couldn't have emptied the Silver Moon more completely," Jeff continued. "It's amazing how self-righteous people can suddenly become."

Arabella must have heard them talking and began calling to Jeff, pleading with him to bring her the opium she had left in her room.

"She ripped her clothes into shreds yesterday," Tennie said. Like Jeff, she was trying to ignore Arabella's cries. "She's covered in filth. She needs to bathe and do something with her hair. She's so thin and weak, I don't know how she manages to stand up, but she can still fly into kicking, screaming frenzies."

Jeff rose from the chair slowly, as if he had aged twenty years in one week. "Let's go see what we can do."

When they reached the second floor, Arabella, seeing them, hit the bars in a flying leap, begging, pleading with them to send the doctor to her. Her eyes were black hollows, and drool and spittle had caused the corners of her mouth to turn red and crack. The few clothes she had not clawed away hung on her like a shirt on a broom.

"The doctor left town this morning," Jeff said.

At this news, she became like a woman possessed by a demon. She screeched and hollered; she climbed all over the bars and shook them in a rage, throwing herself on the floor and kicking in a wild tantrum.

Jeff took Tennie by the elbow, propelling her to the stairs. "Come on. There is nothing we can do with her today."

Once downstairs, he took a look out the windows. "They're already lining up out there."

Tennie walked to the window and peered out. On the street, a group of people stood listening to Arabella's begging moans, pointing fingers up at the windows from which the sound of human misery emanated.

Jeff turned to Tennie. "You don't look much better than she does. Go outside to the back and stay there the rest of the day. I'll come back this afternoon and shove another bucket of water and a plate of food in there. That's all we'll be able to do with her today."

Tennie nodded. "Thank you, Mr. Jeff. I know you can't stand Arabella, and I don't know why you are doing this, but thank you."

He squeezed her shoulder. "I'm just paying back what someone once did for my own kin," he said and left.

Tennie sank down at the table, placing her elbows on it, leaning over and rubbing her eyes with her hands. When she removed them, the newspaper headlines stared at her, reminding her of the mess she and everyone else in Ring Bit was in. She found herself longing for the Granger ranch.

Arabella's begging screams grew louder, and Tennie rose, heading for the back door.

The noon sun shone above them when Shep Davis rode his horse, a chestnut gelding with a glistening coat, around the back of the jail. Tennie and the boys had just finished dragging a table outside to put under the brush arbor.

"Hello, Mr. Davis," she called, trying to be cheerful. "Will you have dinner with us?"

He dismounted, led his horse to a clump of grass and dropped the reins, confident he would not stray far. He stomped toward Tennie, removing his hat and showing his tousled gray hair. "My God, woman!" he said in his loud voice. "You can smell bread baking ten miles out."

Tennie laughed and set an extra plate for him. "I'm sorry about the noise."

"What noise?" he asked as he sat down, surveying the food on the table.

She pointed to the jail.

"Oh that," he said. "Can't hardly hear it out here."

Tennie had spent all morning thinking about the ranch. She eyed Shep Davis as he ate, and later as he sat and talked, giving a long monologue about cattle.

Grateful for the distraction, she listened with interest and wondered how much to confide in him. She recognized his capabilities as a rancher, knew he was a kind man, and yet, there was something about Shep Davis she could not completely trust. When it came down to doing the right thing or what was best for his ranch, he would pick his ranch every time. It had a stronger hold on him than any lover.

"Honey Boy is a-feared you are angry with him," Shep said as he prepared to leave.

"Of course not. Please give Honey Boy my regards."

And that was that. Honey Boy could be the most treacherous, dangerous creature on earth when he was drunk, but when he was sober, Tennie trusted his honesty wholly. Wash Jones would give her excellent advice, but he wasn't around, and unlike Honey Boy, Wash was hiding something.

"Cattle rustling has let up for a time being," Shep said as he swung atop his horse. "I don't know why."

Tennie stroked the thick neck of Shep's horse. "Maybe whoever was doing it got religion and quit."

Shep grunted. She stepped back and waved good-bye as he left, his horse nimbly avoiding the baseball and bat on the ground.

Lucas picked them up. "Play ball with us, Miss Tennie?"

"Let me wash the dishes and put my old dress on," Tennie said, watching Shep and his horse go around the building, disappearing from view. She looked toward the jailhouse. Arabella's begging moans and yells had become a monotonous grating on her nerves.

"I liked it better when she was screaming orders," Rusty said. "All this hollering and begging is worse to have to listen to."

"Are we going to play ball or not?" Badger said.

Jeff came by later in the afternoon after school let out, and Tennie had ceased to play ball, having been superseded by better players. When they went upstairs, Arabella began screaming for help again.

Shorty waited for them downstairs. "What did she think you were today?" he asked when they returned.

"Snakes," Jeff said. "It's not the first time I've been called a snake, but it's the first time somebody really saw me as one."

Shorty shook his head, clicking his tongue and tut-tutting under his breath. "How are things in the saloon?"

"Dismal," Jeff said.

"Lafayette asked for it. He may not have promoted it, but he allowed it." Shorty turned his attention to Tennie. "Just a few more days. I hear tell the telegraph wires between Cat Ridge and

Austin have been smoking, demanding the judge return immediately."

"She's in no shape to stand trial now, anyway," Tennie said, dropping wearily into a chair.

"It won't last forever," Shorty said. "You'll be shut of her soon enough. But I do have bad news. You're going to have to be the one to take her to Cat Ridge."

"What?" Tennie said, bolting upright in the chair. "That lazy good-for-nothing sheriff can't come get her? And what about the deputy marshal? Is he afraid she might mess up his big moustache or something?"

"Tennie! Calm down," Shorty barked. "Be realistic. She's a woman even if she is a whore. What man is going to want to have to deal with a woman prisoner's needs on a long trip?"

"Well, I don't want to have to deal with them!" Tennie cried, and she began to weep.

Jeff took her elbow and propelled her up. "Get outside and stay outside like I told you," he said, exchanging glances with Shorty.

Arabella's screams, retching, dysentery, tremors, and hallucinations peaked Thursday night, and by Friday evening she was down to just lying on the bed, making regular, heart-wrenching pleas for someone to please give her the drug she craved.

Tennie locked the jailhouse and went with the boys to Shorty's, where they played dominoes

360

and cards without interruptions. Some of the smaller saloons had a few customers; the Silver Moon had none. Everyone else was staying home or had fled to Brushwood. There were a few saloons in Cat Ridge, but they were so sedate, the cowboys referred to them as "the old folks' watering holes."

Saturday morning, Tennie sat under the brush arbor shelling peas the Paytons had sent by one of their cowhands. Looking up, she saw Honey Boy riding his sleek grulla around the corner. He dismounted and removed his hat, his blond head gleaming, set off by the soft blue gray of the horse. Tennie greeted him, commenting on the horse's unusual markings, a dorsal stripe down the back and black barring around the lower legs. He blushed with pleasure at the compliment while Tennie bade him to sit down.

Badger, having lost some of his fear of Honey Boy, brought him Rascal to admire.

"That's a mighty fine-looking dog you got there," Honey Boy said. "I hope you are taking good care of him."

"I'm just worried the dog might become crippled," Tennie laughed. "Badger carries him around so much."

"He can run," Badger said. "Let me show you how fast he can run."

"All right," Tennie said with a smile. "You run over yonder and we'll watch. But leave me and

361

Mr. Honey Boy alone for a while. We have some business to talk about."

"Okay. But watch, okay?" Badger said.

"I promise," Tennie said.

They kept their eyes on the boy and dog as they said they would.

"What did you want to talk about, Miss Tennie?" Honey Boy asked.

She placed her bowl of peas on the table. "I guess you heard the bank president is saying I'm just a silly mixed-up female, and he never said he was repossessing the Granger ranch."

Honey Boy nodded. "It's not lost on anybody he started saying it after you sicced a lawyer on him. Winn Payton went over there and cussed him out and said if he heard of one more irregularity, he was running him out of town."

"Mr. Payton isn't afraid of the devil," Tennie said. "I don't know if that's a good thing or a bad thing. Anyway, I need some advice about what to do with the ranch. We can't live out there the way it is now; it's falling down, and I don't know anything about cattle or horses or ranching."

Honey Boy paused before asking, "Why didn't you bring this up with Shep when he was here?"

"Because I'm bringing it up with you now."

Honey Boy leaned forward, elbows resting on his heavy thighs, twirling his hat in his hands. "Somebody's been staying out there off and on, doing a little work here and there."

"What?" Tennie exclaimed.

He nodded. "Nothing major, just fixing a board or two."

Tennie immediately thought of Wash Jones and his men.

"Rusty's been out there, too," Honey Boy said.

"Rusty? Have you seen him?"

"No, but I ride over there every so often to keep an eye on things. Rusty's buckskin has a unique overstep; I know because I broke and trained him. I'd recognize those hoofprints anywhere. A year or so ago, Ashton came out to the ranch to sew up one of Shep's favorite horses that had tangled with a bobcat. He wouldn't take no pay; he said he just wanted to buy a horse, and he picked the buckskin. He's a good daisy clipper, and I sure hated to let him go, but Shep felt obliged to Ashton, so he let him have the horse."

Tennie only half listened to his explanation. Her mind was racing in other directions.

"Don't fuss at him, Miss Tennie," Honey Boy advised, as if he had read everything she was thinking. "Some young'uns you have to watch over careful, like that one over yonder." He pointed at Badger, who was playing chase with Rascal. "Others, like Rusty, you can trust to find the right way."

"Have you seen any signs of cattle rustling there?" Tennie asked, fearful of the answer.

He shook his head. "Shep wants me to fire

Two-Bit. He's got this idea in his head I ain't never gonna get drunk again, so why keep Two-Bit around? I'll talk to Shep about leasing your place to run cattle with the idea of sending Two-Bit over there to do repairs as part of the deal. I'll have to iron out the particulars with Shep."

Tennie nodded. "That sounds fair."

"I'll have to tell him I'm the one who brung it up, or his feelings will be hurt you didn't come to him first off."

Tennie agreed, and they sat talking for a good while longer. She wanted him to remain for supper, but he shook his head. "I don't even want to be near town come sundown. I don't want to be tempted."

That night, they played five-card draw with Shorty.

Things were so quiet at the Silver Moon, Jeff joined their game.

"I saw you had a visit from Honey Boy. Give me two cards."

"That's right," Tennie said. "He's going to work something out with Shep to lease the ranch until Rusty can take over. If he wants to, that is." She looked at Rusty. "Maybe you want to be a doctor like your pa was."

Rusty shrugged. "I don't know."

"I want to be a businessman," Lucas said. "I'm going to be a businessman like Mr. Lafayette."

Shorty scowled. "Let's hope you're not as

364

prone to get embroiled in trouble as he is. Tennie, are you going to take any cards or not?"

"One. One," she said.

Shorty didn't like any fooling around when playing games.

"Honey Boy said he trained the buckskin you have, Rusty. That Shep sold him to your pa." Tennie discarded one card and took the one Shorty dealt her. She didn't glance at it. She looked at Rusty. "He said the buckskin has a distinctive way of making tracks. If you were to get into trouble while riding that horse, it'd be mighty easy for someone recognize it was you."

In the pale light the lantern threw, Rusty blushed. "I'm not getting into any trouble, Miss Tennie," he said, looking down at his cards. "I promise."

CHAPTER 24

On Sunday, Tennie tried to get Arabella to clean herself, but she threw the soap at her. Tennie had been expecting it and dodged in time. For the umpteenth time, Arabella told her and Jeff they weren't human. In between the insults, she spewed degrading, sniveling, begging pleas for them to satisfy her cravings. She wanted to know if Lafayette was going to give her money.

"If the high-priced lawyer Lafayette is paying for gets you off," Jeff said, "there will be money waiting for you in San Francisco."

"That will make both of you happy," Arabella yelled. "To be rid of me."

Tennie and Jeff looked at one another. "Yes," they both said at once.

"Arabella," Jeff said. "The whole dag-blasted town wishes you were dead."

She picked up the plate of food they had brought her and threw it at them. "I'm sick of your orphanage slop," she told Tennie. "You tell Lafayette to have Joe Lee make me something fit to eat and bring it over here."

Unable to control it, Tennie felt blood rushing

to her face. Her biggest pride was she thought she had risen above orphanage food and had learned to cook like the best home cooks of the South. Of all the insults, this one hurt the most because she was secretly afraid it was true.

"I haven't seen Mr. Lafayette since you've been in here," she managed to say evenly.

"Then you tell him, Jeff," Arabella said. "I can't stand this hog swill."

Jeff and Tennie left her to her pacing and walked down the stairs.

"Joe Lee has abandoned ship, too," Jeff said when they reached the foot of the stairs.

"Oh, no."

"Everyone in town is treating Lafayette like he has leprosy," Jeff said, his mouth grim. "All because of that . . ." He jerked his thumb upward.

On Monday morning, Tennie dressed with care, pinned her hair up and put on the only hat she owned. Taking a deep breath, she walked outside, locking the door behind her. From across the street, Maggot Milton scowled even more furiously at her. She was almost overcome with the desire to stick out her tongue at him, but managed to control herself.

Shorty, sweeping the sidewalk, paused to peer at her. "Tennie, where are you going?"

"To the saloon. I have business with Mr. Lafayette."

Shorty opened his mouth, but shut it without

speaking. As Tennie walked past, she had the feeling his eyes were following her.

It wasn't just his eyes, and it wasn't her imagination. She had not been away from the jail for days, and people paused to stop and gawk at her, watching her progress.

She paused in front of the swinging doors of the Silver Moon and looked in. The glass chandelier still hung; the wallpaper was just as flocked, the velvet curtains separating private booths looked just as expensive. The room appeared empty except for a bald, mustached bartender polishing glasses with a white cloth and a listless attitude. He caught sight of Tennie and stared.

She pushed the doors open. "Could I have a word with Mr. Lafayette, please?" she asked, noticing for the first time a gigantic painting of an indolent nude behind the bartender's bald head. Her eyes widened, but she caught the bartender's finger pointing up the stairs.

"He's in his office. First door on the right."

"Thank you." She made her way past deserted tables and chairs. Climbing the stairs, she swallowed hard, feeling uncomfortable and out of place. When she reached the landing, she looked downstairs. The bartender was watching her. He gave a nod of his head, and she turned to the door on the right and knocked on it.

"Come in," said a weary voice from inside.

She opened the door. Across the room was a

massive desk, and behind it, an impenetrable looking black safe with gold trim. The same flocked red wallpaper, the same tasseled gold curtains hung in his office. Lafayette sat in a solid oak chair behind his desk, and Tennie did not know who was more surprised, Lafayette or herself.

His appearance shocked her. Suave and well dressed as ever, he had lost even more weight. His eyes were ringed with dark circles and deep lines radiated from them. The grooves around his mouth had deepened as if in great sorrow.

He jumped from the chair and came around the desk, taking her hands in his. "My dear Miss Tennie, this is an unexpected honor." He kissed her hands.

She smiled. "You are always so kind."

He returned her smile. "Come over here and sit down." He led her to an alcove containing two massive chairs carved in ornate wood, the chair padding covered in plush velvet.

She sat down on the edge of one, while he drew another closer to her before sitting down. He stared at her for several seconds, as if satisfied just at looking at her.

"I know you didn't come here just for a visit. What is it I can do for you?"

Tennie hated to spoil his mood. "I came to see if I could collect some of Miss Arabella's clothes. She has destroyed the ones she was wearing when she came to the jail. She's going to need some clothes for her trial."

He leaned back in the chair, closing his eyes and sighing. "The girls stole all the dresses when they left, including Fanny's." He thought for a moment before speaking again.

"Arabella had gone to her dressmaker for a final fitting the day before the murder. You can fetch it and have it put it on my bill. But you'll have to ask the seamstress to untart it first. Myerson left instructions Arabella was to appear in court as decorous as possible—an impossible feat, I fear." He stared at Tennie. "She has done to me what she always threatened she would do if I tried to get rid of her."

"It is my fault for not being more vigilant in keeping reporters away from her," Tennie said.

"Dear sweet Tennie," Lafayette said. "She would have screamed it from the windows of the jailhouse anyway. It was a stupid plan to bring Fanny here, hoping she could humiliate Arabella into leaving in a huff. Jeff tried to warn me, but I wouldn't listen."

"That's water under the bridge," Tennie said. "And people will get over this and move on to something else. The bright lights of the Silver Moon will shine again."

He smiled. "So speaks my honest little Puritan who finds comfort in hard work and thrift. I'm sorry I put you and Jeff through this. Jeff is worrying himself sick you are not going to be able to hold up and will collapse. He has no idea what a tough little fighter you are at heart."

"Thank you." Tennie smiled. "I think," she added with a laugh. She rose to go. "Will you escort me down the stairs and to the door?"

He paused and stared at her. He smiled and, for a brief second, Tennie thought she saw signs of tears in his eyes, but she brushed it aside. Lafayette never showed deep feelings.

He rose and held out his arm. "Of course."

She took his arm and together they walked down the stairs. She chatted and told him of Lucas's desire to become a businessman. "I hope he has not been overly influenced by the painting of the lady above the bar."

Lafayette laughed. "He can't see it from the back door. The chandelier, maybe." He walked her to the swinging doors.

Tennie became aware that a bevy of outwardly uninterested and apathetic cowboys had placed themselves on the sidewalk near the door.

"Good-bye, Mr. Lafayette," Tennie said. "Thank you again."

He kissed her hand once more. "It has been my pleasure." He held the door open for her, and they exchanged grins as Tennie passed.

She walked across the street and farther north to the dressmaker's shop. Looking into the window, she saw the undertaker's wife inside. She gave an inward groan, wondering if she should return to the jailhouse and come back later. She wouldn't receive the same welcome she got at the Silver Moon, but on impulse she went inside anyway.

A bell above the door tinkled, and both women turned to stare at her, their conversation stopping in midsentence.

Tennie took a step forward to the small, middle-aged seamstress. "Excuse me, ma'am," Tennie said in a voice so low she had to clear her throat and try to speak louder. "Excuse me, but Mr. Lafayette said Miss Arabella might have a dress here waiting."

Tennie had not counted on the curiosity of the dressmaker, who knew Arabella well. The undertaker's wife listened with tight lips to the probing of the seamstress. Tennie did not want to say much for fear every word she spoke would be repeated to reporters who would twist her statements to suit a sensationalist demanding public.

"The attorney wants Miss Arabella to appear, uh, er, sedate," Tennie said, stumbling over her words. "So, before I take the dress, could you make sure it looks"—she searched for the right word—"*modest.*"

"The reporters said Miss Arabella was in terrible condition," the seamstress said. "Dirty, disheveled, her clothes in a state."

Tennie pressed her lips momentarily together. "She hallucinates and becomes so violent, we haven't been able to keep her presentable. But she is getting better. Tomorrow, with Mr. Jeff's help, I'm going to try to wash her hair and bathe her."

"You'll have to chain her up," the undertaker's wife said.

Tennie nodded, afraid to say the word *yes* lest reporters heard about it and made it sound like they were mistreating Arabella. "Do what you can and leave the rest to God," Tennie murmured.

"What was that?" the undertaker's wife said.

Tennie blushed. "Oh, that was just something Papa used to say. I had forgotten all about it until now."

"Is Mr. Dumont planning on taking Arabella back at the Silver Moon if she gets acquitted?" the dressmaker asked with a sort of discreet frankness.

Tennie felt sorry for her in a way. She had lost her best customers, but she had to walk a fine line with her remaining clients, too.

Taking a deep breath, Tennie answered. "It is my understanding Mr. Lafayette is purchasing a one-way ticket for Miss Arabella to leave for San Francisco, with money waiting for her to make sure she arrives there."

The dressmaker and the undertaker's wife exchanged glances.

"I'll deliver the dress tomorrow," the dressmaker said.

"If you have any undergarments, chemises, and petticoats that would fit her, please send them along, too," Tennie said. "She has destroyed almost every stitch she had on."

"And shoes?" the older lady asked. "What about a hat?"

"She doesn't need shoes. She threw hers at us, and we took them downstairs to keep until she needed them," Tennie said. "She will need a hat. I think when those other women left town, they took everything."

"Humph," the undertaker's wife said with a snort. "Murders some woman and gets a new dress, a new hat, and a trip to San Francisco out of it."

Tennie made as quick of an escape as she could, and once outside, took a deep breath, hoping she had said nothing imprudent. She dreaded the thought of bathing an unwilling Arabella.

Back at the jail, she pushed buckets of warm water and soap through the door Big Mike had made, begging Arabella to wash. But the more she pleaded, the more Arabella shrugged it off.

"Bring me something to read," Arabella said. "I'm about to go crazy in here."

Tennie paused, wondering if she should let Arabella see the newspapers.

Arabella became impatient with her. "Look, I know you and those brats read to one another at night. Bring me what you are reading."

"All right," Tennie nodded, relieved Arabella had ceased her relentless pleas and screams. She went downstairs to fetch the book Shorty had loaned them, but she paused, reluctant to take it upstairs. Undecisive, she stood holding it.

"Tennie! Are you going to bring me that book or not?" Arabella shouted. "I'm bored to tears up here!"

Tennie took the book up the stairs and handed it through the bars to Arabella. She grabbed it and turned away. Tennie wanted to beseech her again to please bathe, but with a sigh, she turned and went back down the stairs.

Taking her broom for the first time in over a week, she walked out the front door and began to sweep the sidewalk. Big Mike saw her and joined her, and together they sat on a bench.

"Quieter today," Mike said.

Tennie nodded. "I'll have to ride the stage with her to Cat Ridge," she said, dreading it with all her heart.

"I help with boys. I keep watch on them."

"Thank you, Mike. You've been a true friend to us."

"It's nothing."

She stayed outside with him a long time. Other cowboys gathered around, but no one had the heart to say more than a few words. Down the street, she could see a few cowboys drifting into the Silver Moon.

When Tennie did go back inside, something on the ceiling caught her eye, and she glanced upward. Arabella must have kicked over the buckets; the plaster was wet. With another heavy sigh, Tennie grabbed a mop and began up the stairs. When she reached the top, she saw she had been right, water had been splashed everywhere.

Arabella lay on the cot. When she saw Tennie, she rose and came to the bars. "Here"—she held out the book—"I changed my mind. I don't want to read it after all."

Tennie took the book and stared at it. Arabella had defecated between the pages. Blinking back tears, Tennie placed the book on the window ledge and began to mop up water, while Arabella flounced back to her cot, a sardonic smile twisting across her face.

When Jeff came the next morning, Tennie explained about the water buckets. "We have to get her cleaned up before she can go to Cat Ridge."

A knock came at the door, and a voice called out, "It's me, Shorty."

Tennie unlocked the door to let him in. She was reluctant to tell him about the book and put it off.

"I think the judge finally got on the road and should arrive in Cat Ridge today," Shorty said.

They discussed whether or not Arabella was capable of traveling.

"Let's put her on the stage coming in from

El Paso tomorrow," Jeff said. "Can you keep the reporters from riding with us?"

"Are you going?" Shorty asked.

"I'm not letting Tennie go alone with her. She's over seeing frogs on the ceiling, but she's too unpredictable. We'll have to chain her up just to wash the dung off her."

"Listen," Shorty said. "The army has had so much trouble with bandits, they are sending a special stagecoach through here at daybreak. No one is supposed to know about it. I can hustle the three of you on it before anyone in town is even awake."

Another knock came at the door, and they looked at one another. Tennie went to the door, unlocked it, holding it part of the way open. When she saw who stood in front of the threshold, she opened it wider. "Yes, ma'am?" she asked the undertaker's wife.

CHAPTER 25

"I am here to do my Christian duty," the undertaker's wife said. "You said yesterday you were going to have to bathe your prisoner today, and I am here to assist you." Her lips made a grim line across her face, and she looked like the last thing on earth she wanted to do was to wash Arabella, but her jaw was set in determination.

She started inside the jail, and Tennie, flabbergasted, stood aside to let her in.

Jeff and Shorty stood looking as surprised as Tennie.

"Have you chained her up yet, Jeff Hamilton?" asked the undertaker's wife. "Mrs. Granger and myself do not wish to be assaulted."

Jeff opened his mouth and closed it before answering. "I'll do it now."

"I'll get some warm water from the kitchen," Tennie said, throwing the undertaker's wife a look of bewilderment before fleeing for the kitchen.

"It's going to take a lot of water," the older woman warned Jeff.

When the two women reached the top of the

stairs, Jeff had Arabella standing, hands and feet shackled to the bars. She was tugging on her restraints and cursing Jeff.

When she turned her head to see Tennie and the undertaker's wife, she cried in a loud voice, "Oh my God! It's the Sunday school brigade."

Jeff brought up more buckets of water. Tennie stood helpless, not sure where to begin.

The undertaker's wife gave Jeff a hard look. "We will call you when we need you, Mr. Hamilton," she said, dismissing him.

"Yes, ma'am," Jeff said, nodding his head and backing up. He turned and fled down the stairs.

"We'll have to cut her clothes and peel them off." She took the scissors from Tennie's hands and began to snip away most of what was left of Arabella's clothes. When they began to strip the remaining fabric sticking to her skin with vomit, dried urine, and feces, Arabella howled and accused them of trying to rip her hide off.

The undertaker's wife worked with sure, swift fingers, ignoring Arabella's wails. "You wash her hair, and I'll do the rest of her," she told Tennie. "I've had much more experience changing dirty diapers and cleaning up after bedridden old folks."

Tennie nodded and began the ordeal. Arabella squirmed and tossed her head, in every way making their job more difficult. Tennie narrowly escaped getting bitten. In between times, Arabella cursed and accused them of "getting off" by feeling her.

Tennie didn't understand what she was talking about; she only knew it was the most distasteful job she had ever done in her life.

"You think you're so high and mighty," Arabella shrieked at the undertaker's wife. "Your husband has put his pecker in every whore in the Silver Moon."

As she continued to elaborate on that theme, Tennie, embarrassed, stole nervous glances at the undertaker's wife. But other than a compression of her lips and widening of her nostrils, she did not respond to the jeers and continued to scrub Arabella with lye soap.

"Don't listen to her," Tennie finally said after a particularly vivid description of the pleasures the undertaker had supposedly engaged in. "When her lips are moving, she's lying."

This brought no response from the undertaker's wife, but Tennie received another tongue-lashing.

"If you think you're going to get rid of me and have Lafayette all to yourself, you stupid cow, well, you're wrong. Lafayette would never be satisfied with somebody whose main goal in life is to make good biscuits and probably hasn't seen her own body naked since she was five. He's going to join me in San Francisco, and we're going to live it up. I can do things to Lafayette to make him happy that you wouldn't do in your wildest dreams."

Tennie had to bite her tongue to keep from pointing out just how miserable Arabella had made Lafayette. Instead she looked at the undertaker's wife. "I can't get all the soap out of her hair."

"Pour a bucket of water over her head," she said.

Tennie nodded. "Stand back."

Water went everywhere, all over her, all over the floor, but it got the soap out of Arabella's hair.

The undertaker's wife finished washing and rinsing the soap from Arabella and began to help Tennie comb out her hair. They had to cut many of the tangles out, they were so knotted. All the while, Arabella screamed, calling them obscene names and telling them how much she hated them.

Afterward came the task of mopping the floor and changing the bedding.

"There's no way we can get this gown on her with her chained to the bars," Tennie said.

"We'll wrap her in a sheet and place the gown on her bed," the undertaker's wife said. "She can put it on herself."

"Where's my clothes!" Arabella demanded as they wrapped the sheet around her. "I want my dresses from the saloon!"

"Your friends took them all when they left,"

Tennie said. "When it's time to leave for Cat Ridge, you can put on a new dress the seamstress made for you."

"Mr. Hamilton!" the undertaker's wife called. "We are ready for you."

The women vacated the cell, removing their buckets, rags, what was left of Arabella's clothes, and the soiled bedding.

Jeff climbed the stairs. He went into the cell and unshackled Arabella's feet, throwing the shackles out of the cell. He unlocked the handcuffs and got out as quick as he could, slamming the door and locking it.

Arabella ripped off the sheet and stood sneering in her nakedness.

The undertaker's wife shook her head. "Shameless hussy," she murmured.

"I've seen it all before, Arabella," Jeff said. "And I'm not impressed. Here, let me help you ladies with those buckets."

As they walked down the stairs, Arabella screamed Jeff was some kind of mother, but nobody paid notice.

Tennie followed the undertaker's wife to the front door. "Thank you," she said, brushing tears from her eyes.

The undertaker's wife paused to stare at her. "I know you probably hate me, Mrs. Granger, but I had a brother who turned outlaw and died in the Missouri State Penitentiary. I lay awake at night worrying my boys are going to follow in his footsteps. I panic thinking about some worthless man seducing my girl, causing me to have a grandchild to raise and a daughter with a reputation ruined. If I'm hard and merciless, it's because I'm fighting to keep evil away from my children.

"We all have our own row to hoe," she said. "You have yours, and I have mine."

Tennie nodded. The undertaker's wife turned and walked away.

Tennie shut the door and put her forehead against it.

"What is it?" Jeff asked.

She turned to him. "Life isn't all black and white, is it, Mr. Jeff?"

"That's the reason God gave us a heart and a brain, sis. So we'd use both of them." He looked out the window at the retreating back of the undertaker's wife. "He must have given her a hell of an epiphany to get her over here."

"No questions. Just gratitude," Tennie said, plopping down in a chair and shutting her eyes. Arabella began yelling she wasn't about to put on the horrible shift Tennie made; it wasn't fit for a pig.

Tennie gave a sigh.

Jeff put his hands on her shoulder and squeezed it. "Come on. Let's empty these buckets."

After that task was finished, Jeff left, but

returned that afternoon for another meeting with Tennie and Shorty under the brush arbor.

"The company has their best driver on the coach, but they're having problems finding someone to ride shotgun," Shorty said.

"How much trouble are you expecting?" Jeff asked. "Is it going to be safe, having two women in a stagecoach loaded with payroll money?"

"They will be safer in that stagecoach than they will be in a wagon where any crackpot can try to capture them for ransom," Shorty said. "Nobody knows about this shipment except the army and a handful of men who have been employed by the company for years. It's taking an entirely different route to begin with.

"Besides," he said. "I've decided I'll be riding shotgun on this stretch. Rusty agreed to look after the station until I get back."

Tennie opened her mouth, but Shorty cut her off before she could speak. "He knows what to do. He and the boys will lock themselves in with Bear at night and be just as safe there as here."

"Tennie, you'd better pack a bag," Jeff said. "They may want you for the trial."

"But, but . . ." Tennie said.

"Rusty and Big Mike will look after the boys, and you know Lafayette will have men keeping an eye on them," Jeff said. "And you need to rest this afternoon. I know when you get worried, you start cooking the house down, but let those boys

385

fend for themselves for a while. It won't hurt them, and they will appreciate you that much more when you get back."

Tennie sat forward with one hand over her eyebrow, shutting her eyes, realizing it was just something she was going to have to live through.

She turned and looked at Rusty, who had been standing nearby, listening. "Can you handle that?"

"Yes, ma'am," he said.

Jeff knocked on the jailhouse door at three-thirty in the morning. Tennie was waiting for him with the clothes the seamstress had brought the day before. Together, they mounted the stairs, Jeff carrying a lantern.

"Wake up, Arabella," Jeff said, hanging the lantern on a hook. "We're headed for Cat Ridge."

She rose naked from the bed and stared at them with wide eyes.

"If you hit Tennie or rip these clothes, I'm going to knock you to kingdom come, do you understand me, woman?" Jeff unlocked the door and let Tennie enter, clothes in hand, while he kept his eyes on Arabella.

Arabella seemed to be digesting for the first time she really was going to stand trial for murder. She grasped Tennie's shoulders in fright. "They're going to hang me, Tennie! Don't let them hang me!" she cried.

"They're not going to hang you," Tennie

386

replied with a calmness born of weariness. "You have witnesses who will swear Fanny was provoking you, and your attorney will plead temporary insanity. Because you are a beautiful young woman, an all-male jury will latch on to any excuse to let you go."

"Do you really think so, Tennie?"

"Of course, I do. Now put your clothes on. A lot of people there will be looking at you."

"That's right," Arabella said as if realizing that, too, for the first time. She grabbed the clothes Tennie had brought. "Well don't just stand there. Help me."

Tennie assisted her, looking past Arabella to exchange glances with Jeff. The skirt and jacket were solid dark blue, with a white blouse that buttoned under the chin. It had a sedate jabot, and the matching hat held no feathers, only one ribbon tied around the band. Once the clothes and shoes were on, Jeff handcuffed Arabella's wrists together.

He pulled his kerchief from around his neck. "I'm gagging you until we get out of town. We have to leave as quietly as possible, and I can't take the risk of you suddenly squawking."

She didn't like it. Since her hands were bound, she shot a dirty look at him. Taking the lantern in one hand, he escorted her down the stairs with the other while Tennie followed.

Outside, Tennie gave her stepsons brief hugs.

Shorty held the stagecoach door open. Packer Jack sat up high, holding the reins in his hands. Arabella climbed in, sitting behind the driver's seat.

Jeff pulled her unceremoniously away and shoved her in the seat across from it. "That's Tennie's seat," he said in a quiet voice.

Tennie started to protest it didn't matter, but she remained silent and climbed in. Jeff got in and sat beside her, while Shorty shut the door. He climbed on top, and without a word, with only the cracking of the reins, they left Ring Bit before dawn.

They rode in silence, and it was only after going several miles that Jeff leaned over and removed the gag from Arabella's mouth. She shook her head in anger, but to their surprise, said nothing.

Despite the darkness, Tennie saw they were riding in one of the company's older models. The seats still had padding, but not the plush red tufting the newer ones sported. She didn't know where the money was hidden. She shut her eyes, and the rocking motion of the stagecoach soon had her asleep.

She opened her eyes to daylight reflecting speckles of dust on the seat. Arabella sat across from her, nodding in sleep. Tennie looked beside her to Jeff. He was awake, but his eyes had dark rings around them.

"Where'd you get that dress?" Jeff murmured.

Tennie looked down at the blue dress she wore. "A friend of the man who was shot, the one we took care of at the ranch, had Rusty go to town and buy the material for me," Tennie said, likewise keeping her voice low. "He didn't want me to take the marshal job, and I guess he hoped by encouraging me to dress as feminine as I could, he could save me from being shot at."

Jeff nodded. "It worked with Harden Kane, but it upset the women of the town that you came into Ring Bit with a new pair of shoes and three new dresses. Most women only own two, an old one for every day and another for church and funerals."

"I'm sure that didn't dawn on him. If they had seen me in the dress I came out here in, they wouldn't have wondered if I was a gold-digging hussy."

"A lot of them were in love with Ashton Granger," Jeff said. "Just hoping their husbands would pop off so they could have a chance with Ashton, even if he did have a herd of troublesome colts."

"I was lucky," Tennie said. "He was a kind man."

"Winn Payton wouldn't have put you with anyone but," Jeff said.

They exchanged smiles.

Tennie leaned closer. "Did Lafayette really kill one of his own brothers?"

Jeff, looking at Arabella, nodded. "I wasn't around him then, but he told me about it. He and the brother's wife had fallen more into lust than love, and the brother challenged him to a duel. Lafayette had every intention of letting his shot go wild, but at the last second, he realized his older brother was intent on killing him. He said it wasn't a day for perishing, so he fired hoping to wound him, but instead he accidentally killed him. That's when his life there ended."

"So, he roamed until he ended up in Ring Bit?" Tennie asked.

"That's right."

"Mr. Payton said he was surprised her family hadn't come after him since he had ruined her."

"That's a crock," Jeff said, giving a gentle snort. "She ruined herself. But don't think he hasn't been looking over his shoulder for the past seven or eight years."

Tennie glanced at Arabella. "Too bad he's so prone to getting mixed up with the wrong women."

Arabella woke up and gave them a cross look. "What are you two talking about?"

"Nothing. Go back to sleep," Jeff said.

But Arabella did not go back to sleep. She squirmed. She complained about the handcuffs. She was thirsty. "I have to pee," she announced. "Make them stop this coach."

Jeff drew a deep breath, but hung his head out the window. "Packer, find a place to stop for the ladies, will ya?"

"I heard," Packer yelled. "She can hold it till we get to the big tree."

They rode for another fifteen minutes, with Arabella grimacing at every bump they hit. She leaned closer to the window on her side and shouted, "Are you aiming for every rock and pothole in the road?"

Packer didn't answer, but reined the horses to a stop. Shorty dropped from the coach and opened the door.

"About time," Arabella said when he helped her down.

Tennie stepped down after Arabella and looked around. They were in the middle of a flat plain, the only object in sight a large oak tree with a five-foot circumference. She looked at Jeff and Shorty.

"It's the safest place to stop," Shorty explained.

"Come on, Arabella," Tennie said.

Once they finished and started back, Arabella stumbled. Tennie caught her and helped her upright.

Arabella stared at her. "Do you know what my real name is, Tennie?" she asked, her voice serious, and for the first time, devoid of all pretenses.

"No," Tennie said, shaking her head.

"My real name is Essie. Essie Mae."

Tennie stood silent for several seconds then said, "There was never really anything wrong with the name Essie Mae."

"Tennie," Arabella said, her eyes filling with tears. "Promise me they aren't going to hang me."

"They're not going to hang you," Tennie said.

The men began to call to them and urged them to hurry.

Once back in the stagecoach, Tennie hoped Arabella's mood of honesty and reflection would hold, but it soon vanished.

After an hour of riding, her complaints became almost nonstop. She complained the stagecoach was dirty and rough. She complained her new dress and hat were too plain. The petticoat she had on itched. She complained because Tennie didn't complain.

"You're not human, you know that? You kowtow to all those old men, doing everything they say when you should be out chasing every young buck in this county. Did you have a funny uncle or something? Are you searching for some old man with one foot in the grave? Oh, wait a minute, you already had that," Arabella said with a roll of her eyes.

Tennie blushed, looked out the window, and said nothing.

"Arabella," Jeff said. "That's enough of that."

She started in on Jeff, calling him a dirty old

man among other things. In a sudden shift, she demanded something to eat. "I'm hungry."

Tennie reached into a poke bag and pulled out a biscuit with a slice of ham in the middle. She handed one to Arabella and another to Jeff.

Arabella took one bite, spit it on the floor and threw the biscuit out the window. "I don't want this slop. Why didn't Lafayette have Joe Lee bring me something? You didn't tell him, did you?"

"Joe Lee's gone," Jeff said. "He liked his opium pipe as much as you liked yours, and he left with the doctor."

"God, I wish I had one right now," Arabella said. "It would ease the torture of having to sit here with your disapproving faces staring at me. Judge and jury, right in front of me."

She settled back in the seat. Filled with moody anger, she stared at them. Tennie said nothing, and Jeff, too, refused to comment. Their forbearance only increased her dissatisfaction with them.

"Tennie," she spoke, but watched Jeff in spiteful glee. "Do you know why Jeff came to Texas with Lafayette?"

Tennie did not answer because she knew she was going to hear why anyway.

"Because Jeff came home one day and found his wife's legs wrapped around a nigger. A big, ugly, black, blue-gummed nigger."

"Arabella, don't talk that way," Tennie murmured, knowing even as the words left her mouth they were useless. She glanced at Jeff.

He and Arabella were holding a staring match.

"She wanted a dumb, stinking niggerman's dick inside of her snatch instead of Jeff's little pecker," Arabella mocked. "He killed them both, right then and there, and took off. He started running and ran into Lafayette, and that's why he's in Texas. He can't never go back to the Old South again."

Jeff continued to stare at Arabella. He did not move, but Tennie glanced at the pistol in the gun belt he wore.

"I don't believe Lafayette told you that story, Arabella," Tennie said. "And from what I've heard, killing a spouse when you catch them with another person is not any more of a crime in North Carolina than it is in Texas."

"It is if the woman was the sheriff's daughter, and he hid that niggerman's body so deep in the woods bloodhounds couldn't find it," Arabella said.

"And Lafayette?" Tennie pressed, ready to call her down if she insisted Lafayette had repeated it.

"I heard it straight from the mouth of a man who knew Jeff in North Carolina," Arabella said with a toss of her head. But she glared at Jeff, before returning her gaze to Tennie.

"Didn't you wonder why Lafayette and every other man in Ring Bit never said nothing about Jeff being around you so much?" Arabella asked. "Because they know his pecker died the day he caught his old lady in a clinch with every white man's nightmare."

From the corner of her eye, Tennie saw a finger on Jeff's hand move. "Can't you find something more interesting to talk about, Arabella?" she asked as if bored. "Like how many men were in love with you in New Orleans, for instance."

Before Arabella answered, they heard a series of strange cries. She looked out the window and screamed, "Indians!"

CHAPTER 26

Packer Jack cracked his whip and urged the horses forward. The stagecoach gave a shuddering lurch. Arabella fell to the floor of the coach, but Jeff jerked her back on the seat. The horses picked up speed while the stagecoach rocked crazily.

Taking Tennie's arm, he pushed her to the floor. "Stay down there!" he hollered, pulling the pistol from his gun belt at the same time. Shorty's rifle fired repeatedly. Jeff took aim and began firing out the window.

Arabella fell on top of Tennie, screaming, "We're all going to be killed! They are going to kill us all!" She began crying huge wracking sobs.

Tennie moved, trying to position herself so she could see Jeff. Arabella lay heavily on her, and she finally had to push her over so she could watch Jeff. He fired out the window of the coach as it raced, passing trees and scrubby brush at a terrifying speed. The Indians continued to whoop and fire back, but Tennie thought there was something strange about their cries. They did not sound like the Indians who had attacked her wagon train.

Outside, buckskins and war paint blurred by.

She heard the whistling of a bullet and saw Jeff clutch his chest and crumple back into the seat.

"Jeff! Jeff!" she cried. With as much force as she could, she shoved the hysterical Arabella off her and climbed onto the seat next to him.

"Jeff, Jeff," she cried again. Blood was seeping from his chest through his shirt. She put one arm around his shoulder, clutching his hand in hers.

He gave her hand a feeble squeeze. "Tennie," he whispered.

"It's all right, Jeff. I'm here with you, Jeff. Tennie's here."

He gave her a faint smile and shut his eyes. Tennie's eyes were drawn to the window. For a few brief seconds, a horseman rode next to the coach, and she caught a surprised look on his face as they stared at one another.

He was covered in dirt and war paint; he had on a black wig with a feather in it, and he wore buckskins, but she recognized him as a white man through and through. It was the corporal who had almost strangled her in the jail.

His face was gone in an instant as the horses, driven into a frenzy of racing by Packer Jack's cries and whip lashes, tore through the country-side, the stagecoach rocking violently. Tennie looked down at Jeff. She hugged him, kissing his cheek and murmuring his name, but even as she did, she knew he was almost gone. She removed the handkerchief from his neck and tried to stop the flow of blood from his chest, all the while knowing it was useless.

In the turmoil, she heard other shouts, blood-curdling shrieks she thought she would never hear again, Rebel yells coming from the hills. She peered out the window and saw three cowboys racing down the hill at top speed, firing their rifles, heedless of danger. With a gasp, she recognized the three riders though their mouths were contorted with screams and the gun smoke around them almost obliterated their faces.

She placed her head next to Jeff's, hugging him close as she shut her eyes and prayed. It occurred to her to pick up his six-shooter and fire, but in the wild melee outside the stagecoach, she realized she could hit one of their rescuers. She would have to save the bullets in the gun to protect herself and Arabella if they failed.

In less than a minute, the yells ceased and the gunfire faded away. The stagecoach gradually slowed.

"Tennie!" Shorty's voice called, and Tennie sent up a prayer of thankfulness he was alive.

"We're all right," she called. "Except Jeff," and her voice caught. "Jeff didn't make it." Tears fell down her cheeks as she cradled his dead body next to hers. "Jeff, Jeff," she murmured.

Arabella had not ceased sobbing and screaming the entire time, but as the stage slowed, so did her sobs. She got back up in the seat, but she was so self-absorbed, Tennie didn't think she realized Jeff was dead.

Their rescuers continued to ride with the stagecoach, escorting them to the outskirts of Cat Ridge.

Their leader motioned to Packer Jack and asked him to stop. When the stagecoach lurched to a halt, he rode his horse to the window where Tennie sat, still holding Jeff.

Wash Jones leaned across the window and held out a handkerchief in his hand. "You dropped your handkerchief back there, ma'am."

Tennie stared at him and the strange handkerchief he held out to her. She reached for it and murmured, "Thank you."

He nodded, and with a forward wave of his hand, he, Poco, and Ben McNally rode away in the opposite direction.

"We're much obliged," Packer Jack called, but their only response was to raise one hand in acknowledgment and move on. They didn't even look back.

The handkerchief was wrapped around a crackling object, but Tennie dared not open it in Arabella's presence. She stuck it in her pocket.

Arabella stared out the window in apprehension as they approached the sheriff's office and stopped. Shorty climbed down, but he had to place his hand against the stage to steady himself. The sheriff ambled from his office, eyes narrowing. The major and his men hurried forward, and Tennie could hear the tumbled story of their attack coming from Shorty and Packer Jack.

Shorty opened the door and motioned to Arabella. "We're here. Out."

Tennie took her arm from Jeff's shoulder, reluctant to leave him, but she followed Arabella out of the coach.

"Indians!" the major exclaimed. "We haven't had any problems with Indians this far south."

"It wasn't Indians," Tennie said, and her voice sounded to her like that of a dead woman.

"What?!" the men exclaimed.

"I've been in an Indian attack before. I know what they look like, and I know what they sound like. This was not Indians. It was white men dressed like Indians." She turned to the major. "If you search through your corporal's belongings, you will probably find war paint and wigs."

"Are you accusing him?" the major said.

"A three-second look is not enough to swear to in a court of law, but it is enough to ask you to do a thorough search of his belongings," she said, ready to forget all about the corporal.

She turned to Shorty, but he spoke before she could. "I'll have the undertaker put Jeff's body in a coffin," he said, looking away.

"Tennie!" Arabella cried. "You're not leaving me here?"

Tennie nodded. "You'll be fine." She looked at the gawkers already gathering around them. "Just think, Arabella, if I'm here, people will be gaping at the woman marshal, but if I'm gone, you will be the center of attention all by yourself."

"That's true," Arabella said, considering it. "All right. Good-bye. Get going."

The sheriff stomped forward. "Wait a minute, young lady," he yelled at Tennie. "You're not leaving me to look after this woman prisoner. You're staying right here."

"No, I'm not," Tennie said. "I'm hiring a wagon, and I'm taking Jeff Hamilton back to Ring Bit as soon as I can. I'm not going to allow him to be buried in this godforsaken dump." She turned and began walking away with the sheriff's blustering behind her.

"Tennie, stop!" Shorty called, catching up with her. "You don't even know where you are going."

"I'm going home; that's where I'm going," Tennie said. "I'm going back to Ring Bit."

Shorty took her arm. "You're going to the station to rest first. I'll see about Jeff and getting a wagon and drive. We can leave at dark. The road will be jammed with people heading to see Arabella's trial, and we'll be perfectly safe with so many fellow travelers."

"Tennie! Tennie!" Arabella said.

Tennie turned her head, thinking Arabella was going to say "thank you."

Instead she asked with anxious eyes, "Do I look all right?"

Tennie nodded. "You look beautiful," she said, hoping she never saw or heard from Arabella again.

At the station, Shorty put her in a small room with a cot, insisting they rest and eat before heading back to Ring Bit. He left, closing the door behind him, and in the tiny, hot, windowless room, Tennie removed her clothes, scrubbing herself from a water pitcher and bowl on a small nightstand next to the bed, as if by removing the dust, she could remove the memory.

Sitting naked on the bed with water still clinging to her, she dug into her dress pocket and brought out the handkerchief Wash had given her.

She stared at it a long time before removing the small square of paper folded inside. With shaking fingers, she opened it, reading the words that had been written in haste with a firm, clear hand.

I think of you every minute of every day.
GWJ

Wrapping her fist around the paper, she fell onto the bed and began to weep.

Shorty had men tie Jeff's coffin to the wagon bed so it wouldn't shift, and he had the station maids prepare a pallet for Tennie next to it. He insisted she lie down in the wagon bed while he again rode shotgun on the wagon seat. Tennie agreed, thinking Shorty had the constitution of a bulldog. He insisted she keep Jeff's pistol beside her.

"He had a will leaving all his money to his sister in Mobile, but his possessions to Lafayette," Shorty explained. "Lafayette will want you and the boys to have something to remember Jeff by anyway, so keep it."

Tennie did not know their driver. He was an employee of the station who would return the wagon the next day. A quiet man, he didn't say much; nevertheless, Tennie got little sleep. They passed person after person on their way on horseback, buckboard, and buggy, journeying to Cat Ridge to witness Arabella's trial. Every time Shorty had to explain the coffin contained Jeff's body, Tennie's eyes teared up. She had no idea what it was doing to Shorty, except his voice grew gruffer, and his temper grew shorter. He wouldn't allow her to trade places with him.

Dew fell, making Tennie wet and hot with humidity, but they traveled on, reaching Ring Bit while the coyotes still howled in the moonlight. Stopping at the livery, Shorty had trouble getting out of the wagon. Big Mike walked outside to greet them, and Shorty again had to explain about Jeff.

"Pick Tennie up and put her to bed," Shorty ordered, breathing heavily. "She's suffering from shock and exhaustion."

Tennie did not protest and allowed Mike to pull her from the wagon. She placed her head on his shoulder while Shorty fumbled with the jailhouse keys. He opened the door, and Mike took her inside, placing her gently on the bed, but not before she had kissed his whiskered cheek.

"Thank you," she murmured, and it was the last thing she remembered for a long time.

The boys got her up in time to dress for Jeff's funeral. They walked through the deserted streets, following the horse-drawn hearse. The mayor, the banker, and the rest of the town council were all businessmen who had remained in Ring Bit to mind the store, and they were there, wearing composed looks of mourning. The unmistakable sadness radiating from Lafayette was almost overwhelming.

For the second time, Tennie and her stepsons threw flowers and dirt into a grave.

After the funeral, Tennie and the boys walked back to the jailhouse. Rusty took one of her hands while Lucas took the other.

"Miss Tennie," Rusty said. "We have something we have to show you."

They led her to the backyard.

She stared, uncomprehending of the devastation she saw. The tent had been ripped to pieces and torn down. Someone had demolished not only the brush arbor, but the oven Poco's friends had made.

"They did it last night before you got home," Lucas said.

"Bear started barking like crazy," Rusty said. "But Shorty had told us to stay inside and keep Bear with us no matter what happened."

Tennie didn't know what to think. "Mike didn't say anything about this last night. Maybe he thought I was too tired, and he didn't want to worry me."

"We asked him about it," Rusty said, "but—"

"Yeah," Lucas interrupted. "He said he didn't hear anything."

Mike was lying; Tennie knew he was lying. "It must have been the mayor and the town council's doing," she muttered. "He wouldn't interfere with them. But why? Why would they do this?"

Badger began to cry. "They're bad men!" he sobbed.

Tennie stooped to hug him. "We won't think about it now. We'll think about it later." She led them back to the front of the jailhouse, where she sat down on a bench and stared into nothingness.

"Are you going to fix dinner for us, Miss Tennie?" Lucas asked.

Tennie gave a start. "Yes, of course," she said rising. Life had to go on.

Nevertheless, she did her chores like a person

drifting through a bad dream. Sweeping the sidewalk in the evening, she was only vaguely aware the few men in town were once again wandering into the Silver Moon. She doubted if it would be much consolation to Lafayette. The thought of working another weekend in the jailhouse without Jeff filled her with dread.

The next day, she cleaned Arabella's cell and changed the bedding. When she finished, she turned and gave it a last look. There was nothing left to testify of Arabella's presence, only one more layer of human misery pervading the walls and bars. She picked up her bucket and the dirty linen and headed down the stairs.

That afternoon, she forced herself to dust the downstairs office. A stifling hot breeze blew in through the front windows. The sound of Maggot Milton cursing rode in on the feeble wind. She wanted to put her hands over her ears and scream to block out the sound. A child's cry caught her attention, and she thought of Badger.

Walking outside, she saw Badger and Rascal in the middle of the street.

Maggot stood across the road, shaking his fist. "I told you not to let that mutt come into my store."

"If he did, it was an accident," Badger cried. "He didn't mean to."

A crowd was gathering. Nobody said anything; they stood on the sidelines and watched.

"I'll kill him if he does it again," Maggot threatened.

"Don't you shoot my dog, you old maggot," Badger yelled.

Tennie took steps forward to drag Badger and Rascal out of the street. Before she could reach them, Maggot Milton had pulled a gun from his holster.

"I'll teach you to sass me," he hollered.

As Tennie watched in horror, he aimed at the dog and fired.

Blood spurted from atop the puppy's skull, and he went down. Badger shrieked and began bawling.

Something went off in Tennie's head, and without even knowing what she was doing, she ran up to Maggot Milton and began to shake her fist at him. "If I see you coming out of that store with a gun one more time," she screamed as loudly as she could, "I'll kill you! Do you understand me? I'm shooting your sorry ass dead if I ever see you outside with a gun in your hand again."

Maggot backed up. "Somebody get this crazy female away from me!"

Tennie felt arms around her, pulling on her waist, but she continued to rant at Maggot. "Get in that store. You get in that store right now and don't you ever come out with a gun in your hand again."

"She threatened me," Maggot yelled. "You all heard her threatening me!"

"I'm not threatening you," Tennie screamed even as she was being pulled backward. "I'm telling you what's going to happen if you come out of that store one more time with a gun."

Her feet dragged the ground, but whoever was pulling on her lifted her and carried her into the jailhouse, slamming the door behind them.

She turned, realizing it was Lafayette, and she began pummeling him with her fists and crying. He grasped her so close to his chest, she could no longer fight him. She placed her head against him and sobbed as he held her so tightly she could scarcely breathe.

"Tennie, Tennie," he whispered, rubbing her back and hair.

Minutes went by before she could stop her hysterical weeping. Finally able to quiet herself, she lifted her head to look into his eyes. He bent his down, lips parted, eyes lowered.

"Miss Tennie! Miss Tennie!" Lucas cried, throwing the door open.

Tennie and Lafayette separated.

Lucas, pulled on her. "It's okay. It's okay. Rascal just got his scalp creased. He was knocked out for a minute, but Shorty said he's going to be okay."

"Oh, thank God," Tennie said with relief.

Having delivered the message, Lucas ran back outside, leaving the door open.

"Your face is wet with tears," Lafayette said. "I seemed to have picked the worst time to be without a handkerchief."

"I have one," Tennie said. She dug into her pocket, fumbling to extract the handkerchief Wash Jones had given her without bringing the note he had written with it. But it fell out of her pocket onto the floor.

Before she could stoop to pick it up, Lafayette bent to retrieve it. He opened the note and read it, staring at it as seconds went by. "And this is from?"

"It's from a man who came to the ranch with a hurt friend when I first arrived," Tennie said.

"The same friend Ashton operated on?" Lafayette questioned.

"Yes," Tennie answered. "They stayed several days. After they left, I never spoke to him again until he and his friends came to our rescue during the stagecoach attack. He gave me the note then, before riding away."

"He seems quite taken with you," Lafayette said. "And is this the same GW who taught your stepsons how to fence?"

"Yes, do you know him?"

Lafayette folded the note and placed it into her hand. "Yes, I think I do. I'm the one who taught him those same fencing techniques. Although the initials are slightly different." His voice was even, but the blinking of his eyes and the slight tremor of his hands told of an emotional struggle. "And what do you know about him?"

"Nothing, except he travels in and out of the shadows. I don't know who he is or what he is doing in Ring Bit," Tennie cried. "He pretends not to recognize me, yet he arrives to save my life and slips this note into my hands."

Lafayette stood looking at her for so long, she was about to cry, "What is the matter?"

Before she could, he rubbed her cheek with one finger. "Don't worry, little Tennie. If he does not show his hand soon, I will force it."

CHAPTER 27

Lafayette left Tennie fighting an internal battle of her own. Unable to understand what was going on with Wash and Lafayette and their place in her life, she turned and looked out the window. The crowd had dispersed, and Maggot Milton had gone back into his butcher shop. She wondered if she should walk across the street to apologize and tell him she had no intention of shooting him or anyone else.

She opened the door, but instead of walking across the street, she went to Shorty's.

He and the boys stood in the front room of the station, watching Bear lick the top of Rascal's head as the puppy wiggled, trying to play.

Badger ran to Tennie and hugged her leg in happiness. "See, he's all better now."

She had to confess what happened to their headless horseman book. Shorty said it didn't matter. He'd find them something else to read. Rusty said he wanted to go out to the ranch on a picnic the next day, and Shorty backed him up.

"You need to go, Tennie," Shorty said. "Rascal

413

can stay here with me tomorrow so I can keep an eye on him." He looked down at Badger and reassured him. "He's all right. He was wounded, though, and doesn't need to be traipsing all over the countryside on a picnic."

Tennie wasn't in the mood for a picnic, but Rusty insisted. With the other boys clamoring to go, too, she caved in. "When are we leaving?" she asked, since Rusty already seemed to have all the details worked out.

"In the morning," he said. "At eight o'clock."

She stared at him, but nobody else seemed to think his exact time of eight in the morning was unusual.

"Eight o'clock," Lucas repeated. "That gives me time to collect some empty bottles and take them to Mr. Lafayette."

"I'll go with you," Rusty said.

"Don't you have to get the wagon ready?" Tennie asked.

Rusty flushed. "Oh, I'll get up early and do that."

"Tennie," Shorty said. "Why don't you go back to the jailhouse and start preparing a picnic basket? It will give you something to do to take your mind off your troubles and have a jump on things in the morning."

"All right," Tennie said. "Good heavens. You all act like it would be a sin if we left at eight-thirty instead of eight."

Rusty had the mule and wagon waiting in front of the jailhouse the next morning.

Tennie shot nervous glances at the butcher shop, but Maggot Milton stayed inside. "I'm afraid I have made your task of going to the butcher shop for meat even more unbearable," she said, apologizing to Rusty.

"It doesn't matter anymore," he said, helping Badger get into the back of the wagon.

Tennie opened her mouth to ask him what he meant, but he turned to swing atop the buckskin while Lucas sat nearby on the dun.

"We don't really need to take the wagon," Tennie said. "Badger and I can ride double."

"Oh, I've already got it hitched," Rusty said. "Might as well go like this."

His words sounded too casual, causing Tennie to give him a pointed look. "Is there a reason why we need to leave Ring Bit at exactly eight o'clock with all our animals?" she asked.

"Except for Rascal," Badger cried. "You wouldn't let me bring Rascal, and I wanted to."

"Rascal is better off being looked after by Shorty," Rusty said. "We're just going on a picnic. Now everybody, come on."

Tennie gave a sigh and urged the mule forward. Once away from town, the past weeks fell away, and she forgot about death and trouble and wondering what Rusty was up to.

The scenery around them was in no way as

beautiful as what she had left behind in Alabama, but as Tennie looked around, she had no desire to go back. A peace descended upon her that being outdoors always managed to induce. She knew she was going to resign her post. She would take the boys back to the falling-down ranch house and live there on their meager savings until the railroad came through. They would sell part of the ranch for a right-of-way and go to work for Lafayette in his new hotel. And if the railroad or Lafayette failed them, she would find something else to do.

They rounded a bend, and three men rode out from behind a boulder, blocking them. Rusty and Lucas immediately halted their horses, and Tennie pulled up on the reins, bringing the mule to a stop.

Wash Jones rode up beside the wagon. "You're coming with us, Miss Tennie." He dismounted, grabbing Badger and placing him behind Lucas. Ben McNally dismounted and took the reins of the mule.

"If you please," Wash said, holding his hand out to Tennie.

She looked at Rusty. He flushed, but did not deny his part.

"Shorty was in on this, wasn't he?" Tennie asked Rusty.

He nodded.

"You've got some explaining to do," she said.

"He did what I asked him to, Miss Tennie," Wash said, still holding out his hand.

There didn't seem to be anything else to do but take it and allow him to help her from the wagon. Ben took her place, moving it away from the road, and unhitching the mule. He attached a lead rope to the halter and handed it to Poco.

"You'll have to ride double with me, Miss Tennie," Wash said. "We're kidnapping you. Rusty has to run an errand, so he won't be going with us."

"I guess it would be futile to ask why," Tennie said to no one in particular. "Why should anybody tell me anything?"

Wash got on his horse and again held out his hand to Tennie. "In good time, Miss Tennie."

They took her on a trail an ant in search of sugar would have had second thoughts about following. Brush and cactus reached out to grab at her ankles, and she worried the pink dress she wore was going to get ripped. She hitched her skirt up, better to have her petticoats torn and later mended than her dress. Realizing how ridiculous it looked to be more concerned with her dress than being snatched from a wagon and kidnapped, she started to put it back down, but changed her mind. Let them think what they wanted.

Wash halted the horse in a camp made in a hidden clearing on a hillside. "Be careful of snakes," he said as he helped her down.

"Am I in the presence of one?" she asked.

"Rusty will be back soon. I'll ask you to hold off judgment until then. Ben is going to take Badger and show him a cave with some Indian drawings a little ways from here. In a while, I'm going to ask you and Lucas to hide behind those rocks yonder and keep your mouths shut until I tell you to come out."

Tennie looked at Lucas. "What do you know about this?"

"Only a little bit, Miss Tennie. I think we'd better do what he says."

Tennie nodded and found a rock to sit on while they waited.

Wash busied himself with the horses, and it seemed to Tennie he took care not to look her way.

Poco, in the meantime, smiled at her. "Do not worry, señorita. It will all turn out well."

She wanted to thank him for the outdoor oven, to thank both of them for saving her life in the robbery attempt, but like Wash, she remained silent.

At the sound of a bird calling, Wash turned and motioned them to go behind the rocks. He followed while they sat on the ground behind a small boulder. "Don't say a word; don't cry; don't make a sound," he warned them.

Tennie and Lucas nodded, and he left them as a loud crashing noise came through the trees.

"Where is she?" Big Mike came shouting through the brush. "What have you done with her? I will kill you if you hurt her."

"She's not hurt," they heard Wash say. "She's not kidnapped. Rusty just told you that to get you here with your money. Did you bring it?"

"Yes!" Mike hollered. "But I not give it to you until I see Tennie!"

"She's not here. And I don't want your money. I want information."

"Information?" Mike's voice asked, becoming suspicious. "What information?"

"I'm a Texas Ranger. My men and I have been working undercover, trying to break the rustling ring that's been going in this area for years."

Tennie put her hand over her mouth to keep from gasping. She felt herself almost collapsing with relief.

"We've pinpointed the headquarters of this bunch, and it's in Ring Bit. We know you've been running stolen horses through your livery," Wash said. "They are bringing them in at night; you're holding them in your corrals where they are sold or auctioned off by twos and threes by different cowboys.

"Look. I'm after who's pulling the strings. We think it's the men on the town council. I just want you to confirm it."

Tennie felt sick. No wonder Wash had told her not to cry. Mike! What kind of trouble had he gotten into? He had not spoken, and Tennie knew he was desperately trying to figure out what to do.

"Mike," Wash said. "I am within my rights as a lawman to hang you here and now. I'm not going to. I'm going to give you a chance to leave here with your money and start somewhere else."

"Why? Why you do this for me?" Mike said.

"I think you know why," Wash said.

"Because of Tennie? You will not tell her!"

"I think she'll figure it out herself, Mike," Wash said, and his voice was not unkind.

They could hear sounds of Mike sobbing. Tennie grabbed Lucas's hand and squeezed it to keep from crying.

"Yes," Mike said. "I come to Ring Bit. They say, 'We set you up in shop. All you have to do is keep few horses for us.' When I find out, it's too late."

"All of the town councilmen?" Wash asked.

There was a pause.

"And what about any of the other businessmen? The undertaker?"

"No," Mike said, and Tennie breathed in silent relief.

"And Lafayette Dumont?" Wash asked.

"No, he suspect, but he keep quiet."

Tennie's relief was so great, she had to put her head down to keep from fainting.

"And Milton the butcher? He's selling stolen beef, isn't he?" Wash demanded.

"Yes," Mike said.

"Don't go back to Ring Bit," Wash ordered him. "Ride to Cat Ridge and take the first stage to Waco. Here's the name of a man who will help you get started again." He handed a note to Mike. "Rusty's going to ride with you part of the way to make sure you don't go back and warn the others."

Mike continued to sob. "Tennie . . ."

"Tennie knows you love her," Wash said, his voice harsh. "And she and those boys love you, too. That's the only reason I'm letting you go."

They could hear the sounds of Mike leaving. Tennie looked at Lucas.

"He had a running iron," Lucas said. "He tried to hide it, but I saw it. It was just like Two-Bit described it."

Tennie nodded.

"Wash told Rusty they wouldn't suspect us because we were kids, and they'd think we were too little to understand anything. But he said if they thought you knew anything, they might kill you. That's the reason they hired you, Miss Tennie. They thought you'd never find out, or if you did, they could scare you into doing nothing."

Wash came around the rock. "Lucas, would you go with Poco to fetch Ben and Badger?"

Lucas got up, but looked down at Tennie. She nodded, and he left.

"Of all the boys," Wash said. "He is the most devoted to you."

"I know." She rose and began to walk away.

"And me?" Wash asked.

Tennie stopped, turned and glared at him. "Do I know about you?" she said, almost spitting at him. "I know you let me go into a lion's den so you could go off chasing outlaws."

Wash's face colored. "I'm an attorney by profession. I admit I'd hoped if I'd succeeded, I could win a judgeship further down the line."

"So I was sacrificed so you could get a judgeship?" Tennie shrieked, tears flooding her eyes.

He grabbed her by the shoulders. "I promised to do a job! I had a duty! What kind of man would I be if I sloughed it off so I could go stand in line with the other lovestruck fools in Ring Bit."

"I don't care about your duty! All I know is you deserted me!" Tennie cried, tears streaming down her cheeks.

"That's not true," he said, shaking her. "I watched out for you every chance I got. And how do you think I felt, knowing every man in Ring Bit was in love with you? I could have strangled Lafayette," he said between clenched teeth. "The only thing that kept me from it was because I knew he was looking after you. And Jeff Hamilton! Every man in Ring Bit was sick with

422

envy because Jeff got to work with you. And that giant cowhand, Honey Boy! Everyone knew how you favored him! I was nothing to you! And my hands were tied!"

He grasped her hair, bent her head back and kissed her roughly. A hard kiss holding only hunger and sorrow. He drew back, but kept his grip on her.

"And are your hands still tied?" she asked.

"Yes," he replied. "I have to go in there and arrest those men, and I may not come out alive."

"Don't do this!" she cried.

"I have to," he said.

"Wash!" Ben's voice called.

He let go of her, struggling to rein in his emotions. Tennie wiped the tears from her eyes. Together, they walked around the rocks to face the others.

"We'd best get Miss Tennie on her way," Ben said. "We want to get this over with before school lets out."

Wash nodded. "Tennie, you, Lucas, and Badger take your horse and mule and go back to your ranch," he said, once more in control of himself, although his face was ashen. "Rusty will bring the wagon along to you when he gets back.

"If we succeed, we will let you know," he continued. "If we don't, you can stick with the story that you went on a picnic to your ranch and pretend you know nothing."

"What about the innocent people in town?" Tennie cried. "What if Mr. Payton and his wife are in town?"

"The people of Ring Bit are used to hiding from trouble," Wash said. "Lafayette will stay inside his saloon. We took Honey Boy into our confidence, and he has gone around to all the ranches to warn the cowboys he knows are straight to stay away from town today. If Winn Payton knew, he would want to be in the thick of it, but his cowhands have instructions to keep him busy on the ranch."

"And Shorty?" Tennie asked.

"Shorty will be in the church bell tower to shoot anyone who tries to escape. Once a ranger, always a ranger," Wash said, sounding weary. "I'll lead you out of here. But we must go now."

He helped Tennie onto the dun, while Ben placed Lucas and Badger on the back of the mule.

Wash stood by Tennie's side, as if unwilling to let her go. "My father warned me not to fall in love with a beautiful woman, but he didn't tell me how to keep from it."

Tennie clinched her fist, wanting to beg him again not to go on this mission, but she knew it would be useless. Instead, she leaned down and kissed his cheek. "God be with you, Wash Jones," she whispered in his ear. "Because my heart will be, too."

By the time he led them through the thick

brush and stands of trees, he was back to being stoic, silent Wash Jones, and when they reached the road, Tennie did not press him into showing anything else. He sent them on their way with orders to get on the ranch and stay there all day.

Tennie nodded and urged the dun forward, but when she looked back before getting out of sight, he was still there, watching them.

In was only later she realized she had forgotten to ask him if he had previously known Lafayette.

When they reached the turnoff to go to the ranch, the mule stopped and wouldn't be budged. Lucas and Badger kicked and hollered, but the mule stood with ears straight up and refused to lift a hoof.

"Let's twist his tail," Lucas told Badger.

As if he knew what they were saying, the mule sat down, and the boys slid off his back.

Tennie dismounted and pulled on the lead rope, but that only made the mule dig in his heels. Lucas went to find a switch, and while she pulled, he yelled and popped the mule with the switch.

"This isn't getting us anywhere," Tennie said. "We'll have to leave him here. You boys can ride the dun, and I'll walk." She looked around for Badger. With a sudden feeling of dread, she asked, "Where's Badger?" and began to call his name.

They searched but couldn't find him. She looked for footprints, but the ground was too hard to show a small boy's tracks. She looked down the road and tried to keep from crying.

"I think he went to get Rascal," she told Lucas. "You go to the ranch and stay there. I'll take the dun to town and search for him."

Lucas turned as balky as the mule and refused to leave her.

"All right," Tennie said, fearing they had wasted too much time already. "Come on. We'll both ride the dun and the devil with the mule."

"Hold on," she said once they were on. She wasn't a good horsewoman, but she dug her heels in and yelled "Giddy-up" as loud as she could.

At the same time, Lucas popped the dun with his switch, and he took off.

Tennie slowed him as they neared the town, fearing she would cause comment if they came tearing in. The first thing they saw was pudgy Badger walking down the middle of the street holding Rascal in his arms.

Tennie got down from the horse and swooped him into her arms. "Into the jailhouse, quick," she told Lucas.

"What about the horse?" Lucas cried.

The streets looked deserted. "Bring him in," Tennie cried and unlocked the door.

As soon as all four of them were inside, she slammed the door and locked it. They went through the jailhouse to the back door. Tennie unlocked it and held it open. "Take him to that

426

far tree yonder, the one closest to where you play baseball. Maybe nothing will hit him that far away, but hurry, Lucas!"

He bolted out the door with the horse and did as she said. As soon he had tied it to the tree, they heard gunfire coming from the far end of town.

"Run, run, run!" Tennie urged him, and he ran back into the jailhouse. She slammed the door and locked it.

"Get in the stairwell and stay there," Tennie said, pushing them along.

It seemed as if the whole town had turned into a battlefield. What had started out as a few gunshots had become a volley of rapid fire. She could hear rifles being fired, and when she heard the sound of a shotgun blast, she almost fell to her knees in fear. Creeping to the front windows of the jailhouse, she peeked outside. Men were running up and down the street, firing pistols and yelling.

When she saw Maggot Milton burst out of his butcher shop with both pistols firing, she leapt across the room to the desk, jerking out Ashton's and Jeff's pistols. She ran to the stairwell and handed Ashton's gun to Lucas, thankful his father had made sure he knew how to use it.

"Be careful, but kill anyone who tries to hurt you," she said and ran back to the windows. Before she had a chance to look out, the front door crashed open, and Maggot Milton backed in, firing pistols into the street. Tennie raised hers, but before she could pull the trigger, someone from outside shot in rapid succession, hitting Maggot. As Tennie watched him crumple, she looked up to see Wash rush into the jailhouse.

When he saw her, his face twisted in terror. "Upstairs! Now!" he shouted.

Tennie ran past him, grabbing Badger and urging the two boys up the stairs. "Stay down," she told them when they reached the top.

She ran to the window and crouched down, peering over the window ledge. "I can't see anything!" she cried. "The street is filled with gun smoke." She raised her eyes and saw a cowboy creeping along the backside of Maggot's false storefront. She thought of the cowboys who had stood across the street after insisting she lock up the drovers and realized he was one of them. She raised Jeff's gun, and taking careful aim, fired. She missed, and he fired back. She fell to the floor, looking at the boys. In a second, she raised back up to fire again, but someone on the street beat her to it, and whoever it was did not miss. The cowboy fell off the building, hitting the sidewalk with a bounce.

She found herself being raised and pulled backward, the pistol wrenched from her hand. An arm held like a vise covered her neck. Twisting, she saw the banker's face.

He held a gun on her in his other hand. "Drop

the gun, kid," he told Lucas, "or I'll shoot her."

Lucas dropped Ashton's Colt and sat staring, but Badger, holding Rascal, began creeping away to one side and behind the banker. Tennie did not know what to do except play for time.

"I didn't know you cared," she gasped.

He jerked her. "You didn't know anything," he hissed. "I was invisible to you. You batted your eyelashes at every man in town and avoided me like I had a disease."

Tennie shut her eyes momentarily, willing her mouth to say something, anything. "I was afraid of your wealth and power. I was afraid you would fire me."

"I thought if I held the note on your ranch," he breathed in her face, twisting his arm on her tighter, "you would come running to me. You would let me have my way with you in order to save it."

Tennie gulped. He was holding her neck so tightly she gasped for air. "I thought you were just greedy. I didn't know you were passionate," she said, trying to keep from crying. She looked down and saw Badger making his way to the banker's leg.

Lucas saw Badger, too.

"You didn't even try to know!" he said.

"Mister!" Lucas yelled. "Don't shoot!"

The banker screamed; Badger had bitten his leg. He kicked Badger across the room, but loosened his grip enough on Tennie she was able to twist out of his grasp. Falling down, she rose and rushed for Jeff's pistol. The banker lunged at her, pulling her down. Twisting and reaching as far as she could, she grasped the gun. Turning, with the banker looming over her, she fired into his stomach. He went down, and she scrambled out of the way.

She looked at the boys. "Are you all right?!" she cried.

They rushed to her and hugged her. She sank to her knees, taking them with her. Rascal jumped into her lap. They heard a lone gunshot followed by two more. After that, the streets were silent. She waited several minutes, but nothing was forthcoming. Getting up on her knees, she looked out the windows. The first thing she saw was the man she loved best walking down the middle of the street toward the jailhouse.

Scrambling to her feet, she ran down the stairs, avoided stepping on Maggot Milton's body, and headed out the door, running straight into Wash Jones's arms.

Wash swept her up, hugging her and covering her face with kisses. Lucas and Badger followed Tennie and hugged their legs.

Wash murmured, "Tennie, Tennie."

He paused, his eyes looking down the street. Tennie followed his gaze. Lafayette walked toward them.

He stopped when he reached them and spoke. "Brother."

"Faye," Wash said.

Tennie looked from one to the other. "You are brothers?"

"Half brothers," Lafayette said. "I took my mother's maiden name, and I assume Wash took his. Our real last name is . . . well, it doesn't matter what our real last name is." He stared at his younger brother. "Father?"

"Dead," Wash said. "They are all dead."

"And you? What about you?" Lafayette asked.

"Besides doing turns at being a Ranger," Wash said, "I have a law practice in San Antonio, and a small ranch nearby."

Lafayette rubbed his eyebrow with his fingers. "Ring Bit will have need of an attorney and a new town council."

Lafayette stepped forward, taking Tennie's hand in his. He bent down and kissed it, raising up to look into her eyes. "And now my dearest, sweet, Tennie," he said in slow measured words as he held her hand, "you must allow me to redeem my soul by letting me be the best man in my brother's wedding."

Tennie looked at Wash. He squeezed her shoulder, and she nodded.

Books are produced in the United States using U.S.-based materials

Books are printed using a revolutionary new process called THINKtech™ that lowers energy usage by 70% and increases overall quality

Books are durable and flexible because of Smyth-sewing

Paper is sourced using environmentally responsible foresting methods and the paper is acid-free

Center Point Large Print

600 Brooks Road / PO Box 1
Thorndike, ME 04986-0001 USA

(207) 568-3717

US & Canada:
1 800 929-9108
www.centerpointlargeprint.com